Praise for The Forgotten Goddesses series

How to Worship a Goddess:

"The Forgotten Goddesse   with this
stellar entry by Julian, who
romance. Liberally laced w
triguing characters, her st
surprising conclusions."

—*RT Book Reviews*, 4½ stars

"Paranormal romance scenes run explicitly hot and heavy."
—*Publishers Weekly*

"Romance that makes you smile, cheer, and swoon doesn't
get any better than *How to Worship a Goddess*. It's a wild and
amusing tale… topped off with sizzling sexual chemistry."
—*Long and Short Reviews*

"Hockey players, goddesses, and sex… oh my! A fun paranormal read oozing with sex and passion… it will knock
your socks off!"
—*The Romance Reviews*

"Deliciously steamy. It downright sizzles. Ms. Julian's
books are a guilty pleasure—you can never read just one."
—*Anna's Book Blog*

"Stephanie Julian has crafted her story mostly around
Lucy and Brandon's intense romantic relationship with
generous helpings of sizzling hot and hearty sex."
—*Fresh Fiction*

GODDESS IN THE MIDDLE

WITHDRAWN

STEPHANIE JULIAN

sourcebooks
casablanca

Published by Sourcebooks Casablanca, an imprint of Sourcebooks, Inc.
P.O. Box 4410, Naperville, Illinois 60567-4410
(630) 961-3900
FAX: (630) 961-2168
www.sourcebooks.com

Library of Congress Cataloging-in-Publication Data

Julian, Stephanie.
  Goddess in the middle / by Stephanie Julian.
     p. cm.
  1. Goddesses—Fiction. 2. Werewolves—Fiction. 3. Triangles (Interpersonal relations)—Fiction. I. Title.
  PS3610.U5346G63 2012
  813'.6—dc23

                              2012002342

            Printed and bound in the United States of America
                  VP 10 9 8 7 6 5 4 3 2 1

To the readers who have followed along on this journey. Thank you.

Glossary

Aguane—Etruscan elemental water spirits, always female

Aitás—Etruscan Underworld

Arus—Magical power inherent in the races of Etruscan descent

Candelas—Tiny, glowing Etruscan sprites

Cimmerians—Warriors from Cimmeria, with legendary strength and bravery

Enu—Humans of magical Etruscan descent

Eteri—Etruscan for foreigner, used to describe regular humans

Fata—Elemental beings of magical Etruscan descent

Fauni—shape-changing Etruscan elemental beings with an affinity for animals

Folletta—Etruscan fairy

Gianes—Female wood elves

Involuti—Founding gods of the Etruscans, those from whom all other Etruscan deities were descended

Linchetto (pl. linchetti)—Etruscan Fata, a night elf

Lucani—Etruscan werewolves

Malandante—descended from the Etruscans but born with a bent toward evil, with a taste for power and wealth

Salbinelli—Etruscan satyr

Silvani—One of the Etruscan elemental races

Strega/stregone (pl. streghe)—Etruscan witch

Tukhulka—Etruscan demon

Versipellis—Literally "skin shifter;" shapeshifters including Etruscan lucani (wolves), Norse berkserkir (bears), and French loup garou (wolves)

Chapter 1

"Amity, those two guys have been staring at you for the past half hour. Are you just going to sit here and ignore them or are you going to put them out of their misery?"

Amity Monroe, formerly known as Munthukh, Etruscan Goddess of Health, gave Jill Doyle a wry grin before taking another sip of her whiskey sour—and continuing to ignore the men at the other end of Kelly's Corner Bar.

She and Jill had grabbed a table in the back, away from the constant bustle at the bar, because Amity had said she'd wanted a quiet night out with a friend.

"How do you know they're looking at me? Maybe they're looking at you."

Which would make a lot more sense. A drop-dead gorgeous brunette in her late twenties, Jill had been known to break more hearts than she saved. And Jill was a damn good trauma nurse. One of Reading Hospital's best.

Men typically fell over themselves to get to Jill. She inspired fist fights and more than a few indecent proposals.

Amity... Well, she apparently looked like the kind of woman men wanted to take home to their mothers. Not the kind who inspired panting and dirty talk. She hadn't even gotten that at the height of her worship, oh so many, many centuries ago.

It wasn't that she was ugly. No, men still looked at her with lust in their eyes and fell into her bed when she invited them for fast, hot sex. The problem was, most of them wanted to stick around the next day and the next. They wanted to keep her.

Amity had learned her lesson on that point. She may be the Goddess of Health but she couldn't heal her broken heart. Best never to let a relationship get to that point.

Humans were so very fragile. So easily broken. And she no longer had enough power to fix them.

"They haven't given me more than a passing glance." Jill leaned back and grinned at her over her wine glass. "Why don't you go over and introduce yourself?"

Sighing, Amity took another sip of her whiskey sour. She'd spent more than half her day with two of the worst cases she'd ever seen in her career as a medical aesthetician. And her frustration level at her inability to perform even the slightest miracle had boiled over about two hours ago into a crying jag.

Which was why she'd agreed to come out tonight with Jill and a few of the other nurses. The girls had been talking for two weeks straight about the new bar that'd opened only a block from the hospital on a West Reading side street. The drinks were cheap, the men good-looking and plentiful, and one of the bar owners was a former nurse whose husband was a cop and a Navy vet. Which accounted for all the guys.

"Not tonight." Amity shook her head. "I'm just here for a few drinks."

Okay, more than a few drinks with her friends, thereby avoiding the loneliness of her home.

Maybe she was totally pitiful, especially considering the fact that she didn't even *want* to turn around and *look* at the guys.

Jill raised an eyebrow at her. "Well, I think you should at least give them a chance. Gotta warn you, though. The one's a little rough looking. His face…"

Jill didn't finish and Amity saw pity cross her friend's expression.

Now, her curiosity kicked in. Not wanting to make it obvious—and probably failing miserably, because she was *not* going to go over there and introduce herself—she shifted around and immediately knew which two men Jill meant.

She blinked, caught first by the sure knowledge that she was looking at two Etruscan males. She was an Etruscan goddess, after all, even if she hadn't been worshipped in more years than she wanted to remember.

Her second thought… *Oh, yes, I'll take two to go. Please wrap them and deliver them to my bed.*

The taller one, with his short, dark hair and ruggedly handsome features, met her gaze straight on. He didn't smile, just let their gazes connect and hold until she felt a sizzle start beneath her skin.

Tinia's teat, that one fairly burned her alive with only a glance.

Pull yourself together. You're a goddess, not a horny twenty-year-old.

And she'd do well to remember that.

With effort, she dragged her gaze to the second man.

Her breath stuck in her throat. Oh my. This one had been beautiful. Once. Until someone or something had scarred the left side of his face.

And still, he held her attention for reasons other than those marks. So much strength in that face. And in the body that looked long and lean and lickable. Totally lickable.

As opposed to his friend who was built like a gladiator. And whom she'd rather take bites out of.

They can make me the filling in their sandwich any day.

As she stared, the dark-haired one leaned down to say something to the scarred one, who now turned. He caught her gaze and her chest tightened until she thought she might embarrass herself by having to gulp for air.

Wow. Just… wow.

Where the hell was her reaction coming from?

She wanted to go over and demand to know why they were looking at her like they wanted to devour her. And that was really stupid. She should be flattered. Hell, maybe even grateful.

Then again… Damn it, she was just too old for this flirting non-sense. Why couldn't they just walk over and ask her if she wanted to get naked and get it on?

Probably because she was totally misreading the looks they were giving her.

No, they must be staring at Jill.

Still, that tingling sensation low in her belly continued. How long *had* it been since she'd had mind-blowing sex?

Way too long if she had to think about it.

Jill elbowed her discreetly in the side, knocking her back into the moment. "Go over there and talk to them. You know you want to. You're practically devouring them with your eyes."

Shaking her head, Amity took a sip of her whiskey sour. "Aren't they supposed to come to me?"

Jill laughed. "Honey, what century are you living in?"

Good question. The answer was one she occasionally forgot. Lately, the years had been blurring into one long, slow grind.

But right across the room was, at the very least, a way to relieve some of that grind. Hopefully with a little bump and grind. Or a lot. A lot would be good, actually.

Fine. She picked up her drink, straightened her shoulders, and slid off her bar stool.

"Watch my back. I'm going in."

Jill laughed as she was supposed to. "Good luck, Amity. But I don't think you're going to need much. Those men want you some-thing fierce."

"She's on her way."

"Are you sure this is a good idea? We don't know what the demon wants with her. Hell, I'm still not convinced it's really after her."

Romulus Cangelosi heard the doubt in his cousin Remy's voice but found he couldn't take his eyes off the woman now approaching them through the crowded bar.

"Bullshit." Rom's almost silent curse wouldn't have been heard by anyone in the vicinity except for Remy. "We both know it's targeted her and it's gonna try for her tonight or tomorrow at the latest."

Remy sighed and Rom heard resignation in the sound. Remy had been against this plan from the moment Rom had brought it up.

His cousin still had scruples.

Rom couldn't afford to have any, not when they were so close to achieving their goal.

Still, he could admit, at least to himself, seducing this woman wouldn't be a hardship.

From the first moment he'd seen her, his skin had stretched tight over his body and every one of his muscles went taut with heightened awareness. Of her.

It'd been a damn long time since that'd happened to him. Lust like this—the biting, raging, tearing kind now eating at his insides—was what brought down kingdoms and countries.

Rom refused to let his dick fuck it up.

But, damn. The woman pressed every one of his buttons. And he knew Remy wasn't immune either.

Which should make the seduction that much easier.

"I don't know why the hell you needed me to come tonight." Remy practically growled the words. "You would've done just fine on your own."

True, but then Remy would've been left alone at the house and Rom thought that might have been like waving a red flag at the *tukhulkha* demon they'd been after for almost twenty years.

Maybe it didn't know they were in the area. Then again, maybe it did. Rom was taking no chances. He and Remy needed to stick together or they'd wind up dead.

This woman was the key to tracking down the demon that had

killed their families. For some reason, that same demon had targeted Amity Monroe, a thirty-year-old medical aesthetician who'd been employed by the Reading Hospital for the past five years.

Why the hell it wanted her, they had no idea. But when it finally came after her, they'd be by her side, waiting for it with sharp blades and even sharper teeth and claws.

No, seducing Amity into their bed was *not* going to be a hardship.

But Remy had to do his part.

"Damn it, Remy, at least *try* to look like you're into her."

Remy sighed but finally turned in the direction of their prey. "I don't have to try," he grumbled.

Surprise at Remy's comment made Rom shoot his cousin a quick glance. For the past few days as they'd followed her, waiting for the demon to attack, Remy hadn't said one damn word about an attraction to her. Amity wasn't Remy's type at all, so Rom hadn't been surprised. His cousin usually liked them blond, blue-eyed, and long-limbed.

Amity was short and curvy with dark hair and eyes. She projected a sweet femininity that other men might mistake as being plain. Those other men had been brainwashed by television and by women who believed they had to be runway-model skinny to be attractive.

Which was a damn shame, as far as Rom was concerned. He liked a woman to look like a woman, not a hard plastic doll with fake breasts and lips and hair.

Rom knew better. This woman's soft features perfectly matched the softness of her body, all rounded curves instead of sharp angles.

Her sable brown hair had dark gold highlights and waves that made his fingers itch to sink into them. And her face... He'd been staring at it long enough now to realize how truly striking she was.

Full lips, rounded nose and cheeks. Wide, dark eyes that mesmerized and missed nothing. Intelligence shone from those eyes.

A smart woman. They'd have to be careful or she'd realize they were up to something.

He straightened as she reached their table, making sure he maintained a pleasant expression. One that hid the fact he wanted to strip her naked, throw her on a bed, and fuck her until she was so sated she couldn't walk. Then he'd watch while Remy did the exact same thing.

Then they'd take her together.

And when the demon came for her tomorrow or the next day, they'd kill it, avenging their families' deaths and saving the damsel in distress. Then…

Yeah, what then?

"Hello, gentlemen. My name is Amity. Can I buy you both a drink?"

Out of the corner of his eye, Rom saw Remy's mouth kick into a true grin, an expression he hadn't seen on his cousin's face in months, maybe as long as a year.

"Not that I wanna turn down an offer from such a beautiful woman," Remy responded before Rom could open his mouth, "but I think we owe you a drink since you've provided us with such beautiful scenery all night."

His hand curled into a fist beneath the table and Rom had to hold himself still so he didn't smack Remy upside his thick head. Was he trying to drive her away? Damn it—

Amity smiled, making those beautiful lips even more enticing. And her brown eyes sparkled as she began to laugh, a rich, earthy sound that made all the hair on Rom's body stand on end.

"I have to admit I've been out of the dating pool for a very long time but that might just be the lamest pick-up line I have *ever* heard." She paused as she slid onto the free chair at their table. "But I must say your delivery ranks pretty high on a scale of one to ten, so I'm going to say yes to your offer."

Remy's smile widened even farther and Rom knew his cousin had deliberately used that corny line to break the ice.

Remy stuck his hand out. "Remy."

She took his hand and let her fingers curl around his cousin's for a few heartbeats. Remy's expression transformed from flirtatious to almost slack-jawed amazement.

"And you can call me Amity."

Releasing Remy's hand, she turned to Rom. "Nice to meet you…"

"Rom." He took her hand and felt the same electric connection that had just rocked Remy back on his heels.

Holy hell—

"Do you live in the area?" Amity continued as she released his hand, cutting that connection. "I haven't seen you here before, have I? I think I would have remembered."

"No, this is our first night." Rom forced himself to speak and not to reach for her again. "We're here on business."

If possible, her smile turned even more sultry. "And what business is that?"

"Sales." He'd decided their cover story, if they had to use one, should be something so simple and boringly nondescript, no one would ever question it. "And you?"

"I'm a medical aesthetician at the hospital."

That smile still held and Rom's gut twisted with lust. Damn, he didn't have time for this, but apparently, his cock hadn't gotten the message. It wanted to be inside this woman.

You need to go slow. Don't want to scare her away, do you?

So he shoved the lust down as far as it would go and worked with Remy to draw her into a conversation. Which she deftly steered away from their professions and into the most innocuous subjects: books, films, and music. Nothing too revealing, though she kept the conversation rolling like a pro.

She enjoyed mysteries and any movie where stuff exploded. She and Rom had that in common. Remy went more for political thrillers. Their musical tastes couldn't have been more different. She liked Top 40 and country. Remy loved metal, which Rom could tolerate, but he went more for jazz and standards. He blamed his dad for that.

As they talked, Rom tried to get a sense for which of them she was more attracted to. He and Remy had agreed that if she wound up in a bed with both of them, no problem. But if the only way to get close to her was for her to pick one of them, they were adult enough to deal with that.

But if she didn't choose him, Rom knew it was gonna sting.

He didn't flirt. He wasn't good at it. He'd found intensity worked better for him. Remy had learned how to use flirting to get beyond a woman's natural aversion to his scars.

But Remy didn't have to lay it on thick for Amity.

Maybe it was the fact of what she did for a living or maybe it was just who she was. Either way, she responded to his cousin with clearly evident warmth. And in the exact same way she responded to Rom.

Which just made Rom like her that much more.

And then she dropped her bombshell.

"So, gentlemen," Amity said after more than an hour had passed. "Now that the pleasantries are out of the way, why don't we place our cards on the table? Are you here to talk? Or are you here to find a woman to share your bed for the night?"

Remy nearly spewed his mouthful of beer.

Luckily, he managed not to embarrass himself that badly, but holy hell… Had she really just implied that she'd be willing to share their bed? Or had he totally misread her statement?

He glanced at Rom, who sat with his mouth hanging open, obviously thinking the same thing. Nope. He hadn't misread her.

Holy shit.

Remy opened his mouth to say something, but Amity's bright eyes, teasing smile, and the graceful way she held that beautiful body distracted the hell out of him.

She truly wanted to know if they wanted to take her to bed.

Oh, hell yes.

Remy's gaze shot to Rom again. Amazingly, Rom appeared to have been struck dumb. Which left Remy to fill the void in the conversation.

Leaning forward, he looked directly into her eyes. "If I said that's exactly what we were looking for," Remy's muscles tensed with anticipation, "could we buy you another drink first?"

He was right. He saw no pity, only interest in her eyes as she smiled at him.

"I'd love another whiskey sour, thank you."

Rom stood immediately, his expression a polite mask that had Remy battling back a frown as his cousin nodded at Amity.

"I'll be right back."

What the hell?

He sent the thought directly at his cousin, knowing Rom could sense exactly what Remy was thinking. But Rom didn't answer or look back.

Remy wanted to smack his cousin on the back of the head. What the hell had shoved that stick up his ass?

"I'm sorry. Did I scare him away?"

Amity looked at Remy with a hint of regret in her eyes but Remy shook his head.

"Rom doesn't scare easily. And neither do I."

No, Rom wasn't scared. They'd both had that gene crushed out of them years ago. He didn't know what was up with his cousin. But he couldn't dwell on that. They'd come to this crowded *eteri* bar with one purpose. Get close to Amity.

"Brave words," she murmured. "So, how did you find out about this place? It's a little off the beaten path for the out-of-town crowd."

"One of our clients told us about it." Which was kind of the truth, if you stretched the meaning of client to include a *Malandante* pawn they'd captured four days ago and had questioned relentlessly until he'd given up this woman's name.

The spell he and Rom had worked to pinpoint the demon's whereabouts had led them to this bar, which shouldn't have been a shock.

The city of Reading and the surrounding county still held an old and powerful magic. Many in the magical Etruscan community, into which they'd been born, continued to call this area home. Many years ago, so had he and Rom.

Better not dwell on that now.

"So what exactly does a medical aesthetician do? I don't think I've heard of that profession before."

She paused, her teeth biting into her lower lip before she smiled again. "I mainly work with cancer and accident patients. Look, I hope you don't think I'm rude, but I'd rather not talk about work tonight."

He heard something in her voice that made him rein in his curiosity. Something painful. He didn't want her to feel any pain while she was in their company.

"No problem. Let's make professions off limits. Why don't we just agree not to talk about anything other than how much I want to get you naked and in bed?"

She blinked and her eyes widened just the slightest bit. *Shit.* He probably shouldn't have pushed that far that fast.

Damn it, he should've left the seduction to Rom. He was gonna kick Remy's ass—

She laughed, a slow, deep sound that brushed against his cock like a physical caress. His hands clenched and he had a sudden, vivid image of her spread out on a bed crooking her finger at him.

"I have to admit, it's been a long time since I met a man who made me consider simply jumping into bed with him after a few minutes. Let alone two men."

Fierce, hot triumph licked through him. "And are you considering it?"

Her smile answered for her.

Yes. He wanted to pump his fist in the air. Wanted to toss her over his shoulder and find the nearest bed. Or maybe he'd just bend her over the table and take her now.

Probably attract a little too much attention but, damn, it'd *so* be worth it.

Shoving back the lust that threatened to swamp him, he took a deep breath and forced himself to remember why they needed her. She was a means to an end, one that had been coming for a very long time.

But right here, right now, that need was not based on what they wanted her to do for them but what he wanted to do *to* her.

"So, Remy, would you and your cousin like to come back to my house for a drink?"

Oh, hell yes.

Luckily, Remy didn't blurt that out loud. And not because Rom had overheard Amity's question from his place at the bar and sent a warning thought straight back to him.

Remy half expected Rom to rush back and take over the conversation. Couldn't say he'd blame his cousin. Remy didn't normally do this, the pick-up stage. He usually left that to Rom.

But there was something about her…

"We would love to."

Chapter 2

Conveniently, Rom hadn't bought their drinks yet, and Amity watched Remy catch his cousin's eye and motion him back to the table.

If she hadn't been watching Remy so closely, she would've missed it. She had the feeling these two were much more than business partners, though she didn't get the vibe that they were lovers. Yes, they had ties, but they weren't romantic in nature.

Through her empathy, she felt emotion running between them, a complex mix of love and guilt and responsibility.

Family, she decided. Not brothers. She didn't sense that deep of a blood connection.

But there was a connection. A strong one.

And apparently, they'd both decided on her for this… whatever this was. Pick up. Hook up. One night stand.

Am I really going to go through with this? What if—

No. Mentally, she shook off that thought. She wasn't going to talk herself out of this.

She'd made up her mind. What could one night with two hot men hurt? She sensed absolutely no danger from them and she was a goddess, after all. They couldn't hurt her. Even if they worked together, she still had enough power to knock them unconscious and kick their asses to the curb if they tried to harm her.

But she felt absolutely no malicious intent from either of them. What she felt was desire.

And it made her slightly intoxicated.

"Amity?"

She looked up at Rom, his dark eyes so intent, questions lurking. She let her lips curve in a smile that forced the questions from his eyes and replaced them with heat.

"I'm ready. My car's parked on the street. I don't live far. Would you like to follow me?"

"We can do that." Rom exchanged another glance with Remy then extended his hand to help her up. The gesture made her smile. It was old-fashioned and sweet, totally contradicting the lust etched into the handsome lines of his face and the leashed strength in his hand.

A shiver ran through her and she knew, without a doubt, that these men had *arus* flowing through their veins, the power that was passed from generation to generation in the ancient magical races. It certainly explained the connection she felt to them.

After collecting her purse from Jill, who said good night with wide eyes and a snarky grin that promised a full grilling tomorrow, she walked back to the men waiting by the door. They accompanied her to her car, the silence heightening her awareness of them.

Remy walked by her side, close enough that she could feel the heat of his skin. Her head barely came up to his shoulder. Rom stayed slightly behind them, as if guarding their backs. Which was silly.

What danger could be lurking in the streets of sleepy West Reading?

Plenty. And not all of it from this world. She shivered, knowing she wasn't as safe as she'd like to think.

"Are you cold?" Remy asked. Before she could respond, Rom had draped his suit coat over her shoulders.

The warm, masculine scent hit her low in the gut, made her thighs tighten and her sex moisten. If she wasn't careful, she'd throw herself on them the second they entered her home.

And what would be the harm in that?

She didn't abide by the dictates of *eteri* morality. As much as they liked to believe they'd liberated themselves from their puritanical past, many *eteri* couldn't talk about sex without a guilty grin or a blush.

They still believed sex without an emotional connection, or a legal piece of paper, was wrong. They didn't realize how much energy sex created. Or how you could use that energy.

"Warm enough now." She turned to smile at Rom, who nodded then began scanning their surroundings with that sharp gaze. The man missed nothing.

"My car's parked down this street." She pointed to her bright red Audi convertible about halfway down the block. "I'll wait here for you so you can follow me."

"No need to wait. We're parked right over there."

Remy pointed to a late-model blue Cadillac practically across the street from her car.

Coincidence?

Of course, it had to be. How would they have known which car was hers? Unless they'd been following her.

No, that was her paranoia talking. If they'd recognized her as Munthukh, they would have identified themselves as Etruscan. And she would have recognized them from the *lucani* den, from the small *Fata* community to the north of the city, or from the general Etruscan population who still held to the old ways.

The group grew smaller every year as their deities grew obsolete and wielded much less power. It was a vicious cycle and one she could do nothing about.

Forcing those depressing thoughts to the back of her mind, she glanced up at Remy, who looked at her with a hint of speculation in his eyes.

"My home isn't far. You'll need to turn around to follow me."

"Don't worry. We'll be right behind you."

Her mind automatically produced an image of her bent over a

table while Rom fucked her from behind and Remy sat in front of her masturbating while he waited for his turn.

She tried to hide her indrawn breath as she turned to open her car door, aware that neither man had moved. They waited until she got in her car and started it before they crossed the street to theirs.

The drive to her home seemed to take longer than usual and when she finally pulled into the driveway of her cozy, brick Cape Cod in the small neighborhood next to the county's Catholic high school, she wanted to run for the door, grab whoever came through first, and ravage them. Then, she'd start on the next one.

They'd probably think she was desperate. They wouldn't be too far off the mark. She couldn't remember the last time she'd felt this depth of need, this clawing ache.

She knew she'd get to sate it soon, but that made her almost frantic. She had to force herself to slow down before she ran for the door.

Remy and Rom were at her side before she reached the front door, two large, silent, strong men who looked at her with matching lust in their eyes.

She aimed the key at the lock but missed the mark and had to try again. Her hand trembled as she managed to slide the key home on the second try. The door swung open with little effort and she stepped into the house, feeling the magical wards Salvatorus had helped her put on the house slide by her.

She turned in time to see Rom and Remy exchanged a glance as they followed her.

Definitely Etruscan. They'd sensed her wards.

A question settled on the tip of her tongue but she never got to ask it.

Remy closed the few steps between them, grabbed her shoulders, and settled his mouth over hers for a kiss that rocked her down to her toes, curling them in her pumps.

Maybe she should have been frightened. Or, at the very least, startled.

All she felt was the molten burn of lust as it blazed through her body. All she tasted was the desire on his lips and the lash of his tongue as he licked his way into her mouth.

No intent to hurt or dominate through fear. Well, maybe she sensed a little domination, and she was totally okay with that.

She lifted her hands to place them on his chest, feeling Rom's coat slide off her shoulders. His dark, earthy scent still clung to her but now it blended with Remy's heat and spice.

Pure intoxication. And hard, hot muscle beneath her hands.

Blessed Mother Goddess, she wanted to strip him to his skin right here in the tiny foyer of her house.

She moaned into his mouth as his arms wrapped around her and his hands splayed across her back. His erection pressed against her stomach as he pulled her closer until they were plastered together from chest to thigh.

And the man could *kiss*. No hesitation, no fumbling. Just a masterful touch that made her want to melt into him.

She gave him all the control, let him kiss her until she could barely breathe and she saw stars beneath her eyelids.

Vaguely, she realized her feet had left the ground and she moved her hands up to his shoulders then around his neck. Her fingers curled into his shaggy hair, lacing through the strands as if she thought he might try to get away.

She couldn't stand the thought, couldn't bear to think she could be left alone to deal with this raging hunger.

Slow down. Slow down.

No, she didn't want slow. She wanted fast. A flash fire, not banked embers.

Remy seemed to know exactly how to give her what she wanted.

Stepping forward, he put her back against the wall then crowded even closer. Pressed so tight, he seemed bigger. Harder. And infinitely more male.

Now she swore she felt the beat of his blood pulsing in his cock and her hips arched forward. The ache in her sex demanded relief, demanded to be filled.

She started a slow grind against his cock, needing that pressure, anticipating the burn when he'd fill her.

Even through his clothes she could tell he was thick. She wanted him inside her.

She tried to draw her legs up but her tight skirt had her legs trapped.

And he seemed in no hurry to help her with that problem.

Holding her against him with one arm around her waist, he used his free hand to cup her head. He tilted her head into the perfect position for his mouth to ravage hers, his fingers woven through her hair. The slight tug against her scalp only added to her pleasure.

She moaned into his mouth, and his body hardened even more.

When he pulled away, her immediate response was to pull him back to her. She wasn't finished with his mouth.

But then he looked into her eyes and said, "Where's the bedroom?"

Heat flashed through her body. Her clit swelled and her sex clenched in a burst of lust.

"Up the stairs."

His gaze flashed away from hers for a brief second before he shifted his hold on her, swinging her into his arms and striding toward the stairs. He stopped at the bottom to look over his shoulder and Amity followed his gaze to Rom.

Rom stood by the front door, watching them. Arms crossed over his chest, Rom's expression gave nothing away. Only his erection ruining the line of his pants let her know he wasn't unmoved.

Something passed between the men. The exchange lasted only seconds but she knew Remy wasn't happy with Rom's response, whatever that had been.

And she knew Remy won when Rom's mouth tightened just before he pushed away from the wall.

Remy didn't wait to see if Rom followed him up the stairs but he must've known he would.

Looking over Remy's shoulder, she watched Rom as he trailed behind them. He made brief eye contact with her, as if he were trying to tell her something. She had no idea what that might be but she was so glad he followed.

Since her bedroom occupied the entire second floor, Remy had no trouble finding it.

And when he saw her bed, his lips curved in a smile. This was the reason she'd had the walls removed up here after she'd bought the house.

"Nice bed." Remy's voice held a distinct humor that lit her up inside.

"Thank you. I—"

He tossed her on it and she barely had time to laugh before Remy reached for her blouse and began popping open buttons.

Her laughter stalled at the intensity in his expression. Her nipples tightened into painful points as her gaze dropped to watch his hands. Dark against the white silk of her blouse, his fingers made short work of the buttons then pulled the tails from the waistband of her skirt. He bared the nude lace of her bra. She expected him to put his hands on her breasts, waited for it with bated breath, but couldn't exactly be disappointed when he reached for the side closure on her skirt.

He opened the zipper with the same precise movements he'd used on her blouse. His fingers brushed against her skin, making goose bumps rise before he gripped the sides of the skirt and tugged it off her hips. With a deliberate shimmy, she let him pull the skirt off her legs. He tossed the skirt at the closest chair, an old, butter-soft leather armchair at the head of her bed. But Rom stepped into her line of sight and caught the skirt before it made it to the chair.

She watched as he laid the skirt on the dresser then lowered himself into the chair, sinking back into the cushions, his hands settled loosely on the arms.

Rom was going to watch.

She hadn't realized she was holding her breath until Remy pushed the blouse off her shoulders then lifted her off the bed so he could strip her shirt away.

This time, he tossed it at Rom, who snagged it in one hand. She expected him to drop it. Instead, he kept it, rubbing his fingers over the soft material as he continued to watch her.

Her thighs quivered, her gaze caught on his hand, wondering what it would be like when he got his hands on her.

Would he be rougher than Remy? His hands lay on her bare stomach, calluses lining his palms. The man was no stranger to manual labor. They scraped across her sensitive skin as he dragged his hands up her torso to cup her breasts. Her breath caught in her throat and she arched her back, pushing her breasts harder into his hands.

He squeezed the mounds, his gaze dropping to watch her generous flesh spill out over the cups of her bra, his eyes narrowing to slits of vibrant, burning blue.

She watched Remy caress her, watched as the corner of his mouth curled up as he started to pull her bra down, exposing her breasts fully. Tight and achy, she wanted him to take her breasts in his hands and squeeze them, ease this ache. Instead, he abandoned her breasts, leaving her bra to cup but not conceal.

"Beautiful." Remy's voice had a rough edge that made her lungs tighten and fight for each breath.

Then he bent over her and bared his teeth. He sank them into her nipple, gently at first, rolling the tip between his teeth before he bit down and forced a cry from her.

He hadn't hurt her, unless you considered the almost

soul-destroying ache in her pussy to be painful. Which it was. Just not the kind of pain she wanted to give up. No, she wanted him to use those teeth all over her body.

She reached for his head, her fingers sinking again into those lush waves as he worshipped her breasts with his mouth and his hands. Plumping the mounds, he sucked on the tips then bit until she reflexively yanked hard on his hair.

He didn't release her, just bit harder then trailed his lips to her breastbone where he began a slow descent. She watched Remy as he bit and licked his way down her belly, letting his tongue rim her navel before he continued down to blow on her pubic hair. The cool brush of air made her shiver and her eyes flashed to Rom, whose muted groan had rumbled through the room.

She felt Remy smile against her hip bone, where he'd pressed a kiss as his hands slid under her ass so he could lift her as he sank to his knees. The cool cotton of his shirt brushed against the smooth silk of her thigh-high stockings as he spread her legs, her gaze still locked to Rom's.

His shoulders looked as broad as a barn in his white, button-down shirt, but it was the hand that didn't hold her blouse that held her attention right now. As Remy pressed kisses along the inside of her thigh, Rom unbuckled his belt, unbuttoned his pants, and pulled down his zipper.

Sliding his hand into his pants, he pulled out his cock and wrapped his hand around the thick shaft.

As she watched, Rom began a slow, rough masturbation, almost hypnotic in its beauty.

"Are you watching Rom?" Remy asked, his lips centimeters away from the throbbing lips of her labia. "He likes when you watch. He gets off watching. Watching your expression when I put my mouth on your breasts. When I put my fingers inside you."

Remy brushed his fingertips across her labia, causing her to gasp as electricity shot through her, centering in her clit and spreading into her core.

"Your pussy is gonna taste so fucking good but first I'm gonna fuck you with my fingers so you're slick and ready."

Good gods. She was ready to come just from the sound of his voice and the visual stimulation of Rom stroking himself with an increasingly heavy hand. And when Remy began to sink his fingers between the sensitive lips of her sex, her free hand, the one not entangled in Remy's hair, grabbed at the comforter beneath her and held on.

Remy didn't begin slow and speed up. He started with a steady, forceful rhythm, one that pushed her into a heightened state of sensuality. Her body responded with a fresh surge of lust and she heard Remy suck in a deep breath, as if breathing her in.

Then she heard him growl, a distinct sound that rumbled out of his chest and made every hair on her body stand on end. Her pussy tightened around his fingers, an orgasm beginning to short-circuit her brain.

So much heat. She thought she might spontaneously combust. She wanted to savor the sensations but Remy kept pushing her.

He leaned in and flicked the tip of his tongue against her clit, teasing a sharp cry from her lips. Everything went black as her eyes closed and she tried to hold back the inevitable. But her body tensed in preparation, her brain blank—

And he pulled away.

"No. You can watch me or you can watch Rom but you have to keep your eyes open, Amity. We want to watch you."

It was so hard to do when all she wanted was to lose herself in the maelstrom building inside. Still, she wanted what he was going to give her. She forced her eyes to remain open, her gaze falling first to Remy, his eyes glinting with lust, before she turned to Rom.

He had his hand wrapped around the thick length of his cock.

The dark, distended tip appeared and disappeared rapidly as he pumped with a ruthless rhythm. She nearly lost herself in the motion, felt her breathing shift to mimic his.

"Fuck."

Remy's rough tone barely registered as Rom's hand began to speed up. With his tie loosened, his shirt untucked and his pants unzipped to release his cock, he looked like a white-collar wet dream. The intensity in his expression scalded, mesmerized her so she almost overlooked the fact that Remy was opening his pants with one hand while he worked her with the other.

Her pussy had such a tight grip on his fingers, he could barely move them. And when he finally pulled free and shot to his feet, she nearly demanded he continue, even though she knew she was about to be filled more satisfactorily.

Looking down her body, she watched Remy shove his pants down far enough to release his cock. A little slimmer than Rom's, maybe a little longer. And oh so much closer.

She reached for him as he moved toward her.

"That's it, babe." Remy grabbed her hips and pulled her closer. "Wrap your hand around my cock. Stroke me. Pull me closer. Rub your pussy lips all over the head. God damn, that feels great."

He stood still as she ran her hand along the shaft, marveling at the softness of the skin over the steel-hard core beneath.

She needed him inside, didn't want to wait any longer. Arching her hips, she felt the head of his cock nudge at her entrance then stop. She felt the leashed energy in his body, knew he was holding himself back. His expression tightened, his features honed into sharp planes as his gaze dropped to where they were almost joined.

"So beautiful." His voice had gotten even rougher, if that were possible.

Then he surged forward, burying the entire length of his cock in one hard thrust.

Her head punched back into the bed as a wave of heat rolled through her body. It felt almost like…

She cried out, her hands wrapping around his wrists as his hands gripped her hips and began a pounding rhythm. Remy hadn't taken off his shirt and the tails tickled against her stomach, adding to the sensations already driving her closer to orgasm.

Her eyes began to drift closed but she remembered his directive and forced them to remain open. Through the narrow gaze, she saw dark pleasure flood Remy's face then harden into fierce determination. He thrust again and again, shifting her, moving her until he had the best position for maximum friction against her clit and inside her sheath.

Every motion pushed her closer to the edge but he kept her hanging there for what seemed like forever. Almost to the point of pain, to a point she hadn't felt in years. Power simmered, just out of reach.

She tried to concentrate but these men and their dual assault on her senses had scrambled her brain.

She felt her orgasm blister through her body, twisting her, tearing through her. Remy paused for a second as her sex convulsed around him, then he rode her hard, prolonging the bliss.

Vaguely, she heard Rom's harsh grunt, felt Remy shudder as he pumped his release into her.

And realized, only minutes afterward, that she'd nearly achieved something even more amazing than that orgasm.

For a few seconds, she'd felt more than sated.

She'd felt powerful.

—·—

Rom knew she was going to ask them both to stay.

Which was exactly what they'd wanted. So when the demon attacked, they'd be here.

As he cleaned up in the bathroom, he debated making an excuse to leave her and Remy alone.

She was the first woman in whom Remy had shown any interest. Ever.

And Rom wanted her so badly, his teeth ached with it.

But it was one thing to get off watching her and Remy have sex. It was another to fuck the woman his cousin actually *liked*.

They were so close to achieving their goal. Too close to let a woman screw with their heads.

Frustration burned like a ball of hot silver in his stomach. Looking at his reflection in the mirror, he saw that same frustration reflected in the tight slash of his mouth and the glitter of his eyes.

Closing his eyes, he forced himself to relax, to loosen his muscles, to subdue the desire.

When he thought he had himself under control, he took another look in the mirror. And figured it wasn't going to get much better.

So he'd make a damn fast exit.

Unfortunately, he'd have to walk through the bedroom to leave, but maybe he'd get lucky and she'd be asleep already.

Then he'd only have to deal with Remy.

But he knew he couldn't hide in the bathroom any longer.

Straightening his shoulders, he opened the door to find Remy lying on the bed beside Amity. He'd drawn a cover over her and Rom sensed she'd fallen asleep.

Remy had removed his button-down, leaving a T-shirt to cover the scars on his chest. He still had his pants but he'd lost the shoes and socks.

Nodding his head toward the stairs, Rom headed for them, silently telling Remy to stay.

Of course, Remy didn't obey. His cousin followed him down the stairs to the front door.

"Where the hell are you going?" Remy put his body in front of the door so Rom couldn't leave.

"I'm just going to do a little reconnaissance while she's sleeping. Leave my clothes in the car. I'll be back before dawn."

A run would help get rid of some of this frustration. And as long as none of the neighbors had really good night vision, no one would even know he was there.

Remy's eyebrows lifted slightly. "Wanna tell me why you're heading out for a run when there's a beautiful woman in that bed?"

Not really. "She's worn out. Stay. Get some rest. I'll be outside." He paused. "She likes you, Remy."

Now his cousin's eyes narrowed with speculation. "What's going on?"

Rom deliberately misunderstood Remy's question. "I know you noticed the wards when we walked in. I wanna do a little nosing around. Keep her upstairs. Keep her occupied."

For a few seconds, Rom wasn't sure Remy was going to let him get away with it. Then Remy sighed. "What do you think you're going to find?"

"Not sure yet. Probably nothing. It's an old house. It could be an old ward, previous owner. Don't know. But if we're going to kill that demon and we have to fight here, everything we know betters our chances."

"Then I should come with you."

Rom shook his head. "You stay with her. I'll let you know if I find anything important. Go back up. Keep her busy if she wakes. I'll be back before dawn but warn me if she's an early riser. If I can't make it back in to pretend like I slept on the sofa, tell her I got a cab and went back to our hotel. Maybe we'll get lucky and the demon'll attack tonight."

He wanted this over. Finally.

Remy's mouth twisted. "I think your idea of lucky differs from mine."

Probably. Didn't change facts, though. Rom started to undress. "If I find anything, I'll let you know."

"Don't be stupid." Remy took his clothes and folded them as neatly as any butler. "You see the demon, you let me know."

Rom nodded. "I will. I know I can't take the thing down myself. Don't worry, Remy. I'm not stupid."

Remy just looked at him until Rom gave him the finger.

"Go back to her. I'll see you in a few hours."

—⁓—

Amity walked into the hospital that morning trying not to grin like a fool.

How could she help it, though, when she'd woken with a gorgeous naked man wrapped around her.

Remy had kissed her good morning, made coffee while she showered then asked if he could see her again tonight.

She'd said yes, probably too fast, but she hadn't cared. Then she'd asked if Rom would be joining them again.

"You can ask him yourself," Remy had said. "He wanted me to tell you he's sorry he skipped out last night. He had an early appointment."

They'd exchanged numbers and he'd left with a smile, which had been infectious.

Opening the door to her office, she flicked the lights—

And nearly screamed like a little girl when she saw someone sitting at her desk.

"Jeez, I know it's been a few years, Amity, but did you have to scare the crap out of me?"

Quickly shutting the door behind her, Amity released a sigh as she realized who sat at her desk. "Tinia's teat, Kari. You scared the hell out of *me*. What are you doing here? Did anyone see you?"

Her twin sister sighed as she twirled in circles in Amity's desk chair. "Still so worried about appearances. Of course, since we do look exactly alike and you never tell anyone you have a sister, I guess you would be worried."

Amity didn't bother to conceal her eye roll. "Kari. I love you dearly, but what are you doing here?"

The chair stopped spinning and Kari stuck her elbows on Amity's desk and put her chin on her hands. "Nice to see you too, big sis. I'm fine, by the way. Just returned from Etruria. You remember home, right? The one in Italy? Saw a few old friends, had some great sex with a *linchetto*. Or two. Possibly three. Oh, and I brought some of Fuflun's wine for you because I know how much you love it. And from the looks of you, you could do with some loosening up. We should share a bottle tonight and catch up. You can tell me all about your latest sob stories and I will tell you all about my latest conquests. I did tell you about the *linchetto*, right?"

Amity was laughing and shaking her head by the time Kari shut her mouth and stared up at her with those oh, so deceivingly innocent eyes.

"Yes, but I believe you said there were three." Closing the distance between them, she drew Kari to her feet and exchanged a tight hug. "I *have* missed you and I *am* glad to see you. You just startled me. So, tell me what you're doing here. Usually you at least give me a heads-up when you visit so I know to stock up on Bugles and orange soda."

Kari giggled as she pulled away, her long, wavy hair flying around her like a cloak. These days, Kari, formerly Akhuvitr, Etruscan Goddess of Healing, looked like a reject from the 1960s. A flower child, sometimes complete with actual flowers in her hair to complement the crinkly skirts and gauze shirts. Peace and free love, baby, that was Kari all the way.

"Well, I'm not staying long enough for that. I've got a commune to christen in Southern California tomorrow." Kari hopped onto the wide window ledge as Amity started her computer and stuck her purse in a drawer. "But I'm surprised you didn't know I was coming. This is a command performance, after all."

Amity frowned at her sister. "What are you talking about?"

As she spoke, Amity felt the hair on her arms rise and saw Kari's gaze shift to a point behind her.

"Oh, good. You're here. I thought for sure you'd be late."

Concealing a sigh as she thanked the Great Mother Goddess that her office was in one of the oldest wings of the building with no windows into the hallway, Amity turned, making sure she had a smile for her newest guest.

"Hello, Nortia. And how are you this morning?"

Dressed in a conservative black suit that still managed to be sexy, the Barbie-doll blonde with a body to match shrugged her shoulders. "Same old, same old." Then her blue gaze narrowed. "You, however, look like you had a good night. Anything you want to share with the class?"

"Ooh, sis, did you get lucky last night?" The surprise in Kari's voice made Amity frown. It wasn't like she was a virgin. Or a hermit. "Spill. I want details."

Amity refused to let the blush burning beneath her skin rise to the surface. She loved her twin, but Kari would want to interrogate her, and Nortia would probably tell her all the reasons why last night had been a bad idea. Nortia was the Goddess of Fate, after all.

Shooing Kari away from the window, she pointed at the two guest chairs in front of her desk. Time to move this along. She did have work to do today. "I take it you two are here for a reason other than my sex life. Nortia, what's going on?"

The Goddess of Fate gave her the look she typically reserved for men. The one that said she wasn't getting away with anything.

Amity chose to ignore it.

"Actually," Nortia said, "there *is* something a little more important going on. Kari, sit down. You make me crazy when you don't sit still."

With a huff, Kari flopped into the chair next to Nortia, who gave a long-suffering sigh, to which Kari responded with a toothy grin.

"I know you both heard what happened to Tessa."

Yes, they'd heard. Kari's lack of a smart-ass response was proof enough of the shock they'd all experienced when Tessa, formerly the

Etruscan Goddess of the Dawn, had given up her powers to avoid being consumed by Charun, the Etruscan God of the Underworld. Charun wanted to leave Aitás, the Etruscan Underworld, but doing so would open the gates between his realm and Earth. And that would have catastrophic consequences.

"What you probably don't know," Nortia continued, "is what happened to Lucy."

Amity and Kari exchanged a brief glance before they returned their full attention to Nortia.

"Tell us." Their perfectly synchronized response made Nortia shake her head.

"I sometimes forget you two are identical," Nortia muttered before shaking her head. "And then you do that. It is kind of creepy."

"Nortia." Amity tapped her desk with one finger. "Focus, love."

No one ordered the Goddess of Fate to do anything. Not if they wanted to continue breathing without the help of a ventilator. Not even her sister goddesses pushed her. But Amity was feeling more than a little brave this morning.

Nortia merely rolled her eyes. "Fine. Lucy transferred her goddess powers to Cat. She no longer holds the mantle of Goddess of the Moon. Charun sent a demon after her and, for the safety of everyone involved, she decided it was time to relinquish her duties."

Amity's mouth dropped open in shock, and from the corner of her eye, she saw Kari do the same.

Nortia pinned Amity with her gaze before doing the same to Kari. "You two need to be on your toes. We think Charun has targeted one of you next."

Chapter 3

SHE'D BEEN WARNED.

If anyone asked, Amity would freely acknowledge the fact that she should have heeded Nortia's warning and taken just a little more care.

But had she listened?

Of course not. She hadn't believed Charun would come after her. She was such a minor goddess in comparison to Lucy and Tessa. Even when she'd been in full command of her powers, all those millennia ago, she'd never been what most people might call popular.

Sure, she'd had followers, but mostly, she'd been worshipped only when someone was gravely ill. That made for a lot of weeping people and though she was always glad to help, it was slightly depressing.

Before Paris Hilton, before Marie Antoinette… hell, before Cleopatra, she and Kari had been the original party girls, drinks in one hand and a man, or two, on the other.

And really, who could blame them? It'd been their way of decompressing from the death and destruction inherent in their duties. Amity may have lost some of the joy in life that Kari retained, but that didn't mean she was ready to hand herself on a platter to Charun.

The night sky held no glow from the moon, and clouds obscured the stars as she ran along the trail past the Reading Museum. The creek to her left babbled cheerfully, swollen after a full day of rain, concealing the sound of the demon chasing behind her.

It was late, yes, and she should've stayed inside the hospital but she'd sensed no danger when she'd walked across the street to the park. She'd just needed a respite. After her unsettling meeting with Nortia, she'd spent the entire day working with her patients. She'd needed a few minutes by herself to gather her thoughts before she met Remy and Rom for a late dinner. Remy had called to say they'd be late to pick her up and asked her to wait for them at the hospital.

Since she'd had a few minutes, she'd decided to take a walk on the beautiful grounds of the museum. Yes, the overcast sky made it darker than normal at seven o'clock on an early May night. And the air held a chill from the earlier rain.

But she'd never imagined she'd be running for her life from a wiry blue demon.

With her heart pounding in her chest and her lungs burning, she ran faster than she ever thought possible, considering she'd never been much for exercise. A goddess just didn't have to worry about gaining a few pounds or losing muscle tone. She was as she'd always be.

Since she happened to be five-foot-three and 130 pounds, she had curves other goddesses didn't. Which meant she lost points for maneuverability.

Still, the demon didn't appear to be gaining on her. And that didn't make sense.

Charun's enforcer must be playing with her.

She wanted to call the thing nasty names but bitch and bastard were gender specific and *tukhulkha* demons were gender neutral. No one knew why. That's just the way it was.

And didn't mean a damn thing at all to her situation right now.

She needed to get back to the safety of the hospital, where the demon wouldn't dare enter for fear of being seen by the *eteri*, those humans without magical powers. Screams would be sure to follow if an *eteri* caught sight of the nightmarish creature.

Of course, she'd begun to run in the wrong direction, and if she tried to double back now, the demon would be that much closer.

"Stupid. How could I be so stupid?"

Pretty freaking stupid, apparently, for all she thought of herself as a levelheaded person.

Luckily, she hadn't changed into the heels she'd brought for her dinner date. She still wore the comfy red running shoes she favored for long days at the hospital. They'd never gotten a workout like this before, though.

"Amity." The demon called her name, drawing out the three syllables to creepy lengths. "You know you can't outrun me. You're just not built for speed, dear. But please, keep running. This is so much fun."

Ooh, that blue bastard-bitch. How dare it taunt her?

What she wouldn't give for the ability to conjure a thunderbolt or two. She'd blast the demon's ass back to Aitás.

Barring that, she needed to use her brain. She'd walked these trails so many times, she knew them like the back of her hand.

The tiny bridge at Trudy's Garden. If she could get there and get over it before the demon, maybe she could outrun it back to the next bridge. Then, if she could make it up the small hill, she might be able to get to the emergency room entrance where she could alert the guard.

Not that she could actually tell him what was after her. Chet, the nearly eighty-year-old man who stood at the door in a uniform and directed people, would think she'd lost her senses. But at least he could call the police.

Or maybe she'd get lucky and there'd be a police car there. It wasn't unlikely—

She tripped and nearly fell, a short, startled cry falling from her lips before she could bite it back and right herself. Luckily, she didn't go down but she lost precious ground. She swore she heard the sound of the demon's feet pounding behind her.

"Oh, dear. Are you okay, Amity? Hope you didn't hurt yourself. Don't worry, I'll be there soon, and all this exertion will be at an end."

Her lungs burned, as did her thighs and calves. She didn't know how much longer she could keep up this pace.

Above the din of the creek, she heard the ringing of the chimes that hung from trees in the pretty little garden near the end of the park. She was so close, she thought she could smell freshly turned earth. Just a few more feet before she reached the bridge—

The demon brushed a hand down her back, causing Amity to scream.

Sweet Mother Goddess, this was it. The demon would take her back to Aitás for Charun to consume her soul.

She did trip then. Her feet tangled together and she hit the ground hard. The air rushed from her lungs and starbursts flashed before her eyes as her head bounced off the paved surface of the trail.

Pain flared seconds later, beginning in her temples and radiating throughout her entire body. Still, she tried to scramble to her feet but only got to her knees when she felt a hand grab her shoulder.

"Steady there."

The masculine voice made her head snap up. She realized someone stood in front of her. A tall, masculine shadow whose face she couldn't make out in the darkness of the park but whose voice sounded so familiar.

"Are you ok—"

Amity pushed away the hand he'd extended toward her, terror making her shake. "You've got to run. Go now or you'll be killed."

His hand didn't move. "No, I don't think I will."

The certainty in his tone made Amity blink up at him in astonishment as she realized the man standing above her was Rom.

She opened her mouth to yell at him but felt a chill seep into her body that had nothing to do with the air temperature. Her time was up. The negative energy of the demon began to suck at her positive force, the energy that allowed her to heal those who needed it. If she lost too much of it, she would be no good to anybody.

"Well now, it looks like you've found a hero," the demon taunted. "How nice for you. He'll make a tasty snack for later, won't you, *lucani?*"

Lucani. She blinked up at Rom, standing so tall above her. He was an Etruscan wolf shifter? Why hadn't she realized that last night? Was Remy too?

How had she missed it?

Reaching down, Rom wrapped a strong hand around her arm and pulled her to her feet then drew her behind him.

"You'll have to break me first, demon." Rom's deep voice was filled with palpable menace. "And, trust me, you won't get the chance."

Peeking out from around his shoulder, Amity watched the demon emerge from the shadows, close enough now for her to see the whites of its eyes. Its body was nothing more than another dark shadow sliding through the night.

She shivered, the demon's menace surrounding them like a force field. Blessed Mother Goddess, this was no rank-and-file demon, she realized. This was no minion.

This demon had the blue skin and black hair as all *tukhulkha* demons did, but it also had small black horns erupting from its temples and curving back along its head. And she was sure, if it turned, she'd see the demon's black wings tucked behind it.

It was one of the few generals in Charun's army. A demon didn't earn horns or wings until it'd proven itself to Charun's exacting standards of pain and torment.

This situation became stranger every second.

Why would Charun risk sending one of his high-ranking demons to track her? She couldn't have fended off an attack from a regular demon, much less one with so much power. And how had Rom known she'd needed help?

"So cocky for a lowly dog." The demon's voice dripped with disdain, ripping across Amity's empathy like claws, making her breath catch at the pain. "But you'll bleed just like the rest."

Rom laughed and she detected absolutely no amusement in the sound. Or fear, for that matter. "I may bleed a little but you're the one who's going down. When I rip your throat out, you'll cry just like all those you've killed before."

The demon's head cocked to the side, its expression visible now that Amity's eyesight had adjusted. It looked contemplative and when a demon got that look on its face, you really should run the other way. Because it was either thinking about eating you or tearing you into little bits in preparation to do so.

"We've met before, haven't we?" The demon put its hands on its hips in a strangely feminine pose, making the hair on Amity's neck rise. "Have I eaten your loved ones? Possibly maimed a friend? How awful for you."

"All of the above, actually. And now you're going to pay."

The demon's eyes rounded in mocking wonder. "Is your name Inigo by any stretch of the imagination? You know that would just make my day."

"My name's Romulus Cangelosi."

The demon rolled its eyes as if the name meant nothing. "Pity. I'm a huge fan of *The Princess Bride*. So"—the demon crossed its arms over its chest—"what'll it be, Romulus? A fight to the death—yours, of course—then I'll take the lovely little goddess anyway. Or should we make it more interesting and I could kill the goddess while you watch and then kill you? Which would you prefer?"

"Actually I prefer the version where I take your head off."

"You don't actually think that's going to happen, do you?"

"There's always a first time."

The demon smiled, a mouth full of sharp teeth that made Amity grow faint at the sight. Blessed Goddess, she did *not* want to be on the receiving end of those.

But neither did she want to see Rom ripped to shreds before her.

She laid her hand on his shoulder, feeling the bunch of warm, hard muscle. "Please don't get yourself killed on my account."

He didn't take his eyes off the demon. "I don't intend to, Lady Amity."

The demon actually laughed, sounding so human it was eerie. "Such a brave boy."

"I'm no longer a boy and I've been a little focused on you."

"Much as I appreciate your focus, I think we've delayed this long enough."

The demon leaped, causing Amity to scream and fall backward even as Rom held his ground.

It all happened so fast, she wasn't sure what came next. From her vantage point on her ass behind Rom, all she saw was the demon suddenly fly to the side as if a gust of wind had taken it off its feet and thrown it away.

Then she realized a huge dark shadow crouched over the demon, growling like a wild beast.

Or a *lucani* wolf.

Remy.

With a high-pitched screech, the demon tossed the wolf aside, scrambled to its feet, and shot straight for Amity.

She barely had time to gather breath to scream again before Rom drew a sword from the sheath on his back and slashed at the oncoming demon.

Amazingly, the demon avoided being cut by the huge blade and the wolf set on it with another attack.

"Run, Amity!" Rom shouted at her. "We'll take care of this. Go!"

Scrambling to stand, Amity managed to hold her knees steady when they wanted to fold under her. Proximity to the demon sapped her strength at an alarming rate.

She tried to run but could barely manage to walk. And when she heard the wolf yelp in pain, she couldn't help herself.

She stopped and turned back to the fight.

Remy's wolf lay sprawled on the ground, unmoving as the man cried out, raising the sword above his head. He looked wild, his expression grief-stricken. And he'd left himself wide open to attack.

The demon smirked, sensing an opening, and tensed to leap.

"No!" Her cry made no impression on the demon but Rom flashed her a quick look.

And in that second, the demon saw its opening.

Rom had no chance to save himself from the demon's attack and took the full brunt of its charge. Demon claws caught him in the side, and Rom cried out in pain as the sword fell from his hands. But he managed to get his hands up and around the demon's neck to keep its teeth and, more important, the deadly venom those teeth produced away from his throat.

The demon hissed, his clawed hands readying for another slash as Amity, reacting on pure instinct, scrambled for the sword.

She'd just wrapped both hands around the hilt when she heard the wolf snarl. The wolf moved so fast, he looked like a passing cloud as he shot to his feet and jumped on the demon's back.

The wolf's jaws opened, aiming for the demon's neck. As if anticipating the move, the demon wrenched hard to the right, trying to roll onto his back and bring Rom on top of him.

She realized then that Rom and the wolf had played the demon but she'd messed up their plan.

"Amity! Leave the sword. Run."

No, she couldn't run. If the *lucani* defeated the demon, they would need her help to heal because they were taking a beating. And if the demon won, well…

She wouldn't get far enough away for it to matter. The demon would run her down.

Instead, she struggled to lift the sword. It weighed a ton. She should run, get far, far away. She couldn't.

Adrenaline pumping, muscles straining, she lifted the sword as far as she could, only a couple of inches from the ground. It would have to be enough. She just hoped like hell she didn't hit Rom or the wolf.

The tangle of bodies rolled again and the wolf lost its grip on the demon. The demon shoved at the wolf, raking its claws along its flank.

This time, Remy's wolf wasn't faking the injury. He struggled to maintain his feet but he couldn't get his left back leg to move properly.

Still, the wolf went back at the demon, biting down on its arm and trying to drag it away from Rom. Which only caused Rom to cry out in pain, because the demon had its claws sunk in his side.

Seeing her opening, she pointed the sword at the demon's back. Ignoring the fact that she was about to cause mortal injury to another living creature, something that went against every cell of her being, she stabbed the demon as hard as she could with the pointed end of the weapon.

The demon roared as it lashed out, grabbing the sword and trying to rip it from her hands. Stupidly, she held on and was tossed to the ground along with the sword.

The demon howled, the evil sound cutting through the night like a siren. Surely someone had heard that and would come to investigate.

Would they believe what their eyes were seeing? Maybe it wouldn't matter.

"The sword. Lady, get me… the sword."

Rom's voice sounded strained and weak but he reached out to her with one hand. The other barely held the demon's snapping jaws at bay.

As fast as she could, she got to her knees and crawled toward him, pulling the sword along with her. It seemed to have gained a hundred pounds since she'd first picked it up.

Remy's wolf made another lunge for the demon, catching onto one of its legs with his teeth and holding on, even as the demon kicked and flailed.

A scream ripped from the demon's throat as Rom grabbed the sword from her hand and maneuvered it until he got the point stuck into the demon's side. Skewered, it thrashed as Rom forced the blade farther into its body.

With a grunt, Rom shoved the demon onto its back, keeping one hand firmly on its throat and the sword buried in its side.

Amity heard only the sound of her own breathing echoing in her ears as the demon weakened from blood loss until finally it lay still on the ground.

With a hard sigh, Rom rose to his feet.

As Rom stood over the creature, she turned toward the wolf, lying on its side and panting heavily. Though her healing skills worked best on humans, she could extend them to all living things.

Pushing to her feet, she stood for a second, just to make sure she wasn't going to keel over. She crossed the distance to the wolf, who lay on the ground watching Rom with glazed eyes.

"Will you let me examine you?" She kept her voice low, not wanting to startle him. "You're bleeding pretty badly. I can heal your wounds enough for you to shift, if you'd like."

The wolf spared her a quick glance then huffed, shaking his head as he turned back to Rom.

Amity followed his gaze, just in time to see Rom lift the sword and swing it down. With a gasp, she closed her eyes just in time.

She couldn't see what Rom had done. But she heard the sound of the blade as it cut through flesh.

Shaking with the aftereffects of fear and swallowing against the bile rising in her stomach, she drew in a deep breath.

"It had to be done, Lady. And it was our right to kill the demon."

The air shifted around her and she opened her eyes to the sight of Rom's broad chest directly in front of her. A tight, dark T-shirt stretched across the expanse, the fabric ripped in places.

Tilting her head back, she looked into his eyes.

She'd thought him handsome before. Tonight, he looked fearsome. His short, dark hair stood up in tufts, and dark scruff covered his jaws and chin, so very different from last night's clean-shaven businessman. So masculine. She had the almost uncontrollable urge to cup that jaw in her hands and let his whiskers rasp against her skin. Between her breasts. On the insides of her thighs.

Her blood heated just looking at him. Even after the terror of the past few minutes, she couldn't help but look at him and want to have that hard body pressed against hers on the soft sheets of a huge bed.

The sword made a heavy thump as it fell out of Rom's hand and dropped to the ground next to him. He would've followed it down if she hadn't grabbed him around the waist and held him up.

"Damn, I think I better sit down." His voice sounded slurred and husky. "I don't want to hurt you."

"I'm stronger than I look." And she was, though he must weigh almost a hundred pounds more than she did.

Glancing around, she spotted a park bench not too far from them and began to guide him to it.

The wolf whined, causing both of them to stop and turn back.

"We're not going far, Remy," she said. "Just to the bench."

It took forever to get Rom to the bench. Closing her eyes, she ran her hands over his body, from his head to his shoulders and chest, down his stomach to his thighs and shins.

"You're bleeding internally. I need to stop it now or you'll die, Rom."

The tear in his femoral artery wasn't big but he was already starting to show signs of blood loss. Praying she had power to heal him after such a long day and the damage inflicted by the demon, she smiled at Rom, infusing it with as much confidence as she could.

"I want you to lie still, Rom. Close your eyes now. And let me work."

As her power worked through touch, she let her hands settle onto his thigh.

Tinia's teat, this wound was deep. The demon had cut into the muscle, all the way to the bone.

Healing Rom would drain her. She'd need help returning home afterward. She had to hope Rom and Remy would be able to get her there.

Taking a deep breath, she closed her eyes and let her power rise.

His pain hit her first. It always did. She gasped as she took it in, accepted it, although it made her nerve endings scream and her muscles tighten.

She kept her hands steady and let the power seep from her into Rom. It sought out the pieces of him that needed healing.

She replaced the chips of bone that the demon had broken off, not a difficult task but necessary. Then she tackled the muscle tears. That required a delicate hand. And though she was out of practice, she thought she did a respectable job. She was confident he would regain full use of them.

Moving on to the rips in his skin, she knit them back together, making sure she left no scars. She didn't want him to have a constant physical reminder of this encounter.

She didn't know how long it took. She only knew that when she opened her eyes, the sky was pitch black and she saw the flashing lights of a police car as it stopped at the top of the hill, less than a quarter of a mile from where they were.

"Oh, dear."

Chapter 4

THE COLD, WET SWIPE of a wolf's tongue brought Rom back to full consciousness with a shudder.

"Damn it, Remy. What the hell?"

His cousin nudged him with his cold snout as he heard a woman's heartfelt sigh.

"Oh, thank the Blessed Mother Goddess," Amity said. "I was afraid the police were going to come down here and find you all bloody and unconscious and arrest me for assaulting you."

Sitting up, Rom instinctively grabbed for Amity as she trembled on her knees next to him.

"Are you okay?" he demanded. "Were you hurt? Bitten? Are you bleeding?"

She shook her head though it seemed an effort. "No, but you nearly died. And Remy's injured as well." She nodded to the wolf sitting and panting beside him. "We need to get out of here before the police see us and decide to investigate."

He'd nearly died? Is that why he felt like he could sleep for a week?

Didn't matter. Right now, he needed to find the strength to get the three of them away from here before anyone noticed that they looked like survivors of a massacre.

Standing, he pulled Amity to her feet as he glanced around.

They'd gotten lucky so far. The clouds hid the moon and the museum had no guards at night. It'd just been dumb luck that they'd ended up in an area of the park that had some cover from bushes and trees.

He didn't know how long it'd been since Amity—that wasn't her real name, was it? The woman who'd introduced herself last night as Amity was really the Goddess Munthukh. How was that for a twist in their screwed-up tale?

Well, it wasn't one he could spend any time thinking about right now. They needed to get back to the car.

Remy bled from several cuts on his body. Amity looked pale and disheveled and shaky. Rom looked down at himself. He looked like he'd just killed something and bathed in its blood.

Great.

Remy's wolf gave a low whine, his eyes vaguely dazed. No help there. But at least Remy was alive.

Focusing his attention on the goddess swaying in front of him, Rom reached for her, drawing her close to him and holding her tight. He couldn't believe neither he nor Remy had recognized her last night. His only excuse was that, for the past several years, he and Remy had been single-minded in their pursuit of the demon now turning into a pile of ash a few feet away.

They'd had no time to attend the rituals still held at Uni's Temple just across the Schuylkill River in center-city Reading.

But why hadn't Amity told them last night? Surely, she'd known they were *lucani*, Etruscan wolf shifters.

"Rom," Amity's voice sounded even more weak. "We need to get out of here."

Time for questions later. She was right. They needed to get moving.

He looked into his cousin's eyes and relief at his cousin's clear gaze flowed through him like a shot of fine whiskey.

Thank the Gods.

Shaking his head, Rom sank his fingers in the fur around the wolf's neck. "Let's get the hell out of here."

"Lady, may I carry you?"

"Last night it was Amity." Her voice was barely a whisper and he heard a weakness in it that worried him.

"Yeah, well, last night, I didn't know you were a goddess."

"I can walk. Let's just get out of here now. Remy has injuries as well. He needs to be healed."

Fine. She didn't want him to hold her. But she still needed his help to the car.

With his arm around her shoulders, Rom pointed her in the right direction. She didn't fight him. He'd like to think she trusted him but it was probably because she was too tired. She felt delicate against his side. Too damn breakable.

If the demon had hurt her…

Well, it hadn't. Though why a *tukhulkha* demon would be after a goddess, he didn't have a clue. It didn't make a damn bit of sense.

Remy whined and Rom's gaze snapped down to his cousin. Clutching Amity, Rom drew in a deep breath and stared into Remy's deep blue eyes, searching for reassurance that his cousin was okay. If anything happened to Remy…

The wolf huffed, shaking his head. Remy knew what Rom was thinking and he didn't like it. Remy hated when Rom worried about him. Which just meant Remy was pissed off most of the time.

Shoving those thoughts away, Rom started walking, careful not to go too fast for Amity.

As they passed the demon's remains, he noted they'd already shrunk into a pile of almost unrecognizable ash. When the sun hit it, the remains would disintegrate and blow away with a stiff breeze.

It seemed almost anticlimactic.

All this time, he and Remy had been chasing this demon. All these years spent tracking it and coming so close but always just a step behind.

They'd finally done what they'd set out to do almost twenty

years ago: wiped the murdering scum who'd killed their families off the face of the earth.

And saved a goddess in the process. A beautiful goddess with sable brown hair and a lush body.

"Remy."

His cousin had walked over to sniff at the remains, growling low in his throat then stomping on them with his paws, scattering them.

"Remy, we need to go."

The wolf gave one final growl, glared at the pile of ashes, then lifted his hind leg and gave them one final indignity.

When Remy limped to his side, he looked up at Rom. In his cousin's stormy blue eyes, Rom saw the fierce light of anger still raging.

He'd hoped once the demon was gone, Remy would lose that look.

Rom tried not to let disappointment rise. Hell, he probably still looked bloodthirsty too.

A good night's sleep and they'd be able to get on with their lives.

Yeah, and what exactly does that mean?

Rom shook his head, trying not to think about that. But now that he had, he couldn't contain it.

First things first.

Get Amity somewhere safe. Although now that the demon was dead, she wasn't in any immediate danger.

They made it back to the car without being seen, though they were nearly caught by an early rising dog walker whose dog had to water every damn tree on the block.

And there were a lot of frickin' trees.

Remy wanted to sneak up on the little mutt taking its own sweet time to round the corner and bite it in the ass. Rom sent him a wordless threat to stay put, which Remy reluctantly obeyed. Though Remy did give him a look that Rom knew was a mental middle finger.

He had Amity stand beside the front passenger door while he retrieved the key from the magnetic lock box hidden in the passenger-side front wheel well then opened the doors and got her settled in the front seat while Remy hopped into the back. With a sigh, she slumped into the seat and stared out the window.

Shit, she didn't look good.

Closing the doors, he hurried around to the driver's side and slid into the seat.

Behind him, Rom felt the pull of Remy's *arus* against his own as Remy recalled his pelt. His cousin's body began to contort in pleasurable pain as he retook his dominant human form.

Rom had to fight the urge to let his own wolf come to the surface as their blood connection kicked in. Since they'd been children, growing up together with their families in the forests of northern Pennsylvania, they'd had that connection.

It's what had led to their parents' deaths and driven them for the past twenty years.

And now that they'd killed the demon... What did they do with their lives?

"Rom, knock it off."

Rom turned and found Remy staring at him with stormy eyes and a scowl on his scarred face. Grown men had been known to run the other way when Remy turned that look on them.

Rom glared back at his cousin. "Get dressed before someone sees you, *scassacazzo*. I don't want to get stopped by the police with your dick wagging all over the place."

Remy just raised one brow before he took his sweet time pulling on clothes as Rom buckled Amity into the seat. She seemed to have fallen asleep, which was fine by him.

Dressed, Remy moved forward so he could let his hand stroke along Amity's disheveled hair.

Rom started the Jeep, wincing at the loud growl from the engine. *Vaffanculo*, he needed to get this thing tuned up so it didn't make so damn much noise. Or maybe he'd finally buy a new car since they wouldn't be battered and bloody so damn much now that they'd killed the demon.

"And there you go again, thinking too damn much." Remy's voice held just the right note of sarcasm to fire up Rom's ire. Remy was the only one who could do that so fast.

Rom prided himself on being relatively calm, cool, and collected during most situations.

Even in a fight, he never let his emotions get the better of him. Remy had enough for both of them.

One of them needed to be thinking ahead to the aftermath. Remy often lost himself in the fight, in the heat of the battle.

Even in the thick of things, Rom was thinking ahead to how to dispose of the bodies.

"It's a damn good thing one of us actually does think." Rom deliberately poked at Remy to see what he'd do.

Remy surprised him. He only gave Rom the finger then returned his attention to Amity.

"Why the hell didn't she tell us who she was?"

Rom put the Jeep in gear and pulled out onto the street, careful to keep to the speed limit as he drove away from the hospital and deeper into Wyomissing.

"No idea. Now I feel the vibe coming off her, like a low-level energy current. I didn't feel that at all yesterday."

On the off chance the demon hadn't been alone, he turned left onto Reading Boulevard, meaning to wind through this sleepy little borough just long enough to make sure they weren't being followed.

"Me either. Are we taking her back to her place or the house?"

"Ours. If there's another demon looking for her, they'll look there first."

Remy sighed and ran a hand through his shoulder-length, light brown hair, making a mess of the already tangled strands.

"Shit. Do you think there is?"

Rom cut around the traffic circle on Wyomissing Boulevard then headed west, out of the borough.

"I don't have a clue. We'll take her back to the house and take care of her until she wakes. Hopefully she's not injured." He shook his head. "Who the hell would hire a *tukhulkha* demon to hunt down a deity?"

"Someone must've hired the thing because someone has to pull their strings." Remy let his head fall back against the seat rest and breathed out a sigh.

Gritting his teeth against his increasing headache, Rom turned to take another look at Remy. With Remy's eyes closed, Rom saw the teenager Remy had been the night their families had been ripped apart by the demon.

At the second he thought about them, Remy opened his eyes. "How bad's your head?"

That damn psychic connection cut both ways. "Not that bad."

"You must've had internal injuries. She was worried you were gonna die."

Rom chose not to think about that as he drove the winding road to the home they'd rented in the wooded hills of Bern Township. It was far enough away from the city to avoid the radar of the thousand-or-so Etruscans who still lived in the city, and from the resident *lucani* pack in Rockland Township.

If the *lucani* knew they were here, the pack would've insisted they stay with them, would've wanted to know what brought them.

Rom hadn't wanted anyone to interfere with their vengeance.

Not that he thought the *lucani* king would've denied them the right to kill the demon. But King Colerus, from what Rom knew of him, would've demanded they take backup.

And neither Remy nor Rom had wanted that. It was their kill and only theirs.

"I'm fine. How are you?"

Remy hesitated a split second too long. "I'm fine."

"Bullshit. What's wrong?"

"Nothing."

Remy could be a hardheaded *scassacazzo* when he wanted. Rom gave the Jeep a little more gas.

Silence ruled for the rest of the ride as Rom pushed every speed limit. He didn't want to get pulled over, but every second that passed made his tension level rise and his headache worsen.

Behind him, Remy stared out the window, his mouth drawn into a straight line of pain.

When Rom finally pulled into the dirt lane leading to their small house, sweat coated Remy's forehead and his skin had taken on the pallor of ashes.

"Son of a bitch."

Tearing out of the car, Rom yanked open the back door and reached for Remy, just as his cousin's eyes closed and he listed to the side.

Rom felt his chest contract in on his lungs as he carried Remy through the door and into the house. He didn't bother to turn on the lights. They'd rearranged the meager furniture that came with the place seconds after the real estate agent had left, her memories of the time spent with them altered by one of Rom's spells.

He had a straight shot from the front door to the bedroom at the back and he didn't stop until he set Remy on the bed. He looked like shit and that scared Rom. Remy was his only family. If anything happened to him…

Amity would fix him. She'd fix Remy like she'd fixed him.

He raced back out to the car, flung open the door, and reached in for her. She roused as he curled his arms around her.

"What's wrong? Where am I?"

"You're safe, Lady." He hurried back into the house. "Remy and

I killed the demon. I was injured and you healed me, but then you passed out and now Remy's unconscious."

It took her a few seconds to process what he'd said, but he knew she'd understood him when she turned her head to look around the room.

She saw Remy and gasped, immediately struggling in his arms. "Put me down. I need to see to him."

Which is exactly what Rom wanted. Instead, he hesitated. "Lady, you're in no shape to help him."

"He's injured. He needs me."

"And I want you to help him. But you're gonna do yourself major harm if you try to heal him now."

She hesitated for five long seconds. "Then I need you to have sex with me."

Rom's brain flatlined as he stared into her way-too-serious eyes. "What the—Are you serious? Did the demon knock your head against the ground?"

Shit. He hadn't meant for that to come out so harshly. But still. Her brain must've been rattled pretty severely. Why the *fuck* did she want to have sex with him right now?

Her expression pulled into a frown as he continued to scowl at her. "First of all, I am not crazy. And second, if I'm going to heal Remy, I need to gain strength. The fastest way to get it is to have sex. Otherwise, I need to sleep for a few days, and Remy doesn't have that much time. Please, Rom…"

He opened his mouth to tell her no fucking way then shut it as his gaze fell on Remy.

Vaffanculo, his cousin looked even worse than he had a minute ago.

Turning back to Amity, Rom felt his jaw clench. Damn it, he wanted her. He could deny it until he was blue in the face but it didn't change facts. He'd wanted her last night but Remy—

Remy was dying.

"Amity…"

Her head tilted to the side, as if she were trying to read between his lines. "Don't you find me attractive?"

He tried to stop his mouth from dropping open in shock and wasn't entirely successful. He never would've expected her to be the type to beg for compliments. Then he realized she wasn't. She actually thought maybe he didn't desire her. After last night, how could she doubt it? Then again, he hadn't touched her, even though every molecule of his body had begged him to.

Taking a deep breath, he reined in the mounting frustration. "Lady Amity, I think you are… extremely attractive. Beautiful. You're beautiful." *Yeah, just keep sticking your foot in your mouth, idiot.* "But, tonight… the demon… I'm finding it tough to switch gears."

Her smile lit a tiny fire in his gut. "I understand, Rom. Truly, I do. It's been a rather stressful night for me, too. I'm sorry. I know this is asking too much of you. How about just a kiss? That might be enough to get me going."

She held out her hand to him, palm up. Not a command. A request.

Her delicate fingers trembled the slightest bit as they hung in midair, waiting for him.

Shit.

Why the hell did he feel like he was betraying his cousin if he did this? They'd agreed before they'd set out to seduce her: it didn't matter which of them she chose, or if she chose both. Remy had had her last night.

Why shouldn't he today? Especially if it would save Remy's life.

Because she'd made her choice. She'd chosen Remy.

You want her. Take her. She's handing herself to you on a platter. And Remy needs you to do this.

Right. His cousin needed him. How many times had Remy saved his life in the past twenty years?

Having sex with a goddess didn't exactly seem like a hardship to save Remy's life.

He reached for her, noting how her smaller hand disappeared in his, the coolness of her skin and the tremble just beneath. Lifting his gaze to meet hers, he saw her lips curl in a sweet smile that lit a simmering heat in his gut.

Kiss her.

He wanted to. He'd wanted to from the first moment he'd seen her.

Lowering his head, he watched her eyes darken in anticipation then braced for impact when she lifted to meet him.

Their lips came together in a rush, hers cool at first but warming fast beneath his.

Her eyes had drifted shut just before he closed the distance between them, and he let his close, as well. Let himself shut off the part of his brain that tried to tell him this wasn't right and simply enjoyed the feeling of her lips pressed against his.

So soft. So sweet.

He angled his head so his mouth fit better against hers. Still not good enough. He released her hand and cupped her face in both of his, turning her to get a better position.

Her hands reached for his shoulders, tiny nails sinking into his skin. The pain heightened his awareness of her. The sweet scent of her, the softness of her skin beneath his palms. The fragility of her bones.

He could crush her with one hand. The demon could have damaged her beyond repair with one hand behind its back.

Rom wanted to kill it again, just for daring to touch her.

Which he shouldn't be doing either.

She was a goddess and he hadn't given the deities their due in years. Not since—

He pried open her lips with his own and let his tongue slip

between her lips, nearly groaned as the sweet taste of her exploded on his tongue. Damn, she tasted good. Still cool but heating fast.

Her breath became a little hotter now, and he took it into his own lungs as his tongue tangled with hers. She moaned, the sound vibrating through him, straight to his groin. He couldn't help but wonder what that mouth would feel like wrapped around his cock.

Sucking in a startled breath, he pulled away, and his eyes flew open to see a slightly dazed look in her eyes. *Vaffanculo*, he hoped she couldn't read his mind. She'd probably want to kick his ass from here to—

Then she smiled and he swore she *had* read his mind and wanted the same thing.

No. No fucking way.

He shook his head, but her hands moved to his face, pulling him down with her onto the bed. He obeyed, his fists punching into the mattress on either side of her shoulders to hold him up. To keep his weight off of her.

"Lie down beside me, Rom." Her voice whispered soft and sexy against his cheek as she pressed a string of kisses from his lips to his ear. His own breathing became rough, harsh in his throat. "Please."

The "please" did him in. He brought his knees up onto the mattress by her side, causing her to scoot over to make room for him. He didn't want that much room.

He wrapped his arms around her shoulders and pulled her against him as he came down on her. They sank into the bed, his mouth again plastered to hers. He kissed her harder, his lips and tongue demanding a response she gave willingly.

Her tongue slid against his, teasing, eliciting a response from low in his body. Heat made his balls tighten and his cock throb. He got hard and his hips ground into hers.

She tilted her head to the side so she had a better angle and she chased his tongue back into his mouth so she could taste him.

With any other woman, he would have drawn back. He wasn't comfortable with that level of intimacy.

He wanted Amity to push him onto his back and take what she wanted. What she said she needed.

Her fingers slid into his hair at that moment, sifting through the short strands and tugging on them gently. Just enough to fire the pain receptors on his scalp. He broke their kiss, hissing a breath at the burst of sensual pleasure, magnified because he'd never felt anything like it.

Before, sex had been scratching an itch. Not a sensual assault.

He stared down at Amity as she watched him, her gaze steady, as if she knew exactly what he was thinking. Then she tugged again, making his eyes close for a brief second before she moved her fingers to his scalp, massaging the sensitive area at the base of his neck.

His head tipped back as she rubbed, his hips pressing harder into the soft flesh between her legs, covered by her soft skirt.

The skirt had to go if they were going to do this. And he wanted her now more than he'd wanted anything in his life.

Adrenaline pumped through his blood, making him buzz like he was high.

Sitting back on his heels, he kept his gaze squarely on Amity. On her dark eyes staring back at him. On her lips, swollen from their kisses.

He reached for her waistband, grateful to realize he wouldn't have to deal with zippers or buttons or hooks. The stretchy material was tight enough that it didn't need help staying up.

Realizing his hands were shaking, he curled them into fists for a brief second while he tried to regain some control.

Just another woman. She's just another woman.

Total bullshit. But if he let himself think about what she really was, he'd be toast.

Curling his fingers in the skirt's hem, he started to pull. The material didn't want to move right away, but he gave a hard tug, and it gave up the fight.

He never considered pushing the skirt up around her waist and taking her half-dressed.

No, he needed her naked. Fast.

On its way down, the skirt revealed the soft skin of her stomach. She didn't have the tight body other women seemed to crave. No rock hard abs or muscular thighs.

No, she was curved. Not fat. Just rounded.

"So fucking pretty."

Moving down to her feet, he pulled the skirt to her ankles, then bent her knees and lifted her feet so he could get it all the way off and drop it on the floor. She lay before him bare from the waist down except for tiny red satin panties.

Just the sight of them made his mouth water.

He wanted to lean forward and put his mouth over the tiny triangle covering her pussy but he knew if he did that, he might lose himself in the act, and Remy could die before he found his way back.

Amity wasn't about to let that happen. "As much as I would love to have your mouth on me right now, we don't have time." Her voice, breathy and broken, caught his attention and drew his gaze up to hers.

Her cheeks now held a flush and her breasts quivered each time she drew in a shaky breath.

"Later. I would love to feel your tongue against my clit later. Right now, we need to hurry. Take your clothes off, Rom."

Just her saying the word clit made his cock tighten almost to the point of pain. And his name coupled with her telling him to take his clothes off... Well, shit. She might as well resign herself to a thirty-second fuck, because that's all he was going to last.

When she reached for the bottom of her green T-shirt to pull it over her head, he knocked that number down to fifteen seconds. Damn, she had nice tits. High and firm and more than enough to overflow his palms.

Her bra matched her panties but the cups were red lace and transparent. Her nipples poked through the lace, and he couldn't ignore the temptation. He bent and sucked one into his mouth, lace and all.

Amity gasped and her hands cupped his head. She didn't push him away, though. She held him to her. As if he might try to get away. Like hell.

He wanted to suck on her breasts, which she appeared to really like, before he got inside her and completely disgraced himself. If he could bring her off with his mouth and hands now, maybe she wouldn't notice how fast he came.

And it was gonna be fast. Had to be fast.

As he alternately licked at her nipple through the lace, soaking it completely, and sucked the hard tip into his mouth, he brushed one hand down her body to her mound.

He didn't bother to pet her through the panties. He just sank his hand beneath them and let his forefinger graze her clit on its way to her slit.

Hot. Wet. Silky smooth. He was gonna come in his pants. He groaned against her breast and she arched her back to push her nipple farther into his mouth, moaning. But it put her pussy at an awkward angle so he pressed her down with one hand on her shoulder as he slid two fingers into her sex.

He heard her gasp, her hands gripping his hair tighter, his scalp beginning to burn. He liked that. He wanted to tell her to do it harder but he didn't want to move his mouth.

Sucking harder at her nipple, he grazed his teeth along the tip before he bit her. He didn't let her move this time. He used his free hand to grab her hip and hold her in place as he used his fingers to fuck her. Slow and deep, making sure his thumb rubbed her clit each time he stroked her high inside her channel.

It didn't take long for her to tighten around his fingers like a vise. *Vaffanculo*, he couldn't help but imagine what it would feel like when he got inside her.

She'd be so damn snug, she'd milk his cock dry.

Speaking of… He had to get his pants off or he'd end up coming in them.

The black tactical pants were designed to be form-fitting but not tight. Easy to slip on and off. But even though they'd been designed with comfort in mind, they still needed someone to unhook them.

He pulled away from her breast long enough to say, "Get my pants off."

The hand in his hair immediately dropped to his waist. Or as close as she could get. "Scoot up."

He rose to his knees so she could reach his waistband and deal with the button with a flick of her fingers.

"Take them off, Rom. Hurry."

With one final lick, he released her breast and sat up. Stripping off his own T-shirt, he tossed it behind him then shoved his pants down his thighs.

His skin felt hypersensitive, and her fingers made his nerve endings flame and pop under the skin as his balls tightened.

She stroked over his thighs, his hips, his stomach, not lingering until her fingers brushed against his left nipple. Running a finger around the soft areola until the skin hardened and pebbled, she then took the hard tip between her thumb and forefinger and pinched it. The sharp, pleasurable pain took his breath for a second.

His hands clenched into fists at his sides as she played with him with just her fingers. His cock throbbed with longing, and he had to hold tightly to his internal reins so he didn't throw her down on the bed and ravage her.

Which lasted all of about thirty seconds. Then he ripped his pants the rest of the way off his legs and tossed them aside before tearing away her panties.

He didn't give her time to stare at the rest of his body. Before his pants hit the floor, he covered her with his body, sliding his legs between hers and letting his cock press against her mound.

Her arms wrapped around his shoulders as his mouth fell on hers and devoured. She was ready for him, opening her mouth to him as she opened her legs. Her tongue slid into his mouth as he shifted his hips so the tip of his cock brushed between her pussy lips.

So soft.

He groaned into her mouth, planted his elbows on either side of her head, and began to press his cock inside her.

He didn't want to go so fast but he couldn't help himself. The second she started to close around him, he felt his balls draw up and he thrust forward. He couldn't spill outside her body. He had to be inside her.

She took him all, straight to the base. Then she tilted her hips as if she wanted more.

He wanted more. Wanted everything.

Ripping his mouth away from hers, he sucked in a deep breath and started to pump. She was so tight, he felt huge inside her. But she was wet and he slid easily.

He wanted to slow down and enjoy the sensations. The heat of her surrounding him, the sound of her moans… they snuck inside his brain and stoked his pleasure higher.

His hips began to pick up speed as her fingers sifted through his hair, tugging on the strands as she pressed her mouth against his neck. He felt her lips move on his skin, sucking, biting. Heating his blood, making it pump through his veins like lava.

And when she bit his earlobe, he couldn't hold back any longer. His release started at the base of his spine, pushed through his balls and cock. He cried out, his head tossing and his cry echoing through the room as he came. Thick, hot seed pulsed from him.

Her legs wrapped around his waist and her arms around his shoulders, unbreakable bindings that he wouldn't have chosen to free himself from anyway.

After at least a minute, he thought he could finally breathe again and he came back to himself with the realization that she was unmoving beneath him. He pulled back with a start only to sense that she wasn't harmed.

She was drawing in the sexual energy they'd raised so she could heal Remy.

Rom's gaze immediately turned toward the other bed where his cousin lay, white as a sheet.

Pulling away and scrambling to his knees, he sat as still as he could at the bottom of the bed. He didn't want to disturb Amity, who looked much better than she had before they'd had sex.

He had to admit *he* felt a hell of a lot better. Now, if she could just fix Remy.

Her eyes opened and his body shook in reaction to the glow emanating from them. He bit back the "holy shit" on the tip of his tongue and managed not to give in to the impulse to get the hell out of her way.

She sat up, blinking as if unsure of where she was or what she was doing, then her gaze focused on Rom.

Taking in a deep breath, she reached out to him with her hand and he only hesitated a second before he took it.

And when she smiled sweetly at him, his guard dropped again. Goddess, yes. But still a woman.

Her fingers wrapped around his and she tugged him closer until his lips were only centimeters from hers.

"Thank you."

Her voice whispered across his cheek just before she brushed a kiss against his mouth.

"You're welcome, Lady."

"Now, I need to see to Remy."

She slid off the bed with a sinuous grace he'd either not noticed before or that she hadn't had. Maybe she'd picked that up after sex with him.

Maneuvering until he sat on the edge of his bed, he watched Amity crawl onto the bed with Remy, sitting on her knees next to him. Her lips began to move, though he couldn't make out what she was saying. She held her hands over Remy's chest then moved them down to his thighs then back up again to his head.

Her eyes narrowed and her expression set in lines of intense concentration. And her hands began to shine.

And he didn't mean with the dull glow he could produce when he and Remy worked together to create a rudimentary healing spell. Healing was one of the hardest spells they'd mastered, though they didn't have a one hundred percent cure rate.

After nearly twenty years of working spells together, you'd think they would've come closer to being able to fix more than broken bones, the simplest cuts and scrapes, and the occasional puncture wound.

They had much better luck with offensive and defensive spells—disabling locks, jamming weapons, mass displacement and elemental manipulation.

Apparently, being the culmination of a centuries-old prophecy had made him and Remy more than one-trick ponies. But it'd also gotten their families killed. Something they could never allow themselves to forget.

Which wouldn't matter one bit if Amity couldn't cure Remy. Her hands still shone but they'd dimmed a bit as she let them rest directly on his abdomen. Rom watched Remy's chest rise and fall in a fast, shallow pattern. Not good. Especially not when combined with the pallor of his skin.

Should he pray to the Great Mother Goddess to give Amity the strength to heal Remy? Rom hadn't prayed in years. It did no good. The *Involuti*, the five founding gods of the Etruscan pantheon, had retreated from their plane of existence hundreds of years ago. They'd deserted their people and the rest of the pantheon and they didn't deserve to be worshipped.

Unlike this goddess. She deserved an entire nation of worshippers.

He didn't know how long it'd been since she'd started working on Remy but Rom could tell his cousin's skin tone had lost that death-pale hue. His breathing had become steadier, deeper, and his body appeared more relaxed.

Amity's eyes were closed, and Rom let himself watch her now instead of Remy. She didn't appear to be suffering any ill effects from healing his cousin, though it seemed to take forever.

Rom's gaze shot to the window for a second, not surprised to see the sun had risen. It had to be close to seven or eight in the morning.

He should go to the kitchen and make them something to eat. They'd probably be starving afterward.

Hell, he was, but he didn't want to leave them alone in case Amity needed him for something. To make sure she didn't fall over in exhaustion.

Or if she needed a booster shot of sex.

Yeah, like that's gonna happen.

Shaking the thought out of his head, he forced himself to move slowly. He didn't want to disturb or startle her, but she didn't appear to notice him at all when he headed for the door. Leaving it open, he went straight to the kitchen.

The kitchen was his domain. The extent of Remy's cooking ability was a peanut butter sandwich, but Rom could create a meal any five-star restaurant would be happy to serve.

He enjoyed being in the kitchen. There was something about cooking that gave him a sense of relaxation that nothing else did.

Wherever they happened to land, Rom always made sure the place had a kitchen so he could cook if he had the time.

Honestly, he'd rather cook than run past a drive-up window every night. And Remy had learned not to bitch when Rom decided they were having duck or buffalo for dinner. He'd even gotten Remy to enjoy pâte over the years.

Now, Rom decided to go for comfort foods. Meatloaf, mashed garlic potatoes with blue cheese, roasted Brussels sprouts, and maybe pie for dessert.

It was the least he could do to thank the Lady Amity for her help. And the mind-blowing sex.

Chapter 5

AMITY FOUGHT TO OPEN her eyes. They felt weighted, as if she hadn't slept for days.

Beside her, she felt the warmth of a large body. A male body.

Remy.

Memories of last night ran through her mind. The demon. The fight. Remy and Rom saving her life. Healing Rom. Having amazing sex with Rom. Then healing Remy.

Carefully, she sat up, clenching and unclenching her fingers that felt as if she'd held them in fists all night. It was an aftereffect of running that much power through them. When they felt marginally better, she stretched her hands over Remy's torso, careful not to let them touch him.

He'd had massive internal injuries and if she'd waited even a half hour more he would have succumbed to them.

And she'd nearly gotten lost in Rom's lovemaking...

Her mind wanted to go back over every detail, every second.

No. Taking a deep breath and shaking her head, she forced her eyes open and stared down at Remy. She breathed a little easier as she noticed the color returning to his cheeks and the more natural rise and fall of his chest.

He would be fine after he'd rested.

A yawn caught her by surprise and she lifted a visibly shaking hand to cover her mouth. Actually, she shook all over. Her arms were covered in goose bumps, and her teeth were beginning to chatter.

Cold. She was so cold, a reaction to the length and intensity of the healing. She'd not done anything like this in years. She hadn't had the power to even attempt it.

But with Rom…

What was it about Rom?

No, it wasn't just Rom. It was Remy as well. She'd felt the power surge the night before when she'd had sex with Remy. She'd just been so surprised by it, she hadn't done anything to capture that power and hold on to it.

What was going on between the three of them that had allowed her to heal Rom and recharge fast enough to heal Remy?

And how had they shown up at the exact moment she'd needed them? With a sword strapped to Rom's back?

So many questions.

She yawned again, her eyelids having difficulty staying up. A nap sounded really good at that moment. And she would say she deserved it. There was more than enough room next to Remy to spread out and close her eyes for a few minutes.

And it would be no hardship to sleep next to him, though sleeping wouldn't be first on her list if she were rested.

Wow, for someone who hadn't had much sex in the last few… well, hundred years or so, her libido had definitely been jump-started.

Lifting one hand, she smoothed it over Remy's messy golden-brown hair then along the whiskers on his chin.

As if he felt her touch, which he really shouldn't considering all he'd just been through, he shifted his head toward her.

Her fingers brushed against his lips and she shivered again, though not from cold.

She closed her eyes—and nearly fell on top of him.

With a sigh, she stretched out next to him, the heat of his body drawing her closer until her back pressed against his arm.

His warmth seeped into her, and she closed her eyes.

Remy opened his eyes and stared at the blank white ceiling.

Soft light seeped through the shade at the window and he smelled... Rom's meatloaf. His stomach growled and he put a hand over it, as if he could cover up the sound.

His elbow brushed against something warm and soft. What the hell was Rom—

No, not Rom.

Amity lay beside him, sound asleep. She rested on her side facing him, the brown silk of her hair curling across her face, a few strands fluttering around her mouth as she breathed. Her eyes were closed, obviously, so he couldn't tell their color, but that meant he could study her features more closely.

And realized nothing had changed from the first moment he'd seen her. She was beautiful. So damn pretty he wanted to lean over and press his mouth against hers and—

He drew in a deep breath as he caught the scent of... sex. Musky and earthy and... Fuck.

She'd had sex with Rom. Holy fuck. How the hell long had he been out?

His jaw started to ache and Remy realized his mouth was hanging open. Snapping it shut, he took another deep breath. Just to make sure he hadn't made a mistake.

No. She'd definitely had sex with Rom. His mind conjured up images of the pretty goddess sucking him off while Rom fucked her from behind—

Whoa. Okay, good to know everything still worked properly. Or maybe he was just horny enough to get a hard-on from the scent.

Damn. Rom had had sex with Amity. Remy would've sworn his cousin wouldn't have touched her. Rom had somehow gotten the idea in his head that Remy had proprietary feelings toward her because of the other night.

So do you?

Good question.

Amity drew in a deep breath and her eyelids fluttered opened. She looked bleary eyed and Remy froze as her gaze locked with his.

For several seconds they lay there, unmoving, staring into each other's eyes.

Then she gasped and her eyes flew open wide as she scrambled to her knees beside him. "Sweet Mother Goddess, you're awake."

"Uh…"

"No, no." She put one delicate hand on his shoulder and pressed, as if she were afraid he'd try to get away. Hell no, he wasn't going anywhere. "You lie still and let me see how you're doing."

At that moment, he felt pretty freaking great because she'd started to pet him. Well, she probably wouldn't call it petting but that's what it felt like to him. Her hands slid all over his bare chest, her fingertips soft, feather light against his skin. Starting at his shoulders, she let them drift over his pecs, his nipples hardening into sensitive peaks.

She didn't stop there, though he wished she would have, at least for a few seconds. She continued on to splay her hands across his stomach, which he couldn't stop from flexing. He sucked in a sharp breath and had to practically bite his tongue to keep from groaning.

Tinia's teat, he was naked under a thin sheet that had been washed until it was practically transparent. And he had a hard-on that threatened to burst at any second. Especially if she moved those hands any lower.

But, Sweet Mother Goddess, he wanted her to.

Staring down at her, he noted her intent expression and only realized then that her hands gave off a blue glow and held a heat that seeped into his abdomen.

So good. "Damn, that feels amazing."

"Shh," she scolded, but her lips curled up in a slight smile. "Just lie still for a few more minutes."

"Yes, Lady." He had no problem listening to her commands, as long as she kept her hands on him.

Crossing his arms behind his head, he let his gaze take her in.

He'd thought her beautiful two nights ago. Now… She absolutely looked like a goddess.

He noticed tiny freckles on her arms that he hadn't before. They didn't detract from her beauty in any way. In fact, he wanted to lick them. Or connect the dots because he saw a few on her torso as well, one just above her right nipple and another lower, near her belly button. And another, lower still, right above her mound.

Snapping his gaze back to her face, he found he couldn't hold it there and it dropped to her breasts. She had gorgeous breasts—full and round and soft-looking. He wanted to cup them in his hands and see if they were as soft as he remembered.

He wanted to knead them, let his fingers pluck at the pale pink nipples before he put his lips around one and sucked it into his mouth. Let his tongue flick at the tip for a few seconds, playing with her, until he bit down. Not hard, just enough to make her gasp and bring her hands to his head to hold him there.

He realized he was panting and his eyes had closed as he'd played out that little fantasy in his head.

Now they snapped open. And found Amity staring at him.

Deep and wide, her chocolate-brown eyes mesmerized him. For a brief second, he wondered if that was because she was a goddess, then he totally forgot that fact and saw only the woman.

Her full, pink lips parted slightly and he figured she had to know what he was thinking. When her fingers clenched, pressing into the clenched muscles of his stomach, he watched her blink.

"How are you feeling, Remy?"

Her voice felt like another kind of caress, making his skin erupt in goose bumps. And his cock throbbed. He felt pretty damn horny actually. Like he could roll her under him and fuck her for hours.

Totally not what he should be thinking about.

And yet…

The look in her eyes had darkened, and her chest began to rise and fall in a faster pace, her breasts jiggling the slightest bit and making him harder still. As if she were just as turned on as he was.

He forced himself to relax his hands, which had been fisted in the sheet, and tore his gaze away from her. Then he shook his head, more to clear it than as an answer to her questions. Which he'd almost forgotten she'd asked.

"I'm feeling fine, Lady Amity."

He heard her draw in a deep breath as she withdrew her hands from his body and sat back on her haunches before she twisted to the side and slid off the bed.

She looked completely comfortable in her nudity as she stood, hands on her hips, staring down at him, a slight smile curving her lips. "Please, it's just Amity. And I'm very happy to report everything seems to be healed."

"Thank you. For healing me."

"It was the least I could do after you saved my life."

Remy's gaze narrowed as he ran through last night's events. "Rom and I are glad we were there to help. Do you know why the demon was chasing you?"

Even as he asked the question, he knew he shouldn't have brought up the subject without talking to Rom first. He had no idea what his cousin had told her, if anything.

And she was too smart not to wonder how and why he and Rom had been in the right place at the right time.

"Yes, actually, I do. What I don't know is how you and Rom knew the demon was going to come after me."

Yep. Rom was gonna kill him. Should've kept his mouth shut.

Her head tilted to the side as she crossed her arms under those gorgeous breasts. Remy swore his eyes nearly popped out of his head as she plumped them into mouth-watering mounds. He forced himself to lift his gaze back to hers.

"Can you hold onto that thought for a few minutes? Let's get dressed and go get something to eat. You really don't want to miss Rom's meatloaf."

Her gaze narrowed. "So I'm not wrong. You knew. But—"

"We've been hunting the demon for years, Lady Amity. And last night we avenged our families with its death."

Remy's gaze flew to the doorway where Rom had appeared. Relief at the sight of his cousin looking so damn healthy actually made him weak.

"Lady Amity—"

"Just Amity," she said again, pinning Rom into place with her gaze. "How are you feeling this morning?"

Rom stiffened, making Remy wonder just what the hell had happened between his cousin and her. Considering they'd had sex, shouldn't he feel more relaxed?

Remy shoved down the slight, bitter hint of jealousy that lurked in the back of his throat and tried to wade through the morass of emotions in the room.

Between his, Rom's, and Amity's, it was no wonder his brain was getting a cramp.

"I'm fine." Rom practically bit the words out before turning his back on them and walking away. "Come out and eat and we'll talk then."

Amity watched Rom walk away, her fingers tapping along her arm in a way that reminded him of the annoyed swish of a cat's tail.

Okay. Time to play peacemaker.

Sliding out of bed, he walked over to the chest, grabbed a pair of sweats for him and a T-shirt for Amity.

"You really should take it easy." She tugged the shirt over her head then bent to pick up her panties from the floor. "You were severely injured last night. Both of you. I've healed your wounds, but your bodies will need time to rest and recover."

"I feel fine," Remy said. "And cooking relaxes Rom. I know we have some things to discuss, but you should eat first. Smells like Rom went all out. Meatloaf and mashed potatoes. And apple pie."

"Dinner?" Amity sounded startled. "Did we sleep that long?"

Remy nodded. "It's almost four in the afternoon."

Amity stiffened. "Oh dear. I should have been back at the hospital hours ago."

"You work Saturdays?"

"Oh. I forgot it was Saturday. No, I don't. I had planned to check in, at least for a few minutes. That can wait, though. I want to know what's going on."

Amity sat at the tiny dining table and ate the best meatloaf she'd ever tasted.

Remy hadn't been kidding. Rom cooked like a master chef.

The men had barely spoken during the meal, and she got the distinct impression they were making a conscious effort to be on their best behavior. She imagined they didn't often have a goddess at their table. Especially not one they'd both had sex with.

It was obvious they hadn't known who she was when they'd picked her up Thursday night. It was equally obvious now that they'd had an ulterior motive to do so.

She vacillated between being upset that they'd used her and grateful they'd been there to save her ass. Sighing, she ate the last bite of her meatloaf and set her fork on her plate.

Tension ran through her like high voltage and reverberated through Remy and Rom. She couldn't help but wonder if she'd created some of the strain between the cousins.

She'd basically forced Rom to have sex with her in order to save Remy. He'd been reluctant, to say the least, but she'd pushed him.

Should she apologize? She didn't think he'd found her offensive. She wasn't built like the actresses and models plastered all over the magazine pages. She had curves. Some might say a few too many.

But she'd been born the Etruscan Goddess of Health and, as such, she embodied the ideal picture of health. Sadly, her ideal was a few millennia out of date.

Maybe Rom just hadn't found her enticing. Maybe that was why he hadn't touched her Thursday night. Maybe…

Oh, hell. Maybe she should just get to the point.

"That was delicious." She flashed a smile at Remy then Rom, hoping to draw him out just a little. She sensed such a dark well of sorrow in him, but he covered it so well, she'd almost missed it. However, she couldn't miss the responsibility he felt for Remy.

Rom nodded but didn't smile.

When she flashed her eyes to Remy, he merely nodded, his gaze barely grazing hers in response.

Then she heard Rom stifle a sigh. "I started to cook about seven, eight years ago." Her gaze tripped back to Rom, who was gazing at her with what looked like an apology in his eyes. "The first couple of times… Well, I wouldn't call it edible."

Rom's attention slid to Remy and Amity's followed, catching the slight smile that made the scars on Remy's cheek crinkle.

"Oh, it was edible. It just tasted like shit. Crap." Remy winced. "Sorry, Lady."

She laughed at Remy's chagrined expression. They both acted as if they'd offended their grandmother with their language. Which kind of sucked. Especially since they'd both had sex with her.

Sure, she was ancient, but she wasn't *old*. And yes, she knew that didn't make any sense at all, and she didn't care. She didn't want these men to think of her as anything other than a desirable woman who was falling unexpectedly for two damaged men.

"Would it help if I said 'fuck' a few times?" She batted her eyes at Remy, gratified when his expression eased a little more. "Trust me, there's nothing you can say that I haven't heard before. And in all languages."

Which just reinforced the fact that she'd been around almost as long as the pyramids.

Shit.

"Lady, are you finished?"

Rom stood with his plate in his hand, staring down at hers.

Nodding, she handed it to him. "Yes, thank you. It really was delicious."

"I'm glad you enjoyed it." He picked up her plate and headed to the tiny kitchen just off the dining room.

Her gaze followed him until he disappeared from sight before she turned back to Remy, who was watching her with an inscrutable expression.

"Will you tell me what happened now? Why were you chasing that demon? How did you know it was going to attack me?"

Remy didn't speak right away, but she didn't sense he was going to lie to her. She sensed only hesitation.

"The demon killed our families."

Her head swiveled back toward the kitchen where Rom stood, hands in his pockets, resignation on his face. As if she'd backed him into a corner and he had no choice but to answer her questions.

Damn it. That wasn't how she wanted them to tell her what had happened. But she kept her mouth shut and waited. Obviously the memories were painful ones.

"Remy was fifteen. I was almost twenty. Our families had split from the *lucani* den about two decades ago." Rom's gaze slipped to Remy's for a brief second and the cousins exchanged another one of those looks, as if they were communicating silently. For all she knew, they were. "We headed to West Virginia and got lost in the woods."

She wanted to ask why, but Rom's expression told her she wouldn't like the answer. So she kept her questions to herself.

"They bought up some land, built a couple of houses, and didn't bother anybody. And one night, that demon showed up and massacred everyone except us."

"I had two younger sisters." Rom's voice had deepened and she found him watching her intently. "Remy had a four-year-old brother."

Her heart hurt to hear the pain in those few words. She knew whatever that demon had done to those children, Rom's swift killing didn't come close to being punishment enough.

"What did it want?"

Remy's hands clenched into fists on the table. "Rom and me."

"Why?"

The men exchanged another look, as if debating how much to tell her. Neither of them made any move to tell her anything.

She focused on Rom. "Why did that demon want you?"

When Rom stayed silent, she turned to Remy.

After a few seconds' pause, Remy said, "We were born *stregone*."

Oh my. Her mouth opened, then closed without saying a word.

Well, that would explain a hell of a lot, wouldn't it? About why their parents had wanted to take them away from the Etruscan base of power.

Two male witches born to a single family and so close in age. And *lucani*, to boot. The possibilities were endless. And frightening.

It explained why she'd gained so much power from them. If she bedded them together...

Oh my.

Some of her thoughts must have shown on her face because Remy's expression shut down into a stone-cold mask.

Blinking, she tore her gaze away to look at Rom. Not surprisingly, he wore the same expression.

"When did your parents realize?"

"When Remy was four." Rom's gaze flashed to Remy for a brief second. "My mom had already figured out that I'd been born with a Goddess Gift, though she didn't know for what. I had an affinity for fire but I also had one for metal. Considering I was *lucani* and shouldn't have been able to do some of the things I was doing, it was enough to make my parents suspicious."

Lucani magic was tied to their shape-changing abilities given to them several millennia ago by the goddess of the moon. It wasn't tied to the elements, which was where *streghe* got their power.

A Goddess Gift, a special affinity to a specific element, was much rarer for a *lucani*.

"Did your king know?"

Remy and Rom exchanged a glance and Amity had her answer.

"That was part of the reason our parents ran," Remy said. "They feared the king would draft us into early service. The *lucani* were fighting a war back then and they weren't getting much help."

She thought she heard censure in his voice and wouldn't be surprised by it. Many of the Etruscans thought the deities had deserted them through the years.

He was right. Some had. Others simply didn't have enough power to be of much help.

"My mom was teaching me a basic incendiary spell," Rom said. "I was only supposed to light the candle. I nearly burned the house down around us with one of the simplest spells. Because Remy happened to be in the same house. Our parents packed up that night and left the den before anyone else realized what was going on."

She wanted to go to Rom and wrap herself around him, take away the pain she heard in his voice. "That must have been so hard on you."

The *lucani* were social creatures. If they didn't live in the den located several miles away in Rockland Township, they lived in a city, even if that meant there were no woods to run in.

But two *stregone* in one family. And born so close…

Rom shook his head. "There were five kids. And our parents were close. We had each other."

Until the demon had stolen it. "Why?"

Rom shook his head, and Remy continued the story. "Because the *Mal* hired it to kidnap us. Promised it could have us when they were done."

"The demon was willing to wait a few decades until the *Mal* were finished with us." Rom's voice was practically a growl. "Guess it figured we were so strong, we'd still have enough juice when it finally got its turn."

"Rom and I had gone to the movies. I'd begged him to take me to see some horror movie." Remy shook his head, his mouth twisting in a scowl. "Hell, I don't even remember which one now. I only know I picked it because I knew our parents wouldn't let the kids come along."

The men's grief was an almost-tangible pain in the air around them. Amity had to rein in the empathy that wanted to take it away. She knew they wouldn't appreciate it.

"I was going to college during the day so I wasn't home a lot," Rom continued. "It was the first time Remy and I had been apart for extended periods of time. We didn't realize how that put us at risk. Neither did our parents. We didn't have a guide book. Hell, we still don't. Back then, we didn't know that spending time apart actually made us more powerful. And easier to track."

"Though we didn't know we were being tracked. At least, not right away. And we didn't know by what. If we had…" Remy shook his head. "Our parents never let us forgot we were in danger from the *Mal*. We moved around for years, never staying in one place longer than a few months. By the time I turned eight, the *Mal* had made two attempts to take us. They nearly killed Rom's dad the second time."

"After that, we learned to stick close to the big cities." Rom's hands clenched into fists at his sides. "It was just dumb luck that we met a *strega* in Atlanta who agreed to help us figure out how to control our powers, especially the ones that work together."

"What was her name?"

"Tullia."

Amity had to work hard to school her expression because she was pretty sure she knew the *strega* Rom was talking about. "How did you meet her?"

Remy and Rom exchanged another of those glances before Rom answered. "She approached our parents after she followed Remy and me home from one of our unscheduled outings. We thought our dads were going to kill us, but it turned out to be the best thing that could've happened. We never would've learned so much on our own. She worked with us for a month, never asked for anything in return. Of course, our parents thought she'd been sent by the *Mal*, but somehow she got them to trust her."

Yes, the Tullia she knew had a way with words. One she'd been developing for many, *many* years.

"After Tullia showed us how to use our powers to shield ourselves, our parents finally decided the younger kids needed a place to call home."

"We were all so fucking sick of running." Remy's voice held a weariness she wasn't sure he realized she could hear. "So our parents bought a few thousand acres of nearly uninhabitable forest in West Virginia, and we basically lived off the grid for five years."

"And then I got cocky." The edge on Rom's voice could cut through steel. She tried to suppress a shiver. "I forced my parents to let me go to college. I got our families killed because I wanted to take art history and read *The Canterbury Tales*."

"Rom—"

"Don't *fucking* say it's not my fault again, Remy. We both know it is."

Remy's mouth slammed shut but he shook his head, his eyes narrowing to slits.

"Why do you think it's your fault?"

Rom's expression tightened and his mouth became a thin slash. She thought he wouldn't answer and the pain she felt coming off of him in waves made her stomach hurt. These men had such deep scars.

She thought about another way to ask the question, how to get Rom to open up to her, when he finally answered.

"The demon must've followed me home."

"You don't know that." Remy bit each word out. "We have no idea how the demon found us."

"It had to be me." Rom turned to Amity, and she saw the grief and the anger so clearly on his face. "Tullia helped us set up wards around the house strong enough to deter any spell thrown at us. Yes, by that time, we were that good. But then I wanted to go to college. I pushed and pushed until finally they agreed. And somehow the demon found me."

Remy kept shaking his head. "It could just as easily have been me. I was sneaking out to run past the borders of the wards. They could have picked up on me just as easily as you."

"But I was the one who insisted on using my magic." With a muted growl, Rom stomped toward the front of the house, but there wasn't much room to run and he stopped only a few feet away.

"The girl would've died if you hadn't!"

"Then I should've let her die! If I had, our families would still be alive."

Remy opened his mouth but Rom slashed his hand through the air. "No. I'm not doing this again." With a conscious effort, Rom dialed down all the rage she felt emanating from him. It only took him seconds, as if he'd had a lot of practice.

When he looked at her again, he showed no trace of any emotion. "Forgive me, Lady. I didn't mean to yell."

"No apologies necessary," she assured him, attempting a small smile to see if Rom would respond. She wanted to know more about what had happened, about the girl who had almost died and how she'd affected Rom but...

His expression remained stoic. "When you feel strong enough, Remy will take you home. I'm—I'd like to go for a run, if you don't mind?"

A quick glance at Remy showed he wasn't thrilled with that idea but she could tell Rom needed some space.

She softened her smile and watched a bit of the stiffness ease from Rom's expression. "Of course I don't mind."

"Rom—"

"Remy," she turned, her smile widening, "I would appreciate it if you would assist me with something."

Rom took the opportunity she'd given him to head for the door. By the time Remy had taken a breath to respond, Rom was gone.

Remy turned to her with frustration in the thin line of his mouth. She wasn't sure Remy wouldn't just ignore her and go running after Rom.

"He shouldn't be alone." Remy spoke each word through clenched teeth.

"Everyone needs a little time to come to terms with things in their own way."

She watched Remy closely, feeling the pull of the seething emotion beneath the surface. The man needed more help than a solo run could ever give him. He needed someone to ease his pain.

She just wasn't sure he would ever give it up.

"I know what you think." His voice had a hard edge that was

so at odds with his almost placid expression. "You think he'll go out, he'll run for an hour, maybe two. He'll come back and he'll be good as new. But you don't know him. He won't be back for hours. He'll run himself ragged and, if we're lucky, he won't decide to tangle with any wild animals while he's out there. If he does, he'll come back bloody and exhausted, and tomorrow he'll act like nothing happened."

Amity's fingers ached to reach out and take his hand. "He's blowing off steam. Do you ever do that, Remy? Or do you keep it all inside?"

He shook his head, a nervous tic if she'd ever seen one. "I don't hold onto any of it. It's not worth it."

"You're telling me nothing affects you?"

Holding her gaze, he stood then stepped closer. She wondered for a brief second if she should worry that he'd take his frustration out on her. But in the next, she knew he'd never consider it. The man who'd made love to her had shown his true colors. He may be trying to intimidate her right now but he would never hurt her.

He wanted her to back off. And she couldn't do that. Not when he hurt so badly.

When she merely met his gaze and stood her ground, she saw frustration in his clenched jaw and narrowed eyes.

When she lifted her hand to stroke her fingers along that jaw, she felt the tightness of his muscles. He would've stepped away immediately, but she reached for his hand, lacing their fingers together.

He froze like a deer in headlights, and she knew he was replaying their time together in bed.

A flash of heat shimmered through her. Heat so unexpected, she almost let herself get lost in it.

And while she would enjoy another few hours of sex with Remy, it wouldn't do him any good. He needed to talk, and it didn't seem that he was getting that from Rom.

Though the two cousins seemed to be closer than brothers, she wondered if they ever really talked. About their parents, their lost siblings.

About what they were going to do when they'd finally killed the demon.

"Remy, tell me about your brother."

He looked like he'd taken a sucker punch straight to his lungs. As if she'd reached into his chest to wrap her hands around his lungs and squeezed until he truly looked like he was going to pass out.

She could tell his immediate response was to tell her to fuck off but he was too well-mannered to do it. He couldn't bring himself to say those words to a goddess, much less one he'd had sex with the night before.

His lips parted to deny her but no words came out. His focus had turned inward to his memories.

"Rom and I already had our pelts. Danny was almost six years younger than me but he tried so hard to keep up."

His voice seemed to startle him, it sounded so loud in the quiet of the room. His gaze refocused on her, standing so still in front of him. Her fingers stroked along his jaw, as if she were gentling a wild animal.

"Did he look like you?"

"Mom… always said no." He took a deep breath, and she swore she could hear the rapid beating of his heart. "Dad said we were more alike than she wanted to admit."

"Why?"

"Because I was a pain in the ass, and Danny wanted to be just like me."

She felt something warm her inside at the expression on his face. His lips curved up in just the slightest hint of a smile. And it totally transformed him. Here was the man she'd met two nights ago at the bar, the man she'd fallen for. His blue eyes glowed as he focused inward on his memories. That mouth softened. Even the scars on his face appeared to lessen.

She had the almost uncontrollable urge to lean forward and take a bite out of his bottom lip. Instead, she forced herself to stay in her chair and listen.

"He followed us around constantly, like a shadow. Of course, I probably did the same to Rom when I was younger but Danny... Danny had the devil in his eyes. Mom always swore he had *salbinelli* blood in him."

The Etruscan satyrs were notorious for their impish ways.

"She also always said it was a good thing he was so damn cute or she would have leashed him outside when he pulled one of his stunts. I knew she'd never do it. She loved him too much to ever put a leash on him. She died protecting him. That bastard demon killed them all, then locked them in the house and burned it down around them."

The smile was gone, but the rage that she sensed from both Remy and Rom had turned cold, so cold it felt like ice against that part of her that only wanted to help others.

"The demon knew we would realize they were dying. Our parents tried to block us, but we heard their screams in our heads. We were sitting in a movie theater, watching a stupid movie about some fake monster killing off idiotic teenagers while a real, live demon was slaughtering our families in our own home."

His gaze sharpened, and she felt him stare down into hers with something close to a blow.

"Rom's wrong. It wasn't his fault the demon found us."

"Then why does he think that?"

"Because a few days before, he saved a girl from an accident he witnessed at college. It was so fucking stupid, really. She tripped, something people do every day, but she fell. Rom just happened to be walking beside her at the time and he saw her heading straight for a rock on the side of the path. She could've died if she'd hit her head on it. He used his magic to knock her aside."

"So he believes because he used that tiny amount of power, the demon found you."

Remy nodded.

It was possible, she conceded to herself. If the demon had been searching for them, it could have tracked their specific magic signatures and, when Rom used his power outside of the protection of the wards, then yes, it was conceivable the demon had tracked them that way.

"But if that was the case, it would've had to know what general area to look at in the first place. Not even a *tukhulkha* demon can cast that wide a net for a specific magical signature."

"Rom thinks his constant back and forth through the wards gave the demon our general location, and then it just waited for one of us to use our magic so it could hunt us down."

"But you don't believe that's what happened."

Remy shook his head. "It doesn't matter what I believe. Nothing matters except that the demon that killed our families is dead."

She paused before she asked the next question, knowing she might not like the answer but having to ask anyway. "So what are you going to do now?"

~~~

Rom watched from the window, arms crossed over his chest as he shielded himself from Remy and Amity.

He hadn't lied when he'd stormed out. He'd fully intended to go for a run to cool down. He'd torn off his clothes and shifted into his pelt but then he'd stopped and taken a deep breath.

He could still smell her. Her scent was all over him. It made him stop, forced him to think about what exactly he was running away from.

With a huff, he shook his head, recalled his pelt and redressed. He'd meant to head straight back in and apologize, but he'd caught the gist of the conversation, and it'd been everything Rom had wanted to ask Remy himself but had never been able to force out of his mouth.

His heart pounded so hard, he thought for sure Remy would be able to hear it as he waited for his cousin to answer Amity's question.

"We used to talk about returning to the den," Remy said after a pause. "Years ago. When we were young and stupid and thought it wouldn't take long to track down a demon and kill it."

They'd been chasing that fucking demon for so long, Rom had forgotten that, at one time, he'd actually had a plan for what to do after.

Not that he and Remy had ever talked about what they were going to do. Rom had felt disloyal whenever he'd thought about life after killing the demon. As if in thinking about the future, he wasn't concentrating enough on the present and their quest to avenge their families.

It didn't matter that he knew their parents wouldn't have wanted them to become soulless killing machines, intent only on death and destruction.

It was what they'd wanted so badly to avoid when they'd packed up their families and run all those years ago.

But what the fuck would they do now?

"I'm going after the *Mal*."

Remy's softly spoken words held the weight of a vow that Rom could hear clearly through the glass.

"Do you know who you're going after?" Amity asked. "Do you actually know the name of the man who hired the demon?"

Rage hit Rom low in the gut. Damn that demon for forcing them to kill it before they'd been able to ask it any questions. He and Rom had wanted the demon to tell them who'd sent it after them. Who'd ordered it to kill their families.

But that hadn't happened. Now they were back at square one.

Rom wasn't sure he wanted to continue on. For so many years he'd sought vengeance, and now that they'd killed the demon... Damn, he was tired.

But Remy... Remy wanted more blood. And he was afraid his cousin—

Shit.

Rom wouldn't leave his cousin's side. He owed him too damn much. And yet...

"No," Remy finally answered Amity's question. "But I won't stop hunting until I have it. And I think I might have found a way to track the guy."

Rom's heart skipped a beat. What the hell was Remy talking about? He'd never mentioned anything about this.

"And how's that?"

Remy paused, and Rom's heart pounded out a staccato rhythm.

"An *auscultatus* spell."

Rom's heart stopped beating for a few seconds.

Rom hadn't known Remy even remembered what an *auscultatus* spell was. Tullia had spoken of it in hushed tones and with a healthy sense of fear the first and only time she'd ever mentioned it during their training. Then she'd told them never to attempt it, even though they might be tempted.

Tinia's teat. That spell required a shitload of power and precision control, so the caster didn't leave his mind open to whoever's mind he was trying to read. It could backfire big time.

Remy knew that. They'd never even spoken about using it before because either one or both of them could fry their minds if they tried.

"We've tried everything else," Remy continued. "The demon was our last chance to figure out who'd hired it. Now we need to take another approach."

"Remy, that spell..."

Obviously Amity had heard of it, too. And rightly feared it.

"I know what Tullia told us. I know how dangerous it is, but we're out of options." Remy shook his head. "We stayed ahead of that demon for years. Then a month ago, we felt it getting closer, trying to get a lock on our position, and we knew we'd have to move again. We tried to draw it out a few times, staying in the same place for a couple of months, daring it to come and take us, but the damn thing must have known what we were doing. It never took the bait. The few times it's come close to snatching one of us have been when we thought we were safe. So we've learned never to think we're safe."

"It was playing with you."

"Yeah, like a cat with a mouse." Remy's voice could have cut glass, it was so sharp. "I'm done being prey. The demon got sloppy when it went after you. Or it just got arrogant. Whatever happened, Remy and I managed to track it here and save you."

"And I can't tell you how grateful I am for what you and Rom did for me."

Rom watched Amity lay her hand over Remy's fist clenched on the table top. At the touch, his cousin actually seemed to relax the tiniest bit.

"Do you have any idea why the demon was after you, Lady?"

It was Amity's turn to pause, and Rom could tell by her expression that she knew.

"Yes," she finally said. "But I can't tell you what you want to know. It's complicated and… nothing for you to worry about." She smiled, but he could tell it was forced. And so could Remy because his cousin's gaze narrowed to slits.

Rom knew that look. When Remy got an idea in mind, he was like a dog with a bone, no pun intended.

"Amity, I don't want anything to happen to you."

Amity smiled at Remy, lifting one hand to cup his jaw, and lust moved through Rom like a tidal wave of heat, threatening to take him under.

He wanted her, craved her on a level he hadn't thought possible. But the way she returned Remy's intense gaze made it clear she desired his cousin.

Fucking hell.

Remy had never looked at a woman the way he was looking at Amity. With desire instead of animal lust. Remy viewed sex as a necessary part of life, like eating and sleeping. He needed it to sustain him, but sex wasn't for pleasure. It was for release.

Remy didn't just want to fuck Amity. He felt an emotional connection with her.

Of course the first woman Remy would fall for would have to be a goddess.

"Thank you, Remy. I feel the same about you and Rom."

Hell, hearing his name come from those beautiful lips just made him want her all the more. His skin felt too tight, and his hands curled into fists. He wanted to walk into the house, grab her, and throw her back down on the bed and fuck her senseless.

No way would he ever do that to a goddess but, gods damn, he so wanted to.

"I have a favor to ask of you, Remy. One I'm not quite sure how to broach."

"Anything. You can ask anything of us."

Shit. *Shit.* He and Remy might not have been raised in the den, but their parents had made sure they knew the ways of their people.

You didn't refuse an Etruscan goddess anything.

But when a goddess wanted something from you, it probably wasn't anything good.

Still, she'd saved both of their lives, and they owed her.

"Would you be willing to make love to me again? This time with your cousin."

Chapter 6

AMITY THOUGHT REMY'S EYES might pop out of his head.

Maybe this hadn't been such a good idea.

"I'm sorry." She started to backpedal. "Forgive me. That was incredibly ru—"

"No. No, Amity, I'm sorry." Remy blinked several times, looking like she'd smacked him across the face. "You just took me off guard. Please don't mistake my response for anything other than surprise."

But he still hadn't said yes, she noted. "Maybe I should have prefaced that by telling you why I'm asking."

He nodded slowly, looking a little dazed. And confused. And why wouldn't he be?

"I'm not sure whether you realize this or not, but I gain power from sexual contact." She waited for him to nod before continuing. "I'm sure you also know that most deities' powers have greatly diminished over the years."

She didn't add that two of her sister goddesses had given up their powers in the past year. Or that they'd done so for the men in their lives. Not that she blamed them. After so many millennia alone, she'd do the same, though she held no illusions she'd ever find that one man who could fulfill her needs. Or who'd be able to put up with her.

At least, she hadn't found one yet.

Remy nodded in response to her statement, and she forced her thoughts back to the situation at hand. Rather, back to talking

Remy, and eventually Rom, into her bed. All for a good cause, of course. Not simply because she wanted them.

Although, truthfully…

"Some of us have found other ways to make ourselves useful, for our lives to have some meaning in the world today." And some merely existed, a state Amity despaired of ever finding herself in. "That's why I work at the hospital. I use my limited remaining powers to help my patients."

Remy's eyes narrowed. "Aren't they mostly *eteri*?"

She could see confusion in his expression and she felt frustration creeping up on her. Yes, the deities had a reputation for being selfish and petty. And yes, as a young goddess, she'd had more than her share of arrogance.

Vast amounts of power could do that to a person. Over the years, though, she'd learned how to temper that arrogance. Losing most of her power had certainly helped.

But maybe she hadn't been as successful as she'd hoped if she'd thought Remy and Rom would simply fall at her feet and say "Of course, we'll both run right back to bed with you so you can recharge your batteries."

"Yes," she answered, "they are. I still provide services to the Etruscans as well, but… I'm not exactly on anyone's speed dial. I like to be useful, and I am at the hospital."

"Everyone wants to be useful." Remy's lips curved in a slight smile and she returned it, cautious optimism creeping in.

"Yes, becoming obsolete sucks, Remy. I hope you never experience it."

Some dark emotion shadowed his eyes for a second before he blinked it away. It could have been her imagination, though she didn't think it was. She didn't want to lose his attention now by refocusing the conversation on him. "I have two patients at the moment who are the worst cases I've ever had to handle."

The hospital employed two medical aestheticians and they split the caseload between them. Because of the intensive nature of the injuries, Amity would have expected Sue Ellen to handle at least one of them, but Sue Ellen had been on vacation the week both patients had been brought in and the cases had fallen to Amity alone.

Remy flipped his hand under hers to lace their fingers together. "Tell me about them."

Surprised and secretly delighted at his interest, she continued. "Bobby's ten. He's got pale blue eyes and the sweetest smile you've ever seen. He got trapped in his bedroom when his apartment building went up in flames."

Remy's eyes widened, and the horror she saw in them mirrored what she'd felt the first time she'd met the boy. "His parents and younger siblings slept on the second floor and they got out, but the electrical fire started in a wall in his room on the third floor. His parents nearly died trying to get to him before the firefighters arrived."

"I've been working with him for a month, trying to heal some of the damage to his face and body, but I don't have the power necessary to do it on a large scale."

Remy nodded. "And the other patient?"

Perrin Winston. Amity felt her stomach tighten just to think about Perrin. This woman was a much tougher case.

She took a deep breath, wondering how to explain Perrin's case. The facts were straightforward, at least. "Perrin is a gifted artist who works wonders with metal. Her abusive boyfriend rigged her workshop to explode while she was in the room. He caused a short in an extension cord that led to the kerosene heater exploding, which sent the contents of the tool chest in front of it straight at her face."

"Wow." Remy's eyes widened as he shook his head. "That sounds… like something you'd see in a movie."

"I know. She's lucky to still be alive. That bastard thought he'd get away with murder. I saw photos of how she looked when they brought her in. Like a macabre pin cushion. But she was lucky. None of the projectiles hit anything vital. No arteries severed, no internal organs damaged."

"But…?"

Remy stilled, like a wild animal scenting danger. Amity deliberately kept her gaze on his, resisting the almost overwhelming urge to look at his cheek.

"Her face took the brunt of the explosion. And she's refusing to allow them to reconstruct it so she might have a chance at a normal life."

She fell silent then, waiting for Remy.

After at least thirty seconds, he didn't disappoint. "Why does she refuse to do it?"

"She won't talk about it. But I have my suspicions."

"And they are…?" he prodded when she stopped to take a deep breath.

"Perrin's had a troubled life. She left home at seventeen on an art scholarship but gave it up after a year when she met a guy."

"The guy who did this to her?"

She nodded. "He wasn't abusive at first. He appeared to be everything she could want. Kind, funny, sweet. But then he changed."

Amity felt her stomach roil, just as it had done the first time Perrin had relayed the story. "She once told me she should have known he was evil because he was too good to be true. How awful to go through life thinking that."

"Did they arrest the guy?"

Her mouth curved in a hard smile and she saw Remy's eyebrows lift, as if he were shocked by her response. "Yes. And I hope the bastard never sees his freedom again. And that case of gonorrhea and psoriasis I gifted him with on his way out of the courthouse will never clear up. I made sure of that."

Remy's mouth quirked in a weak smile. "Remind me not to get on your bad side."

"He hurt her so badly, I wanted him to suffer."

"You like her, don't you?"

She nodded. "Very much. But that man stole her will to live and I hope he never tastes freedom again."

Behind her something popped. Remy's gaze shifted to see what had happened as she closed her eyes and tried to rein in the pulse of empathic power that surged through her.

When she finally opened them, she found Remy watching her carefully. "I'm sorry. Did I break something?"

He shook his head, his mouth curving until she actually thought he might laugh. "Uh, no. But the people who own this house are going to be a little surprised to see their end tables sprouting leaves."

She turned in the direction he pointed, and her eyes widened at the sight of live branches growing from the wood tables on either side of the couch.

"Oh, dear. That's going to be a problem, isn't it?"

"Yeah, I think we might have to forfeit our security deposit for that one." He lifted his eyebrows, looking at her with questions in his eyes. "I wouldn't even know how to explain it."

"My powers are geared toward healing. They connect with the life forces around them. This time it chose the wood in that table and brought it back to life for that brief period."

His eyes brightened even more. "I don't think that's the explanation I'll be giving to the real estate agent."

"No, I don't think they'll believe that, will they? I'll ask a friend to take care of it."

"No problem. We'll handle it."

She had no doubt Remy and Rom could take care of most problems that came their way.

Except Remy hadn't yet given an answer to her request that he and Rom join her in bed.

"So…" Remy's expression turned serious again. "You want Rom and me to have sex with you so you can heal your patients."

She wondered what he'd say if she told him she just wanted to have sex with him and his cousin, and the fact that she'd gain power to help her patients was more of an added benefit?

It had been so long since any man had intrigued her the way these two did. And she knew the *lucani* were much less hung up on puritanical sexual mores than the *eteri*.

With a smile, she said, "Yes."

And watched his gaze narrow in thought.

"Is there a reason you don't want to be alone with me again?"

Shock made her mouth drop open for a few brief seconds before she caught herself and closed it.

"Remy, why would you…"

Oh. The scarring on his face and body.

He held her stare, almost as if he were daring her to say something about it. So she deliberately let her gaze slide to his marred cheek before she lifted one hand to cup his jaw, letting her fingertips caress the scars. Remy tensed but didn't pull away, watching her with narrowed eyes.

"These marks, they tell me how brave you've been. How much adversity you've had to overcome. They don't turn me off. They don't make me pity you. They're a part of you and they don't make me see you differently as a man. You're strong, handsome, and I can't wait to have you inside me again. Does that clear things up for you?"

Remy's expression didn't change. "But the main reason you want to have sex with Rom and me is to boost your power?"

Was it? At the moment, she couldn't honestly say yes or no to that question. "What if I said that's only part of the reason? Would you believe me if I told you how intrigued I am by both of you?

How my body flushes with heat when either of you are near? Please believe that I will completely understand if you don't want to fulfill my request. I know what I've asked of you is unorthodox and—"

He moved so fast, she could barely track him as he leaned over and covered her mouth with his. Since her lips were already parted, he slid his tongue between them and kissed her until she thought she might pass out from lack of oxygen. Which would be extremely embarrassing for a goddess.

His taste, so well remembered from the first time they'd kissed, flooded her body with desire, making her nipples peak and her thighs quiver. His mouth moved over hers with a hunger she felt in the fierce lash of his tongue against hers and the heavy pressure of his lips.

Her hand slid from his jaw along his neck then back into his hair, slipping through the long strands before clutching at them so he couldn't get away. She tilted her head to get a better angle and felt his tongue stab deeper into her mouth. She had a brief flash of an image in her mind, an image of her with his cock in her mouth as Rom thrust into her from behind.

She shuddered as her skin felt electrified, and the flesh between her thighs swelled and moistened.

Then suddenly, she was gasping in air as he pulled back, his eyes looking as dazed as she felt.

"I'll talk to Rom." His voice sounded as if he'd sandpapered it. "Just give me a few minutes."

She blinked, trying to get her brain to function normally again. "Isn't he out for a run?"

Remy's gaze shot to a point over her shoulder. Turning, she realized he was looking out the front window, where she saw Rom watching from the front porch with a narrow-eyed stare.

How long had he been there? Long enough to hear what she'd said? What was he thinking? Did he feel left out? Rejected?

"No." She drew in a breath, trying to calm her thundering heart. "No, I think I need to talk to him."

"If this is really what you want, Amity, don't take no for an answer. And I can tell you that's exactly what he's going to say."

She turned back to see Remy staring at her with an intent gaze. "I don't want to force him—"

Remy's panty-wetting smile cut off her train of thought like a scalpel through butter. "Trust me. He wants you. But he's stubborn enough to say no to what he wants if he thinks…"

"If he thinks what?"

Remy stared back out the window. "If he thinks he'll upset me."

"And will this upset you?"

He shook his head, his gaze steady on Rom's. "No. In fact, I think it's the best damn idea anyone's had in a long time."

The absolute conviction in his voice made her smile. She sensed no trace of a lie in Remy's voice. Only barely leashed anticipation.

Which made her tingle all over.

She had to force herself to head for the door, to grip the knob in her suddenly sweaty hand and turn it. Nerves weren't something she was used to. Actually, she didn't think she'd ever felt nervous.

The past twenty-four hours had been a roller coaster, and she felt like the train had just taken a dip before beginning another climb.

Good thing she loved roller coasters.

Stopping in the doorway, she was almost surprised to find Rom standing in front of her. Waiting for her.

Arms crossed over his broad chest, expression impassive, his gaze never wavered from hers until she almost felt the urge to drop her gaze. Like a coward.

Stiffening her spine, she tilted her head back so she could continue to hold his gaze. His beautiful mouth tightened, as if he expected her to turn tail and run.

"You heard." She didn't make it a question. She saw no point in beating around the bush. "Are you willing?"

He didn't answer right away. She could tell he was thinking fast and hard. And she wasn't at all sure he was going to decide in her favor.

She didn't want to railroad him into having sex with her again. She wanted him. Had wanted both of them from the first moment she'd seen them in the bar.

She'd thought maybe Rom truly didn't want her. That maybe he hadn't wanted to touch her, only to watch.

But she'd felt his desire for her, felt how much he'd wanted her as they had sex before she could heal Remy.

She was usually very good about reading people. Here… she was making such a mess of things.

"Why do you need both of us? Why not just Remy?"

Undercurrents flowed between them, thick and dangerous. She wished she knew exactly what he was asking.

Did he really not want her?

And was that so hard to believe? Perhaps there was a reason she was more forgotten than most other goddesses.

The thought put an edge on her words. "The amount of power I could gain from both of you together would be exponentially more than what I'd get from one-on-one encounters."

Damn it. She hadn't meant to sound so clinical, so cold.

And Rom's raised eyebrows displayed his lack of enthusiasm with her offer.

Uni's ass. She'd always been told she had a great bedside manner. Where the hell was it?

"I'm sorry." She shrugged, surprised to feel a flush heating her cheeks. "I'm not normally so bad at this."

"At what? Talking men into sharing your bed? I can't believe that, Lady Amity."

Was that sarcasm she heard in Rom's tone?

Some of her sister goddesses believed she was too soft for her own good.

Which was a crock of dung, if you asked her.

She dealt with pain and death on a daily basis. She'd seen the worst people could do to each other. It took strength to forge ahead every day, to treat those who'd been so cruelly abused or who suffered so much.

She was no cream puff.

Drawing her spine straighter, she watched Rom's eyes widen as wariness crept in.

Good. She was still a goddess, after all. She deserved a little respect, at the very least.

"Forgive me, Lady." His gaze dropped. "That was uncalled for."

Shit. Just… shit. She didn't want him to come to bed with her because she commanded him to. "No, please forgive me, Rom. I would never want to force you into anythi—"

"Lady Amity, trust me." He raised one hand as he shook his head. "You wouldn't be forcing me. I'd be more than happy to share your bed. It's just—I don't want…"

"Rom." Remy's voice sounded from behind her. "Just shut up and say yes."

Chapter 7

ROM'S HEAD SHOT UP as his gaze sought Remy's.

His cousin had shocked the hell out of him. Rom had never in a million years expected Remy to go for this.

That he wanted to…

It made him wonder what the hell Remy was up to.

Yes, they'd shared women before. The women Rom—and it was always Rom—chose were always *eteri*. Any female from the magical races would have known what they were immediately and would have raised too many questions they couldn't answer.

Remy had used those women like they were food or water, a necessity of life. Not a pleasure.

He wasn't looking at Amity like that. Remy's expression held nothing of his normal detachment.

Remy wanted her. Rom could admit, at least to himself, that he wanted her just as badly. But if his cousin had feelings for Amity that went beyond simple lust, Rom should start walking fast and far.

"Remy," Amity started to turn, "wait—"

"No, we can't wait." Remy's gaze held his steady. "You can't give him time to think about it because he'll talk himself out of it. He wants you. He just won't admit it. But I'm not that stupid."

Amity drew in a sharp breath and Rom's gaze dropped to watch Remy's hands curve around her hips. Remy's fingers spread, tightening and she went still. When he looked into her face, he realized that she was also intently watching him.

He saw worry in the way she bit her bottom lip, but she couldn't conceal the rapid rise and fall of her chest. Or her nipples as they poked through the T-shirt she wore. He had the almost overwhelming urge to bend and suck those stiff points into his mouth.

Instead, he watched Remy bend his head and put his mouth against her neck, causing her eyelids to fall and her lips to part.

Rom had never seen another woman as sexy as Amity in this moment. It made his cock thicken as his pulse thundered.

Remy knew all of Rom's secrets. A casualty of sharing a telepathic bond with another person. Remy knew how much he liked to watch.

He enjoyed seeing a woman get lost in passion. And Remy had a gift for getting women to let go.

Remy's hands hadn't moved, but Amity put hers over his. She wanted him to move higher. To her breasts. But Remy wasn't giving her what she wanted. Instead, his hands actually moved down, lower on her hips, causing her to moan. Sweet and powerful, that sound practically reached between his legs and grabbed his balls.

The air around them became heated and thick, and he caught the scent of her arousal. Fuck, she smelled amazing.

It was the same scent he'd caught this morning when he'd woken with her. He nearly growled with hunger.

He caught back the sound, not wanting to break the spell she appeared to be under.

Instead, he reached for her. His right hand cupped one breast, letting it settle into his palm. The weight felt good there, the heat of her seeping into his hand. He squeezed the plump flesh, his thumb and forefinger pinching the tight little nipple and teasing it.

"Sweet Mother Goddess, don't stop."

Her breathless plea made him freeze for several seconds, waiting to hear her voice again. He had no idea who she was begging not to stop but he figured the plea extended to both of them.

Remy had plastered her back to his chest, his hands holding her hips tight against his. His mouth had moved from her neck to her ear, where his teeth alternated between nibbling at the lobe and the sensitive skin behind it.

Her head had tilted to the side to give Remy more access, her eyes closed. He didn't want her to close her eyes. He wanted to see everything she was feeling.

Moving closer, he bent his head until his eyes were on a level with hers. Then he used his left hand to cup her jaw and tilt her head back. "Amity, look at me."

He'd thought maybe he'd have a hard time giving her orders. She was a goddess, after all. He had to disregard everything he'd ever been taught about the deities, especially the number one rule… Never demand anything. You were likely to get your ass singed by a bolt of lightning.

But when she opened her eyes immediately and looked into his with that glaze of passion hazing her vision, everything else ceased to matter.

She was a beautiful woman, one he wanted with a burning passion.

"I want you to keep your eyes open. I want to see you."

She sucked in a rough breath and her lips parted. He couldn't help himself. He closed the few inches between them to kiss her.

He didn't think, he acted. The hand on her breast tightened as the one holding her chin tilted her head so he could get a better angle.

His tongue licked at her lips, slicking over the plump curves before slipping into her mouth. He vaguely registered Remy pulling back as he used his lips to get her to open hers.

As she moaned into his mouth, he crowded closer. Since she had nowhere to go, he had her body pressed tight against his, and Remy's, in seconds.

Her stomach cradled his cock. She wasn't tall enough for him to rub against her mound but he was content for now to have her breasts crushed against his abs and her hands clutching at his shoulders.

She kissed him with a sense of urgency that quickly infected him. His kiss became more demanding as she gave him everything he wanted. His tongue played with hers, deepening their connection. Damn, she tasted so good, he swore it made him drunk.

When he had to pull back or risk suffocation, he opened his eyes to see hers blinking up at him. Satisfaction at her dazed expression made him long for more. Much more.

"Strip her."

The words were out of his mouth before he realized he was going to say them and, for a second, he wondered if Remy would obey.

Typically when they shared a woman, they were both careful to rein in their natural dominance. Neither wanted to tip that delicate scale between them.

Of course, they'd never been in a bedroom alone with a goddess.

One Remy had feelings for. A goddess Rom wanted more than he wanted to breathe.

Remy's gaze caught his and held for a few seconds. In that short time, he saw exactly what his cousin wanted him to see. How very okay he was with all of this.

The strap he'd been keeping on his libido snapped, allowing his brain to shut down so all he could do was feel.

Crossing his arms over his chest, he nodded then watched Remy's mouth curve in a wicked grin just before his hands began to move.

They rose along her hips to the hem of the oversized T-shirt. She blinked as he slid his fingers beneath the material, and Rom let his gaze drop as Remy's hands disappeared.

Amity gasped and Rom figured Remy's fingers were playing along the edges of the red lace underwear he'd caught brief glimpses of.

How soft was her skin there? Remy already knew. He'd had his hands all over her last night.

Rom felt no jealousy. The anticipation wiped out any trace he might have felt.

Instead, he bit back a demand for Remy to go faster.

As if he were moving in slow motion, Remy gripped her shirt in his fingers and began to lift it. He bared her stomach inch by inch, his mouth settling on the curve of her neck and shoulder to bite her.

She shuddered and Rom's gaze flipped back to hers. "No. Don't close your eyes. Watch me."

Her eyes on his, her lips parted as she reached behind her to grab Remy's hips as if she needed to anchor herself. Maybe she did. She certainly looked dazed enough to need support.

Damn, that made him so fucking hard. He almost reached down to adjust himself then stopped. The sharp ache helped to focus him as Remy bared her stomach and the lower curve of her breasts. But her arms stopped him from taking the shirt over her head.

"Lift your arms," Rom said. "I want to see your breasts."

She obeyed without hesitation, and Remy drew the shirt over her head.

"You're so fucking beautiful. I want you naked."

The words were out before Rom could censor them. So not appropriate for a goddess but totally right for the moment.

She must not have taken any offense because her breasts began to quiver with her faster breathing.

The pebbled tips were dark raspberry, and his mouth actually watered for a taste of them.

Remy dropped her shirt to the floor then cupped both breasts in his hands. The contrast between her pale skin and Remy's darker flesh sent Rom's pulse thudding through his veins.

"Goddamn, your skin is amazing, sweetheart." Remy's voice was barely audible as he whispered in her ear. As she shivered, Rom swallowed a groan.

She continued to stare at him as Remy lingered at her breasts, caressing them, pinching the nipples until they stood at attention and begged for Rom to put his mouth on them.

Swallowing so loudly Rom heard it over the sound of their tortured breathing, she tried to speak. It took her at least thirty seconds before she could get the words out.

"Rom said naked." Her voice, low and husky, reached somewhere deep inside him. "Get with the program, Remy."

Remy snorted and Rom's lips curved in a grin.

"You heard the lady." Rom crossed his hands over his chest. "You'd better listen to her."

"And why is it that I'm still taking orders from you?"

Remy's words held a bit of an edge and Rom stilled as he carefully watched Remy for any sign of trouble. But the glint in his cousin's eyes wiped out all fear.

Even here, Remy was going to bust his ass.

Fine. He could deal with that. As long as Remy was okay.

"Because you know I'm always right."

"At the moment, I'll have to agree."

Releasing her breasts with one last pinch, Remy grabbed the waistband of her panties and, in one swift movement, yanked them to her knees then let them drop to the floor.

Their goddess stood naked in front of them, not a hint of embarrassment in her expression. And absolutely no need for it.

"It's no wonder men fought to worship at your feet, my lady." Rom could barely get the words out around the lust threatening to cut off his air supply.

Her smile was bittersweet. "That was a long time ago."

Did he hear sorrow in her tone? He wanted nothing like that to intrude.

"Then we heartily apologize for the male gender's idiocy." Remy settled his hands on her shoulders. "And trust me when I say we will fight to the death for you."

Her expression softened with wonder and Rom knew Remy had come up with the right thing to say.

"I don't want you to fight for me. I want you to take me."

"Oh, we will." The hint of a growl in Remy's voice made her visibly shiver. "But first, we're going to make you scream."

Remy turned her in his arms and dropped his mouth over hers. From this angle, Rom couldn't see her face so his gaze dropped. He watched Remy's hands splay across her back, watched them stroke and knead the soft flesh, slowly drifting down until he reached her waist.

As Rom fought to breathe, he watched Remy smooth his hands over Amity's hips then go even lower to cup her ass. She had a gorgeous ass, rounded and feminine.

Perfect. Absolutely perfect.

Remy's skin was at least a shade darker, and the contrast to her skin was vivid, arousing as all hell. Remy stroked her ass with one hand and kneaded with the other, causing her to shift beneath his hands, for her ass to clench as she tried to rub her mound against him.

Their height difference made it impossible for her to align their bodies how she wanted, so she lifted onto her toes, causing her leg muscles to tighten into sleek curves.

Remy shifted, turning his head to get a better angle on her mouth, one hand reaching up to cup her chin and angle her head, and Rom saw total concentration on his cousin's face. Rom usually only saw that expression when Remy was fighting.

But it was the expression on Amity's face he wanted to see. Shifting a few inches to the left, he looked... and lost himself in the bliss on her face. She fairly glowed with it.

When her eyes opened to stare into his as she continued to kiss Remy, Rom felt the impact of that gaze throughout his body. His stomach clenched, his skin felt too tight for his body, and his cock pounded against the zipper of his jeans.

He was torn between wanting to watch and wanting to put his hands on her.

His fingers curled into fists but he forced them to loosen as Remy released her mouth to trail kisses down her neck.

Reaching for her hair, Rom threaded his fingers through the curls then tugged, not hard enough to hurt, just enough to let her know what he wanted her to do. She obeyed, tilting her head back so Remy had better access.

Remy didn't waste time. He bent to suck a nipple into his mouth, cupping them in his hands and drawing hard on the tip, the pink flesh disappearing into Remy's mouth. With one hand still in her hair, Rom put his other on her shoulder.

The heat of her skin seeped into his, causing his blood to pound through his body and his stomach to curl into a tight knot of want.

"Does it feel good, Amity? Does Remy's mouth feel good on your breast?"

"Yes." Her voice was barely audible this time. "Like wet fire."

"Think how much better it will be when we're fucking you. When Remy has you impaled on his cock and I have mine in your mouth."

A heavy blush suffused her cheeks. Shit. Maybe he shouldn't have been so crude. Maybe—

"Then maybe you should both be naked."

She punctuated her statement by reaching for him. For his cock, actually. She grabbed the waistband of his jeans to tug him closer then molded her hand to the ridge behind his zipper.

He hissed, the sensation making every muscle in his body clench in anticipation. She petted him, squeezed him, as his hand tightened in her hair. She played with him for endless minutes, until the barrier of his jeans became a torment.

"Open my jeans, sweetheart. Take 'em off."

She didn't obey right away, mostly because Remy was using one hand to caress between her legs, almost mimicking what she was doing to Rom.

Her chest rose and fell in short, rapid bursts as she fell deeper into the sensations Remy was creating.

But Rom wanted her hands on him and he was selfish enough to demand it.

"Amity. My jeans. Now."

She blinked, as if coming out of a daze, and her hand tightened around his aching erection for several seconds. With one hand on Remy's shoulder to steady herself, she stared into Rom's eyes as she slowly slid her fingers to the button.

She tugged him closer, just a couple of inches but enough that she didn't have to stretch to reach the button. Then she worked her fingers between his skin and the jeans, as if testing how tight they were.

Brushing against the sensitive tip of his cock, she made him suck in a short gasp. His cock throbbed beneath his jeans, but she withdrew before he could push into her. After several torturous seconds, she slipped the button through the hole. He gritted his teeth against the sensation of the denim rubbing against his shaft.

From the corner of his eye, he caught Remy pulling away from her breast, his gaze falling to his hands on her lower body.

As Remy's hand disappeared between her legs, her lips parted in a short moan and her hand slipped away from Remy's jeans.

Stepping closer, until his chest just barely brushed against her shoulder, Rom leaned down to whisper in her ear. "And here I thought you had more willpower. Concentrate, my lady, or we're never going to get to the good stuff."

"I wouldn't say this isn't good."

The hint of amusement in her voice made Rom smile and coaxed a snort out of Remy, who pressed an openmouthed kiss to her breast, just before he released her and stepped away.

Her gaze flew to Remy, who'd backed up to sit on the couch. With one arm draped over the back of the couch, he looked like he was settling in to watch TV. Only the intensity of his gaze and the low growl of his voice gave away the strength of his desire.

"Don't worry. I'm not going anywhere. Finish undressing Rom. I'll wait my turn."

"Are you taking turns?" Her tone indicated that wasn't what she wanted.

"For now. Rom hasn't had the chance to get to know you as well as I have." His lips curved in a way that made Amity suck in a deep breath. "Trust me. I'll be right here. Watching."

⁓

Amity felt the desire behind that last word stroke over her skin with the same sensation she felt as Rom's hand caressed her breast.

Sweet Mother Goddess. These two *lucani* men made her hotter than she'd ever felt in her very long life.

She wanted to force them to skip the foreplay and get to the good part, but she realized she was enjoying this way too much. Her heart felt ready to pound out of her chest with desire for these two men.

She liked the way Rom had looked at her while Remy stroked between her legs. She especially liked the way he looked as she toyed with the button on his jeans. As if he wanted to take a bite out of her.

Her neck tingled in anticipation of that bite but Rom had a firm grasp on the lust pulsing through his body.

And Remy… Remy's heavy-lidded gaze made her thighs clench and her sex moisten.

Dragging her gaze from Remy's with significant effort, she let it drop to where her fingers had stilled on Rom's jeans.

She swore she saw his cock swell more than it already had. The thick ridge behind the zipper made her mouth water with anticipation.

Taking a deep breath, the heady scent of Rom's desire filling her lungs, she put both hands on the waistband of his jeans.

She didn't rush, because she knew she'd give away her almost rampant desire. And a goddess just shouldn't do that. No matter that she could barely control the tremble in her fingers or the quiver in her thighs.

Instead, she pulled the material away from his stomach, only a few centimeters but enough to get her fingers between the denim and his skin again.

So hot. She wanted to shred his shirt and press against all that heated flesh.

And why shouldn't she?

"Will you take your shirt off, Rom?" She let her gaze flash up at him, caught the blazing heat in his eyes, and couldn't resist slipping her hand lower until she felt the smooth head of his cock beneath her fingertips.

Rom sucked in a sharp breath, and his hand tightened in her hair, tugging until she felt the sharp bite of pain. She had no idea she'd like that so much. Obviously, she'd been missing out on a few of the more… painful pleasures in life.

"You take it off for me."

Oh yes. That would be her pleasure.

Sliding her hands out of his jeans, she used both to grasp the hem of his soft cotton shirt and tug it up. Washboard abs came into view first, almost distracting her from pulling the shirt higher. She wanted to lick along those beautifully defined ridges, then follow the thin line of fine hair up to where it spread over his pecs.

Pushing the shirt higher, she uncovered the broad chest she'd seen earlier today. Lightly covered with brown hair, she wanted to brush her nose against it, then take that flat male nipple between her lips and suckle, just like they'd done to her.

"Lift."

She was surprised she was able to speak, with her heart pounding and the dryness in her throat. She wasn't sure he was going to obey, since he didn't release her hair right away. But finally, with one last tug, he did, raising his arms so she could get his shirt over his head.

Since Rom stood at least six inches taller, she had to lift onto her toes to do it. And he made no concessions for the height difference, forcing her to press up against him.

Her naked breasts met the heated skin of his abdomen and they both hissed in response. Her nipples tightened until they ached and her sheath clenched tight.

By the time she had them both naked, she'd be begging them to fuck her.

Not very goddess-like. And she didn't care one bit.

Hunger like she'd never felt in centuries had its claws in her, and she found she'd missed this feeling. This ache. For so long, she'd felt lacking.

Now she realized what she'd been missing. And she had two fine specimens of exactly what she needed right here.

She hadn't forgotten that Remy sat only a few feet away, watching everything she did.

Dropping Rom's shirt on the floor freed up both hands to pet the chest that enticed her.

Blessed Goddess, the man should be immortalized in marble.

Beginning at the top, she settled her hands on his shoulders and soaked in the strength radiating from him. Strength she admired so much.

"Amity." Rom's voice intruded on her thoughts on what part of him she wanted to taste first.

"Hmm."

"You need to take my jeans off."

"Aren't you capable of doing that?"

"Yeah, but I like when you've got your hands on me."

She smiled and petted her hands down his chest. "And I like having my hands on you."

"If you take off the jeans, there'll be much more to touch. Do it."

The harsh demand in his tone made her shiver and her hands fell once again to his waistband. She figured she'd have more than enough time to explore that wide expanse of chest a little later.

Her lungs struggled to keep up with her need for air as she grabbed the tiny silver tab of his zipper. The already undone button looked sexy as hell.

Just think how much sexier he'll look with the zipper down.

Cautious, knowing he wasn't wearing underwear beneath the denim, she released the zipper, the snick of metallic teeth machine-gun loud in the room where she heard only the sound of their heavy breathing. It was a wonder the windows weren't fogged. By the time they actually got down to the sex, they probably would be.

Before she could consider her actions, she went to her knees in front of Rom, dragging his jeans just below his hips. He reached for her immediately, his hands on her shoulders ready to pull her back to her feet. Or hold her there.

She wasn't sure which. As she stared up at him, she wasn't sure he knew what he wanted, either.

Wouldn't matter. She wasn't going anywhere.

His cock stood straight and proud, thicker than Remy's but not as long. She wanted him in her mouth.

Her lips parted and Rom froze, every inch of him except his cock. That thick shaft throbbed, as if straining toward her.

She blew out a rough breath. Rom groaned and threaded his fingers through her hair again. She expected him to pull her closer, to rub his cock against her lips. Instead, he put his other hand under her chin and tilted her face so she stared up at him.

"Amity."

She heard the question he didn't voice and let her lips curve in a smile.

Then she wrapped both hands around his cock, maintaining eye contact the entire time. His cock felt like silk over a steel core as she stroked one hand up the shaft to the tip and the other down to cup the heaviness of his balls.

His expression tightened into sharp lines, his eyes blazed.

Blessed goddess, how wonderful it felt to have a man stare at her like this. It'd been so long since she gotten this close to one. And she didn't mean sexually. She meant emotionally.

Desire wasn't the only emotion charging through her blood. Something that felt very much like compassion flooded her system as well.

But of course she'd feel something other than physical desire for these men. They'd saved her life. And she'd done the same for them.

What they did wasn't about repaying a debt, however. It was about something far more, something that made all her empathic abilities hum to life.

It was almost like she wanted to heal him, although she knew he had no injuries.

Instead of lingering on that thought, she redirected her attention back to the heated flesh in her hands.

She wanted to lean forward and put her mouth on the tip, suck it inside. But she also wanted to stoke that heat in his eyes just a little higher.

Twisting her hand around his cock, she stroked him with a firm motion at the same time she squeezed his sac.

How he managed to stay so still... The man had incredible control.

Which she swore she was going to break. She was a goddess, after all, and what she wanted, well... sometimes she got.

"So hard." She made sure her voice held every ounce of pleasure she felt. "So beautiful. You're going to feel wonderful in my mouth."

His cock jerked in her hand and his hand tightened.

"Anything you want." His voice sounded like five miles of gravel road. "I'm yours."

A shiver caught her off guard and she bit down on her bottom lip to control it. She'd had men say the exact same thing to her before. But she'd never felt anything like the wild joy spreading through her when these men said it.

She had no idea what to say in return. Could only express herself through her actions.

She leaned forward and pressed a kiss directly over the slit, her tongue slipping out to tease the tiny opening.

Rom's groan reverberated throughout her body as she opened her mouth to take him in. Her tongue licked along the heated shaft, the taste making her yearn for more.

How long had it been since she'd felt such desire? Decades? Centuries? She couldn't remember the last man she'd had sex with. These men made her forget everyone else.

She had the overwhelming desire to consume them, to push them to heights they'd never experienced with another woman.

Sinking farther down his shaft, she took more of him in, increased the suction and felt his hips thrust. He froze as if he'd done something wrong and she moved one hand to his hip to encourage him to do it again.

She wanted him to participate, not just give her what he thought she wanted.

Pulling back, his cock slipping from her mouth with a slight pop, she looked up at him. "Don't stop. Fuck my mouth, Rom."

The heat in his eyes scorched her, and she didn't see his hands move until he'd cupped her cheeks and pulled her forward. He held her face steady as she took him in her mouth again, then he began a rough, thrusting motion.

Holding onto his hips, Amity let him control her. She barely registered the fact that no one had ever dared to treat her like this, which might have been part of the reason she felt a bone-deep thrill at this intimate act.

He wanted her. He took her. She burned.

His cock slid over her tongue, though he made sure he didn't thrust too deep or too fast. At least, not at first. Quickly, she grew hungry for more, began to pull him closer, take more of him.

Cock swelling even thicker, he moved harder, faster. One hand threaded into her hair, tugging on the strands, providing a stinging counterpoint to the caressing motion of the other on her jaw.

His breath hissed through his lips as she let her teeth scrape along the sensitive shaft. He jerked and groaned—and pulled away.

Before she could utter a protest, he pulled her up, holding her against his body with her feet dangling inches from the floor and her eyes almost on a level with his.

"I want to come in your mouth." His voice had lowered at least an octave, resembling a growl. "I want you to make me come with your lips and your tongue and I want Remy to fuck you while I do. I want you to come at the same time we do."

Her sex clenched and she nearly came just from the rough sound of his voice. She couldn't get her vocal cords to work so she merely nodded, her lips parted so she could breathe.

Her heart beat so fast, she knew they could hear it.

"Remy's going to sit on the couch and you're going to straddle his lap, your back to his front. He's going to sink his cock deep inside you, then you're going to open your mouth and take me back in."

Yes. Absolutely. That would be wonderful.

She wanted to say the words but couldn't speak because the expression of total domination on Rom's face rendered her mute.

She nodded again, deliberately and slowly so there was no misunderstanding.

Rom's gaze shifted over her shoulder and she heard the couch springs shift as Remy stood.

"Turn and let Remy pick you up. Put your legs around his waist."

Rom's tone demanded compliance and she obeyed without thought. Remy lifted her effortlessly, her legs wrapping around his waist and baring her sex. She gasped as the heated skin of his abdomen caressed the lips of her sex.

Remy's expression held her spellbound as he took the few steps to the couch then set her on the edge of the nearest cushion before taking a step back. She almost reached for him, thinking he was leaving her, before she realized he was shucking his jeans.

For a few brief seconds when he straightened, she got a glimpse of just how beautifully Remy was made. Lean and sleek but firmly muscled. Her gaze tripped over the scars on his chest but they in no way detracted from his male beauty.

He moved then, breaking the spell, and she blinked. In that instant, he dropped onto the couch beside her, put his hands around her waist and lifted her over his lap, facing away from him, as if she weighed less than a feather.

Which certainly wasn't true.

Her legs spread as he set her on her knees over his lap, cooler air brushing against the heated flesh of her exposed sex.

Her eyes closed for a few brief seconds as she felt the brush of his cock against her pussy lips. She tried to lower her hips to continue the contact but he kept his hand on her waist and held her exactly where he wanted her. High enough not to touch but close enough to feel the heat of his skin.

Heart knocking against her ribs like a trapped bird, she opened her eyes and found Rom standing in front of her, his expression tightened with lust. "Finish removing my jeans, Amity." He took another step forward, then another until she could reach him. "Take them off for me."

Her hands reached for his already undone jeans, but her gaze lit and stuck on his broad, powerful shoulders and chest for several seconds before falling to his defined abs and thick, muscled thighs. Absolutely beautiful.

She reached for Rom, Remy's hands steadying her hips as she leaned forward to push Rom's jeans down to his ankles. She hadn't had much time to explore Rom earlier. She planned to indulge her senses, just as she had with Remy.

Knowing Remy wouldn't let her fall, she stretched to put her hands on Rom's chest, petting the soft mat of dark hair on his chest. His chest muscles flexed and rippled beneath her palms and she had to bite her bottom lip to make sure her mouth didn't hang open.

"Don't stop there. I want you to touch me."

The command in his voice made her shiver. "I don't plan to stop. I'm simply taking my time."

"Don't take too much."

"Don't listen to him," Remy whispered in her ear. "Anticipation makes everything better."

She *liked* Remy. He made her smile. And smiles had been few and far between in her life recently.

Rom carried the weight of the world on his shoulders, a weight he seemed to have no trouble supporting. But her empathy sensed the deep well of rage and uncertainty that constantly bubbled under the surface.

Remy had learned how to compartmentalize. The only thing she sensed from him right now was his desire for her and the pleasure it gave him to have his hands on her.

Rom needed more encouragement to let go.

Curling her hands slightly, she let her fingernails scratch a trail from his shoulders to his nipples, where she raked across the tiny nubs and felt him shudder beneath her hands. Her gaze dropped to his waist, to the dark, throbbing mass of his cock. She couldn't wait to have him in her mouth again.

Sliding one hand behind his back, she pulled him closer until her lips touched the skin of his taut stomach.

As she bared her teeth and prepared to take a bite of his skin, she felt Remy's hand slide from her hip to her thigh. Then between her legs. She gasped out a quiet breath as Remy's fingers began to pet her slick lower lips. No more than a whisper of touch but enough to make her bite harder than she'd anticipated.

Rom groaned and she pulled back, only to feel his hand on her head, pulling her back.

"No. I like it. Don't fucking stop."

Her pussy clenched at the rough sound of his voice, then she nearly toppled over as she felt Remy slip one finger between her lips and into her channel. He went slowly, as if afraid to hurt her, but she was slick and ready.

Impaling herself farther onto Remy's hand, she began to lay a series of biting kisses along the rippling muscles of Rom's abs as her fingers blindly followed the thin line of hair that led from his belly button to his groin.

She brushed against the base of his cock, his skin furnace-blast hot as she wrapped her hand around that thick shaft just as Remy inserted another finger and began a slow, torturous pump that stole her focus.

Her hands stilled, gripping Rom's cock as she breathed against his skin.

Rom groaned, putting one hand over hers, urging her to continue. Liquid heat moved through her body as Remy fucked her with his fingers. So good. So—

"Come on, babe. I know you can multitask better than this."

Rom's voice, heavy with lust, stirred her out of the haze. Blinking, she looked down at the thick shaft only inches from her mouth.

She moved, bent her head, but had to steady herself when Remy flicked at her clit with his thumb.

The sensation buzzed along connections deep inside. Her body wanted to melt but she knew she had to hold on.

Even when she felt Remy's silky cock nudge the inside of her thigh.

Yes.

Her hand began to move on Rom's shaft, urged on by his hand as Remy's fingers continued to stroke inside her.

The rhythms differed and she gave herself over to them for long minutes.

Above her, Rom's heavy breathing echoed in her ears, while she felt Remy's against her neck.

Her own brushed against Rom's cock.

"Damn it," Rom growled, "suck me."

Because that's exactly what she wanted, she pushed Rom back to get the right angle to take him in her mouth.

Which she didn't do right away. Instead, she licked around the head, listening for Rom's groan. He didn't disappoint. Lacing the fingers of one hand through her hair, he reached out with the other to tweak her nipple.

"You look so fucking hot, I could come right now."

His voice spurred her to open her mouth over the head and take him in. Just the head, sucking hard until he groaned again.

Behind her, Remy's fingers continued their slow plunge and withdrawal even as he shifted, pushing her forward until her knees were on the very edge of the cushion. His fingers continued their slow plunge and withdrawal. Drawing in a deep breath, she tried to take Rom deeper.

And moaned when she felt Remy's tongue slide across her slick, swollen lower lips.

"Fuck," Rom's voice deepened even more. "Do that again and I will come in your mouth."

He'd do that anyway but not yet. And if she wasn't careful, she'd go over the edge too.

It was so damn hard to concentrate while Remy made a feast of her, but she forced herself to give Rom at least enough attention to make it good for him.

And from his response she must have been doing something right.

Rom's heavy breathing filled the room, his vocal pleasure enticing her to suck him harder before she backed off to tease the head with the tip of her tongue.

With her eyes closed, she imagined how they must look, the three of them naked and in such a carnal act. Heat flashed through her, threatening her resolve.

No. She'd hold on as long as she could. Remy and Rom made her feel too good to want it to end quickly.

The scent of sex warmed the air around them. Remy had a masterful way with his tongue and lips, stroking, penetrating. Nipping. Destroying her control as she tried to do the same to Rom.

When Rom finally reached his breaking point, she nearly cried out in relief.

"Remy. Do it now. Take her."

She barely understood what Rom had said but she felt Remy shift behind her again, felt his hands grab her hips.

In the next second, she was impaled on his cock. Spread wide enough to burn.

Crying out, she felt Rom pull away as Remy settled her more fully on his lap. Remy allowed her only a few seconds to adjust the fullness, to the wonderful thickness of him, before he started to fuck her slow and easy.

Her hands fell to Remy's knees but she had no need to steady herself. He held her tight, even as his hips thrust in a strong rhythm.

She let herself fall under his spell then, her eyes closing and her pussy tightening around him with every stroke.

So close…

Her head tilted back but it wasn't long before Rom cupped her cheek with a demanding hand. She opened her eyes and got caught in Rom's blazing hot gaze. For several seconds, he held hers as Remy lifted her on and off his cock.

Rom liked what he saw. Glancing down, she saw his other hand wrapped around his cock, stroking himself. The sight of that deep red cockhead disappearing into his fist then reappearing made her mouth water.

When she glanced up again, her body on the very edge of orgasm, she knew he saw exactly what she'd wanted him to see.

Taking that small step forward, Rom used the hand wrapped around his cock to angle it perfectly for her mouth.

"So hot. So hot."

The words became a chant as Rom began to fuck her mouth in an alternate rhythm to Remy.

She felt her power rise, but she sought more. Behind her, Remy leaned forward to press an openmouthed kiss to her shoulder before he spoke in her ear.

"Are you close?"

She pulled off Rom for just a second. "Gods, yes. Don't stop."

"Not planning to. You feel amazing."

It was too much. The sound of Remy's voice in her ear. Rom's taste flooding her senses. The scent of the two men loving her.

Her Goddess power, normally a quiet, warm well deep inside her, began to swell and spread throughout her body. Making every one of her senses sharpen to a fine point between pleasure and pain.

She broke first.

Her sheath clenched around Remy as she convulsed in an orgasm so fierce, she saw stars behind her eyelids.

Moaning, she felt Rom grab her head to steady her. Or maybe he just wanted to hold her steady as he came down her throat.

The rush nearly knocked her unconscious as the power coming from the two men flooded into her. It filled her, made her shiver and shake until she thought she might overload. There was too much. She couldn't process it, couldn't hold on to it.

Luckily Remy had a good hold on her because, when she finally broke, she didn't hit the floor.

Chapter 8

AMITY COULD BARELY OPEN her eyes, she was so sated.

And warm. So warm.

Lying between two male bodies giving off so much heat, she should have been uncomfortable. Instead, she wanted to rub up against them like a cat.

As she was pretty sure she'd done so all night after she'd nearly OD'd on sexual energy.

She'd never imagined she could do that. Never came close before.

Perhaps it was a result of being obsolete. Or maybe it had more to do with Remy and Rom.

Sweet Mother Goddess. She'd never felt anything like that. Not in all the many centuries of her life.

Last night, she felt as if she'd been struck by one of Uni's lightning bolts. The patriarch of the Etruscan deities had been known to occasionally let them fly at his children. Usil, the Sun God, had been a frequent target, but Nortia had gotten singed a couple of times for her sharp tongue.

Of course, that had been before the *Involuti*, the five founding deities of the Etruscan pantheon, had retreated to *Invol*, barring the gate behind them and leaving their children to exist on the mortal plane.

An old sorrow hit her, one that always brought her close to tears. But not now. Not when she felt so much power flowing through her blood, nearly equal to what she remembered from her heyday.

Her skin tingled with excitement—and her sex pulsed, clenching. Amazing didn't begin to cover her feelings.

Drawing in a deep breath rich with the men's unique scents and the smell of sex, she let her eyes drift closed once again.

"You seem… happy."

The male voice held no menace and Amity, floating somewhere between sleep and wakefulness, smiled, although she had no idea who might be talking to her in her mind. Most likely it was a dream. "I am."

"Why?"

"Because I had an amazing night and soon I'll be able to help two people who desperately need it."

"And why would you do that?"

The genuine curiosity in that voice gave her pause. Whoever she was speaking with sounded like an adult but asked questions like a child. "Because I enjoy helping people."

"So you give your help freely."

"To those who need it, yes."

"And if I asked you to help me, you would."

She frowned. "If I could. Are you in need of help?"

A pause. "I believe so, yes."

"Are you in pain?"

"I guess that depends on your definition of pain."

That didn't sound at all like a child, and she felt her teeth sink into her bottom lip, worrying the flesh. She still didn't sense any menace, even though she couldn't see a thing. Which should have made sense, considering her eyes were closed.

It was her turn to pause. "Who is this?"

"Are you happy in your life, Amity?"

The first prickle of fear rolled up her spine. "How do you know my name?"

"Would you deny me the chance to find my own happiness?"

"Why would I do that? I don't even know who you are."

"Yes. You do. You just don't want to believe."

Her breath froze in her lungs, which began to burn as her heart pounded. "Charun."

"Ah." The voice actually sounded pleased. "Now we're on the same page."

"How did you find me?"

"It wasn't difficult, honestly. Not when I knew what I was looking for. And I had help. Hinthial can be… accommodating. Then the power surge you recently experienced drew me straight to you."

Tinia's teat. She'd given herself away.

"Oh, don't worry. I'm still locked away in Aitás."

He sounded so bitter about that, and it freaked her out even more.

She should rip herself back to consciousness but she knew the opportunity to speak to Charun was too good. If she could find out what he wanted, why he was hunting goddesses…

"Why did you send demons after Tessa and Lucy? And why send one after me?"

He paused long enough that she wondered if he wasn't going to answer.

Finally, he said, "You killed Thufltha."

That must have been the demon from last night. "Why did you send it after me?"

"Maybe I just wanted to talk to you."

"We're talking now. What do you want?"

A cold agony slid through her mind. Just a brief flash that was gone in an instant. So brief, she almost wondered if she'd imagined it. Fear made her skin crawl, and part of her brain began to fight against the tide of sleep.

"What if I want only what you and our brothers and sisters have?"

"And what's that?"

"Can you be so dense, baby sister?"

Coming from any other man, the term might have sounded like

an endearment. Coming from the God of the Underworld, well… It wasn't exactly menacing, but it wasn't warm and fuzzy either.

"I guess I must be, because I have no idea," she said. "Tell me what you want, Charun. What would make you murder your sisters?"

"I haven't murdered anyone."

"Then where's Mlukukh?"

Another pause, so long she thought he'd gone. Then finally, "I want out."

She shivered at the hard edge of desperation in his deep voice and didn't know how to respond. She had the irrational, but almost overwhelming, urge to ease his pain. He had so much of it.

But the rational part of her mind wanted to rip out of this dream before she didn't have the strength and might never again wake.

"You can't leave." She kept her voice soft and easy, not wanting to anger him further. "You know that will upset the balance. The souls of the dead are tied to you. Culsu commands the gate but you… If you leave—"

"At one time," he cut her off, "that argument would have swayed me. No longer."

"Charun—"

"Why should I be the only one banished to this plane?" His tone grew colder, harder. "No one understands."

She held onto her calm with everything she could muster. "Then explain. What do you want?"

"I want what I've been denied all these millennia. What you and the rest have taken for granted."

"And what is that?"

"Freedom. And rest assured, I will get it."

If she hadn't been assured of Charun's intentions up to this point, she never would have doubted his intentions when he said those last four words.

She woke, gasping for air.

Sitting straight up on the bed, she choked in deep breaths, heart pounding almost painfully against her ribs.

"Hey, you okay?"

She barely heard Remy's sleepy voice through the rush of blood in her ears and when she didn't answer right away, she felt the bed shift as he sat up.

"Amity, what's wrong?"

The low growl of his voice was tempered with genuine concern, and she turned toward him, winding her arms around his waist and sighing in relief as he wrapped his arms around her shoulders and drew her closer.

"Hey, what happened? Come on, babe. Tell me."

Her lips curved in a surprised smile. She'd never had anyone call her babe. She had to admit she kind of liked it.

Sure, she'd had men hit on her. Lots of men, actually. But none of them had made her blood heat the way Remy and Rom did.

"Charun. He came to me."

"*What?*" His arms tightened around her, so much so it was almost hard to breathe. And she liked that too. "How?"

"He said he had help from Hinthial. But…"

"But what?"

"But I don't believe Hinthial would do that. She knows what Charun has been trying to do. She knows he's been hunting goddesses for their power. I don't believe she would just give him information that would lead him straight to me."

"Are you sure you can trust her?"

Amity turned toward Rom, lying on his back, hands behind his head, his gaze steady on hers. He almost looked relaxed. But those dark eyes hid so much.

"Yes. If he says Hinthial helped him, it probably means he's taken her powers. And if that's true then we're all screwed because Hinthial remained strong."

"Hinthial is the Goddess of the Spirit, right?" Remy's voice drew her attention back to him.

"Yes. She guides souls to the Underworld after death. But she's also able to navigate through the sleep plane because it's the closest to death a person gets without actually being dead. It's where the soul goes when the body's sleeping."

"So now Charun knows where you are?" Remy said.

She shook her head. "No, not exactly. But his connection with me on the dream plane will make it easier for him to track me down."

Remy and Rom exchanged a glance before pinning her with remarkably similar stares.

"How easy?" they said in unison.

Her mouth twitched but she quickly got it under control. These men wouldn't understand why she was smiling at their obvious concern for her. "Not that easy. I mean, Charun probably suspects that I'm in eastern Pennsylvania. It's not a huge stretch, considering most of the Etruscans relocated to this area. But if he plans to send another demon after me, he has to be careful. The demons don't have the necessary magic to disguise themselves as anything remotely human, so they have to get close enough to contain me and take me back to Charun."

"The demon last night almost had you," Remy pointed out. "Who's to say that one didn't tell all the others where you were?"

"Because they don't play well with others. They're solitary and territorial. I don't think you have to worry about another demon showing up, at least not for a little while."

But she had a new fear forming. If Charun could navigate the dream plane, he might be able to interact with other Etruscans and track her, or any of the other goddesses, that way.

And when he caught her, he would consume her powers. And she would cease to exist.

"Your expression doesn't exactly scream 'no worries.'" Rom's voice held a sharp edge that belied his calm expression.

She tried to wipe away the anxiety that flooded her system. "Sorry. I don't mean to burden you both with all of this."

"Amity, you're not a burden." Rom laid one huge, warm hand on her shoulder.

She tried to hide the flash of arousal that flooded her body, but they were *lucani*. They could scent the rush of moisture between her thighs. Even though she continued to shake with fear.

She wanted to forget the fact that Charun invaded her dreams and concentrate on the strength of Rom's arms or the way Remy kissed.

But she couldn't. She needed to get in touch with her sister goddesses, see if they'd had any dreams of talking to Charun. She didn't know if she'd be able to contact Tessa. She and her mate, Cal, had taken to wandering. The last she'd heard, they were in Europe, most likely Tuscany. Lucy and Brandon, however, remained in the area.

She'd call Nortia, who she knew was almost always in town, and she'd try to reach Artumes, though who knew if she'd be able to pin down the elusive Mistress of Animals.

Same went for the Lasae. At one time, the four goddesses had been the handmaidens of Turan, Goddess of Love and Beauty. Today... well, no one really knew what they were up to. The last she'd heard of their whereabouts, they'd been working the Southern beauty pageant circuit, but that had to be at least five or six years ago.

"Amity, are you okay?"

She smiled, the motion coming more easily at the genuine concern she heard in Remy's voice.

"Yes. I'm fine. But thank you for asking. And now I'm afraid I must ask you for one more favor."

"Of course," Remy said. "Anything you need."

Oh, she wanted so much more from them than one night. But she didn't have any right to demand they stay with her.

She knew they wanted to continue their search for those who'd killed their families. She didn't want to interfere in that.

Still, wouldn't it be nice to wake up warm and safe between these two men again?

"I could use a ride home."

———∾∾∾———

Rom drove, only because Remy had the good sense to realize he might scare the shit out of their goddess if he got behind the wheel.

Remy liked to drive fast. Really fast. In a different life, he might've been a drag racer. Or a getaway-car driver.

So Rom got behind the wheel of his sedate, but powerful, Mercedes, and Remy let Amity sit in the front seat, ostensibly because he was being a gentleman. In reality, Rom knew Remy was watching their backs for anyone who might try to sneak up on them.

She settled into the leather passenger seat, aimed an indirect smile at both of them, then stared out the window with a sigh.

A quick glance into the back seat at Remy and he knew his cousin wasn't fooled either. Something was wrong.

"Amity, are you sure you're okay?" Rom asked about five minutes after they'd left. He'd heard her stifle several sighs and she couldn't seem to sit still.

She'd given him another distracted smile and nodded. "I'm fine."

Right.

If he didn't know any better, he'd think she didn't want to go home.

And it wasn't like they'd forced her to leave. Of course, they hadn't really asked her to stay either.

Hell, he wasn't even sure he wanted her to stay. She was a temptation he didn't need. But Remy…

He checked the rearview mirror and saw Remy frowning hard at the back of her head.

Remy didn't look ready to give her up. This situation had all the makings of a clusterfuck. Remy had feelings for Amity. Rom could sense them like they were his own. Remy was already trying to figure out a way to get Amity to agree to let them stay with her.

And that would be one *giant* clusterfuck. Because Rom wouldn't leave Remy, not now that he knew Remy planned to go after the *Mal*.

Not that Rom wasn't all for going after the bastards who'd hired the demon to kill their families. He'd gladly focus his still-untapped rage at another target, and the *Mal* were next on the list.

But he didn't need the complications that came with being consort to a goddess, even one who no longer had enough power to save herself from a demon.

And one who made heat build low in his gut.

Damn it, I don't need this. Not now.

But what would it hurt to do our research from here?

They'd have to find another place to live because their lease was about to run out and the family they'd rented the place from was set to return within the month.

He looked in the rearview again and caught Remy's gaze for a long second.

We have to get her to let us stay, Rom. What if another demon comes for her?

His cousin's thought rang through Rom's brain clear as a bell.

Shit.

His hands tightened on the wheel, but he knew Remy was right. He turned the problem over and over in his head for the length of the short drive but didn't come up with another plan that Remy would have agreed to and that would've given Rom the chance to get the hell out of town. And away from Amity.

Before he knew it, they were in front of her home. As he put the car in park and turned off the engine, he felt the pull of the magic from the city across the river, the magic that had drawn the Etruscans here all those years ago. The ley line that ran beneath Reading gave those who knew how to use it a boost in magical powers.

Yet, even with all that energy, the deities had weakened until they couldn't manage to save themselves from attack.

That really had to suck.

Amity sat quietly for a few seconds before she turned from the window. "I... don't really know how to thank you both." She gave them that trembling smile again as she reached for the door handle. "I owe you my life."

In the rearview, he caught a glimpse of Remy's mouth tightening and knew his cousin was swearing silently.

"We're just glad we were able to help." Rom watched as she bit down into that full bottom lip. That mouth had been wrapped around his cock last night. He wanted to feel her mouth on him again. Wanted to sink inside her ass while Rom fucked her pussy and—

Yeah, really not what he should be thinking about.

Except now that was all he *could* think about. Shit.

He glanced at Remy, who stared back at him with raised eyebrows. Waiting for Rom to agree.

Shit.

Remy huffed and leaned over the front seat, putting his hand on Amity's shoulder. As if he didn't want her to get away.

"Amity, why don't you let us come inside with you?" Remy said. "We could check out the house, make sure everything's okay. You can never be too careful."

Was that excitement or gratitude that flared in her beautiful eyes for a few brief seconds before she slowly nodded?

"I'm not going to turn down such a kind offer. If you really don't mind..."

"Trust me." Remy's grin made her smile in return. "It's not a hardship."

Rom slid from the car before she could say anything else. Remy knew enough to keep her there until Rom could open her door. Smiling up at him, she put her hand in his and let him help her from the car. Thank the Blessed Goddess his mother had instilled some manners in him.

Remy stepped in front of Amity while Rom fell into place behind her. As if they actually knew what they were doing.

Imagine that. Maybe all those years of paranoia had finally paid off.

Before they got to the steps leading to the porch, Amity stopped to lift a brightly colored garden gnome from the flower bed and pulled a key out of the bottom.

As both he and Remy's mouths dropped open at the idea that anyone could have access to her home, she shrugged, her expression only slightly chagrined.

"It really is a safe neighborhood."

Holy shit, she left a key to her front door in the most obvious place.

He opened his mouth to tell her how stupid that was—

And stopped just in time. Amity wasn't just another woman. She was a goddess.

Sure, she was dressed in Rom's T-shirt and Remy's sweatpants because her clothes had been ruined. She wore no makeup, and her tousled hair looked like she'd spent the entire night in a man's bed.

She smelled like them and that turned him on too. Hell, everything about her turned him on.

Vaffanculo, this was one big freaking mess waiting for a train wreck to make it even more fun.

Mentally slapping himself, he made sure he kept alert for anything. Anything at all.

Maybe Charun had already sent another demon. Maybe he had something else planned.

Since it was close to midnight, the only light came from the widely spaced streetlamps. The nearest light was two houses away, and it didn't really cast enough of a glow to see the front door clearly from the sidewalk.

Rom visually checked the shrubs surrounding the house's foundation, not big enough to hide a full-grown man but full enough to make him look hard to make sure no one was hiding there.

In seconds, they'd reached the small wooden porch that matched the Cape Cod home. Remy walked straight to the front door, holding out one hand behind him to motion Amity to stay off the steps. Rom wrapped his fingers around her upper arm, just to make sure she didn't follow along after Remy.

And nearly lost himself in the softness of her skin beneath his fingers.

Damn, keep your head on straight, asshole, or she could end up dead.

That made his spine straighten, and he concentrated on using his wolf-sharp hearing to listen for anyone in the house.

All he heard was the beating of her heart.

Remy turned and took the key from her then opened the door as silently as he could. Unfortunately, the door looked to be the same age as the house, probably built sometime in the sixties. And it creaked like a sonuvabitch, announcing to anyone who might be there that they were home.

"Shit." Remy spoke under his breath, so low only Rom could hear him. "Gotta fix that."

Remy flashed a look at Rom, and Rom nodded. He'd keep Amity out here until Remy had checked the house.

After slipping through the open door, Remy closed it behind him as Amity's muscles tensed and bunched beneath Rom's hand.

When she turned, her lips parting to ask him why, he placed two fingers over her soft lips and shook his head.

Her eyebrows raised and her expression told him she knew what he was up to, and that she really didn't think it was necessary.

Too bad. Remy wants you and now you're stuck with us. At least for a little while.

She remained silent, but he couldn't resist the softness of her lips. He stroked his fingertips across them, blood rushing through his body to pound through his cock.

Which, of course, made him remember last night. Which made his cock harden even more.

At the rate he was going, he'd have her naked and up against a wall in seconds. Or maybe he'd watch as Remy fucked her over a table. He'd watch her pleasure build as Remy made her come. Then he'd take her from Remy and make her come around his cock.

They'd made her come so hard, she'd nearly passed out. And the energy they'd created together… Holy fuck, it'd rated off the charts.

So… what? Had it meant anything to her other than being a way to recharge her batteries? Did he want it to?

Amity's head tilted to the side, eyes narrowing as she watched him. Her lips shifted under his fingers and he felt her smile.

Shit. Remy better fucking clear the house soon.

As if thinking about Remy managed to conjure him, Rom saw and heard the door open and Remy appeared, his expression impossible to read.

Withdrawing his hand, Rom took a step back, which made her head tilt even farther before she drew in a deep breath and turned to Remy.

"All clear," he said. "Come on in."

She sighed. "Thank you. I really do appreciate all you've done." She turned to include him in her smile. "Both of you."

Rom heard clear relief in her voice and felt like he'd saved the goddamn world for her.

Then her smile faltered a bit. "I know it's late, but would you like to come in for a drink before…"

Before what? They left? Did she want them to leave? When the hell had he reverted to a sixteen-year-old?

Remy beat him to an answer. "Sure. That'd be great."

As Rom moved to her side, he saw the smile that lit up her face. "I'm pretty sure I have a few bottles of Stoudt's in the fridge. Or there's whiskey or tequila." Then she clapped her hands together. "Oh, wait. I know. Have you ever had Fuflun's Prosecco? I just got a bottle. I think you'll really like it. Unless you don't like wine?"

Remy looked at him—his eyes bright and a grin on his face—for a second before he turned to Amity. "I'd love some."

Guess we're staying.

Following her into the house, Rom's gaze dropped to her ass. He'd always been an ass man, and she had one of the best he'd ever had his hands on.

Remy shoved his elbow into his side, after making sure Amity couldn't see him as she walked through the front living room into the back of the house. A light came on and he saw her moving around in the brightly lit kitchen.

"Dude," Remy said. "What the hell?"

Rom barely restrained his own eye roll. Much of the time, he forgot Remy was still in his twenties. Not by much and not for long, but his cousin sometimes reminded him in odd ways. And though Rom acted like it annoyed the hell out of him… honestly, he liked seeing his cousin act his age.

He hadn't had much chance to since he'd been a teenager.

Remy leaned in close enough that Amity wouldn't be able to hear him. "You were checking out her ass like some douche in a meat market."

Rom made sure his expression was sufficiently scornful as he pulled back to look at Remy. "And you didn't have your eyes glued to her chest?"

Remy's mouth curved in a grin that was pure hound dog, and damn if Rom's mood didn't lighten.

"What can I say? She's a beautiful woman."

Except she wasn't just a woman. She was a freaking goddess who was looking for a bottle of a god's wine to serve to them.

When had their life passed through the Twilight Zone and into the Outer Limits?

"Ah ha! I found it."

Amity appeared in the doorway leading into the kitchen, holding a bottle in one hand. Her smile made his lungs forget how to work.

That was bad. Totally and completely fucked up. He didn't do nerves. He couldn't. He'd be dead if he'd let his nerves paralyze him like they wanted to.

"Why don't you both have a seat? I'll open this bottle, put together some munchies, and we can chill for a while before…"

Before what? Before they left? Or before they all got naked and jumped into bed again?

Hell, Rom figured he was going to need more than a few glasses of Prosecco to chill out.

He was afraid nothing he drank or did would quench his desire for Amity.

And that could drive a wedge between him and Remy that might never be fixed.

Chapter 9

REMY COULD PRACTICALLY HEAR Rom thinking.

Which was *so* not a good thing.

Rom tended to overthink everything, which generally led to a disagreement that usually ended with a couple of punches thrown before they worked out a plan they could both agree on.

But Remy had a raging disgust for waiting and generally took what he wanted before life took it away.

Yeah, yeah, he had issues. But he thought he'd dealt with them pretty well up until now.

Hell, if you considered the situation, most people would think the same thing.

Rom didn't. Rom thought he was fragile from the damage to his face and his psyche and, yeah, to some degree he was. But Rom had decided to take the weight of their world on his shoulders, and nothing anyone could say would convince him he didn't need to.

Usually Remy took it on himself to make sure Rom didn't burn out from all the stress.

And spending a few more hours with a beautiful, totally hot goddess would certainly reduce some of that stress.

Sure, Remy wanted to pursue the *Mal* bastards who'd put that demon on their asses. He would hunt them down and make their deaths slow and painful. But they'd waited this long to kill the demon. A few more days for the *Mal* wouldn't matter.

He and Rom could use some time to regroup. Spending another couple of hours in Amity's bed would give them that time.

And when they left to pursue the *Mal*... they'd leave her vulnerable to Charun.

He had a hard time keeping the frown from his face.

"We'd love to stay for a while." Rom bowed his head and gave the slightest bit of a smile, which made Amity's expression fairly glow with happiness and shocked the almighty hell out of Remy.

So much so, he turned to his cousin after Amity gave Rom the bottle to open then disappeared back into the kitchen.

He stared until Rom turned to glare at him.

"Why the hell are you staring at me like that?" Rom's barely vocal growl made the hair stand up on Remy's arms. But he wasn't about to let Rom intimidate him.

In fact... "Are you sure you didn't have your brain knocked loose during the fight? I think that might've been the fastest decision you've ever made."

Remy expected Rom to totally ignore his dig, which is what he usually did. The guy just didn't have the snark gene.

Instead, Rom scowled. "My brain works just fine. Not sure about yours yet. I'm not the one who got myself knocked out during the fight."

Rom was steady as a rock and had absolutely no sense of humor. He definitely needed to have a stickectomy on the one shoved up his ass.

"Wow. I swear your brain is full of gears and cogs. When—"

"Here we go." Amity slid through the doorway from the kitchen into the living area, an overburdened tray in her hands. "I didn't know what you liked so I put on a little bit of everything. Maybe a little too much, actually. This tray is really hea—"

"Here." Remy reached for the tray. "Let me take that for you."

Her smile brightened the room and made Remy's heart beat just a little faster.

"Thank you, Remy. Just set it on the table there and you two sit down. Please."

Remy slid onto one end of the couch, hoping she and Rom would get the hint and sit there too. Amity did.

Rom, the idiot, sat on the chair across from her.

They fell silent as Amity poured the wine and he and Rom dug into the food. She'd made a huge antipasto plate with all sorts of cheeses, meats, and olives; a bowl of thick-cut potato chips; and another bowl of pesto with crackers.

He and Rom fell on the food like hungry wolves, though both of them managed to remember their table manners before they embarrassed themselves.

"Did you make this yourself?" Remy pointed to the pesto. "I've never tasted anything like it. It's great."

She smiled at him and he swore he felt the earth shift under this feet. He nearly choked on a piece of mozzarella and had to wash it down with a sip of the awesome Prosecco. The God of the Vine absolutely knew what he was doing.

"Remy, are you okay?" The concern in her tone struck a place deep inside his chest, one he thought had been hacked out long ago. It made every protective instinct he thought he'd gotten rid of rise up until it nearly choked him.

"Yeah. Yeah, I'm fine. Lady—"

"Please. Just Amity. Both of you. I'd really prefer that."

He'd call her whatever she wanted to make her happy.

Did that make him a sap? At the moment, he didn't give a fuck. He only wanted to please her. And if Rom said something stupid, he'd—

"Then we'll call you Amity." Rom's tone had a note of finality that should have rubbed Remy the wrong way, but since it was basically exactly what he was thinking, he figured he'd let it go.

"So, Amity." Remy put his arm on the back of the couch, letting his fingers graze along her nape and smiling when she shivered. He figured he might as well dive in headfirst, because Rom would take the rest of the night to ask for what they both wanted. "Would you mind if we crashed here tonight?"

—〰—

Amity tried to temper her delighted grin but figured why bother.

Remy's question simply meant she didn't have to ask them to stay and possibly guilt them into it.

"I wouldn't mind at all. If you're sure it won't be an imposition? I'd certainly feel safer with you both in the house."

"Not a problem," Rom said. "And since we've got some time, why don't you tell us a little more about this situation with Charun. What's it gonna take to get him off your back?"

Her heart gave a little extra thump at Rom's oh-so-serious gaze. He was worried about her. How sweet was that? "Short of me getting rid of what he wants, I don't think there's going to be any foolproof way to do that."

"You said he's done this before. With whom?" Remy asked. "And how did they get him off their back?"

Amity sighed, unsure how much she should tell them.

Two Etruscan goddesses had already given up their powers. What would they think of that? Not many people in their relatively small community knew what was happening. And that was probably a good thing.

If the Etruscan people realized what was going on, would they lose faith in the entire pantheon?

Hadn't they already?

Such a depressing thought, one she really didn't want to dwell on.

"Amity." Remy reached for her hand, which she hadn't realized she'd clenched into a fist on her knee.

His hand felt so warm, so comforting, she wanted to grab hold and never let go.

"Thesan gave up most of her powers and Lusna has… passed hers on."

For a second, both men looked confused. Then, as realization struck, the exact same expression of stunned disbelief settled on their faces.

"You can do that?" Rom said.

She nodded. "Apparently so."

Remy opened his mouth then shut it before finally asking, "Why? How?"

And now it got tricky. "Tessa did it for love. Lucy…"

"Lucy what?" Rom's gaze narrowed even more.

"Lucy had another choice."

Remy opened his mouth to ask another question she really shouldn't answer, but from the corner of her eye, she saw Rom shake his head, just once.

And Remy shut his mouth. But not before he gave Rom a glare sharp enough to cut glass.

"Okay." Rom's voice had fallen into a low, steady tone, as if he were gentling her. "That's fine. So what are your choices?"

Good question. The entire situation felt surreal, like she'd come into a movie midway through and suddenly found herself the subject of it.

"I honestly don't know. Tessa and Lucy had extenuating circumstances." Namely, they'd fallen in love for the first time in their very long lives and had had something more to live for than being Forgotten Goddesses.

Amity didn't have that choice.

"Well, I know I won't be giving up my powers." She stared straight into Rom's eyes so he could see her conviction. "I use them on a daily basis as part of my job. I am damn proud of what I do. And I enjoy helping people."

Not to mention her job had saved her sanity. There had been

a few deities who'd run amok when the burden of everlasting life became more than they could handle.

She'd had to deal with that herself, at least on a smaller scale. Several centuries ago, when the world had been an even bloodier mess. The death and destruction wrought by the *Malandante* against the rest of the Etruscan race had been minor in comparison to what'd been going on in the rest of the world, but their methods had been particularly brutal.

She'd almost given in to despair then. Barely stopped herself from turning her powers on herself and draining the life from her body after she'd lost a young, mated *silvani* and *fauni*.

They'd been savaged by the *lucani* under the control of the *Mal*, their bodies bloodied and battered, their minds broken.

She hadn't been powerful enough to save them. Why should she continue to give her heart and soul for those she couldn't save? Better to simply disappear than be forced to watch the death and destruction.

"Amity. Hey, talk to us."

She came out of those bloody memories with a deep breath, sensing both men's visceral concern. For her.

It made her blood heat and her heart stutter a beat. She couldn't remember the last time she'd had a man care for her like this. And never two.

Or maybe she'd just never let any other man get close enough to get to that point.

She and Remy and Rom had shared so much in the past twenty-four hours, they'd slipped past all of her normal safeguards.

And for a goddess who dealt with the very real world of pain every day, who knew better than most the cost of physical and emotional pain, they'd become dangerous.

"I think… it's been a long day."

Rom watched her with the sharpness of the predator he held inside. He wanted to keep digging, get to the heart of what bothered her.

But the memory of having to repair their broken bodies had risen too close to the surface now.

She needed space. Just a little. Time to think. A little space to breathe without their combined scents making her brain hazy.

She was being selfish in allowing them to stay, knowing Charun would come for her again. But she didn't want them to leave, either.

Damn it, she needed a plan to deal with Charun. Before Remy and Rom came up with one she'd be tempted to allow them to put into action. To put themselves in more danger because of her.

At least for tonight, she thought they'd be safe with her. She didn't think Charun would send another demon so soon.

A little alone time would not be out of line here.

"If you both don't mind, I'm going to take a hot bath. The house has been warded against unauthorized intrusion, though I'm sure you know those spells won't work against deities. But since Charun is still locked in Aitás, I don't think I have more to fear from him tonight."

She hoped.

"And I have some paperwork to catch up on before I return to work tomorrow."

The men exchanged a glance she could read, even though their expressions never changed.

"Yes, I will be going to work. I will not allow Charun to affect that. And I have so much lovely energy now, thanks to both of you."

As a distraction, it worked for several seconds. At least until they figured that's exactly what she'd intended.

But by that time, she'd turned and was headed toward the steps to the second floor. "There's a guest bedroom on the second floor to the left as you come up the stairs," she called over her shoulder. "There's another, smaller guest room off the kitchen. Please make yourselves at home."

Her feet felt like they had lead weights attached to them as she trudged up the narrow flight of stairs at the back of the living room.

She hadn't been kidding about the hot bath. She wanted to soak for hours. Sure, she wished she'd have some company to wash her back. But she also knew she needed to talk to someone with more intimate knowledge of what was going on.

As she ran the water, she used the old-fashioned landline phone in her bedroom to make a call. The line was magically warded, enchanted, and connected a select network of homes and businesses.

The female operator with the incongruous name of Phil agreed to put the call through. She must have been in a good mood because she didn't give Amity grief over the time.

The phone clicked several times before the line connected.

"Hey, sorry it's so late, but we need to talk."

There was a pause on the other end before Kari answered. "I sensed something had happened last night and I tried to reach you, but you didn't respond. I was worried. He's come after you."

Not a question. Amity had figured her twin would realize what had happened. They were connected by such a strong thread of fate.

"Last night," Amity continued. "A *tukhulkha* demon came for me outside the hospital. I had… unexpected champions come to my rescue when I was attacked."

"Champions?"

"Yes, I'll get to them in a minute. Of bigger concern right now is that I also had a dream visit from the man himself."

"Charun contacted you personally?" Surprise sounded loud and clear in Kari's voice. "How did he manage that?"

"He told me he had help from Hinthial."

"No." Kari's answer was firm and clear. "She wouldn't."

"I agree. Then you know what that means."

Another pause. "We need to talk to Sal."

"Yes, we do. But we'll have to meet here. I'm afraid if I leave the safety of my wards, I'll alert Charun."

"No problem. I'll contact Sal and have him meet me at your place."

"Why don't you have Sal transport you here, Kari?"

Kari's bright laugh eased something inside Amity. "Always the worrier. Charun's not after me, sister. At least not yet. But to put your mind at ease, I'll contact Sal. Haven't seen the horny little devil in a while. It'll give us a chance to catch up. Now, about these champions…"

"You'll meet them soon enough, Kari. They've agreed to stay with me tonight."

Amity sensed Kari's surprise. "Well then, I'll be right over."

Chapter 10

REMY AND ROM SHOT Rock-Paper-Scissors to decide who went back to the house to get their gear.

Rom lost because Remy had long ago learned how his cousin thought. Brute force, all the time. Rom didn't hold much stock in subtlety or trickery.

Those tactics had their times and places.

Not that Remy played dirty to win. He just couldn't help knowing what Rom was going to throw before he threw it.

Of course, Rom might've lost because he didn't want Remy to leave the relative safety of Amity's home. In which case, Rom had played him.

Remy's face screwed up in a frown as he lost all interest in the repeat of *The Waltons* he was watching.

"Huh. That sneaky bas—"

"Remy, we're about to have guests."

Whipping his head around, he saw Amity standing at the bottom of the stairs.

She looked somewhat more relaxed than she had before she'd gone up for her bath. Her cheeks were flushed pink, her hair sat in a high ponytail and the form-fitting T-shirt and tight black yoga pants made his mouth hang open.

Beautiful. Absolutely beautiful.

When the hell—

"Wait. What did you just say?"

"I said we're going to have visitors in a few minutes. Is Rom here?"

"No, he went back to the house to get our stuff." He hopped off the couch and started toward her, trying to figure out how to tell a goddess there was no way in hell he was letting anyone enter her house.

"Amity, I'm not sure that's such a good idea."

"Then I guess it's a good thing this isn't your house."

The male voice coming from behind him made Remy spin on his heel, his hand reaching for the *pugio* concealed in his pants pocket. The short Italian blade was perfectly weighted for his hand and lethal.

Shock stopped him from releasing the knife.

"Holy shit."

Goat legs. The guy had goat legs. And little black horns on top of his perfectly human head. As a matter of fact, the guy looked totally human from the waist up. Except for those horns sticking out of the glossy black curls.

He looked to be in his late thirties. Definitely of Etruscan descent.

"Son," the guy's voice sound totally human with a thick New York accent, "trust me when I say you don't want to throw that at me. You'll miss and you won't see it coming when I toss it back."

Out of the corner of his eye, he saw Amity rush by, headed for the woman at the guy's side. The woman who looked almost exactly like her. So close, in fact, they had to be twins.

Another goddess. *Crap*. Remy dropped into a belated bow as the women embraced, his stunned brain sifting through decades-old lessons from his mother.

Who the hell was she?

"This one doesn't seem too bright now, does he?" The male's voice held laughter. "That's okay, kid. You've had a hard day, haven't you?"

Remy bit back the obscenity-laden response on the tip of his tongue. At least some part of his brain still worked.

"Sal, don't hassle the boy." The new goddess gave him the once-over. "Uni's ass, Amity. Where'd you find him?"

"This is one of the champions I was telling you about. Kari, this is Remy. Remy, this is my sister, Kari."

He nodded, surprised he didn't hear his brain rattle.

"And I'm Sal." The goat man's hooves made little snicks across the wooden floor; the sound was surreal. "What's your last name, kid?"

Long-ingrained caution made Remy hesitate until finally Sal's eyebrows lifted. "Well, isn't that interesting."

Salbinelli. The connection finally clicked in Remy's head. He remembered his mom teaching him about the *Fata* races as a child. The *Fata* were the elemental beings of the Etruscan races, descended from the three elemental races—the woodland *silvani*, the water-loving *aguane*, and the animal guardians, the *fauni*.

Remy had never met one of the *Fata*. They were like the *eteri*'s unicorns or dragons. Sure, they might actually exist, but no one had ever seen one in person.

"Are you really…"

Sal rolled his eyes. "Yeah, yeah. I'm *salbinelli*. Don't feed the animals, kid, unless you want your fingers bitten off. Now, Amity, why don't you tell me why I'm sensing off-the-chart power from you. And why he's got way too much of the wrong kind of magic for a *lucani*."

Remy's gaze skipped to Amity, whose expression held an apology.

Shit. Rom was going to have a heart attack. This was exactly what they'd been trying to avoid for years.

Remy swore he felt a noose tightening around his neck.

"Whoa, kid." The *salbinelli* held his hand in the air, palms up. "Hey, I'm not gonna turn you over to the police for murder. But now I gotta know. What the hell's going on?"

Definitely the end of the line for his and Rom's anonymity.

"Sal." Amity moved to Remy's side, as if to lend him her support. "Maybe we should all take a seat before we start getting into particulars."

Sal snorted. "I've got most of them figured out already." He pointed at Amity. "You're Charun's latest target. *And* you had sex with him." He pointed at Remy. "Which made you light up like an overdecorated Christmas tree. You called her," he pointed at Kari, "because you're worried she's going to attract the same attention you're getting from Charun. How'm I doing so far?"

Amity nodded as Remy felt the noose tighten a little more.

"Batting a thousand. Okay." Sal slapped his hands together in front of him, the sharp sound stinging Remy's sensitive ears. "Now, the only piece of the puzzle I'm missing is, where's the second *lucani* I smell? And why the hell do you want to avoid the *lucani* den so badly I can practically taste it in the air?"

Yep. He was so screwed. Rom was gonna kill him if another demon didn't get to him first.

He let his gaze connect with Amity's, saw the worry in her eyes. Worry about how he was going to react.

Okay, he could handle this. No need to panic. He just needed to get the lay of the land.

And if Amity trusted this man, then maybe he could too. He and Rom had been on their own for so long, Remy had almost forgotten that not everyone was out to kill them.

Remy walked over to the *salbinelli* and held out his hand. "Remus Leone."

He watched the guy's gaze narrow for a brief second before he took hold of Remy's hand and shook. Then Sal started to shake his head, his expression turning serious. "Well, I'll be damned. You're alive. And Romulus? Has he survived, as well?"

Remy froze, though his heart started to bang inside his chest like it was exploding. Shit. He knew who they were.

"Now, son, don't pass out on me. But I think you might want to sit down."

"Sal?" Amity's tone held a question as she looked between

Remy and the *salbinelli*, who ignored her, keeping his gaze locked to Remy's.

"I know some people who've been looking for you both for a very long time."

Slowly withdrawing his hand, Remy fought against the urge to run. To hide. That's what they always did when someone got too close. But... he didn't want to run this time.

"Maybe we haven't wanted to be found."

Sal nodded, his expression softening just the slightest bit. "I can understand that."

"Then you also understand why the fewer people who know we're here, the better."

"Have you considered," Sal stared up at him, totally not intimidated by their height difference, "that maybe there are people here who could help you?"

"People who try to help us tend to end up dead." The edge in Remy's tone could've cut glass.

Kari drew in a sharp gasp and Sal actually dropped his gaze for a second. Amity just stared at him with those warm, dark eyes.

"Your families." Sal's now laser-sharp gaze returned to his. "We thought—"

Remy sliced his hand in front of Sal, cutting him off. Definitely not going there. "All I'm saying is, we've had our reasons for being... for not wanting to spend a lot of time in one place." There, that sounded somewhat diplomatic.

Sal's gaze narrowed. "And yet, here you are, throwing down with Charun's minions."

"That was personal."

Sal nodded. "Yeah, I'm beginning to get the picture."

Remy was sure he was. Time to change the subject. "So, you're here to help Amity with the Charun problem."

For a few seconds, Remy wasn't sure Sal was going to let him get away with the change of subject. Then the little *salbinelli* released a harsh breath and waved at the couch.

"Why don't we get comfortable and see what's what."

It took only seconds for everyone to find a seat. He and Amity went back to the couch. Kari and Sal took the plush chairs directly opposite.

"All right, so tell me what happened tonight." Sal's hooves hung several inches off the floor, momentarily distracting Remy with a sudden bout of absurdity that made him almost burst out laughing.

He was sitting in a room with a *salbinelli* and two goddesses. Of course, he was a *lucani stregone*, a werewolf witch who shouldn't exist.

There had to be a joke in there involving a bar.

As Amity recounted the events of the previous night, Remy forced himself to listen for anything she hadn't mentioned before, something they might have missed or that didn't seem important before.

Nothing. All he got for the effort was the start of a tension headache, which Amity would probably insist on healing when she realized he was trying to hide it.

"So he sent Thufltha for Amity." Sal pulled a cigar out his shirt pocket and stuck it in his mouth, though he didn't light it up, just gnawed on the end as he stared at Remy. "And you and your cousin killed it. Gotta say, kid, Charun's not gonna be real thrilled about that. I can't honestly remember the last time he lost one of his Named."

"Yeah, well, this one had it coming."

Sal nodded, his gaze narrowing for a second. "I'm sure it did, kid. I'm sure it did. This isn't the first time I've heard about the *tukhulkha* moonlighting. The *Mal* have been contracting them for centuries, bribing the demons with whatever they wanted. But I've never heard of one so high up the ranks allowing the *Mal* to pull its strings."

"Maybe the *Mal* held something over the demon's head." Remy shrugged. "I don't really care. We killed it. We're moving on."

"To the *Mal*."

Sal didn't bother to make it a question so Remy didn't bother to answer. The *salbinelli* was doing just fine coming to conclusions of his own.

"Maybe you wanna rethink that strategy, at least for the time being." Sal's mouth twisted in a rueful expression. "There've been some developments…"

When Sal didn't continue, Remy pressed. "What kind of developments? Something that has to do with the *Mal*?"

Sal nodded. "And the *lucani*."

Shit. That was… Shit. Sal shook his head and Rom knew whatever was going on, it wasn't going to be anything he or Rom wanted to hear.

"Why don't we wait for your cousin to get back to talk about that angle." Sal let his gaze slide to Amity. "Right now, let's figure out what we're going to do to keep Amity safe."

Remy thought the answer to that was pretty straightforward. He and Rom would stay until Charun decided to leave Amity alone.

Even if it means putting off your pursuit of the Mal? And alerting the lucani *to your presence? And what if Charun doesn't stop? How long do we stay? How long will she* let *us stay?*

"What do you suggest?"

Sal shrugged. "That's the tricky part."

"I'm not giving up my powers."

It was the first time Amity had spoken in several minutes and Remy swore he saw Sal's jaw tighten just a little.

"No one's saying that's even on the table." Sal shook his head. "I've never suggested that and I never will. But Charun's changing the rules."

"This is no game." Kari piped in, her tone razor-sharp and utterly serious. "Tessa nearly died. Lucy…" Kari exchanged a glance with Amity and didn't continue her thought. "We need to stop Charun. For good this time."

Amity shook her head. "And how do you propose we do that? We can't kill him. The gate to Aitás will fall without him. We need to talk to him, find out why he's doing this."

"You can't reason with Charun, sister. The man's brain just isn't wired for rational thought."

"But there's got to be a reason he wants out. After all this time, why now?"

Kari shook her head, her pretty face screwing up into a frown but not detracting at all from her beauty.

And yet, Kari raised no arousal at all in Remy, even though the goddesses were practically identical.

How weird was that?

"Who cares?" Kari said. "Seriously, Amity. It doesn't matter. If Charun achieves his goal, who's to say he'll stop at goddesses. Will he go after everyone else? This entire plane could become Aitás if that happens."

"But maybe if we find out what he wants," Amity said, "we can give it to him and he'll stop."

Kari wore a dumbfounded expression. "Since when did you take on Tessa's eternal optimism?"

Remy felt like he was at a tennis match, watching the ball bounce between the sisters. He noticed that Sal hadn't stuck his nose in, either.

"And when did you become such a cynic?"

"I always have been." Kari shrugged. "I just hide it well. Charun's not going to stop after a few therapy sessions. We've got to find a way to block him from finding us. Or we need to kill his demons before they attack again."

Now that was a plan Remy could get behind. Except Amity's horrified expression said more than words ever could. "How can you even suggest such a thing?"

"He tried to take you, sister. I would kill Charun just for thinking about it."

"And I love that you care for me so much. But that's not the answer."

Kari huffed. "So what are you going to do while you wait for Charun to track you down?"

"I can't go into hiding. Not now. I have two patients who I will not leave right now."

Kari's huff showed exactly how she felt about that. "You know I admire your dedication, sister, but if they ever discovered what you are… Do you think they would treat you with the same compassion you treat them?"

"That doesn't matter because they won't ever find out. The *eteri* believe only what they want to believe. We are an impossibility, so therefore we don't exist."

"And yet you continue to treat them like precious commodities, possibly at the expense of your own life."

Amity opened her mouth to answer, but Remy beat her to the punch. "It won't come to that. Rom and I are staying."

He hadn't realized he was going to speak until the words fell out of his mouth.

And he meant every one of them.

—···—

Amity blinked, her eyes flashing bright as she tried not to smile too widely.

She hadn't wanted to appear clingy and ask Remy and Rom to stay for any extended period of time. But it had been lurking in the back of her mind, taunting her.

"Are you sure Rom will agree? I don't want to—"

Remy shook his head, his expression a tiny bit rueful. "Lady, trust me, he'll agree. If he were here, he'd have said the same thing."

"Well, look at that. The pretty *lucani*'s brave, too. And there are two…"

Kari's tone was light and teasing, and more than a little interested.

And Amity refused to admit she felt any jealousy when Remy smiled at Kari.

"Okay, so the wolf boys are going to stay with you for protection from the demons." Sal leaned back into the chair, his hooves hanging even farther from the floor than before. "But that doesn't solve the underlying problem. What do we do about Charun?"

"Maybe it's time to speak to him on our terms."

Remy turned back to her as he worked that statement through his brain. She saw the effort it took for him to bite back the immediate response he wanted to make.

But he did bite it back before he asked, "And how do you propose do that?"

"By setting up a meeting."

As three voices told her in various and creative ways how that wasn't going to happen, Amity let them wear themselves down before she continued. "I understand why you're all against this. I do. But I also think someone needs to speak to Charun, find out what he hopes to accomplish. Maybe if I can get him to talk, we can figure out how to give him what he wants without having him leave Aitás."

Kari rolled her eyes. "Amity, seriously. Have you totally lost all common sense? If you talk to him for any length of time, he'll be able to pinpoint your location and send more demons. Yes, your *lucani* stopped the first one but what happens if the next isn't as easy to kill?"

"We're stronger than we look, Lady Kari."

The growl in Remy's voice made Amity's thighs quiver.

"I'm sure you are, son," Sal broke in before Kari could open her mouth again. "But what if Charun sends two next time? Or three? What if Thufltha told another demon or Charun where to find you and they're already on their way?"

"Then it won't matter, will it?" Amity shook her head, frustration starting to make her angry. And it took an awful lot to make her lose her temper. "I'm not saying I'm going to be stupid about this. I'll take each and every precaution to make sure he can't track me. But I want to try this."

Kari looked ready to tear her hair out. Sal shook his head. Remy… Remy looked at her with a slight smile.

"Then we'll set it up," he said.

Her smile felt so wide, she thought her lips might split.

At least Remy trusted her.

"Well, then." Sal sighed. "I think I have an idea. It might take a little while, though."

"That's fine, Sal. I'd like to put it off for a few days, anyway. I have patients to attend on Monday. Later next week will be great."

Sal continued to shake his head, not looking at all happy.

"You want to tell me a little more about this plan?" Remy asked. "You're not instilling much confidence here."

Sal gave him a look that made Remy want to crawl under the table with his tail between his legs. "How'd you like to visit dreamland?"

<hr />

Rom scented two other signatures the second he walked in the door, but since Remy sat on the chair in front of the television flipping through channels, he didn't go ballistic immediately.

He figured he'd let Remy explain then chew out his ass for allowing anyone in the house.

Remy looked up and nodded at him. "Don't freak. Yes, there're two people here. There's an explanation."

"It better be a goddamn good one."

"One is Amity's sister."

He paused. "Wait. That means…"

"Yes, she's a goddess. Akhuvitr, Goddess of Healing."

Okay. He could deal with that one. "Who's the other?"

"That would be me."

Rom turned toward the voice, did a double take then stood a little straighter, waiting for the *salbinelli* to speak first. An old memory had popped into his head, something his mother had taught him. His mother had always had a deep and abiding respect for the elder races, the *Fata*.

"Huh. I see someone's had some training in the old ways." The *salbinelli* walked over to him, hand out. Rom took it immediately. "Salvatorus. Nice to meet you."

"Romulus Cangelosi. It's my honor. My mother was—she had a great respect for the *Fata*."

Sal's gaze narrowed but didn't point out Rom's clumsy attempt to hide something. "Nice to know, but there's no need to stand on ceremony with me. I'm Sal. And you and Remy are cousins, yes?"

Rom stiffened. "Yes, sir."

"Now, son, no need to be worried. I'm not about to out you and Remy. Besides, we both want the same thing… to keep Amity safe."

"And how are we supposed to do that exactly?"

Sal's grin made Rom feel like he should run for cover.

And when Sal had finished explaining the plan to Rom, which Remy had apparently already heard, all Rom could do was shake his head.

"So you want us to accompany Amity into her dream where she can speak to Charun so he can tell her all his troubles and hopefully not want to consume her powers anymore."

Sal shrugged. "Basically. Yeah."

Rom was struck speechless. But not for long. "And you actually think this is a good idea?"

Sal shook his head. "What I think doesn't matter. You're forgetting she's a goddess, son. She gets to call the shots. Besides, if the prophecy's right, aren't you two supposed to be the most powerful *lucani* ever born?"

Rom felt everything go still around him, felt Remy's shock reverberate through him. "I don't know what you're talking about."

Anyone else might've flinched from the menace in Rom's tone.

Sal held his gaze steady. "Yeah, you do. Trust me, Romulus. You don't want to fuck with Fate. She knows where you live and she will hunt you down."

"Is that a threat?" Rom's skin felt like it was burning from the inside out.

"No, it's a warning." Sal's gaze softened. "Look, I'm not trying to piss you off or frighten you. I'm trying to bring you up to speed in the easiest possible way. I understand why your parents ran. Knowing your sons are part of a cryptic prophecy is not usually cause for celebration. And yet, here you both are. The two wolves whose hands hold the red fire and whose hearts hold the strength of the Goddess Yet-to-Be."

The words triggered the memory so clearly.

Rom had been sixteen to Remy's twelve. Their dads had taken them aside, out of hearing of their mothers and their siblings. Rom had known, by the looks on their faces, it wasn't anything good.

And after they'd heard what their fathers had had to say, they'd both wished they'd never known.

The two wolves who hold the red flame will fight with the strength of the Goddess Yet-to-Be in their hearts and bring the past forward until the balance is no longer and the Rasenna *face the future without light.*

The *Rasenna*, they knew, were the Etruscans. The Goddess Yet-to-Be... no clue.

The red flame, now that one they knew. Both he and Remy had been able to conjure the red flame as children. But with no one to teach them how to use it, they'd lost the ability as they'd gotten older. They'd never missed it.

And Rom knew their dads had secretly believed maybe that voided the prophecy. No red fire, no dire consequences, right?

Nothing would ever be that simple.

Rom's gaze narrowed down to watch Sal's response. "Do you know what the prophecy means?"

To Rom's complete shock, Sal nodded. "Some of it, yeah. Some I've got a pretty good idea about. The rest… don't have a clue. But I do know where you might start to find some answers."

Rom sighed, knowing where they were headed. "The den. You want us to talk to the king."

"Yeah, you need to talk to the king. No way to get around that one. But I think you might want to send Remy to deal with the king alone the first time."

Rom's shock must have been written all over his face. "Remy? Alone?"

His cousin turned to him, eyebrows lifted. "What? Don't think I can handle it?"

Rom stifled a sigh. "No, that's not what I'm saying. I—"

"If you go together," Sal broke in, "it might appear to be a show of strength and, while Cole is by no means insecure, there are… other considerations."

"*Vaffanculo*, could you just spill already?" Remy's tone held a whole lot of pissed off, perfectly echoing Rom's thoughts. "I'm so fucking sick of everyone talking like we're in a fucking episode of *Lost*."

Sal grinned then started to laugh. "Get used to it, son. Like it or not, your life just veered into another lane. Better get up to speed as fast as you can."

* * *

Perrin Winston knew she was dreaming.

For one thing, the pain she lived with constantly was a faint, dull throb.

And while that was nice, it was also somewhat scary. That pain helped her get through the day, no matter how twisted that seemed.

Still, here… wherever this dream had taken her, it was nice.

The twilight in this stand of trees didn't hurt her now-sensitive eyes. The cool, misty air felt wonderful against her ravaged skin.

Even the man watching her from the shadows beside a thick tree trunk made her only somewhat uncomfortable. Not fearful. Just… hyperaware.

"Who are you?"

Her voice sounded husky, like she had a bad cold and a five-pack-a-day habit. Another gift from Ralph's attempted murder.

"No one you need to worry about."

Wow, the guy had a rasp much deeper than hers but he probably hadn't gone through hell to get it. In fact, his made her shiver. And not in fear.

"Considering you're in my dream and I have no idea how you got here, I think I'm allowed to worry, don't you?"

The man didn't answer right away, and her eyes strained to see into the shadows. She wanted to see what he looked like. She *needed* to see. It was almost a compulsion.

But the shadows clung to him, as if they were an extension of him.

"I understand your concern, but that doesn't change the facts. I'm not going to hurt you."

She snorted, moved to cross her arms over her chest in a motion she'd taken for granted before but stilled before she finished. Her body would hurt, her skin would burn, and her muscles ache if she completed the action.

Amity told her she needed to keep using those muscles and eventually the pain would lessen.

"Forgive me if I've learned the hard way that some men lie and then try to kill you."

A slight shift of the shadows and a face came into view for a few tantalizing seconds before being obscured again. What she'd seen made her take another step closer before her feet simply wouldn't go any farther.

But why should she stop? This was a dream. Nothing here could hurt her. And this dream was a hell of a lot better than the nightmares she'd been having.

Nightmares that consisted only of pain and fire and the scent of burning flesh.

So she took another step forward, and another, careful not to trip over the tree roots that had erupted from the ground. Tree roots that hadn't been there a second ago. As if he'd conjured them to stop her.

She didn't recognize this place. She'd been born and raised in the city of Reading, spent many summers studying in New York City. She'd been to nearby Nolde Forest on class trips in elementary school, but those trips were faded memories now. She preferred living in the city, in her nineteenth-century townhome in Centre Park, where there were always people to talk to, always something to do, something to see.

She stopped when she stood only inches from the man, though even now, she still couldn't see his face clearly. It almost seemed as if he *was* a shadow. "Who are you?"

"No one you know."

"Then what are you doing in my dream?"

"I'm not really sure."

Okay, how weird was this? A strange man had invaded her dream and even he didn't know what he was doing there. Of course, this was all in her subconscious, so obviously she had some reason for him being here. "What's your name?"

He paused again. "Karn."

"Karn. Really." Resting her hands on her hips, she bit back a gasp at the pain that sliced at her as her skin stretched. Still, she didn't put her arms back down. She refused to let Ralph win.

Amity would be proud of her. The hospital's medical aesthetician had been saying for weeks how strong Perrin was. In her dream, she actually felt a little stronger.

In the hospital… let's just say, the hospital tended to sap all her strength.

"What kind of a name is Karn?"

"It's the one I've given you to call me."

So how weird was this dream going to be? Considering how fucked up her life was right now, probably pretty damn weird. Might as well just go with it. She'd wake up soon enough. And in her real life, she didn't talk to many people.

"Fine. So why are you here, Karn? In *my* dream?"

The shadows swirled again and his face began to materialize. A hard face. Not at all what she'd consider handsome. At least, not before she'd been burned.

Her perceptions had changed recently. Go figure.

His square jaw looked almost cruel. His nose too sharp, his dark eyes sunken, and his cheekbones too pronounced. He looked Greek. Or Italian. Maybe in his thirties or forties. His personality felt sharp, hard, like he'd done some time in jail. She thought maybe he should still be there.

But his hair… those black curls looked so soft. She wanted to touch them. And that was truly scary.

No way in hell should she ever want to touch a man ever again.

Blinking, she took a step back, putting more space between them. He didn't move, but she swore she could see him more clearly now.

"Are you leaving already?"

He almost sounded disappointed but she knew that was ridiculous.

"None of this is real. Why should I stay? I don't know why you're here, why I'm talking to you. Is this dream supposed to mean something?"

He smiled and stole her breath. Not that his smile changed her previous thoughts. If anything, it almost made him appear more dangerous. Like a rattlesnake poised to strike.

Still, it made her heart skip a beat. And fear began to eat at her.

She took another step back and watched his smile disappear and his eyes narrow down.

"You're afraid of me. Why? This is your dream, after all. Why would I hurt you?"

Why would he hurt her? Why had the man who'd said he loved her tried to kill her?

Because Ralph was a sick bastard.

Wasn't that what Amity had been telling her for weeks? That what Ralph had done to her had been no fault of her own?

Maybe all that shrink-speak was finally starting to get to her.

Or maybe this was her subconscious way of asking the questions she refused to consider when she was awake.

More likely, she was just losing her mind.

"Why would you hurt me?" she repeated aloud. "Good question, isn't it? Why would my lover plot to burn me alive in my studio? I don't have much money. And what I had, I would have given him. I loved him."

"A man did this to you?"

It took everything in her to keep her head up, to not turn away when she knew he was looking at the scarring on her face and body.

"Yes."

"Is he paying for his crimes?"

"He's in jail. For now. At least until the trial."

Where the bastard was going to tell the jury the explosion and fire had been an accident. That he'd had nothing to do with it.

He hadn't rigged the explosion. Why would he? He loved her. He didn't know how she, the woman he loved more than life, could accuse him of this crime.

Or maybe he thought she'd be too embarrassed, too mortified to show her face in public... the way she looked now.

Maybe he was right.

"That man should burn for what he did to you."

That's exactly what she thought. Her gaze refocused on Karn, whose eyes met hers without a shred of pity in them.

Amity looked at her the same way, though Amity's gaze was empathetic. This man's promised retribution.

She liked that. Her lips curved in a smile, though it pulled at the skin of her neck that was so badly burned in the fire and made her eyes water with the pain.

"Thank you."

He looked startled, as if he'd never heard the words before. "For what?"

"For saying what I'm too afraid to say."

"You're not a coward."

"Yes, I am. And I hate it."

"So you're okay with what you're going to say if anyone asks who you are and what you're doing with me?"

Rom sighed, rolling his shoulders under the gorgeous Hugo Boss suit Sal had delivered that morning before he'd left to take Remy to see Cole. She and Rom had left her home at the same time, driving separate cars in case anyone happened to notice them when they arrived.

Rom had parked right next to her in the garage and had dogged every step she took to the main building.

But she couldn't help but notice how carefully separate he kept himself. He didn't touch her once.

"I'm a product rep shadowing you for the day."

"Yes, that's correct." She smiled over her shoulder at Rom

as they began the trek through the main building of the Reading Hospital. Various renovations and additions had made the hospital a maze, and they had to walk through several different areas before she got to her office.

She was careful to make her smile pleasant rather than let-me-rip-your-clothes-off hot. She knew many of the people who worked in the hospital, and someone was bound to notice she couldn't take her eyes off the man.

Of course, no one was looking at her.

"So what am I supposed to talk about?" Rom had lowered his voice though he didn't attempt to smile. It would have looked forced, and he was drawing enough attention as it was.

Last night, the man had made tight, faded jeans and clingy T-shirts look good. Damn good. Now, wearing a suit that retailed for a couple thousand dollars... oh my.

This morning when he'd pulled on the coat, shot the cuffs, then adjusted the tie, she thought she might have moaned just a little.

She'd always had a soft spot for a man in a suit and tie. And a hat. The 1940s, '50s, and '60s had been good decades. Today's men didn't realize the effect a nice fedora had on a woman. Which was why she loved watching *White Collar* and *Mad Men*. Matthew Bomer and John Hamm could wear hats like nobody's business.

Honestly, if more men wore hats, she swore they'd have better sex lives.

Rom hadn't been too keen on the suit when he'd first walked out of the bedroom. Remy's good-natured ribbing probably hadn't helped.

She'd nearly swallowed her tongue. Sal deserved a box of Selvans's special cigars for choosing this suit.

Forcing herself to focus, she answered his last question. "We can talk about anything, really. Since no one's seen you here before, they'll assume you're new and will steer clear. Usually the new reps tend to be more aggressive, which is why the department usually ships them off with me first."

"Why's that?"

She snuck a quick glance at him then decided that'd been a bad idea because she couldn't look away.

And Rom had made it so very obvious that the only reason he had agreed to stay was because Remy wouldn't leave.

The longer she stared, the more his gaze narrowed until finally she looked away.

Damn him. Damn both of them.

She'd slept alone last night, tossing and turning as the men took turns grabbing cat naps on the couch and standing watch. She should've slept like a baby. Instead she'd been horny as all hell.

"Because I'm good with them. They like that I listen to them."

He didn't say anything for a few seconds. "I bet that's not the only thing they like about you."

They stopped at the elevator where she stabbed the up button with a little more force than normal. Her lips parted to set Rom straight and noticed he was shaking his head and grimacing.

"Sorry. That… didn't come out right. Shit." He sighed. "I meant no disrespect."

"Then what did you mean, Rom?"

"It means I've got a lot on my mind and I shouldn't be taking it out on you. I'm sorry."

Damn. Didn't that just take the wind out of her sails. Yes, she had an underworld god on her ass, but Rom had more than a few things on his mind as well.

She wanted to reach for him, to touch him, reassure him, but she knew he wouldn't appreciate it.

And that was good. That was fine. She had no business fooling around with these two men right now. No matter that she wanted them so badly, just the remembered taste of him made her wet.

"No, you don't have anything to feel sorry for. Let's just get through the day. I don't want to add to your stress."

"Lady, the only thing you're adding stress to is my zipper."

Her mouth dropped open at his blatant statement just as the doors to the elevator opened. Luckily no one was in the elevator or waiting for it.

With another sigh, he put his hand on her back to get her moving. "Sorry. Again. Guess my sense of humor leaves a lot to be desired."

Was he serious? Had he been trying to make a joke?

She stared up at him as he stared straight ahead into the elevator doors.

"I... I didn't..."

"Know that I had a sense of humor?" His mouth twisted in a wry grimace. "Yeah, I get that a lot."

"I'm sorry." She gave him an apologetic smile and felt some of the weight lift off her shoulders when his expression lightened the tiniest bit. Maybe he wasn't as immune to her as she thought. Maybe... "You just seem to be a little..."

"Scary?"

Was that how he saw himself? "How about intense? You don't scare me, Rom."

"Good to know." He nodded. "So tell me a little more about what you're doing today."

Conversation closed, according to Rom. Fine. Really.

The cousins were getting too far under her defenses.

"Well," she forced a bright smile, "I'm going to use all this wonderful energy and give my patients' healing a bit of a boost."

Actually, she'd have to be careful not to heal too much, too fast. There'd be too many questions for her patients. Too many questions she couldn't answer.

The elevator dinged and the doors slid open. Two nurses she recognized from labor and delivery hurried on just before the doors closed, effectively cutting off their conversation. The women gave Rom a quick once-over then glanced at Amity with sly smiles, which she returned.

Yes, he certainly was handsome.

But not yours. Never yours.

She felt her lips twist in a grimace and quickly wiped it away. He was watching her in the mirrored doors.

The elevator dinged again and she realized they'd reached her floor. "Oh fudge."

Sticking her hand out, she caught the doors before they closed again then gave Rom an apologetic glance. "Why don't you come down to my office, Mr. Cangelosi. We can talk there for a few minutes before I give you the tour."

With a nod, Rom followed her, his impressive bulk a comforting presence behind her.

Not that she was afraid. Not really. The hospital felt safe to her. Like all the others she'd worked in over the centuries. Though procedures and equipment changed, sometimes weekly, she still had that sense of belonging in a hospital that she'd never had anywhere else.

Pulling her keys from her pocket, she opened the door to her office and ushered Rom through. Even before she'd closed the door behind her, Rom was shrugging out of his coat and hanging it on the back of the visitor's chair in front of her desk.

"So you've done this before?"

She thought about simply ignoring his question, but in the short time she'd known Rom, she knew he wouldn't let her get away with it. Goddess or not.

Thinking about her answer as she stowed her purse in her desk, she went through her daily routine, including turning on her computer, a necessary evil these days. She much preferred paper and direct contact to virtual anything. Then again, she'd been born more than two millennia ago.

As she shuffled through the files on her desk, she watched Rom lean against the door frame, a solid wall of muscle carefully hidden behind fine silk and cotton.

You'd have to be blind not to notice the air of danger surrounding the man.

"Amity."

Stubborn, stubborn man.

With a sigh, she let the folder she'd been pretending to study drop on the desk, then met his intense gaze. "No, I haven't." She put on her best goddess face and stared into his eyes. "Is that what you wanted to hear, Rom? I've never had to resort to these measures to gain power before."

And quite frankly, she'd never had it happen before. But there was no way she was going to tell him that.

Even while they were having sex, she felt the wall Rom tried to keep between them. And that was fine too. She even understood. Apparently he had more self-preservation than she did.

Besides, Remy's blatant affection made up for Rom's lack.

Which just added another layer of tension to the soap opera she seemed to have stepped into. Although hers resembled *Dark Shadows* much more than *The Young and the Restless*.

"Amity—"

"No. Just… no. So, are you worried about Remy's meeting with Cole?"

Surprisingly, Rom let her get away with the subject change with little more than a sharply released breath. "No. Remy will do what he does best. He'll charm him."

The slightly disgusted look on his face made her struggle to hide a smile. But when he raised his eyebrows at her in that way, she couldn't help herself.

She wanted a kiss from those firm lips, wanted him to wrap his arms around her and hold him against her while he opened his mouth over hers and consumed her. Wanted to heal that deep, hidden well of sorrow. Knew he'd never allow her to. He guarded those feelings so closely.

"I know you're worried about Remy, but Cole is not an unreasonable man. So much has changed since your parents left the den. And you and Remy are no longer children. Maybe you can stop running now. Come home."

Rom didn't even blink. "We don't have a home, Lady Amity. And we never will. Any chance of that was destroyed the day the demon killed our families."

"Remy Leone. This is *Rex* Colerus Luporeale, *legatus* of the *lucani* legions."

Remy was rarely intimidated, much less in awe of anyone.

So when Sal introduced him to the man who claimed the title King of the Etruscan werewolves and commander of the sole remaining legion of the ancient Roman army, Remy's first instinct was to shake his head and laugh like hell.

Luckily, he curbed the impulse. Rom might be right to call him an idiot occasionally, but he wasn't stupid.

So, instead of insulting the man who looked like a well-dressed businessman who spent his days tied to a desk, Remy merely bowed and waited for the king to say something, hopefully before Remy opened his mouth and stuck his size eleven in it.

Remy was a little surprised when the king stuck his hand out but took it and appreciated the firm grip.

"Nice to meet you, Remy. Please accept my condolences on the murder of your family. I share your sorrow at the loss."

Taken aback by the man's bluntness, Remy could only nod and say, "Thank you."

"Now," Cole pointed to the door to his left, "please come in and we can get down to business. Sal's told us some of your story. I'm hoping you'll fill in the rest of the details so we can help you help Amity."

Bracing himself, Remy walked through the door into a room decorated with warm earth tones and comfortable furniture.

From the outside, no *eteri* would ever think a king ran an army of werewolves from this place. The building looked like any other midcentury bilevel constructed of tan brick and brown siding. It was so nondescript, it seemed to fade into the surrounding forest.

Which, of course, was exactly what it'd been designed to do.

Inside though, it was obvious the place was all business.

First, you had to get through the front door, which required either a biometric eye scan or a key. Most Etruscan children were given a skeleton key at birth from their parents. Remy kept his on his body at all times. It was a charm, imbued with special properties geared for that person only. It could be used in various ways, one of which was to open most locked doors.

He doubted his would open this door, though. The lock had probably been set to accept only certain magical signatures.

He figured several of them were in this room. He'd scented three women and six men before he'd opened the door, including Sal.

Four large, dangerous-looking men took his measure the second he walked in. They watched him like most predators did, with a healthy sense of suspicion. He understood so he didn't take offense.

The two women sitting at the table... shit, he recognized them. Remy stopped just inside the door, straightened, then bowed low.

"Ladies."

More goddesses. Okay. Life had just gotten a little more interesting.

The blonde smiled and, before she'd uttered her first word, Remy knew exactly who she was. Thesan, Goddess of the Dawn.

Damn, the woman was gorgeous. He felt his eyes widen, and

he prepared to smile back when he noticed the glare from the dark-haired, leather-clad man standing behind her. Okay, next goddess. Another stunner with long, dark hair and moonlight-gray eyes. Lusna, former Goddess of the Moon. She didn't smile, just stared straight at him. The man sitting next to her rested his hand on her shoulder like he had every right to. Lusna's man looked like a bruiser and had a shiner on his left eye to back up the supposition.

The goddesses' men looked proprietary enough to take off his head if he looked at either of them the wrong way.

The third female sat on the window seat at the far end of the room, mostly hidden behind the man standing in front of her. He looked to be only a few years older than her and Remy would've sworn she couldn't be much older than twenty. The guy looked like the front man for a metal band. Dark, spiky hair, tats covering muscled arms left bare by a sleeveless black band shirt with guns and skulls.

This guy would kill him if he so much as looked at the girl cross-eyed. In profile, she looked deep in thought, sun glinting off her bright copper hair as she stared out the window. As if she hadn't noticed anyone had come into the room.

Remy had no idea who she was. She didn't look like any of the goddesses he'd studied as a kid. Still, her power filled the air around them, so thick he swore he felt it rub against his *arus*, his magic, calling to it.

Frowning, he forced it back down, surprised it took so much effort.

The last two guys… Well, at least they didn't look like they wanted to take Remy's head off. The one was tall and lean, with a kind face, bright eyes, and a shaggy appearance that reminded Remy of a surfer. And holy hell, he had a smile.

The other older, dark-haired man sat quiet and expressionless at the far end of the table. That one could kill you with his hands tied behind his back, and you'd never see it coming.

The door shut behind Remy with a barely audible swish and Cole waved him into a chair at the nearest end of the table, across from all the oh-so-friendly people.

Oh, yeah. This is gonna be fun.

"So." Lusna's voice had a rich, smoky quality that felt like velvet rubbing against his skin. "The prophecy's true. I guess that explains a few things, doesn't it?"

Well, shit.

Remy stiffened and his breath stuck in his throat. His gaze shot to Lusna, whose expression had softened into a smile. He must have put on his mean face without realizing because all of the bruisers bristled.

Only Sal, Cole, and the surfer dude seemed unaffected.

"You're making the natives restless, Lucy." Thesan reached over her shoulder to lace her fingers with those of the man standing behind her then gave Remy a bright smile. "I'm sorry. Everyone's just a little on edge. There have been a few… changes in our corner of the world recently."

That didn't sound good, no matter that it came with a smile.

"Lady Thesan—"

"Oh, please call me Tessa." Another smile, which he felt compelled to return.

"Of course, Lady Tessa." He bowed his head briefly.

"Uni's Ass," Tessa's guy rolled his eyes and sighed. "If he keeps bowing every time one of you talks, we'll never get anything done."

"Hell, Cal." The surfer dude rolled his eyes at the guy he'd called Cal. "Give the guy a break, will you? We all know patience isn't your strong suit, but you're gonna need to find a little right now. Remy, right? I'm X. Please forgive my idiot brother for his manners."

As Cal gave the finger to the guy named X, Lucy's man started to laugh. "Yeah, Conan's not exactly housebroken."

"You wanna talk housebroken?" Cal turned to give the other

guy a double salute. "I'm not the one who has to file down his claws before his games."

Remy didn't have a clue what the men were talking about, but it was obvious they knew each other well enough to get a few shots in.

The banter should have put him at ease, at least a little. It should've reminded him of Rom.

Instead, all he could think about was the power rubbing against his skin.

At first, he thought it was from the presence of the two goddesses in the room. But when he started to try and sort out his feelings, he realized they weren't the source.

It was coming from the girl.

He glanced at Cole, whose attention had never shifted away from him.

"You feel it, don't you, son?"

Sal's question had been pitched low, but Remy had no trouble hearing him. As the three guys on the other side of the table finally quieted, Remy nodded. "Yeah. I feel it. Maybe someone wants to fill me in. Or maybe we can discuss why the girl has more power than two goddesses."

Remy had the feeling he wasn't going to like the answer. He realized he was going to like it even less when the girl in the window seat finally turned away from whatever had been so fascinating outside and settled her blue, blue gaze on him.

He felt the change hit him low in the gut. He sucked in a deep breath, tried to stave it off. His wolf hadn't been called involuntarily since he'd been a teenager.

"Remy. What the—shit." Sal's voice, a growl barely registered in his ear. "I didn't think—"

"Cat, honey. Rein it in. You can do it." Lucy's voice, calm, controlled. "You have the strength. No, Ty. Stop. You can't keep stepping in for her. She can do it herself."

"I don't think I can, Lucy."

Remy fought the compulsion to turn for the simple reason that he hadn't initiated it. But he was losing the fight and, if he didn't give in soon, his wolf would be ripped out of him. And that would hurt like hell.

"Yes, you can," Lucy said. "Release the power. Don't try to control it."

"But what if it gets away from me? What if I can't call it back?"

"You will, Cat. Let it go."

Remy heard the girl gasp, and then a rush of sensation nearly made him double over. Not in pain. It didn't hurt. It brought his wolf so close to the surface, his skin itched with imminent eruption, which never happened.

Just as suddenly, it was gone.

After a few seconds, though he wasn't really sure of the time span, Remy felt he had a handle on his wolf. Pain continued to radiate through his body until he realized his fingers had clamped onto the edge of the table. His lungs strained to drag in air and all he heard was the sound of his own labored breathing.

Shit, shit, and double shit.

Swallowing was difficult through the clenched muscles of his throat, but he forced himself to do it. Then he started to make sure everything still worked correctly. That he didn't have claws or paws or a tail.

Questions raged through his mind, most of them starting with *What the fuck?*

He bit his tongue so he didn't let that slip. Around him, he heard the low murmur of voices, as if they were afraid to speak too loudly. He recognized only Sal's voice and Lady Lusna's. The others were a jumbled mess.

Kind of like the emotions tangled in his gut. Some of which weren't his, he realized. His eyes shot to the girl, staring at him from across the table. She had tears in her too-wide eyes and she looked devastated. He had the almost burning compulsion to go to her and tell her it was okay. That everything would be all right. That he'd take care of her.

Then he realized the delinquent next to her looked ready to kill him and figured he'd probably be safer if he kept the table between them.

"Remy. Hey kid, how you feeling?"

Sal's voice pulled his attention away from the girl and Remy swore he heard everyone release a sigh of relief.

"I'm fine. I'm… just processing."

Sal harrumphed. "Sure. You take all the time you need to process."

Feeling the weight of everyone's stare didn't exactly help with that. Still, after a few minutes, he managed to wrestle his feelings into some kind of submission. And the feelings that weren't his… well, they began to fade. Actually, it felt more like they were being blocked.

Fucking weird. All so fucking weird.

A deep breath. Then another. Instinctively, he looked at Lusna, the patron goddess of the *lucani*. She'd first given the gift of the ability to shift into wolves to his ancestors in Etruria so many centuries ago. Whatever had just happened, she had to have an explanation.

So why did she look so lost?

"Remy. Let me introduce you to Catene." Lucy held her hand out to the girl who now looked sick to her stomach. "The new Goddess of the Moon."

"Hello, Perrin. How are you feeling today?"

Rom forced himself not to show any emotion as he caught sight of the woman on the exam table. He'd seen worse. He'd seen the dead bodies of his family.

This woman was still alive, though she looked… well, she looked exactly like someone had tried to kill her by blowing her up.

Vaffanculo, how had she survived?

Perrin didn't smile as she turned toward Amity. Rom wasn't sure if she couldn't because of the scarring or if she just didn't smile anymore.

"Good morning, Amity. I'm actually… I'm actually feeling okay this morning."

Amity moved to the side of the table, a bright smile on her face. "Well, that's great news. Have you been sleeping well since I saw you last? Are you happy to be home in your own bed?"

As Amity reached for Perrin's hand, Rom noticed how the other woman took it immediately. No hesitation.

"Yes, but I had a strange dream last night. Not a nightmare this time. Just a weird… I don't know what to call it, really. It wasn't a nightmare but it didn't feel like a dream either."

Amity never lost her smile, even as she checked out Perrin from head to toe, and Perrin let her gaze connect with his.

He carefully held her stare, not letting his instinctive rage about her situation show. Her head went back, and he wanted to nod and commend her for not hiding in shame. She had nothing to be ashamed of. She'd survived. He wanted to give her roses.

He could tell from the undamaged half of her face that she'd been a beautiful woman before the explosion and fire. Now… He understood Amity's drive to help her.

"Forgive me for not introducing you sooner. Perrin, this is Rom Cangelosi. He works for the company that makes the wrappings we've been using on your burns. He's here to see how well they've been working. If you don't mind showing him."

Stepping forward, he held out his hand to Perrin. "Nice to meet you, Perrin."

After a second, she took his hand and he made sure not to squeeze.

He released her after only a second and caught Amity's expression. Tears lurked at the corners of those soft brown eyes and he had to restrain the urge to kiss them away.

"So, Perrin." Amity transferred her attention back to the other woman. "Why don't we take a look at your back to start? Last time, we talked about trying some different treatments to lessen the discoloration and pain. Mr. Cangelosi has been kind enough to provide a few samples of new products that I thought we could try."

Retreating to the other side of the room, Rom watched Amity open the huge white toolbox she'd brought with her. Now he saw that it was filled with tubes and tins and makeup, swabs, cotton balls and applicators. And a whole bunch of stuff Rom couldn't identify.

Amity's fingers rooted around in the perfectly packed compartments. Every item had a place in one of the many bins and slots and, after a few seconds, she pulled a white tube from the depths.

She shot Rom a quick glance, which he interpreted to mean watch the door because she was about to do her healing.

He felt the pull along his *arus* as she smoothed whatever was in that tube onto Perrin's back. The cream was thick and white and Perrin visibly relaxed as Amity spread it, talking all the time. Telling Perrin how much better her skin looked, how much better Perrin looked in general.

Amity's voice felt just as smooth to his ears as the cream must have felt on Perrin's skin. His body unclenched as he relaxed into the chair next to the door. His *arus* rose as Amity began to apply her magic.

Warmth suffused the room, though it never became hot. He didn't think anyone else would've noticed unless they had a hint of magic in their blood.

Maybe he was just hypersensitive to her magic. Then again, maybe the heat wasn't related to her healing at all.

He watched Amity's hands, slim and elegant. Then his gaze moved up her arm to her neck, where he'd bitten her last night. He remembered the sound she'd made as he'd licked at the hurt, remembered the feel of her pussy tightening around him.

Lust rose, thick and powerful, as memories flooded his mind. He no longer saw the two women in front of him, he only saw Amity. Naked and crying out for him and Remy to fuck her.

He wanted her. So much, he could barely breathe. And that was fucking dangerous to their health.

Snapping to attention, he forced himself to drag his gaze away from her, stare out the window, at the door, at the wall. Anywhere but at her.

Wanting her could go nowhere. He and Remy had enough shit to deal with without adding consort to a goddess to the list.

Might as well call a spade a spade and just say fuck buddies. Consort was too civilized. At least for them.

Glancing at the clock, he realized he'd been sitting here for more than an hour. His gaze shot to Amity, who had given up any pretense of hiding what she was really doing to Perrin.

Her hands glowed that bright, eerie blue and her eyes had closed. Glancing over his shoulder to check that the door to the exam room was closed, he stood and headed over to the bed.

The closer he got, the more he realized Amity didn't look good. Her skin looked flushed.

No, not flushed. She looked burned. As if she'd stood in front of a hot fire for too long.

Or she'd taken some of Perrin's injury onto herself. He looked at the other woman's back. The scars, or at least what he could see of the scars, were noticeably better.

Like really fucking noticeable.

He reached for Amity's arm but stopped just before he touched her.

Perrin seemed to have fallen asleep, but if she hadn't and turned around, how freaked out would she be if she saw Amity?

And what would Amity do if he startled her? Would it damage either her or Perrin?

Still, he had to stop her. Amity looked pale beneath the red tinge to her skin and close to passing out.

"Amity." He kept his voice low, his tone as even as he could, considering he felt frantic enough to howl.

She didn't respond, didn't look as if she'd heard him. And her hands began to shake.

"Amity!"

Her eyes fluttered but she didn't open them, almost as if she couldn't. As if she were locked into the power of the healing spell and couldn't get out.

Fear tightened his guts into knots. What the hell should he do?

Moving behind her, he wrapped his arms around her shoulders, enfolding her against him. The heat radiating from her body scared the shit out of him. She felt like she might spontaneously combust.

Putting his mouth against her ear, he tried to keep the fear out of his voice. "Amity. You've got to stop. You're going to hurt yourself. Come back to me."

He put a hard command in his tone and felt her shudder against him. "Amity. Stop. *Now*."

She gasped and her hands fell to her sides, the glow fading away in a matter of seconds. But the burn marks on her face remained.

Vaffanculo. He should have known she healed by taking the hurt into herself.

When she'd healed him and Rom, she'd taken their pain, taken their *wounds*. He wanted to pound the walls. He wanted to tell her she was *never* to do it again. Yeah, he was being an idiot. He didn't care.

Damn it, she was a goddess. She was the goddamn goddess of healing. This is what she did. What she'd been doing for millennia.

And every instinct in him wanted to forbid her from harming herself ever again. Yeah. Idiot wasn't strong enough.

"Amity. Can you hear me?"

He felt her body moving as she breathed, uneven and rough. Was she going into shock? What the hell would he do if she passed out?

She felt so slight in his arms—

Wait. He knew one way for her to gain strength. Except there was no way he was bending her over and taking her here.

On the bed, the woman made a sound like a sigh and shifted. He froze, trying to figure out what the hell to do if she turned over and saw Amity. What the hell would he tell her?

But Perrin fell silent again. Asleep.

Rom had never felt such a sense of relief.

Checking to make sure the door was still closed tight, he gathered Amity in his arms and took the few steps to the chair in the corner. Sitting on the edge, he settled Amity on his lap.

Then he attempted to pull himself together before he lost it and started kissing her, trying to force some of his strength back into her.

He wanted her to open her eyes and smile at him, tell him she was fine. Staring down at her, he realized the scarring on her face looked a little better.

Relief wanted to crash through the fear, but he kept it at bay. He and Remy hadn't kept themselves alive all these years by leaping to conclusions.

So he kept watching her, taking his eyes off of her only for brief seconds. Luckily, this section of the hospital didn't seem to be busy on a Sunday. There were no patient rooms, only exam rooms and offices.

But their luck wouldn't hold out for long. Sooner or later, a nurse, a doctor, someone would come through that door and want to know what the hell was going on.

His wolf wanted to say fuck it and take Amity home. The human part wanted that too, but at least he was smart enough not to act on the wolf's instincts. Besides, Amity would skin him if they left Perrin alone.

After a few more minutes, he sensed a change in her scent. She shifted in his arms. Her ass brushed against his thighs and kick-started his libido.

Relief. That's all it was. He couldn't want to fuck her just because she had started to come around. What kind of asshole would that make him?

Good thing Remy wasn't around to read his thoughts and possibly answer that question.

"Amity, hey. You gotta wake up, babe."

"Rom?" She curled against his chest, putting one hand on his shoulder while the other found its way under his suit jacket to rest against his hip. "So tired."

"I'm sure you are, but you can't sleep now. We have to get you out of here."

"Out of where?"

"Out of this exam room."

Her nose crinkled as she grimaced, and he tried not to want to lick along her lips before he sank his tongue into her mouth and kissed the hell out of her.

"Why are we—" Her eyes shot open and she drew in a sharp breath. His arms tightened around her so she wouldn't make a sudden move and make him lose his grip on her. "Oh my… What happened?"

He had to force his jaw to unclench to get the words out. "I'm not sure. You need to tell me. What the—" No. Couldn't go there. Couldn't say that. "You looked like you were going to pass out. And it looked to me like you were developing her injuries. Tell me that wasn't what was happening."

She didn't answer and her gaze slid away to look at Perrin. "Has she woken?"

Gods damn, he was gonna develop lockjaw at this rate. He reached for patience, something he was normally good at attaining. Today, not so much.

His gut kept tying itself in knots when he thought about the pain she must have endured.

"No. She didn't." He made sure he kept his tone even but she was empathic. Of course, she knew he was upset. Okay, maybe pissed off would be a better way to describe what he felt.

She stiffened and began to draw away from him.

"Put me down, Rom. I'm fine now."

But she wasn't. He felt the tightness in her body and saw the lines around her mouth. Yeah, that could be anger but he hadn't seen her angry yet, so he was betting on pain.

And he wasn't doing anything to help her. In fact, he was adding to her stress.

Shit. With an effort, he wrestled his inner asshole back where it belonged—stuffed in a deep, dark hole—and maneuvered her around so she was sitting on the bed and not on him. He didn't want to accidentally hurt her.

"No, you're not fine."

She huffed but it sounded weak. "I just need a few minutes to rest. Then we can send Perrin home and go back to my office. I'll have to wait a little while before I see the boy—"

"Hell no. Not happening today."

Okay, maybe he hadn't stuffed the asshole down far enough. Still, he wasn't going to let her hurt herself again. Not today. He couldn't take it.

He stood directly in front of her, staring down at her pale face, knowing she couldn't take any more today either. Goddess or not, she was still a woman who needed someone to look out for her right now.

Not that she thought so, apparently. She glared at him, her narrowed eyes glittering, her beautiful mouth set in a tight line. If he'd been a good Etruscan, he would've bowed his head and given her whatever she wanted.

Good thing for her, he wasn't a slave to devotion.

Crossing his arms over his chest, he just stared down at her until her eyes widened.

When he wrapped one hand around her nape, bent down and kissed her, he tasted astonishment on her lips. And on the heels of that, a fast-building heat. He let that heat sink in, let it take him under. Not far enough to be dangerous, just for Amity to gain a little strength. And for an ache to begin burning in his gut.

When he pulled away, he saw that her cheeks had regained a little of their normal color and the haze had cleared from her eyes. Relief made him almost light-headed.

Fuck. Just… fuck.

Seconds ticked by as she stared up at him and he tried not to want to pick her up and carry her back to her office where he could close the door and pin her up against the wall.

Her office had no windows except for one on the outside wall that looked out onto a small courtyard. They could lock the door…

The thought wouldn't let him go now that it was stuck there.

He wanted to feel her naked body under his, her pussy stretched around his cock, sucking him in, holding him tight.

He felt the blood begin to travel south, his cock twitching and filling.

Something of his thoughts must have shown on his face because Amity's gaze dropped to his lips and hers parted to draw in a deeper breath.

Lust filled the air between them. Her gaze shot back to his and she held out her hand.

He didn't hesitate to take it, pulling her to her feet. Her head barely came to his shoulder. The lushness of her femininity struck him, the lush curves of her breasts and hips. He wanted to get his hand on those curves; his desire was a palpable force that she had to be able to sense.

Amity didn't say anything as she dropped his hand. He forced himself not to grab for her, which would have been extremely embarrassing because she only wanted to check on her patient.

Perrin slept, her breathing slow and deep, no hint of distress.

His gaze snapped back to Amity's. Her chin lifted and her mouth firmed, as if daring him to say something. He practically had to bite his tongue not to.

"I'll wait outside for you."

It took Amity fifteen minutes to emerge with a visibly rested and still scarred Perrin, who nodded at him before walking away as she promised Amity she'd set up her next appointment for Monday.

Finally, Amity turned to him, her expression coolly professional. What the hell?

"I'm so glad you were able to see how well those bindings are working," Amity said. "Why don't you let me buy you a cup of coffee and we can talk a little more."

Hell no, he didn't want coffee and he opened his mouth to say so before he realized two female medical staff stood at the desk at the end of the hall.

"Sure, I'd love some coffee."

As they walked past the desk, Amity stopped for a few minutes to type something into one of the computers while he continued to the end of the hall to give her some privacy. He pulled out his phone to check his email and messages. It wasn't like he couldn't hear everything the women were saying, anyway.

"Whoa, Amity, who's the hottie? I'd love to get him alone in an exam room for a few minutes."

"You know, I've got a few scars. Maybe he'd like to show me his products."

"Damn, he's biteable."

He nearly choked on a shocked laugh. Holy hell, they talked

about him like he was a lion on display in a zoo cage. It almost made him turn and tell them he could hear them, though he'd never embarrass them like that.

"The man definitely knows how to wear a suit," Amity said. "All he needs is the hat."

The women didn't bother to keep their laughter to a low level. They didn't think he could hear them so they figured he had no idea what they were laughing about.

"High praise coming from you, Amity."

She knew he could hear her, so he knew her next words were deliberate. "Yes, I do have a thing for men in suits, though... I'd love to see him out of it."

That set the women off again. And made his cock throb. He hoped like hell they didn't look below his waist.

"Wouldn't we all. Damn, he's got a nice ass."

He didn't know whether to be shocked or grateful. And he refused to blush, even though he felt the heat below the surface of his skin.

He'd never realized women could be... so much like men.

Amity let the women continue for several minutes while he pretended not to hear them, though he found it harder and harder not to react to what the women were saying.

They'd critiqued him from his shoes to his hair, and he guessed he should be happy he passed muster. But Amity was the only woman he wanted to rip his clothes off.

When Amity finally said, "Gotta go, I've got a hot date with a hot cup of coffee," he nearly sagged with relief.

"You certainly do. Go burn your fingers, girl."

Amity gave a little wave over her shoulder to the women as she walked toward him. Her dark eyes shone and she looked so much better than she had back in the exam room that he had to restrain the urge to grab her, bend her over his arm, and kiss the hell out of her for taunting him like that. Her friends would probably hoot and holler like frat boys at their first strip club.

He shoved the impulse into the dark corner with that inner asshole. Following her to the elevator, he waited until he was sure no one was within hearing distance.

"Are they always like that?"

She turned to him with innocence all over her face. "Always like what?"

His lips twitched but he fought back the grin that wanted to break free. "So... vocal."

Now her lips curved, just enough to make his hands curl into fists before he sank his fingers in her hair and pulled her toward him for a hard kiss.

The elevator chose that moment to appear and they stepped into the cage, where another woman in scrubs already waited. She gave Rom a discreet once-over as he pretended ignorance then gave Amity the same look the other women at the nurses' stand had given her—raised eyebrows and a smirk.

Shit, had he and Remy ever been this bad? Maybe he should feel flattered, but the only person he wanted looking at him like that was Amity.

She smiled at him in the door's reflection.

When the elevator door opened on the floor of her office, it took everything he had not to throw her over his shoulder and make a run for it.

They walked in silence through the hall. Since it was Sunday, this area of the hospital was probably a little less crowded than it would have been during the week. The offices on both sides and across the hall from hers had their doors shut tight. In fact, he heard no movement in any of the offices. The only *eteri* he sensed were around the corner. Out of sight.

She opened the door and, by the time she'd turned to wave

him in, he'd crowded against her and hustled her through the door, trying not to slam it behind him. He made sure he twisted the lock as he kept her pinned against him with one arm around her waist. Then he walked her straight toward the desk.

As her hips met the edge, his pressed against her ass, nestling his cock into her ass.

He tried. Gods damn it, he'd tried to stay away from her.

"Amity."

He shouldn't do this. Shouldn't touch her like this. Alone. Without Remy.

He couldn't make himself release her, either.

"Yes."

That one word, spoken in an almost breathless whisper, cut his restraints and obliterated his good sense.

All his pent-up lust rushed into his blood stream like adrenaline. His cock throbbed against his zipper, threatening to burst through.

Shrugging off the suit jacket, he tossed it at the chair, not caring if it fell to the floor. With one hand, he opened the button on his pants and released the zipper. With his other, he flipped her skirt off her ass and dragged down her underwear. He didn't want to rip them, but the delicate silk tore and fell to the floor in a heap. Amity didn't seem to care as she bent forward, pushing her ass back against him.

Working his cock out of the pants, he let the head brush against the soft skin of her ass, even softer than the panties. He had to grit his teeth against the urge to sink fast and deep into her body.

Slow. Go slow. She's not a nameless fuck in a dark hotel room.

"Hurry, Rom."

Maybe not so slow.

She bent farther, her arms stretching across the desk, hands curling around the opposite edge. Her ass was at the perfect angle, and he briefly considered falling to his knees and putting his mouth on her but he wasn't exactly thinking with his brain right now.

He grabbed her hips, his hands sinking into the soft flesh. Fitting himself to her back, he bent his knees to position his cock between her legs.

His breath hissed between his teeth as he felt her moisture coat his shaft. Hot and wet and ready for him. So fucking ready for him.

He bent until his forehead touched her back, still covered by her silk shirt, then took a deep breath. Her scent sank deep, that light floral fragrance mixed with the heady aroma of her need.

Standing still, he let his body take in all the sensations. Her smell, her heat. He lifted his head, using one hand to brush the hair from her nape, while his other shifted to play with her clit.

The tiny bud had thickened and swelled and she moaned as he used his fingers to pinch and pull. Baring his teeth, he sank them into her skin. Not to hurt. He never wanted to hurt her.

Hell, he didn't know why he did except it'd been instinct. Hold her to him. Keep her close. Don't let her get away.

She gasped, her head falling back against his shoulder, her ass pressed back against him.

"Now. Take me now, Rom."

Her words barely registered but the pleading tone made his hips withdraw, pulling his cock through her pussy lips as every muscle in his body clenched.

His balls drew up tight and, on his next thrust forward, he let the head of his cock sink between those swollen folds. Not enough to penetrate, just enough to get the tip wet and hot from her juices.

Electricity shot through his cock and up his backbone, making him groan with repressed need. And when she shimmied her hips, he swore he saw stars behind his eyelids.

"Stay." His voice vibrated through the air as his hands clamped onto her hips. But whether to stop her or help her, he didn't know. Whatever the case, he held her steady as he pushed forward again, sinking deeper this time.

He knew they didn't have much time. That this was not the time or place.

But Rom didn't think a bomb blast could've affected him right now. Every molecule in his body was focused on her. On the tightness of her hands gripping the table. On the heat radiating from her body. On her moisture coating his cock.

So fucking hot.

His hips swung forward again and this time, he pierced her completely. She was so wet, he slid inside in one smooth glide.

Perfect. Absolutely perfect. He wanted to stay here, like this, forever. His dick surrounded by her, his body covering hers.

Only one thing could've made it better but he shoved that aside and concentrated on what he had right now.

He had Amity. And he wasn't giving her up. Not for anything.

Slow. Go slow.

He pulled out, her tight sheath reluctant to release him. Amity's back arched as he nearly left her body then flattened as he pushed back in, this time with a little more force.

The friction was enough to send him over the edge. He held onto his orgasm by the barest fraction of a margin. Each thrust and retreat hit the spot on the underside of his cock that made him want to blow. How he managed not to… Hell, he didn't have a clue. Except, maybe he did. He wanted her to come with him. Wanted to feel her convulse around him as he pumped into her.

One hand slid from her hip and across her stomach until his fingers brushed her clit again. She moaned, the sound low and deep and so fucking hot, his cock pulsed inside her.

Shit. Too late.

He tweaked her clit and she froze for a millisecond before she tightened on him, her internal muscles squeezing him, massaging him, taking him.

His release punched out of him with the force of a bomb blast.

His shouted triumph split the air and drowned out Amity's muted cry. He pulsed inside her for what seemed like forever. Her sheath quivered around him and didn't slow until he had nothing left to give.

As sanity slowly returned, he took several deep breaths before he eased away. When she didn't move, her body draped over the desk, fear made him icy cold.

His too-tight throat barely allowed him to speak. "Amity. Are you okay?"

The lazy smile spreading across her lips made his relief an almost painful emotion.

"Yes, I'm okay. Actually, I'm more than okay."

Relief wanted to steal his breath, but he couldn't let it side-track him.

Quickly tucking himself back in his pants, he zipped up before she could move and gathered her into his arms, holding her against his chest. She sighed as she settled her cheek against his chest, her hair so dark against his white shirt.

"I didn't mean for that to get so out of hand."

Uni's ass, he really could've hurt her. He wanted to check for marks from the desk or his hands even more than he wanted to leave.

Because this had been a mistake. A huge fucking mistake.

Her soft exhalation sounded amused. "Sweetheart, we really need to get you to loosen up a bit. Remy's right." Her hand curved around his nape, her fingers starting a gentle massage. "Your ass is tighter than Joan Rivers's face after a visit to the Botox bar."

His lips parted but nothing came out. How the hell was he supposed to respond to that? What finally emerged was laughter. He couldn't help himself or contain it. Finally, he just let go and laughed until his stomach hurt.

When he stopped, he saw Amity staring up at him with a bemused but happy smile.

"I don't think I've heard you laugh until just now."

No, she probably hadn't.

With a heartfelt sigh, he set her on the desktop then bent to pick up the scrap of silk that would never again be worn on her body. He had the brief thought that maybe he'd just stuff them in his pocket.

Instead, he used them to clean her gently between her legs.

As he did, she sank her fingers into his hair again, her nails scraping against his skull a drugging pleasure. He wanted to rub against her like a frigging cat.

When he was done, she held out her hand for the panties. He gave them to her reluctantly, and she held them cupped between her palms for several seconds. When she opened them, they looked freshly laundered. And whole.

Damn, he would've liked to think about her naked under that skirt for the rest of the day. Which would've made him even crazier.

Crossing his arms over his chest, he let himself really look at her. "How are you feeling?"

Her brows curved in a graceful but so-expressive arch. "I told you. I'm fine."

He'd started to shake his head before she was finished. "Sorry. Sorry, that's not what I meant. I'm asking if you were having any lingering effects from the healing. You scared me. I don't—" He took a deep breath and tried to get his thoughts in order, knowing it might be a lost cause. "For so long now, it's just been me and Remy. We've got each other's backs. I'm not used to having to worry about anyone else." Shit, that sounded like he didn't want to look after her. "But you don't have to worry. We'll be here. However long you need us."

Amity had to bite her bottom lip to keep from breaking out in a triumphant smile.

This was the first time Rom had actually indicated he might be willing to stay longer than just a few days. And if she had her way, he and Remy would be staying much longer.

She hadn't even admitted to herself how much she'd wanted to hear him say he was staying. It didn't make a damn bit of sense how badly she wanted these two men.

They were *lucani*, yes, but they were still mortal, and she, especially, knew how fragile mortal lives were. How they could be broken and destroyed. How they could be taken away in an instant.

If Remy and Rom left, she'd be devastated. Which meant she was getting way too attached to these cousins.

As she wrestled with her unruly emotions, she nodded at Rom, avoiding his gaze.

He sighed. "Okay, let's try this again. Are you done for the day so we can get home and find out what Remy learned?"

Home. It had a nice ring when he said it. Not that it meant anything. Not really. Still, a shiver of longing went through her. "Sure. I'll check on the boy tomorrow." She forced some enthusiasm into her tone. "I'm ready to go. I can do my paperwork there."

He watched with a narrowed gaze as she collected what she needed. She loved her job but absolutely hated the mounds and mounds of paperwork modern hospitals required. She understood the need for most of it and, with computerization, it'd gotten easier but still…

She missed the good old days when she could heal someone and voila! It was proclaimed a miracle. These days, people were entirely too suspicious. And she had so much more to hide.

"What's wrong?"

Rom's softly spoken question startled her, she'd been so deep in thought, and her gaze flew to his. "Nothing's wrong."

It was his turn to raise his eyebrows at her and she sighed as she shouldered her work bag and moved toward him.

"I was just thinking," she said, "about how much things have changed."

Motioning for her to stay behind him, he opened the door

then stuck his head out to check the hallway. After a quick nod, he stepped out and motioned for her to follow.

If anyone would see him, they'd know Rom wasn't merely a product rep peddling his wares. How anyone could miss the leashed danger in his walk, in his gaze, she'd never understand. The man was a predator, beautifully lethal.

And for that moment, he was hers.

They made it back to the parking garage without running into anyone she absolutely had to speak to. Most of the female staff they passed gave her a wide smile or a thumbs-up behind Rom's back, but she didn't stop to talk to anyone. She wanted to get home. Actually ached with the need to see Remy, to know he was okay.

They didn't speak much on the drive but it wasn't an uncomfortable quiet, more an expectant silence. And her expectations were running high.

Her success with Perrin today had given her hope that the woman might one day be free of her scars. Not that she'd ever be over the emotional scars, but they'd take it one day at a time. Amity would see Perrin through to the end of this.

With Rom at her back, Amity opened the door to her home. Her lips parted to call out for Kari…

And gasped at the chaos spread out before her.

Chapter 11

REMY HAD MANAGED TO get his blood pressure out of heart attack range only a few minutes ago.

The rocker dude, who Remy had since learned was none other than Tivr, God of the Moon and Lusna's son, had scooped up Catene and swept her out of the room, all the while shooting daggers at Remy.

Not wanting to get himself impaled by a lightning bolt, Remy lowered his head, though the submissive gesture grated against his already on-edge nerves. He caught the gaze of the girl-goddess Catene just before she left the room though and apology shone so clear in those bright blue eyes, he couldn't help but offer her a smile just before the door closed.

When it did, silence descended around the table. For about two seconds.

"So who wants cake?"

Remy turned to the surfer dude, who looked like he belonged on a SoCal beach, partying and picking up beach bunnies.

"For fuck's sake, X, nobody wants your goddamn cake."

Lady Tessa's male reached out and smacked the surfer dude on the back of the head as Tessa allowed a bright grin to surface. "Don't hit your brother, Cal. And I'd love some cake, X." She turned that bright smile on Remy once again and he swore he felt the warmth of the sun in it.

Even though, according to Amity, Tessa had given up her powers. As had Lusna, who watched him with her steady gray gaze.

"X's cake really is to die for," Lusna said, completely throwing Remy out of his thoughts. "You should try it."

Seriously. They wanted him to try the cake. He was beginning to think someone had spiked the Kool-Aid but he hadn't seen anyone drinking anything.

"Hell, if X brought cake, count me in." Lusna's male leaned over to fist bump the surfer dude. "That lemon tart thing made my eyes cross, it was so damn good. The team wants you to make more of those dark chocolate raspberry cupcakes you brought to the last game. If you're not careful, you're gonna find yourself the love slave of some horny hockey player."

Remy had the surreal feeling that he'd stepped onto the set of a TV sitcom in an alternate dimension. And when the guy everybody was calling X turned to him and grinned, Remy decided he wanted a little of whatever they were drinking.

"You look kinda like you just fell down the rabbit hole. Welcome to Wonderland. I'm Extasis, by the way." He held his hand out over the table, and Remy leaned forward to shake it. "Just call me X. Wasn't sure if you'd remember my name after all the drama."

"Yeah, about that." Remy looked at Cole then at Lusna and Tessa. "Maybe someone wants to tell me what's going on now."

X got up and walked toward the other end of the table, where a gorgeous white-frosted cake waited. "Everything goes down better with cake, I've found."

Cal sighed, but Remy swore he saw pride in the guy's eyes as he looked at his brother. "Unless that cake is laced with alcohol, you know my response to that."

X started slicing. He made it look easy, and soon enough, Remy had a thick piece of white chocolate cake with raspberry filling and vanilla icing with coconut shavings sitting in front of him.

The first bite practically melted on his tongue. The next made him groan in pleasure. By the fifth, he'd settled to letting his eyes roll back in his head in ecstasy.

"See?" X looked at him with a grin. "I told you."

He finished the cake and realized, yeah, he did feel a little better. But he hadn't come for a sugar rush. "If you all don't mind, I'd really like to get some answers now."

Lusna set aside her fork, her cake only half finished. Pushing it toward her male, she caught his gaze and held it before turning back to Remy. "The short version… Tessa and I gave up our goddess powers to live as mortals with our mates after Charun sent demons after us. Tessa nearly died. I transferred my powers to Catene.

"We know Charun seeks to be released from Aitás and we know he's found a way to consume goddesses' powers so he can do so. We've lost one goddess that we know of. Obviously Amity has been targeted next. We don't know what Charun's end game is. We only know that he cannot be allowed to leave Aitás. Without him, chaos would reign and the gates would open."

And the souls of the dead would be able to leave Aitás.

Holy shit. No wonder no one had mentioned that. It was too scary to think about.

"We also know," Tessa continued, "that you and your cousin Romulus—Great names, by the way." Tessa beamed at him. "Romulus and Remus. Your parents certainly had a sense of history, didn't they?"

"Tessa"—Lucy looked toward the ceiling for a brief second as if trying to hold onto her patience—"don't get sidetracked."

Tessa actually stuck her tongue out at Lucy before she continued. "Okay, okay. Anyway, you and your cousin are actually the heralds of the new order, though we didn't realize that until Amity told us about you."

Remy's brain got stuck on the word heralds. "Wait. What new order? I've heard of the band but—"

"Hey, they had some good music," Lucy's mate, Brandon, broke in.

Lucy smiled at Brandon. "Yes, they did, and you and Remy can discuss that later. But first," she turned back to Remy, "you and Rom were born to be the guardians of the new Goddess of the Moon. That's what the prophecy has led us to believe. And it actually makes sense."

Of course Lucy would know about the prophecy. That shouldn't be a shock. And they'd get back to that in a minute. First things first. "How can we do that if we're protecting Amity?"

Lucy's brows quirked. "Well, that's the dilemma, isn't it?"

"Not to mention," Cole injected, "there's no way in hell Ty'll let anyone close to Cat, least of all two *lucani* who've been AWOL from the den for years." Cole raised his hand before Remy could defend his parents, which he would until the day he died. "That's not a criticism. I completely understand why your parents took the measures they did. I'm just explaining why, for now, we would appreciate if you and Rom would stick as close as you can to Amity."

His expression must have shown his surprise because Tessa started to laugh. "Not what you expected to hear, is it?"

"Actually, no, it wasn't."

Tessa turned to give the hard ass standing behind her a sweet smile that the guy actually returned. Remy hadn't thought Cal had it in him. Except Remy totally understood how no one could refuse Tessa anything.

The goddess exuded warmth like she was a heat lamp. The same couldn't be said for Lucy. Her cool, gray gaze watched him with an intensity that should've burned his skin.

Until she smiled, and Remy realized why she didn't do it all the time. If she did, there'd be riots on the street. And the man sitting by her side, watching her every move, would have more than a black eye.

"Which brings us to why X is here," Sal finally spoke up. "X thinks he has a way to talk to Charun that doesn't include taking Amity to the gate to Aitás."

"And that is…?"

X and Cal exchanged a glance before Cal nodded.

X's expression had turned intense and Remy saw much more of a resemblance between the brothers. "Have you ever heard of Cimmeria?"

Something tickled at the back of Remy's brain, but he couldn't quite pull out the reference so he shook his head.

"No problem," X said. "Cimmeria is the world between the planes. It's where Cal and I grew up. And it's the only access point to the other planes."

Remy recalled a snippet of the story his mother had once told him about the land of mist and shadows where you could access the world of the gods. He remembered being fascinated by the thought. He never actually believed the damn place existed.

"Seriously?"

X gave a wry grin. "Yeah. Seriously. Look, we know Charun's been contacting the goddesses through their dreams. I propose to take Amity into the dream plane and let her talk to him there. I think it's safer than actually taking her to the gate."

"No way does she go without us. And do you really think it's safe to take her anywhere near Charun?"

Cal and Brandon nodded, as if he'd finally done something they approved of, even as Tessa and Lucy shook their heads.

"Amity is not without her strengths," Lucy said. "To imply that she's too weak to merely speak to Charun is an insult. And one I hope you won't repeat to her."

He knew he'd just been dressed down by the Goddess of the *lucani* and he bent his head once more in submission. "Forgive me, ladies. I meant no disrespect. I just don't want anything to happen to her. She saved our lives. Rom and I will do everything in our power to make sure she's safe."

"Glad to hear it." Cole's quiet tone held a note of approval that inexplicably made Remy swell with pride. "Because you may not only be fighting off demons to keep Amity safe. We may be going to war against the *Mal* as well."

―――

"Kari! Kari, where are you?"

Rom took one look at the mess of Amity's living room and had his gun in his hand a split second later.

With his free hand, he reached for Amity before she could run farther into the room and shoved her behind him.

"Close the door and put your back against it and don't move."

To his complete relief, she did exactly as he said. Then he stood in the middle of the room and took a deep breath, trying to scent anyone else in the house.

Damn it. Two men and one woman.

Kari. He knew her scent because it was so like Amity's.

The men were *Malandante*.

Shit.

"Rom." Amity's voice trembled and that pissed him off. "What's—"

He cut her off with a sharp hand gesture, trying to use his senses to pinpoint the men's location.

Turned out he didn't need to. They walked out of the kitchen, marching Kari between them like a prisoner. Kari's expression promised furious retribution, but her mouth remained closed.

"Huh. I'll be damned. There are two of them."

The shorter of the two men looked through Rom as if he were no danger at all. Instead his gaze settled on Amity.

Which pissed Rom off.

"Who are you and what do you want?"

With his thinning brown hair, brown eyes, and nondescript looks, the guy could have walked down a city street and gone unnoticed. But Rom felt the force of his *arus* like a physical presence. The guy held powerful dark magic in that spare body.

"I think you already know the answer to that," the guy said. "Where's your cousin, Romulus?"

When he remained silent, the *Mal* merely shrugged. "Fine. I can sense he's not here. Pity. I would have left the Ladies alone if you'd been prepared to come quietly. Now I guess we do this the hard way. Den, take Lady Kari. I'll follow you in a few minutes."

"No!" Amity cried out and tried to push past Rom, but he reached for her and shoved her back behind him.

"Amity, stop." Rom didn't take his eyes off the trio in front of him. He noticed how Kari didn't look at all afraid, and how Den, whose sole purpose was probably to provide muscle and intimidation with the sheer bulk of his body, didn't take his eyes off Rom.

"We won't hurt your sister, Lady Amity. Ah, you're surprised we know who you are, aren't you? You shouldn't be. The *Mal* continue to practice many of the old ways, though the deities wouldn't know that, would they? Most of your kind abandoned the *Mal* many years ago."

Amity huffed. "Only because you declared war on your own people—"

"After they declared war on us centuries ago." The *Mal* didn't raise his voice but Rom heard his tone change. This guy was lethal. "We will take Lady Kari with us—"

Rom threw himself forward, the element of surprise allowing him to get the jump on the men.

He sensed their momentary shock and hoped it would be enough to give him the upper hand. He hit the shorter guy hard, a no-holds-barred roundhouse that landed with the distinct crush of bone. He stumbled back into Kari and the three of them went down like dominoes.

Behind him, he heard Amity cry out but he couldn't stop now. He followed the guy down and started to pummel him. The big guy lost his hold on Kari, who scrambled away, kicking at him with her spike-heeled boots as he tried to grab her back.

The *Mal* beneath him began to fight back and it was clear he knew how to defend himself. Rom couldn't afford to split his concentration between the men but he knew he couldn't hold both men off on his own for long.

Rom took an uppercut that caught him in the temple and pain exploded through his head. The guy went to throw another but Rom intercepted it before it connected. Using his greater weight, he tackled the *Mal*, hoping to get him pinned against the bigger guy and tie them both up so Amity and Kari could get away.

It worked, but not as well as he would've liked. They got tangled together, fists and feet, arms and legs, until Rom wasn't sure what was attached to whom.

All he knew was that he needed to keep the men away from the women long enough for them to get the hell out of there.

Rom took another shot to the gut that had him gasping for air, and someone's foot came too close to making him a soprano, but he fought to hold his own against the two men.

Getting back to his feet, he aimed a kick at the smaller guy's head, hoping to knock him out. He moved at the last second, and Rom's foot grazed his shoulder instead. The big guy also got to his feet, and Rom prepared for an attack. Instead, the guy turned and ran back toward the kitchen.

What the—

He turned for a brief second. "Amity! Run!"

She obeyed him without hesitation, grabbing Kari by the arm and pulling her toward the front door.

"No, up—"

Rom caught a roundhouse in the face that nearly spun him around just as the door opened. He didn't know whether Amity or Kari had opened it. Didn't matter.

Kari screamed in fury as the goon grabbed her and dragged her out of the house.

Amity would have followed if Rom hadn't grabbed for her arm, just before he felt the muzzle of a gun stuck in his side.

"I can't kill you. You're too valuable." The *Mal*'s voice was calm as he spoke in Rom's ear. "Don't worry. We won't hurt her. She's too important. Consider her leverage."

Rom contained the urge to knock the gun out of the guy's hand, just to get it away from Amity. He didn't think she'd be injured if it went off. More likely he'd take the brunt of a close-range shot. But he wasn't taking chances. "What the fuck do you want?"

"You know what we want." He nodded at Amity. "Next time we come, Lady Amity, it won't be just the two of us. We'll take them both. And they will do what we want."

Rom lunged for the man but he'd already turned to sprint for the back door. Torn between giving chase and protecting Amity, he realized there wasn't much of a choice.

He grabbed Amity and pulled her against him. She came willingly, wrapped her arms around his waist and held on.

"Are you okay?"

Her question caught him off guard because it was exactly what he was going to ask her.

His heart beat like a bass drum in his chest and he felt hers pounding as well.

"Fine. They didn't hurt you?"

If they had, he'd tear their fucking throats out.

She shook her head. "We've got to get to Charun before they decide Kari's worth more to Charun than to them. I've got to talk to him, Rom. I've got to put a stop to this."

"What we've got to do is get you somewhere safe so the *Mal* can't get to you. I'll go after Kari. You and Remy—"

"No."

He cut off a growl before it started and reached for patience. "Yes. You and Remy will get the hell out of here. I'll—"

He cut off as she put her fingers over his lips.

"No. I'm not saying I won't agree to go somewhere you deem safe, but wherever we go, it has to be close. I won't abandon my patients. And you will not go after Kari without help."

She didn't plead, didn't bat tear-stained eyes, didn't beg. She just stared at him with an unwavering resolution. He nodded, though his jaw felt ready to crack as he bit back the demand that she obey him. "Fine. It'll be close. Let's just… Go pack a bag. I wanna be out of here in a few minutes."

She nodded and headed toward the steps, and he found himself following on her heels. Watching her ass sway as she walked up the stairs.

Damn, he was a total dick.

He forced his gaze to look anywhere but at her as she headed for her bedroom and started sifting through drawers and pulling things out of her closet to neatly fold and place in an overnight bag. He knew he should call Remy and let him know what was going on but he lost himself watching her pack. He had no idea how she managed to fit all the stuff inside that bag but she was ready in less than five minutes.

Her hands shook, but she didn't ditz around, didn't open and shut drawers without purpose. She gathered her stuff together and didn't complain once about having to do it or cry about her sister, though he knew she was worried.

She stayed focused. And he forgot to call Remy.

Shit.

Pulling his cell from his pocket, he dialed his cousin.

And started to sweat when Remy didn't answer right away.

Three rings. Four. Five.

Rom had his finger on the button to disconnect when Remy finally answered.

"Yeah. What's up?"

Rom paused at the strain he heard in Remy's voice though he hadn't answered with the phrase they'd agreed on if either of them were in trouble. That would've been, "Can I call you back?"

"What's wrong?"

It was Remy's turn to pause. "When can you get out here?"

Rom's palms went instantly clammy. He turned and headed for the hall as Amity finished packing. "We're heading out now. There were two *Mal* waiting at Amity's house. They took Kari."

"Shit." Remy's voice had lowered almost to a growl then paused as someone spoke to him, too softly for Rom to hear. "I'll text you directions. Get here as soon as you can."

Behind him, he heard Amity say, "Rom, I'm ready. Is everything okay?"

He turned to find Amity watching him with wide eyes. Without thought, he held out his hand and breathed a little easier when she let him draw her into his side. Her shoulders fit perfectly under his arm. And the ding as he received a text message made him stiffen all over again.

"Did you get the text?" Remy asked.

"Yeah. We're leaving now." Rom felt the stiffness of her body and wanted to gnash his teeth at the helplessness he felt. They were fast losing control of things.

And that was unacceptable.

"Make it fast," Remy replied. "Life just got a hell of a lot more interesting."

⁓

Rom had just opened the passenger door and was helping Amity out of his truck when a dark-haired stranger who didn't look much older than Remy stepped out of the barnlike building in the middle of the den.

In khaki pants and white button-down shirt, he didn't look like a king.

Until you looked into his eyes. Then... Yeah, this definitely was the *lucani* king. *His* king. Rom's jaw tightened until he thought it might crack under the strain.

Amity smiled at the guy, and Rom had the almost overwhelming urge to step in front of her and keep her away from him.

"Cole." Amity's voice held a warm note that made Rom's gaze narrow. "How are you, dear?"

The guy bowed perfectly, without hesitation or awkwardness. "I'm fine, Lady Amity. We've been waiting for you."

"And here we are." She curled her hand around Rom's bicep and he nearly bared his teeth in satisfaction.

"Romulus Cangelosi." Amity's hand tightened on his arm, and her fingers began a slow, soothing rub. "Meet Cole Luporeale."

King Cole—Rom would bet his best sword no one ever cracked wise about that to the guy's face—walked down the stairs to stand in front of Rom then held out his hand and looked him straight in the eyes without a shred of domination.

Turned out the guy didn't need to be showy about his strength. All you had to do was shake his hand.

Rom took the guy's hand and bowed his head, which felt like the right thing to do. When he met Cole's gaze again, he felt some of that stress drain away.

"Nice to meet you, Rom. Sorry it's under these circumstances. Why don't you come into the center and get caught up. I know Remy's... anxious to talk to you."

That pause didn't sound good. "Who'd Remy piss off?"

Cole smiled, transforming his stern expression into something much more approachable.

"Actually, your cousin's been informative. And entertaining."

A little more of that stress drained away. They'd definitely made the right choice about who to send because, if they'd sent Rom, the king would probably be telling Remy he'd been uncommunicative and a pain in the ass.

Cole released him and bent to kiss Amity on the cheeks, short pecks on each cheek that put Rom's back up. *Idiot.*

"Lady, I've got Kaisie inside ready to track her, and the *sicari* on standby when he finds her."

"Thank you, Cole. Rom, why don't you go speak with Kaisie and I'll go see Remy and my sisters."

He didn't want to let her out of his sight but he didn't want to start a pissing match with the king. Not unless he had to. Besides, if this Kaisie guy was going to find Kari, then he needed to talk to him. And he definitely wanted to meet the *sicari*. The king's assassin.

Still… he balked at letting her out of his sight. *Shit.*

She smiled up at him, which did screwy things to his insides.

"I'll be fine here. I promise not to leave the building without one of you at my side."

She lifted onto her toes and pressed a kiss to his lips that nearly rocked him back on his heels. She didn't hold anything back, and he felt the wall inside him begin to crumble. She clung to him and when he would have pulled away, she leaned closer. And he kept kissing her.

He only pulled away when he felt Remy's presence. Remy stood behind them, watching. Rom couldn't decipher his expression.

Shit. What was Remy thinking? For the first time, Rom couldn't tell. Could Remy tell he'd made love to Amity without him? Was he pissed?

Remy nodded as Rom put his hands on Amity's shoulders and moved her a few inches backward so Remy could wrap one arm around her shoulders from behind and press his mouth against her neck.

Rom felt no jealousy as Remy kissed her. If it'd been anyone else, he would have torn his head off.

Damn, this was so fucked up. And they had no time to hash it out now.

When Rom turned back to Cole, the king got points for showing absolutely no surprise or shock. Of course, the woman who stood just inside the doorway of the community center had enough surprise for two people.

Until she started to smile. And then giggle.

The woman giggled like a teenage girl, her blonde hair bright as sunlight, and her blue eyes sparkling over the hand she'd placed over her mouth so he wouldn't see her laughing, or so he assumed. Which made no sense at all.

Then she motioned to someone he couldn't see, and a dark-haired woman with solemn gray eyes and an expression to match moved into the doorway with her.

Amity had followed his gaze and her face lit up as she saw the other women. The blonde took that as an invitation and tripped down the stairs to grab Amity in a bear hug. The other woman followed at a more sedate pace but she hugged Amity just as hard.

And when she turned to face Rom, he bowed low to the goddesses.

"Wow." The blonde had a smile a mile wide. "Guess all those Doublemint ads weren't wrong. Double your pleasure, double your fun."

"So the *Mal* took Kari." Lucy settled into a huge leather chair and curled her legs under her. "I wondered how long it'd be before they got bold enough to attempt something like this."

Amity and her sisters had retreated to a private sitting room, complete with mini bar, after she'd promised Remy and Rom she wouldn't leave the room without a chaperone.

Not that she needed one here. It'd been over a year since the *Mal* had breached the *lucani* defenses and taken Cat, a child, and another woman by force. Since then, the wards had been strengthened, most recently when Cat had assumed Lucy's powers.

Tivr had worked on those wards for weeks on end. No one could get through them using magic and, if the wards sensed even a whiff of *Malandante*, the *lucani* sentries would be alerted and the wards would shock the offenders with a spell rendering them unconscious. The only people the spell didn't work on were deities and those given a specific charm to carry on their bodies at all times.

"Nortia said they've been planning something," Tessa said. "She just hadn't been able to figure out what."

Amity rummaged through the mini bar. She needed a drink, and Cole was bound to have a bottle of Fuflun's wine here. And maybe, if she was lucky, he'd have some of the Etruscan God of the Vine's personal stock of beer. Hops grew on vines, too. Most people tended to forget that little piece of trivia.

Yes! Slim brown bottles filled an entire row in the refrigerator. She grabbed one, twisted the cap, and took several grateful swallows.

Finally, she turned and waved the bottle at Tessa, who scrunched up her nose and shook her head, then Lucy, who nodded.

She'd have to get a case of Fluff's beer for her guys. They'd love it.

If they even liked beer. The thought made her pause, her teeth sinking into her bottom lip.

Did they like beer? Or did they like liquor? Steak or pizza? Well, really, they were *lucani* after all. Steak it would be.

Country or rock? Mystery or sci-fi? Boxers or briefs?

Okay, she did know the answer to that last one.

Commando.

She smiled but couldn't hold on to it for more than a second.

"Amity, I know you're worried about Kari and so are we," Tessa said. "But you know Cole. He won't rest until he finds her."

Setting her beer on the table, Amity dropped onto the couch next to Tessa and rested her head on her sister's shoulder. "I know. I just feel like it's my fault. They came for me. Charun is after me. If anything happens to her, it will be my fault."

"Kari can take care of herself." Lucy's rational tone eased some of Amity's anxiety but not all. "And the *Mal* wouldn't dare hurt her."

"Kaisie will track her," Tessa said. "He's the best. And when he finds her, Cole will get her back." Then her smile turned downright wicked. "But right now, why don't you tell us what's going on with the cousins? They look more than capable of finding missing goddesses. Your Remy is certainly the charmer, but that Rom… he's got hidden depths, doesn't he?"

She knew Lucy and Tessa were trying to take her mind off the situation. Her gut tightened with jumbled emotions, but one comment about Remy and Rom and she went wet between the legs.

How the curve of Remy's mouth could turn her world upside down. And how a glance from Rom was all it took to make her burn.

"It's… complicated."

Which was totally the truth. Complicated by the fact that they were mortal and she wasn't. That she'd been marked for extinction by a god. That she could do very little to save herself, much less protect them. That she wanted them desperately and knew she should be pushing them away rather than letting them take care of her.

"I've never felt this way about anyone before, much less with two men who make me feel like I'm a necessary point in a circle we create together."

Sighing, she reached for her beer and took a few more gulps before she realized Tessa and Lucy were staring at her with identical wide eyes.

"What?"

Tessa blinked and looked at Lucy who'd started to shake her head.

"Amity." Tessa voice held a hint of tears. "That's… beautiful."

Yes, it was. But she had no idea how the men felt about her and she felt guilty about wanting her men when her sister was missing.

Lucy leaned forward and gripped her hand. Trying to comfort her.

An odd feeling, she realized, to be the one needing comfort. For the past few millennia, comfort had been her stock in trade.

Amity laced her fingers with Lucy's and held on tight as she abruptly changed the subject.

"We know the *Mal* have been recruiting *eteri* who are descended from the bloodlines, even if they can't access their power. Remy and Rom believe the *Mal* hired a demon to capture them and kill their families. Now, the *Mal* are ramping up their plans. We need to figure out why and if they're working with Charun."

"They have been awfully quiet the last century." Lucy's voice dropped to a low murmur. "And we haven't been monitoring them like we used to."

"We've overlooked them and that was our mistake."

Tessa's gaze narrowed down to a glare. "They're gathering power. While we fade, they've been amassing a power base. They've been biding their time."

"Do you think Cole's aware of this?"

"I'm sure he is, though he hasn't said anything to me." Lucy sighed. "And before you ask, no, I don't think he purposely kept the information from us. You know how meticulous Cole is. I believe he didn't have enough evidence and didn't want to raise an alarm without proof."

Tessa's pretty face screwed up into a frown. "And it's not like we could do anything about it. Our powers have been fading for so long, we've gotten used to being obsolete. And now…"

Tessa and Lucy exchanged a glance that said so much without using any words at all. Tessa's remaining powers could only be used in conjunction with childbirth. Lucy… Amity didn't know if Lucy had any powers left at all. She didn't talk about what had happened when she'd transferred her mantle of power to Cat.

And none of her sister goddesses had wanted to ask for fear of hurting Lucy.

Amity had lain awake at night, wondering what she would do if she lost her powers completely. She hadn't thought life would be worth living. And, for an immortal goddess, life had a very different meaning.

The only way she could end her life would be to give her soul to Charun. Then she would cease to exist. Or be reborn again. No one really knew because no one had ever gone through the process. Only one goddess had been missing since Charun had started his campaign against them, and no one was absolutely positive that she'd been taken by Charun. He certainly wasn't revealing what had happened.

"You knew about Cat, didn't you, Lucy?" Amity asked. "You've known for years."

Lucy's gaze held steady. "Yes, I knew she was born to be my replacement. I felt it the moment she was placed in my arms only hours after her birth. For years I told myself I was wrong. And when it became obvious I wasn't, I foolishly did nothing to prepare her."

"What I don't understand," Tessa chimed in, "is why I don't have a replacement."

Lucy shrugged. "Maybe you just haven't met her."

"What if there isn't one?" Frustration began to creep into Tessa's normally even-tempered tone. "What does that mean?"

Amity shook her head. "I don't have any answers."

Tessa's mouth twisted. "And maybe I was never really needed in the first place. Let's face it, our people never really needed a Sun Goddess. They had Usil and Catha. Needing a third Sun deity never really made sense."

"Maybe because Usil and Catha were always more concerned with devastation," Lucy said. "And you have always been a bright spot in the dark, Tessa."

Amity repressed a shiver at the thought of the dueling Etruscan sun deities. The God Usil and the Goddess Catha were always at odds. It was a wonder the world had survived their constant bickering. The scorched places of the earth bore Usil and Catha's distinctive marks.

Tessa grabbed Amity's free hand and squeezed. "And you give so much of yourself to others. Maybe that's why you don't have a replacement. No one can replace you."

"Then why have my powers been waning along with everyone else's?" Amity's frustration seeped into her tone. "There's just so much I don't understand about what's happening between me and Remy and Rom. Like why did I gain so much power from making love with Rom and Remy?"

Tessa's mouth got that wicked grin again, and even Lucy began to smile.

"I think maybe you need to tell us all about it." Lucy leaned forward, her gray eyes sparkling. "And be sure not to leave anything out."

"And you're sure this will work?"

Rom must have asked the question three times already, but Remy totally understood. He'd had trouble wrapping his head around the idea when X had first proposed it.

Now… well, he didn't think it was a downright shitty idea. But Rom did.

"I understand your reticence, Rom." Cole's voice held absolutely no impatience, no anger. "But this is what she wants and it's our duty to do what she wants."

Yeah, Remy got the whole "she's a Goddess, we do her bidding" deal. But she was *his* goddess. His and Rom's. Rom might not be fully on board with that concept yet, but Remy had no doubt he'd change his mind. He'd have to. Because Remy wasn't giving her up.

Something had happened between Rom and Amity earlier today. They'd gotten closer. Probably because they'd had sex.

And, contrary to what Rom probably thought, that wasn't a bad thing. Remy would have to make him see that.

At least they were in total agreement about how much danger they'd put Amity in. Basically none.

That possessiveness was making Rom twitchy. And when Rom got twitchy, Remy had learned to keep his own anxiety under wraps.

"If it makes any difference," X said, "I've done this before. And I'm not half bad with a sword if it comes down to a fight."

Remy didn't doubt what the Cimmerian was saying. X had a grip that spoke of sword training and a lean, muscled body. Of course, the guy owned a bakery—a high-end, world-famous bakery, but still, the guy made cupcakes.

His brother, Cal, had the air of a man who wouldn't be afraid to kill you if you looked at him wrong. And Cal had the utmost faith in his brother.

"So we're just going to walk into the dream plane and confront Charun?" Rom's tone held a shitload of disbelief, but the look he shot at Remy held much, much more. "And no one else thinks this is a catastrophe waiting to happen?"

Rom caught Remy's gaze and held it, but Remy wasn't backing down. This plan was their best option. The faster Rom realized that, the faster they could get it over with.

Rom must have sensed his thoughts because his cousin sighed and started to pace along the back wall. "Fine." The word sounded like he'd bit it off. "Then what about Kari? We can't let the *Mal* get away with this. They're after *us*. They need to be shut down, now, before they get bolder."

"We know that." Cole's expression showed no surprise, no shock. "We're working on it."

Cole glanced at the two men to his left. The older one with the scruffy brown hair and five o'clock shadow had intense green eyes that missed nothing. Rom figured that was a good thing for a tracker. He didn't look dangerous, but he didn't look like he'd be an easy mark either.

The other guy, the dark-haired one who looked to be around Rom's age... This one was dangerous. Built like a brick shithouse, the guy exuded menace from the tats on his muscle-bound arms to thighs the size of tree trunks.

Kyle Rossini was the king's lead assassin, a job he apparently took to heart because he looked ready to murder at the hint of a gesture from Cole. Dangerous seemed like too tame a word for the guy, but that didn't mean Remy and Rom couldn't take him.

"We've suspected for a while that the *Mal* have been gearing up for something," Cole continued. "We just didn't know what until you two showed up to fulfill a hundreds-of-years-old prophecy. We get that they want your power. What we can't figure out is how the *Mal* knew to target Amity."

Cole paused but he didn't have to continue. Remy realized where this was going.

"Because someone's feeding them information," he said. "Someone's been watching Amity."

Cole nodded. "That would be my guess."

"But how'd they know how to find her?" Rom asked the question aloud but he'd already come up with the answer. "They were with the demon the night of the attack. We missed them. *Gods dammit.*"

Remy wanted to pound his fist into something. How the fuck had they missed that? Sonuva—

"I'd cut yourselves some slack before you take responsibility for this." The *sicari*, Kyle, finally opened his mouth. He hadn't said a word the entire time and his voice pulled Remy's attention. "You were a little busy killing a *tukhulkha* demon. Nice job, by the way."

"Thanks." Remy looked at Cole. "How do we get her back?" The guy was king, after all. Maybe he had some bright idea—

"You don't." Cole held up one hand before Rom could break in. "You two shouldn't go anywhere near the *Mal*. It'd be like offering you up on a silver platter, and we don't want to give them any help finding you. Kaisie will find Kari. Kyle and the *sicari* will bring her back."

Remy wanted to argue and he felt Rom's angry frustration mirror his own. He had to bite back the snarl building in his chest at the tone of command in Cole's voice. He might be the *lucani* king, but they weren't his subjects.

Except technically, they were.

Fuck.

And he couldn't argue with Cole's logic.

"You two are going with Amity to Cimmeria." Cole continued on in the same calm tone of voice, though he had to realize Rom wanted to chew the furniture. "She needs you with her. And so does Cat."

Gods damn right, Amity needed them. And, if the prophecy was correct, so did Cat.

Still, this mess with the *Mal* was theirs. They would be the ones to clean it up.

But they couldn't be two places at once, and neither one of them wanted to let Amity out of their sight.

Cole turned to Kyle, who hadn't taken his eyes away from Remy or Rom the entire time. Remy thought the guy didn't like them. Put enough alpha males together in one room and, sooner or later, they'd try to kill each other.

Instead, Kyle shocked the shit out of both of them.

"Cat's my daughter."

Remy's mouth fell open for several seconds before he closed it. Holy shit. No wonder the guy looked tense enough to chew nails.

"I will kill anyone who tries to harm her and I would give my life for her," Kyle continued. "So would her other father and her mother and every member of this den. But there are only two men who were *born* to fulfill a prophecy that's directly linked to her. Apparently you two are it. I will do whatever it takes to get you to stay. I'll beg if I have to. My daughter means the world to me. She needs you here."

Remy wanted to accuse Kyle of hitting below the belt with that one. The *sicari* knew their story, knew what had happened to their families. Pleading for them to stay because of his daughter… that was almost like saying Bambi's mother would get to live if they stayed behind to protect her.

But Remy also understood. If his brother was alive… If Rom's sisters had lived, he knew they would've done anything for them.

Remy glanced at Rom and knew exactly what his cousin was thinking.

Baciame il culo.

"You don't have to be on your own anymore," Cole added, dangling the most tempting carrot in his arsenal. "Not if you don't want to be. You are members of this den, just as your parents were before they left. They did what they felt they needed to do to protect you. I understand that and I will never hold it against them or you. But now you need us and we need you. Let us help. Come home."

Chapter 12

KYLE OPENED THE DOOR to the small house a short walk from the community center and practically smack in the middle of the den.

"I know it's not real big but it's one of the only houses in the den that's empty at the moment." Kyle waved them in then handed the key to Rom. "You won't be bothered, and the fridge and cupboard are stocked." Kyle turned and bowed. "Lady Amity. Sleep well. We'll see you in the morning. We hope Kaisie will have a lead by then."

With a nod to Remy and another to Rom, Kyle left, leaving silence behind.

Amity's gaze flitted though the cozy little house, checking out the comfortable looking furniture in the living area, the small, wood dining table and the tiny kitchen to the right.

At the back, she saw two doors that she assumed led to the bedrooms. She really hoped she wouldn't be sleeping in one of them alone.

She didn't want to sleep alone. Worry about Kari made her stomach tighten into a ball. She knew her twin hadn't been taken to Aitás, because she still *felt* Kari in that place inside where she held her sister. If Kari had been taken off their plane, she would know.

She didn't think the *Mal* would hurt Kari. She didn't think they'd dare.

But Kari had a way of pissing people off. And not knowing when to keep her mouth shut.

And maybe you're not giving Kari enough credit.

Her twin had been known to talk her way out of any number of sticky situations. It would take much more than a simple kidnapping to make her cower in a corner like a frightened child.

"They won't hurt her. She's too valuable."

Rom's voice drew her out of her thoughts and her gaze automatically sought his. The steady rumble of his voice, the way he held her gaze without faltering, the way he held his body straight, as if he could stop an army onslaught by himself... She felt her lips curve up at the corners, and finally she let herself smile at him.

"I know you're right. Of course you're right. I was thinking the same thing. Kari's strong. She'll get through this. She may actually be able to talk herself out of it. Kari can charm blood from a stone."

Strong arms encircled her from behind and she let her head fall back against Remy's firm chest as her hands gripped his forearms. Such strength in the firm muscles under her fingers. So much heat seeping into her body from his.

Tight muscles relaxed as Remy drew her closer. The fear for her sister's safety remained a steady beat in the back of her mind, but she knew she could do nothing about Kari's situation at this moment.

She needed to clear her head so she could think straight tomorrow. She needed to speak to Charun about his desire to leave his post and destroy the gate to the Underworld, allowing the souls of the dead to wander through as well.

Most of those souls you wouldn't have to worry about. There were some, though, who should never be allowed to see the light of the sun again.

She took a deep breath and felt Remy's arms tighten as his lips pressed against the sensitive skin behind her ear.

Arching her neck, she kept her eyes open, watching Rom's reaction with a fast-moving lust rushing through her veins. His expression showed nothing at all. Stoic described the man perfectly. Beneath the exterior, however, she felt the raging emotions he kept so well hidden.

Today had been pretty much a train wreck for all of them.

Remy understood. She needed him. She needed them. And they needed her. They needed to drown themselves in sensation and be taken out of reality for however long they could manage to hold the rest of the world at bay.

The thick ridge of Remy's erection pulsed with heat against her lower back and she pressed into him, trying to get closer.

Rom's gaze dropped to where Remy's hand had spread across her stomach, the tips of his fingers brushing the top of her mound. She gasped in a breath, her lungs suddenly having to work much harder. And when Remy bared his teeth and nipped the curve of her shoulder, her knees went weak and she let her head fall back to rest on his shoulder.

She refused to close her eyes, though it became harder to hold them open. Rom remained on the other side of the room, unmoving. She willed him to look at her and got her wish when he lifted his gaze.

"I'm not sure I can give you what you want right now, Amity."

She felt Remy's split-second hesitation before he moved the hand on her stomach lower. Each centimeter he got closer to touching the center of her desire, the harder it became for her to breathe.

And the harder the lines of Rom's face became. He wasn't unaffected by the scene before him but he was fighting his desire to join them. She didn't understand why.

Reaching one hand behind her to curve around Remy's neck, she held out the other to Rom. "I only need you to be here. To want me."

She couldn't disguise the need in her voice, the note of pleading, as she sucked in a quiet gasp. She realized Remy had frozen behind her.

Damn it. She hadn't meant to slight Remy in any way. She tightened her grip on him, her nails scraping against his skin, raising goose bumps and causing him to shudder. He needed to know he was equally desired, equally wanted.

She probably should be ashamed of her weakness, of how much she wanted them. Her body had never responded to anyone the way it did to these two men. Her eyelids fluttered closed as she soaked in the sensation of Remy's hands on her body, then she forced them open to stare at Rom again.

The intensity of his gaze burned as he stared into her eyes. She willed him to come to her, to join them. But he refused to move.

Fine. She could play dirty when she needed to.

"Remy—"

"Shh." He spoke directly into her, so quietly she didn't even think Rom could hear him. "I'm right here with you, babe."

His words acted like an aphrodisiac. She didn't think she'd ever heard anything whispered to her with such passion before, with such raw want.

Before, most Etruscan men spoke to her with such reverence that passion was almost an afterthought. And *eteri* men never connected with her the way she needed them to.

Putting her hand over the one Remy held on her stomach, she pushed his hand lower, a centimeter at a time. But instead of angling his hand between her thighs, she moved him down to her thighs, covered by her silk skirt.

She knew Remy understood what she wanted when he continued the downward slide to the hem. Since she wasn't wearing stockings, he brushed against bare skin as he pushed his fingers beneath the skirt then began to tunnel back up.

Pulling her skirt up, as well.

Each inch of skin Remy exposed tightened at the brush of cooler air even as it sizzled at his touch. She held Rom's gaze as long as she could before his dropped to watch Remy's hand.

Her stomach muscles contracted at the desire that transformed Rom's face from expressionless to pure carnality. Heat drenched her sex, and moisture coated her slick lower lips until her panties clung to her folds. Every time she took a breath, she could smell her own arousal.

With their heightened sense of smell, Remy and Rom had to know how excited she was.

But Remy continued his glacial pace, even though she felt his heart pounding against her back at a gallop and the rush of his breath across her neck.

Her thighs shook as he stroked along the skin, the roughness of his fingers inciting her passion to higher levels.

He'd nearly reached the thin silk of her underwear, and she found herself holding her breath as the inferno-hot passions of the men battered against her senses from all angles. Her breath stuck in her throat as Remy slid one finger beneath her panties, only to pull away and trail his fingers back down her thigh.

She moaned her complaint, but it fell on deaf ears as Remy breathed out a hard laugh and let his fingers fall a little farther down her leg.

"So fucking soft." Remy's voice had her sheath contracting with a spasm. "I'm going to lay you on that couch and put my mouth on your pussy very soon. Then I'm going to lick you until you come."

She nearly came just from the sound of his voice and those provocative words. Each one caused her body to tighten and release until her clit throbbed.

Opening her eyes—not having realized she'd closed them—she found herself staring at Rom's chest. He'd moved closer, stealthy as a shadow, and now stood only inches away.

Her hands flexed as her gaze dropped to where she'd dug her nails into Remy's arm, wrapped around her waist. She was surprised he wasn't bleeding, her nails were dug that deeply into his skin. He didn't even seem to notice.

Rom's hand moved into view, and she watched him reach for her shirt. As Remy's hand moved back up her thigh, Rom's began to unbutton her blouse. But he wasn't nearly as patient as Remy. Rom's large fingers bullied the buttons from their holes, working them through with an urgency that made him work for each breath he took.

As Rom pulled the shirt from the waistband of her skirt, Remy finally slid his fingers beneath her panties and touched her clit.

She tried to cry out but she couldn't seem to make a sound. Her eyes closed again as Remy slid his fingers through the slickness easing from her pussy, and Rom spread her shirt wide before putting his hands on her breasts.

Kneading the soft mounds with strong hands, Rom plumped and cupped her in his palms while he used his fingers to pluck at her nipples.

Electric flashes of sensation accompanied each twist of his fingers, every hard tug of the sensitive tips. She found herself falling into a haze of sensuality that she had no desire to rise out of.

"That's it." Remy strung a line of kisses along her shoulders as he used both hands to lift her skirt to her waist and ease her panties down her legs. "Let go."

When the bit of silk fell in a puddle on the floor, Remy found the catch and the zipper at her side and her skirt followed seconds later.

Her naked skin barely had time to catch a chill before the furnace-hot heat emanating from both men surrounded her. Between Rom's hands on her breasts and Remy's on her hips, she thought she might combust.

Leaning forward without conscious thought, she used her teeth and tongue on Rom's nipples, biting into his flesh. Not to hurt. Never to hurt. Just enough to make him hiss in a breath between his teeth.

Her ass pressed even tighter against Remy's erection and now he groaned.

"God damn, you've got a pretty ass."

Remy's low growl made her wiggle that ass against him as Rom sank one hand into her hair to press her mouth harder against his chest.

"And a gorgeous fucking mouth. Gods, I love your mouth."

The hard edge of Rom's tone made her sex moisten and, with unerring instinct, Remy worked his hands between her legs and slid two fingers into her aching heat.

She moaned, the sound muffled by Rom's chest. Remy began to pump his fingers, the rough texture of them providing a delicious friction.

She wanted to sink inside these men, let them take care of her as she fell headlong into their desire and let it consume her.

Surrounded by the blazing fury of their emotions, Amity felt like an incandescent bulb, burning from the inside out.

Someone threaded his hand through her hair and tugged her head back as Rom's mouth covered hers. His lips parted and he slid his tongue into her mouth. Conquering, invading, seducing.

Her arms slid around his shoulders as she hung between them. Remy's fingers stroked her into an ever-deepening pool of sheer bliss while Rom's tongue mimicked Remy's movements below.

Reality fell away and she barely noticed. All she knew was the scent and feel of the men surrounding her.

Her hands slid into Rom's hair, tightening on the short, silky strands until she was sure it had to hurt. Rom continued to kiss her, seducing her with his mouth.

Suddenly Remy withdrew his fingers and the loss made her cry out, but Rom's mouth captured the sound so only a hint of it escaped.

She wanted to turn, to reach for Remy, to make him continue, but Rom refused to release her. Instead, he kissed her with more force, his fingers pinching her nipples harder, just to the point of pain. But the pain made her want more.

Her heart thudding, she bit at his tongue, not knowing whether she was trying to get him to pull away or if she wanted him to kiss her even harder.

One hand reached behind her for Remy, and she thought she may have brushed against him but she couldn't be sure because Rom wrapped an arm around her waist and hauled her up against his body. She felt the smooth texture of his suit pants on her thighs, the starched cotton of his shirt against her breasts as he crushed her to him.

Allowing him to take her weight, her legs wrapped around his waist and she arched her back so she could rub her aching pussy against the ridge of his erection.

Vaguely, she heard the sound of a zipper releasing behind her but it was an almost abstract thought. Because all she knew now was the need to be filled.

Rom's tongue in her mouth simply wasn't enough. She tried to draw away, to put a little distance between them so she could get his shirt off, but he refused to release her. He had one hand tangled in her hair, holding her where he wanted her.

Frustration added to the desire, making her body ache all over. A delicious, wonderful ache.

She tugged on his hair, trying to get him to pull back, but she was like a kitten batting at a bowling ball. He was immovable.

He kissed her like he couldn't breathe without her, like he couldn't bear to release her mouth for more than a second, and she felt his desire for her like a blowtorch on the inside of her skin. So—

Rom ripped his mouth away from hers. Her eyes flew open and rose to meet his. She felt so weak-kneed, she would have fallen if Rom hadn't held her so tight. Then he pushed her away from his body.

For a split second, she didn't understand, until Remy slipped his arms around her and gathered her against his naked chest.

"Let's go find a bed, my lady." His smile made the scars on his face twist and pull but she didn't see deformity. She saw such strength.

Cupping his jaw in her hands, she pressed her mouth to the scarred flesh on his cheek. She felt him stiffen but didn't sense any embarrassment or a need to pull away. She sensed he felt only desire at her touch.

The tip of his thickly erect cock brushed against her hip as he walked with her in his arms. Instead of watching where they were going, she turned her head so she could get her mouth on his skin.

Blessed Mother Goddess, he tasted salty and male and went straight to her already dizzy head like Fuflun's wine. She was drunk on Remy's scent. She liked it.

As she spread her hands across his back then scraped her nails on his skin, he took her through one of the doors at the back of the house.

Remy didn't bother to turn on a light and when he placed her on the bed, she had a few seconds to see why.

Moonlight streamed through the skylights above the queen-size bed, limning everything in silver. Not that there was much in the room besides a bed, a chest on the far wall, and a ladder-back chair in the corner beside the two windows that were covered with drapes.

Lifting onto her elbows, she had a second to smile up at Remy before he dropped to his knees by the side of the bed, spread her legs open and pressed his mouth to her sex.

She cried out in sharp ecstasy as his lips sucked at her clit. Falling onto her back, she tried to concentrate on the sensations spreading through her lower body. Remy sucked on the tiny organ until she arched her back and reached for his head to hold him to her.

So good. So absolutely incredibly amazing. Every nerve ending in her body tingled and her womb contracted as he pushed her closer to orgasm. Almost there. Almost—

She cried out as Remy pulled away. Her fingers tightened in his hair before she let go, not wanting to hurt him. She barely had time to think before Rom reached under her arms and pulled her across the bed. She slid easily across the smooth surface of the quilt until her head hung slightly over the side of the mattress.

And she stared directly at Rom's cock.

Oh, yes, please.

Her gaze shifted to his as she smiled before opening her mouth. Her tongue slipped from her lips to lick from his balls, up the shaft, to the tip. Since the old-fashioned four-poster bed sat higher than a modern frame, her head was at the perfect height for what he wanted. What she wanted.

Grasping his cock at the root, she tilted the head down until she could take it in her mouth. She closed her eyes as he thrust forward, the smooth, hot surface of his cock sliding over her tongue. His groan caused her sex to clench and her hips twisted as Rom eased his cock in and out of her mouth. Each careful thrust built that ache between her legs until she could barely stand it.

She writhed, begging Remy with each movement of her body to come back to her. Every second he delayed stoked the ache that much higher.

As she sucked Rom, finally, *finally*, she felt the bed dip. Her breath caught and Rom paused to give her a moment to anticipate what Remy was going to do.

But she didn't want to stop. She wanted to be taken out of herself and transported. She could feel the looming sense of obliterating ecstasy just out of reach.

Sucking Rom deeper, she felt Remy's hands push between her thighs, spreading her open and leaving her exposed for several seconds. Her excitement built almost to fever pitch, and her free hand slid down her body, stopping to pull at her nipples for a second before reaching the small patch of hair on her mound and then, finally, the slick lips of her sex.

"Go ahead, sweetheart," Remy said. "Show me how you like it."

His voice struck a chord somewhere deep in her body and when her finger brushed against her clit, she shuddered with the sensation. And pulled back until only the tip of Rom's cock remained in her mouth.

As her tongue played over the silken head, Remy's hands tightened on her thighs. She couldn't tell if he was watching her hands or her mouth, but figured it might be a little of both.

Rom's taste flooded her mouth, his scent clung to her, in her nose, her throat, deep in her chest. When he reached down with one hand to play with her nipples, she felt the bed shift beneath her and she shivered with anticipation.

And when Remy's hands slid around her thighs to beneath her ass, she very nearly came.

She felt the rough hairs on his hard thighs tickle the backs of her legs just before Remy pressed the tip of his cock to her entrance. Moaning, she felt Rom go very still as he groaned.

Seconds passed as she waited for Remy to penetrate her, only to moan again when he began a slow, teasing glide through her sensitive lips. Her pussy ached to be filled, but Remy merely tormented her with his proximity, with his heat.

Abandoning her clit, she reached for Remy but he caught her hand and laced their fingers together. Frustrated and aching, she tossed her head, causing Rom to pull out of her mouth just before Remy pulled her onto his shaft, burying himself deep inside her.

Moaning out a heartfelt "Yes," she arched to take him deeper as he used his hands to pull her on and off his cock. He kept the rhythm deliberately slow, drawing out each movement until she could barely breathe.

Every subtle shift of flesh on flesh, every one of Remy's harsh exhales sent magic racing through her veins. Yet it still wasn't enough to send her over the edge.

Then the mattress dipped at her head and her eyes flew open. Rom lifted her off her back without dislodging her from Remy's lap. The angle of penetration deepened and she arched her back so she could lift her hips to ride him.

Rom's hands curled over her shoulders, resting there for several seconds as she worked her body up and down. Then she felt Rom move closer, the hair on his chest just brushing her back.

"Will you take us both, Amity? At the same time? Remy in your pussy and me tight in your ass?"

Sinking down onto Remy as far as she could go, she stopped and paused, held him inside her body as her eyes adjusted to the dark, and she looked into the mirror hanging above the chest. She shivered. The image was so carnal, it made her break out in a sweat.

Remy's long, lean back gleamed in the moonlight, her hands pale against his skin. She lifted one hand to sift through his hair, letting the silky strands fall back against his skin. As her gaze drifted up, she saw Rom staring back at her in the mirror, saw him move even closer to her.

"We'll make it good," Rom whispered in her ear. "We'll make you come until you can't move. And then we'll make you come again. We want you so damn much. Remy can only hold on for so long. You wreak havoc on his control. And if I'm being honest, I have to admit you blow mine out of the fucking water. I look at you, and it's like a fist in the gut how much I want you."

She shuddered at the raw emotion in Rom's voice. At the unvarnished lust. And the thread of gentleness that made her blink back sudden tears.

As if he'd scented the tears, Remy turned to nuzzle his cheek against her hair, his hands kneading her thighs.

"You're so tight around me now, just think how much tighter you'll be when Rom takes you too."

"Yes."

She barely heard her voice in her own head, then suddenly she was moving. Rom pulled back as Remy untangled her legs from around his waist and lay back.

Though she'd done this before—she *had* lived through the Roman Empire, after all, and the nineteenth century in England had been so much more debauched than one might think—she hadn't had the reaction she was having now.

She was so excited she could barely breathe.

Because the men who held her between them meant so much more to her than any other man ever had. Even though she knew she wouldn't be able to hold onto them forever.

They could never belong to her. Not truly.

Shoving those thoughts away, she sprawled full length along Remy's body, her legs spread over his hips. Her hands came up to cup his face as his gripped her hips and held her steady as he began to thrust in a slow, measured pace. Each stroke became a lesson in delayed gratification.

Behind her, she felt Rom's presence, the bulk of his body, but couldn't see him as she lowered her mouth to Remy's.

Their lips met in a rush of heat that stole her breath and caused her body to tighten around him until he moaned into her mouth. His hips picked up the pace, filling her, sending waves of heat up her spine to spread throughout her body.

She reveled in the sensations, trying to keep her emotions in check before she blurted out something she couldn't—or wouldn't—take back.

With a groan, Remy tore his mouth away from hers, sank his hand into her hair and pressed her head down. She turned her face into his neck as he spread his legs even farther, widening her even more. Then the bed shimmied, and she shuddered in anticipation.

Remy's hands moved up her back to her shoulders as Rom

grabbed her hips, stilling her motion and making her pussy clench around Remy's cock.

"Ah, fuck, that feels amazing." Remy hissed in a breath between his teeth. "Hurry the fuck up, Rom. I'm not gonna last."

"No fucking way." Rom's hands began a slow massage of her rear, spreading her cheeks then pressing them together again. "I'm not rushing this."

She wanted to order him to hurry but she knew it wouldn't make any difference to Rom. He would do what he wanted. He would never hurt her, but then, this was such a wonderful torture, she didn't want him to stop.

So she opened her mouth over the warm skin of Remy's shoulder and let her teeth sink into the flesh. Remy's head tilted back and his hips thrust up, stretching her even more.

As cooler air caressed her, Rom began to spread a thick layer of gel around the sensitive pucker of her anus. Where he'd gotten it, she had no idea and didn't really care at the moment.

Amity realized she was holding her breath as he began to work his thumb into the tight opening and she turned her mouth away from Remy before she bit too hard. His body had enough scars. She didn't want to add to them.

Her body tensed against the small intrusion of Rom's thumb and she forced herself to relax, to let him in. She wanted this. Wanted the burn, the pleasure-pain that came from the dual penetration. That sense of overwhelming fullness.

Mostly, though, she wanted them.

She pushed back and his thumb entered her all the way, filling her but not enough.

Her pussy ached for friction, the burn in her ass not enough to send her over the edge. She needed more.

"Rom, please."

"I'm planning to," he murmured. "But not just yet."

Remy shifted, and his cock eased deeper as Rom's thumb pulled back. When she started to wiggle in an attempt to get Remy to give her some kind of relief, Rom pulled out completely.

Bereft and feeling as if she was losing control of herself, she wiggled, trying to get Remy to move, to make Rom hurry.

Neither man obliged her fully, yet they gave her just enough for her to cry out for more.

Remy eased back slowly, while Rom surprised a moan out of her by using two fingers this time.

Yes. Better.

The burn intensified as the men began a contrasting rhythm. She wanted to move too but Remy had one arm tight around her shoulders, the other clamped around her waist.

Her breasts ached, crushed against his chest. Her fingers flexed into the quilt, unable to move, muscles tight with desire and a feeling that went beyond anticipation into pure greed.

An inarticulate cry crossed her lips as Rom's fingers thrust and retreated while Remy held still. It cost Remy to do it. He shook beneath her, his cock throbbing in her sheath as her back passage loosened a bit more.

She didn't know how long Rom fucked her with his fingers. Time had become inconsequential. All that mattered was when he'd finally give her what she wanted.

"Such a beautiful ass."

His words barely made sense, though the tone caused her to struggle against Remy's hold.

"Mine now."

Rom's fingers disappeared and, through the haze of her arousal, she knew… She knew…

Hands spread her cheeks and the blunt tip of Rom's cock pressed against the opening his fingers had just left and she seemed to melt into Remy as Rom pressed relentlessly forward.

The sense of fullness increased until she thought she'd explode like a bottle of soda that'd been shaken too much.

The hot, thick rod forged into her, spreading her, spreading heat until the pain became almost unbearable. Almost. But even then it wasn't enough. She needed more.

When she thought Rom couldn't possibly get any deeper, he paused, his hands tightening on her ass until she couldn't distinguish that lick of pain from the other, deeper throb inside.

She waited for Rom to say something, anything, as they held so still. But it was Remy who finally whispered in her ear.

"Now we make you scream."

Rom's first retreat made her whimper as two cocks abraded the delicate tissues of her sex and her ass. Delicious sensations flooded her body as her men began a rough, alternating rhythm.

Slow at first, too slow.

"Faster. Please. Remy, please… Rom. Harder."

She had no idea if she was making any kind of sense because the men ignored her, keeping their own pace that was designed to drive her mad.

And it wasn't going to be that far a trip. She'd already lost all sense of reality. She felt only their skin, breathed in only their scents. Heard only their voices as they told her how beautiful she was and how good she felt. And how they couldn't hold on much longer.

But still they continued to move inside her.

She turned, seeking something, and Remy's mouth was there, kissing her. Biting at her lips, sliding his tongue along hers. He kissed her like he was losing control and he needed to anchor himself. He groaned into her mouth and his hips began to move faster, forcing Rom to increase his pace as well.

Behind her, Rom bent closer, his lips pressing against her spine, his fingers petting her ass.

Then Rom lifted his head. "Now, Amity," he growled as he slid one hand up her back to sift through her hair and tug on the ends. Another sensation to send electricity through her body, straight to her clit. "I want you to come now."

At the same time, Remy shifted beneath her, pressing his cock higher and hitting that internal spot that lit her on fire.

Her orgasm broke inside her, beginning at her clit and sinking deeper until her pussy tightened around Remy and her ass clenched on Rom.

Crying out, she melted against Remy as convulsion after convulsion racked her. As her womb tightened almost to the point of pain.

Rom was next to break. She heard his harsh shout and then felt the heated pulse of his seed flooding out of him and into her. He froze, his hips plastered to her ass as his cock throbbed.

And still Remy continued to thrust. Once, twice, again and again. Drawing out her climax until she was so drained, she felt light-headed.

When she thought she might actually pass out from the pleasure, Remy arched, sinking as deep as he could then released with a guttural groan.

Then the magic they created together broke over her with the force of a hurricane, sinking into her skin, into her bones and her blood and filling her with strength.

Left her feeling like she could heal every sick and injured person in the hospital. After she had taken a nap, of course.

With a groan, Rom pulled away first, going slowly. She gasped at his cock moving again through those now ultra-sensitive tissues.

The bed shook as he stood, but not before he brushed the hair from her face and gave her the gentlest kiss he'd ever given her.

His fingers trailed over her cheek before he walked away. She was too tired to ask where he was going but she could only hope he would return soon.

Then Remy shifted her up his body until he slipped from her sheath and rolled until they both lay on their sides.

Drowsily, she opened her eyes and stared into his beautiful blue eyes.

"You should get some sleep." Remy smiled at her, looking pretty sleepy himself.

Snuggling closer, she tucked her head under his chin. "I will. If you two do."

"We plan to." Rom walked back into the room at that moment. She felt the bed dip, and a large hand moved her leg before Rom began to clean her. "Let's just make you a little more comfortable first."

"I'm comfortable right here."

She refused to think about how many more times she would get to lie here with them.

"Pick her up," she heard Remy say. "I'll change these sheets."

There was a pause before Rom slid his arms around her and when he lifted her against his chest, she felt his sudden reluctance. And the briefest flash of regret.

She struggled against the lethargy that was taking her under, wanted to know what had made him feel like this.

"Rom?"

She wanted to see him but he pressed his hand against her head to keep her from moving.

"Everything's fine, Amity. Go to sleep now."

Whatever emotion he'd felt was gone now and she sighed because she really couldn't keep her eyes open anymore.

Chapter 13

PERRIN KNEW AS SOON as she opened her eyes that she was back in that dream. The one where she'd met Karn.

She'd been so tired after her session with Amity that she'd wanted to go straight home to bed. But she'd forced herself to stop for takeout at the Chinese place in West Reading. She was a regular there and the teenage girl behind the counter smiled at her as she walked in.

"Wow, you're looking much better today." Su handed her a menu over the counter, unabashedly checking out Perrin's scars. "I guess you started the treatments with that medical atheist, huh?"

Perrin stifled a laugh. Though her parents' accents were hard to understand, Su spoke perfect English. But she was still an American teenager who hated school and would rather be at the mall shopping with her friends than working in a takeout restaurant.

"She's a medical aesthetician and yes, I did." She reached self-consciously for her cheek then forced herself not to attempt to hide her scars.

"Well, she must work miracles."

Perrin had wanted to smile for the girl because she knew Su must be exaggerating. Not that Perrin had looked in a mirror after leaving the hospital. Amity had warned her she might not see an immediate change in her appearance. But over time, she'd promised that the severity of the scars would reduce.

Today had been only her third treatment. Of course the healing would have been minimal, if it'd affected her scars at all.

The only reason she'd agreed to let Amity try this treatment was because she'd told her it was experimental. How she reacted to the treatment could be useful in how it was applied to others.

So really, Perrin was doing Amity a favor.

Yeah, right.

Deep inside, where her hope had gone into hibernation, Perrin knew she was hoping for a miracle. That one day, she'd no longer look like Frankenstein's monster after the villagers had torched him.

Which was why she hadn't looked in the mirror yet. She didn't want to be disappointed.

"I don't believe you will be. Your scars are noticeably better today."

She gasped and turned toward the sound of the voice coming from behind her.

He was there, in the shadows on the trees. No, not trees this time. Pillars.

Karn leaned against a marble pillar, one of several that sprouted from a cracked marble floor. Vegetation spread across the floor, flowering plants she'd never seen before growing over the ruins of what looked like an ancient temple. Like one you'd see in a History Channel program on Rome or Greece.

"Where am I?" She heard the demand in her tone and wasn't surprised when he didn't respond right away. She had the feeling he wasn't used to people demanding things from him.

His head cocked to the side and she sucked in another breath. She hadn't let herself dwell on how handsome he was. He was a figment of her imagination. A creation of her mind.

Although, if she'd actually thought about coming up with the perfect man to dream about, he wouldn't have been it.

His eyebrows lifted and the look he gave her was filled with arrogant disbelief.

As if he'd read her mind.

Which was so stupid. Of course he knew what she thought. He was her.

"You're in my domain." He spoke suddenly, pushing away from the column against which he'd stood, and began walking toward her. "This is where I live. I wanted you to see."

She forced herself to hold her ground and was absurdly proud when she looked up into his eyes when only inches separated them.

"Of course you did," she said. "It has nothing to do with the fact that this is my dream and *I* wanted to see where *you* lived."

Those unrelentingly straight eyebrows rose above his black eyes, and the corners of his lips twitched as if he might smile. She wanted him to smile. *Smile, damn it.*

Her mouth set in stubborn lines when he refused to obey her silent command. Christ, this was her dream. She couldn't even get her dream man to do what she wanted.

"What's wrong?" he asked. "Are you in pain?"

Out of habit, she took a moment to assess herself and found, to her complete shock, that she didn't hurt at all.

"No, I'm feeling no pain. Guess this really is a dream."

"Or maybe I took it away."

Now she laughed and the sound was so rusty, it sounded strange to her.

"Wouldn't that be wonderful if you could?"

"Who says I can't?"

"Since it's a dream, I guess anything's possible."

"Ah." Karn nodded, as if she'd confirmed something for him. "So if this is your dream, where are we exactly?"

She looked around again, trying to place the setting. Had she seen it on TV? In a movie? A book? It really didn't look familiar at all.

"Since you're having such a hard time figuring this all out," Karn waved a hand out to his side, "why don't you let me show you around a little?"

What could it hurt? "Sure. Why not?" With a wide smile that didn't hurt at all, she curved her hand around his arm just above his elbow. "Maybe I'll find out some deep dark secret about myself while we're wandering around down here. Maybe I'll have something to tell Amity at our next session. She's always asking me to talk about my feelings. Maybe I'll ask her to interpret this dream."

Karn's arm tensed beneath her hand. "Amity. How do you know Amity?"

"She's the medical aesthetician the hospital assigned to me. She's…"

Someone she trusted. And Perrin no longer trusted many people. But Amity had worked her way into that very small circle.

"I guess you could call her my friend."

Karn fell silent as they walked, staring off into the distance, allowing Perrin to stare at him. "And what hospital does she work at?"

"The Reading Hospital."

"So she's in the States, too." Karn's voice fell to a murmur, one she had to strain to hear.

Perrin shook her head as they stopped at the door of the temple. This was the weirdest freaking dream she'd ever had, more because it really didn't feel like a dream. It felt absolutely real.

"So where are we?" They'd stopped to look out over a vast plain covered by ruins as far as she could see. In the distance, she thought she saw a river and possibly mountains, but the sun had set so she couldn't really be sure. "Ancient Rome? Greece? Tunisia? I heard there are beautiful ruins in Tunisia."

"Do you like it here?" Karn stared down at her, the intensity in his gaze soon making her uncomfortable. And had his eyes actually begun to glow? How freaky was that?

She pulled her hand away from his arm and looked out over the beautiful, but desolate, landscape.

"It seems lonely."

"It has been. For far longer than you can imagine."

Was this her subconscious talking? If so, she already knew this about herself. She'd admitted it, spoken the words aloud to her therapist, cried herself to sleep thinking about it.

Why was she rehashing all this in her dreams?

Maybe because this isn't a dream.

The voice in her head wasn't hers.

With a gasp, she sat straight up in bed in the little home she rented down the street from her real home, where a work crew continued to rebuild the charred shell.

Glancing at the clock, she realized it was almost 7:30 in the morning.

Too early to call Amity at the office.

But she had to warn Amity. Had to warn her about… Karn? What about Karn?

That she'd dreamed about a man who made her feel something other than abject horror for the first time since Ralph had tried to kill her? That she thought the man wanted to harm Amity?

Amity would think she'd finally gone off the deep end. Dragging herself out of bed, she headed for the bathroom.

And nearly fell on the floor in shock as she caught sight of her face in the mirror.

Her mouth hung open, and her eyes were the size of dinner plates, which was a really stupid saying but the only one that fit at the moment.

What the hell? Was she still sleeping? Was this a dream? And if it wasn't, she really needed to talk to Amity. Right now.

<hr>

"I still think this is a monumentally bad idea."

Remy snorted at the growl in Rom's voice as he strapped a blade to his side. He checked and rechecked the binding. It'd been a while since he'd used his dad's short sword. "Yeah, well, you think any plan you didn't come up with is a monumentally bad idea. At least we're going with her."

"That was never under discussion. Of course we're going with her. I wouldn't have given a flying fuck if Cole had ordered us to stay home."

Yeah, Remy agreed silently. He would've fought Cole and his entire army tooth and nail if he'd tried to keep them from going with Amity. But Cole hadn't and that moved the guy up in Remy's estimation.

Still… "What about the other stuff, Rom? The prophecy? Have you thought about that at all?"

Remy had. Sure, he'd practically passed out last night after he'd come so damn hard he thought he might have shaken a few teeth loose. But he'd woken around 5:00 a.m., after only a few hours of sleep, and couldn't fall back to sleep because all he'd been able to do was think about that damn prophecy.

The one where they were supposed to be the guardians of the brand-spanking-new Goddess of the Moon, who just happened to be a beautiful twenty-year-old girl, who could control their ability to shift and who didn't seem to be all that hyped about her new position in life.

Couldn't say he blamed her. Seemed like the perks might be great, but the actual job required a whole hell of a lot more than they revealed during the interview process.

"No, I haven't had time to think about it."

Remy let his gaze catch Rom's and just lifted his eyebrows. Rom immediately shot him the finger.

"And now's not the time." Rom yanked a T-shirt over his head before strapping matching dagger sheaths to his forearms. "We don't have any idea what we're gonna find in this dream plane. We should talk about what the hell we're going to do if Charun actually shows up for this little powwow."

"According to Amity, he can't leave the dream plane because he isn't really there. The *Involuti* made sure he couldn't leave Aitás."

Rom loaded blades into the arm sheaths then started strapping another to his thigh. Apparently, they couldn't take guns into the dream plane, something about the chemicals being incompatible with crossing between planes.

X had told them bad things happened when you broke that rule.

Actually X had said, "You go naked. Something about the field generated by a living organism. Nothing dead will go."

Rom had just stared at the guy like he was nuts, but Remy had realized X was quoting *The Terminator* and couldn't stop laughing. Damn, he liked X. The guy was pure smart-ass.

"I still don't like it." Rom shoved another blade into his left boot. Good thing they didn't have to go through a frigging metal detector. They'd be in for a TSA cavity search.

"I know you don't. But I appreciate the fact that you're going regardless."

They both turned. Amity stood in the doorway dressed in hiking boots, well-worn jeans, and a plain gray T-shirt that managed to cling to every one of her luscious curves. She'd gathered her hair into a ponytail, revealing the fine bones of her face and emphasizing the pale cast of her skin. She looked frightened and Remy hated that.

Walking over to her, he wrapped his arms around her and dropped his mouth over hers for a hard kiss. She responded immediately, her arms circling his waist and holding tight.

He loved the way she tasted, the way she felt in his arms. The way she'd melted into them last night. The way she managed to temper Rom's morose moods. Damn it, he hated not knowing what the future would bring.

Before, he and Rom had had a purpose in life. A single goal. Kill the demon.

What the hell do we do now?

Breaking the kiss, Amity laid her head on his chest and sighed against his skin. His gaze caught Rom's and they exchanged a silent message. They didn't need to speak. They knew what the other was thinking.

Rom tried hard to control his fear for Amity, but Remy felt it eating him from the inside out. He also felt the emotions Rom tried to cast aside. The hopeful ones. The ones that revealed emotion. The ones he thought made him vulnerable.

Remy understood. He did. He just didn't agree with Rom trying to submerge his emotions, rather than dealing with them.

Remy was sick of living day to day, on the run and always looking over his shoulder.

He wanted a home. He wanted to be part of the *lucani* community, to fight for something other than vengeance. Wanted to come home at night and share a bed with Amity. And he wanted Rom to be there with them.

A subtle vibration against his hip caught his attention and Amity shifted against him, pulling her cell phone from her back pocket.

She frowned as she noted the name on the screen.

"Perrin, is that you? Is everything okay?"

Rom's stress level spiked and Remy shot him a look before the name registered. Perrin was Amity's burn patient.

"Perrin, slow down, honey. I'm not quite sure what you're trying to say."

Amity fell silent and Remy was able to hear the other woman's frightened voice coming through the cell.

"I had a dream last night that I'm not sure was a dream. I know how that sounds but I— Something happened and I don't know how to explain it and I don't know who else I can talk to. Because… Because something happened yesterday. Something happened after our session. Or during it. I just… I think we need to talk. In person. So you can see for yourself."

Amity's face continued to pale until her skin looked like the color of milk. But her voice remained calm when she spoke. "Of course. We can meet. I can be in my office—"

"I don't think we should meet in your office. I think there might be too many questions. Is there somewhere else?"

"Yes. Absolutely. Let me give you the address."

As Amity recited an address somewhere in the city of Reading, Rom began to shake his head, staring up at the ceiling as if praying for strength.

Remy wanted to join him but figured she didn't need both of them looking like they were about to start chewing the walls.

"Give me an hour, Perrin, but I promise I'll be there."

"I just need you to see what's going on. To talk about this. I don't want to cause any trouble—"

"Perrin." Amity's tone soothed. "Everything's going to be fine. We'll figure this out, and I'll see you soon."

"Okay. Okay, I just… I need to talk to you."

"And I won't let you down. I'll be there, Perrin. I'll see you in an hour."

She hung up the phone, her gaze shifting to Remy then to Rom. "I told her I'd meet her at Sal's. Remy," she handed over her phone, "would you please use my phone to call Sal and tell him we'll be there in thirty minutes?"

He took the phone without comment because he knew Rom was about to stick his foot in his mouth and tell her no way.

But his cousin surprised the shit out of him. "I'll contact Cole, let him know we're not going today." Then Rom reached for her and pressed a kiss to her forehead. "Perrin will be okay. We'll make sure of it."

Remy heard something in Rom's voice he hadn't heard in a long time—compassion. And Remy knew it was for Perrin. Obviously something about her had struck a chord in him.

Amity nodded, but she didn't look convinced. "I'm just going to… I should…"

Rom took her by the shoulders and moved her a couple of steps closer to the nearest chair. "You should sit for a few minutes. Let Remy and me do what we have to do, then we'll be on the road."

She nodded again and sat, worrying her bottom lip between her teeth.

Rom gave Remy a quick nod then headed for the front door, pulling the door closed behind him as he pulled his phone from his back pocket.

Remy turned his attention to Amity's phone for Sal's number. He wondered when the other shoe was going to drop. Remy called Sal, who grunted his assent after Remy explained why he was calling then hung up as if he'd been in the middle of something and too busy to talk.

"All right." Rom came back in the house and headed straight for Amity. He reached for her, taking her hands and pulling her to her feet. "I brought Cole up to speed. Told him we're leaving now. He said he'll send a *lucani* guard to Sal's if we decide we need one. All we have to do is call."

Remy had no doubt Cole would come through if they needed him. Nice to know they had an army waiting at their backs if they needed one.

"Remy, you get Sal?"

He nodded. "We're good to go."

"Then let's move. I want to be in place before Perrin gets there."

Amity's attention refocused on Rom. "You think this is a setup?"

That's exactly what Remy was thinking, and he knew Rom was too. Not that Perrin was in on the deal. Just that she was being used to get to Amity.

Which just meant they should leave her behind with the *lucani* until they knew more.

But Remy wasn't foolish enough to suggest it and, for once, Rom didn't try to tell her what to do.

"I'm not sure what I think yet," was Rom's mostly diplomatic response. "We can talk in the car."

But they didn't. The twenty-minute ride was silent. Amity stared out the passenger window, Remy kept his gaze fluid, making sure no one followed them. Rom's usually strict regard for all rules of cautious driving had given way to a lead foot.

By the time they reached the nondescript townhouse on the south side of Reading, Remy's hands hurt from being clenched into fists and he had the start of a pretty decent headache. Rom's jaw looked ready to crack, and Amity had worried her bottom lip almost bloody.

Damn. God damn it. She was empathic. She was picking up their emotions, amplifying her own fears.

Shit.

With a conscious effort, he pushed back the fear. Submerged it under the fiery emotion he felt for her. Let that emotion rise up and consume him.

Could he call it love? Surely three days wasn't enough time to fall in love? Love had to build over time. Gradually. Right?

Vaffanculo, this situation was fucked up enough without him injecting emotions he had no business even considering with her.

She was a freaking goddess, for fuck's sake.

And he was a mortal *lucani*. Whose life might not even belong to him.

That damn prophecy…

Stress began to rise again, so he shoved everything but the thought of Amity out of his mind.

The way she felt in his arms. The way she looked when she came. The smile she had only for him and Rom.

He wanted that all the time. Not just for a few stolen days.

Rom opened his door and slid out, ripping Remy's attention

back to the present. Where Amity stared at him over the front seat, her lips curved in a soft smile. As if she'd read his mind.

She didn't say anything, and when Rom opened her door seconds later, she slid out silently.

He followed, making sure no one got too interested in them.

But this wasn't the type of neighborhood where people hung out on their porches and talked to each other. The houses all looked like their owners took some pride in the facades, but no longer had the money for new paint jobs or doors made in this century.

The residents probably had nine-to-five jobs, and their kids were in school. They said hi if they happened to pass you in the street but they didn't stop and they made sure their smile wasn't too friendly. They did live in the city, after all.

With Rom's hand on her elbow and Remy at her back, Amity climbed the few stairs to a house that looked just like all the rest, until you noticed the unusual decoration in the wood trim around the front door.

Protection runes. Old, powerful, and so well worked into the decoration that, unless you knew what you were looking at, you wouldn't have a clue they were there.

As they stepped onto the porch, the power emanating from the building hit him. Remy drew in a quick breath, which Rom echoed.

"Yes," Amity murmured. "Amazing, isn't it? And only noticeable to those with Etruscan blood. This building has been here for more than a century and it sits directly over the ley line that runs through the city."

"As long as it's safe." Rom reached for the bell set into the trim but Amity simply reached for the doorknob and twisted.

It opened to reveal a small hallway and a staircase that led to the second floor.

Rom entered first, holding one outspread hand behind him. Rom wanted him to keep Amity out of the house until he'd swept it.

But Amity was having none of it. She slipped by Rom and headed down the hall.

"Sal, we're here."

Remy watched Rom bite back a curse and take a few long strides to catch up with her. Luckily, Rom kept his mouth shut.

"I'm coming, I'm coming." Sal's voice drifted down from the second floor and Remy heard the light click of hooves on hardwood floors before he caught sight of the *salbinelli* heading down the stairs.

"Holy shit."

Rom's low exclamation reminded Remy that Rom hadn't met Sal yet. And Rom's expression was enough to make Remy grin.

"Dude, your mouth's hanging open." Remy leaned over and mock-whispered in his cousin's ear.

Rom shot him a burning, split-second glare before he straightened as Sal stopped in front of him.

Though Rom towered over the *salbinelli*, he bowed his head in deference.

"Aw, hell, not you, too." Sal put his hands on his hips, an unlit cigar clenched between his teeth. "Tinia's teat, I'm feeling my fucking age today. Knock it off with the wide-eyed reverence already. I'm *so* not in the mood, boy."

Remy bit back a smile as Rom's eyes widened even more before he blinked and cleared his expression as Sal stomped past him, took Amity's hand, and drew her along with him.

After a few seconds, Rom turned to Remy. "You could've warned me, *ceffo*. He's a fucking *salbinelli*."

Remy shrugged, trying to hide a smile at Rom's obviously stunned amazement. "Kinda slipped my mind with everything going on."

Which was the absolute truth. But still cool to see the usually unflappable Rom knocked on his ass by someone two feet shorter and half goat.

Rom shook his head and his mouth began to curve in a grin. "Holy shit, he's a *salbinelli*."

"Yes, he is. And he's a pretty decent guy, but let's not keep him waiting. I don't want to end up with a tail."

—⁓—

Rom tried not to stare at Sal and he thought he succeeded. Mostly.

Still, it was hard to keep from watching a guy who had goat legs trot around the kitchen making coffee.

The New York accent had been a surprise, but after a few minutes Rom thought he'd caught an underlying accent, and he was tying his brain in knots trying to identify it. He couldn't let it go, trying to puzzle out what it was, but reality intruded when Sal began to question Amity about Perrin's phone call.

"And you're sure she's not working for the *Mal*? They'd love to know where this place is. They've been looking for it for decades."

"I've been working with Perrin for the past several months." Amity shook her head. "She's not working for the *Mal*. She's not working for Charun. She has no idea that the magical races exist. I know this because I've been in her head. I know what she's felt. And the only things she's felt recently have been pain and fear."

The pain in Amity's voice was clear and Rom reached for her without thought. His arm curved around her shoulders just as Remy reached for her thigh, squeezing. Her tight muscles relaxed under their hands and she gave each of them a sweet smile before turning back to continue her conversation with Sal.

And Rom knew that what he felt for this woman, this goddess, went beyond reverence. Beyond duty or gratitude.

He was pretty sure Remy had already come to the same conclusion earlier today but Rom would admit, if only to himself, that he was a little slow on the uptake sometimes. Especially when it came to emotions.

He didn't like them. They fucked him over every time. If he could keep the damn things in line, then life was a hell of a lot easier to handle.

But he'd had enough of living life without emotion.

He wanted a life. One that didn't involve packing up and moving from crappy hotel to rented house to crappy hotel every couple of months.

And even if he had to kill a god, they were going to have it.

"Rom, you okay with that?" Sal asked.

Shit, obviously he'd missed some of the conversation.

"Okay with what?"

Sal lifted one eyebrow at him. "Okay with me opening the door and saying, 'Hi, Perrin. Please don't run screaming. I don't really have goat legs and horns. It's just your imagination. Come on in and have a drink.'"

Rom's mouth dropped open and, in his head, he had one brief, surreal image of Sal doing just that. Then he laughed.

And laughed harder when Remy and Sal stared at him like he'd gone off the deep end.

Only Amity's expression lightened. She leaned forward, one hand outstretched to run her fingers down his jaw. "Thank you."

"For what?"

"You have a very sexy laugh."

He felt a flush burn his cheeks, but his smile remained, and he managed to force a few mumbled words through his lips. "Only for you."

Which was apparently the right thing to say because her lips split into an unrestrained grin. She looked ready to speak again, but the doorbell rang at that moment and the tension level in the room rose by two hundred percent.

"Game time," Sal muttered.

In his peripheral vision, Rom saw something happen to Sal, but until he turned from Amity to really look, he hadn't understood what it was.

Rom blinked and barely heard Remy's quiet "holy shit" as Sal slid from the chair and headed for the front door.

Sal looked like a young teen, wearing a Phillies ball cap, jeans, sneakers, and a black T-shirt. Even his face had undergone a transformation.

No one would look twice at him on a city street. Unless they looked into his eyes.

Fuck, that was freaky.

"Look lively, boys." Sal's voice hadn't changed, though, and that came as another shock. "Let's not have the girl run screaming in the first five minutes."

Amity rose and followed Sal, which made sense considering Perrin was expecting to see her.

Remy motioned him to follow and they headed through the dining room and a sitting room into the front living room.

But as soon as Amity opened the door, she gasped.

"Perrin…"

Amity's voice held a note of shock that had Remy and Rom on their feet and heading toward the hallway and the front door. They stopped just before moving into the doorway where Perrin would be able to see them, standing frozen, waiting to come to Amity's rescue if she needed them.

"So I'm not just seeing things. You see it too." Perrin's voice held a palpable sense of relief. And an almost desperate amusement. "Thank God. I thought I was going crazy."

"No. No, you're not going crazy." Amity's voice had gained a little strength but not much. "But we need to talk. And what I have to say may come as a shock."

"Believe me, nothing could shock me as much as seeing my face in the mirror this morning."

"Don't be too sure of that."

As Amity appeared in the doorway, Remy and Rom stepped back as she waved a hand in front of her and Perrin stepped into the room.

She froze like a deer in headlights when she saw Rom then quickly looked at Remy.

Rom knew she remembered him, knew she was trying to figure out why a man who was supposed to be a product rep was in Amity's home, along with a man who had scars much as she did.

And then he realized what his eyes had seen but his brain hadn't been able to process.

"Tinia's teat."

"Amity." Perrin's eyes grew wide and fear made her blanch to the color of cream. "Why is he here?"

"Because I wasn't honest with you at the hospital yesterday." Amity's voice had fallen into that soothing cadence. "Obviously you remember Rom. This is his cousin, Remy. They're my bodyguards and my lovers."

Spoken so bluntly, the words made Perrin's eyes widen even more. And it was even more powerful for the fact that it was true. Having Amity say the words made it more real somehow. And made it that much more believable.

"*Both...*" She shook her head, as if trying to get her brain to think how she wanted. "But..."

Finally her eyes narrowed and she looked at Rom. "Are you going to hurt me?"

His heart twisted at the resigned expectation in her voice and he knew Remy had barely bitten back a vicious curse aimed not at Perrin, but at the man who'd made her fear so deeply.

"We will never hurt you, Perrin." He wanted her to hear the vow in his voice, wanted her to know the truth in his words. "And we won't allow anyone to hurt you ever again."

Perrin began to blink rapidly and Rom could scent tears forming.

But she didn't let one fall. Then her chin tilted up. "I've learned that you can't trust anyone. Most especially men."

He couldn't blame her for that. "Do you trust Amity?"

A slight pause. "I did."

Amity winced and he wanted to reach for her, but he didn't want to startle Perrin. She reminded him of a terrified rabbit, frozen in the sights of a predator. "No. You do. You know she's done nothing except try to help you. And she has. I know you're confused right now. I completely understand. But if you can't trust me, then trust her."

Perrin held Rom's gaze for several long seconds, her chest rising and falling rapidly. Remy had taken his cues from Rom and stood stock still behind him.

Sal was still out of sight in the hallway but Rom knew he was waiting, as well.

Finally Perrin took a deep breath. "I do trust Amity."

Rom nodded. "Then let her explain. Because I think we all deserve an explanation."

Perrin turned to face Amity again, and Rom bit back the curse that flew to the tip of his tongue.

Absolutely fucking amazing. No wonder the woman had demanded to see Amity. She'd been the recipient of a miracle, after all. One that had almost completely removed the scars from her face.

―――

Amity couldn't stop staring.

Blessed Goddess, she hadn't realized…

Perrin must have thought she'd finally gone mad when she'd looked in the mirror this morning. Or maybe she thought she hadn't yet woken up from a dream.

Her face…

Yes, you could still tell she'd sustained some damage to her face, but the scarring was now minimal.

Perrin looked almost normal. No wonder she'd felt so drained last night. She hadn't meant to heal quite so much.

And now she was faced with a huge problem. One she wouldn't be able to explain away as just a remarkable ability by Perrin's body or an experimental treatment.

This was miracle territory.

And Perrin knew it.

"Amity." Perrin's gaze pleaded with her to explain what had happened. "What did you do to me?"

Blessed Goddess, what did she say? What *could* she say?

The truth was out of the question. Telling a woman who had no idea there was magic in the world that she'd cured her with Goddess powers probably wasn't the smartest idea in the world.

Then again, what other explanation could she give?

"What if—" Amity took a deep breath as Perrin watched her avidly. "What if I told you I could do things people might think of as..." Did she dare use the word magic? Or simply explain it as power? "As impossible?"

Perrin just stared at her for several seconds. Then she blinked and took a deep breath. "My mother claimed my grandmother could heal her headaches just by putting her hand on her head. Is it... Are you like that? Like a faith healer?"

That would be the easy way out, wouldn't it? Let Perrin believe in this simple lie because the truth was so much harder to comprehend.

And so much more dangerous. She couldn't really tell her the truth. Well, she *shouldn't* tell her the truth. Amity's existence relied on her ability to keep her true nature hidden.

But... Amity didn't want to lie to her. Perrin didn't deserve it. After all she'd been through, Perrin would be able to tell that Amity was lying. And Perrin would hate her for it.

Amity had spent months getting Perrin to trust her. She didn't want to lose that trust now. Especially not since she had the ability to give Perrin back a normal life. If she managed to live through the next day.

"Yes, it's kind of like that but...."

How did you tell someone you were an ancient deity without them thinking you were crazy? Or they'd gone off the deep end?

Perrin's gaze narrowed, and Amity felt her own tears start to form. Damn it, this *so* wasn't fair.

Suddenly, Rom reached for her hand and squeezed. "Tell her. We'll deal with the fallout." He smiled. "Then we'll introduce her to Sal."

Her own smile cracked her lips and she nodded before catching and holding Perrin's gaze again. "My name hasn't always been Amity. I was born Munthukh, Goddess of Health, more than three thousand years ago in the region you now know as Tuscany, Italy. For a thousand years, the Etruscan pantheon was worshipped. Until the Roman deities usurped our roles and most of our power."

Amity paused to gauge Perrin's mood, but the other woman just continued to stare at her.

"I've worked most of my life as a healer and most recently as a healthcare provider. I've taken care of the sick and the dying my entire life, but the longer I've lived, the less powerful I've become. I still try to be useful where I can. For the last several hundred years, I haven't been able to provide more than fleeting comfort for those dying slow, horrible deaths. And then about fifteen years ago, I discovered the new profession of medical aesthetician. And I realized that I could still provide a meaningful service."

Amity stopped, biting her bottom lip until it hurt, watching Perrin's eyes for any hint of impending hysteria.

It wasn't every day the woman you trusted to heal your body after a horrific attack told you she was an ancient goddess.

Perrin had every right to tell her she was crazy. Gods, this had been a disas—

"Prove it." Perrin's voice had calmed, though Amity still heard a slight tremor running through it.

"How?"

"Are your absent scars not proof enough?" Rom asked.

"They should be, shouldn't they?" Perrin hadn't taken her eyes off Amity. "But I need something I can touch, something tangible."

"How about a little show and tell?"

Sal's voice sounded in the hall a second before he appeared in the doorway to the room, goat legs and horns in plain sight.

Perrin's sharp gasp filled the room but she held her ground. Sal didn't come any closer, just leaned against the door jamb, arms crossed over his chest as he looked back at her.

Perrin blinked several times before she turned back to Amity.

"I'd like three fingers of whiskey and a couple shots of Jägermeister. And then I think we need to talk about my dream about someone named Karn."

Chapter 14

"How the hell did he find out about Perrin?"

"And why the hell would he even approach her? She's useless to him."

"Unless he planned to take her and use her as leverage against Amity."

"Then why hasn't he sent a de—ah, sent someone to take her?"

"And how the hell did he even find Perrin?"

"No idea, but I think it's time to get some answers."

Amity had listened to Remy, Rom, and Sal circle back and forth for the past several minutes while Perrin sipped her whiskey and Jägermeister and stared at Sal. Mostly at Sal's horns.

The woman was fascinated more by those horns than by Sal's legs, which had been known to cause grown men to feel faint.

Amity wondered if Perrin was going into shock, but she didn't look pale.

She looked amazed.

"So, Perrin," Sal asked when Rom and Remy finally paused in their conversation, "you wanna touch 'em?"

Amity cringed at the *salbinelli*'s teasing question, knowing Sal wasn't trying to embarrass Perrin. It was just how he was.

But Perrin had been through—

"I would love to, if you don't mind. Are they bone or cartilage?"

Sal leaned forward across the table so Perrin could reach out and touch him. "Bone. They grew in when I was in my twenties and I've had them ever since."

After caressing the blunt little obtrusions for a few seconds, Perrin sat back, shaking her head.

"Amazing." Then she turned to Remy and Rom. "So what exactly can you two do? I'm assuming since Amity is a goddess and Sal's a *salbinelli* and that a God has been visiting me in my dreams, you two must have some special power, or you wouldn't get to hang with the cool kids."

Sal snorted out a laugh and Amity hid a smile as Remy and Rom exchanged a glance. It was their secret to tell, but Amity hoped they would. At this point, what could it hurt?

Perrin already knew much more than most other *eteri*.

"We're *lucani versipelli*," Rom answered after Remy nodded. "Wolf skinshifters."

Perrin didn't miss a beat. "You mean werewolves."

"Some people call us that, yeah."

"Huh." She sipped at her Jäger again before pushing the half-finished glass aside. Then she did the same with the almost empty whiskey glass. "So now what? What are you going to do to keep Charun off Amity's back?"

Amity reached for Perrin's hand and squeezed. "We'll make sure you're safe, no matter what."

"Charun doesn't want to hurt me. Actually…"

"Actually what?"

Perrin frowned. "He seemed kind of lonely if you ask me."

Amity didn't know what to say to that. After all Perrin had been through, Amity had thought Perrin might think of Charun as the Boogeyman. Instead, she felt sorry for him. Amity felt it beneath Perrin's fear and confusion.

"What makes you say that?"

Shrugging, Perrin shook her head. "I don't know. Just a feeling. I'm probably wrong. The dream, or whatever, was just so freaky. So real and yet… I knew it wasn't. I never believed anything like magic, like *salbinelli*," she turned to Sal with a wry look, "or werewolves were possible. I just couldn't imagine things that are so far out of the box. So maybe my perceptions are a little off."

"Don't doubt what you feel," Remy said. "I understand why you may be a little gun-shy about trusting your instincts, but you weren't wrong about Amity. You can trust us. What else did you sense during your dream?"

She loved these men. So strong. So amazingly perceptive. How she wished they could be hers forever.

Though it could never be. She had no successor to whom she could pass her powers, what little remained, anyway. And she would not give them up when she could still use them to help people.

With war brewing between the Etruscans and the *Mal*, her people would need her powers.

And Cat would need Remy and Rom.

No, when this was done, and Charun was dealt with, however that came to be, then she needed to break her ties with these men.

Even if it broke her heart.

"So we're agreed?"

Rom's question brought her back into the conversation, which she'd been listening to with half an ear.

Remy and Rom wanted to bring Perrin with them. They didn't want to leave her alone, in case Charun sent someone after her while they were gone. And they all thought she might be of use against Charun. He had seemed to take a special interest in Perrin. Maybe they'd learn more with her by their side.

Perrin squeezed her hand and nodded when Amity looked at her. Excitement shone from her eyes. No fear at all.

For her, this must seem like an amazing adventure. An almost unbelievable one.

Amity only wished everything wasn't moving quite so fast.

"We're agreed," she said. "Perrin comes along."

———

Remy knew something was eating at Amity. He just couldn't figure out what.

As X and Cal led them along a barely passable trail in a thickly wooded forest near Hawk Mountain, Remy wanted to pull Amity aside and find out what was wrong.

Considering he was wearing his pelt, that would've been a good trick.

She'd had something on her mind since they'd left Sal's. Something that made her distance herself from them. She hadn't made it obvious, but she'd been careful not to get close to either of them.

She'd stuck by Perrin's side the entire time, which he totally understood. But her normal placid attitude had been replaced by stress. Again, not a shocker. This whole situation was a fucked-up mess.

Still, Remy felt her distance like a void in his gut. The warmth he associated with her, the heat she directed at him and Rom, was missing. He didn't like it and his wolf hated it.

He wanted to stick to her side, rub against her legs and mark her as his. As theirs. Rom felt the same way, except he wanted to sandwich her between them and fuck her until none of them could see straight.

The images coming from Rom, combined with his own anxiety, made him work twice as hard to keep his attention on their surroundings.

They walked through thickly forested state gamelands. No homes, no buildings. Just trees and rocks. And a palpable sense of magic whose location he couldn't pin down. He didn't sense any danger, just a very old, very powerful force.

Amity had to have picked up on it but she hadn't said anything. By the time they reached the spot where the building should have been, Remy felt ready to crawl out of his skin.

Until his eyes realized what he was seeing.

"Wow."

Rom spoke for both of them.

"I didn't realize this still existed." Amity's hushed response drew Remy's attention back to her. Even she looked dumbstruck. "It's been so long since… How did you know about this place, X?"

"My mother is Etruscan, Lady Amity. She'd learned its location years ago."

"What is this place?" Rom said.

"Artumes's circle." Amity's voice had dropped almost to a whisper. "I haven't been here in more than a century. Didn't think anyone kept it up."

From what Remy could see, no one had.

If an *eteri* had stumbled on this place, they might have thought it was nothing more than a rise in the earth. If they'd looked closer, they might have seen the stone foundation. Or they might have dismissed it as a natural outcropping of rocks.

You had to be standing right next to the structure to realize that what you were looking at was man-made.

Some people called them fairy mounds and believed they were the gateway to fairyland. Some believed the indigenous American tribes had used them as burial mounds centuries ago. Others had more far-fetched explanations.

This one, as Amity had indicated, was man-made.

"What's an Artumes's circle?" Perrin asked.

Amity gave Perrin a bittersweet smile. "Artumes is another goddess and this is where she was worshipped for many years by the Etruscan *Fata*. The mound was Artumes's home. And the circle," Amity pointed into the forest, "is right beyond that stand of trees."

"And what exactly are the *Fata*?" Perrin was shaking her head as if she were trying to get the information to settle.

"Sorry. I guess you would call them the fairy races."

Perrin's mouth dropped open for a second before she closed it again. "You mean like Tinker Bell?"

Amity began to laugh and sounded much closer to normal. "Not like… Well, actually some do kind of look like Tinker Bell. But the *Fata* are pretty diverse. Sal is *Fata*. So are the *folletti*, who have wings. And the *linchetti*, who have pointed ears."

Remy watched Perrin as she took in that information like she was swallowing a bitter bill. Finally she sighed and shook her head. Again. "Okay. At the risk of blowing what little brain I have left, I'm going to ask one more question. So what's the circle?"

Amity took Perrin's hand and started to walk again, following X and Cal into the trees. "It's probably just better if I show you."

Remy was about to follow them when he caught a whiff of human.

He stopped, eyes narrowed as he sniffed the air. The scent was faint but he knew he wasn't mistaking it for something else.

Humans. Headed straight for them.

From this distance he couldn't tell if they were *Mal*. Only one way to find out.

Remy growled low in his throat and sent Rom a mental warning just before he melted into the forest and backtracked.

He knew Rom was cursing him for breaking away and going off on his own but Rom wouldn't leave Amity's side.

Making sure he stayed hidden, Remy used all his senses to try to figure out if these men—two of them—were innocuous hikers or something more sinister.

Turns out he only needed one. As soon as he came within a hundred yards, he knew these guys weren't here to bird-watch.

They stank like *Mal*. The hint of rot that underlaid their natural scent grew more potent the closer he got.

Remy stood motionless in a thick stand of brush, his fur blending in perfectly. They didn't know he was there. He could've ripped out their throats before they knew what was going on. He had a hard time getting his wolf not to lunge. Not because they didn't deserve it but because Cole would want them alive for questioning.

And so did Remy. He wanted to look into their eyes when he told them they'd never take him and Rom alive. They would fight to the death because they had something worth living for, and it wasn't revenge.

He began to retreat, to circle back and meet up with Rom. He'd need Rom's help to take care of these guys. They couldn't be allowed to get anywhere near Amity.

To be on the safe side, Remy made a wider circle on his way back. And that's when he scented the third man.

And this one didn't smell *Mal*. He just smelled… wrong.

Remy had never come across anything like it before. Etruscan but different. Powerful. Wrong.

Wrong how, he couldn't say. This guy was trouble. And he was close.

Remy tried to get a lock on his location, but it was almost like something was interfering with his tracking ability.

As if the guy had a deflecting spell. Remy had never heard of one, but then maybe his mother just hadn't gotten around to teaching it to him. Or maybe his mother hadn't known about it either.

Who the *fuck* was this guy?

Using every skill his father and uncle had ever taught him about being a wolf, Remy began to move silently through the brush. He wanted to get a look at this guy, wanted to get closer. He needed to look at the guy, see his eyes, his face.

But he had to find him first.

His scent seemed to be everywhere, but nowhere, in particular.

Where the fuck was he?

Silently, Remy stalked a ghost. He slid away from the two *Mal* who had stopped moving forward and appeared to be waiting for instructions, probably from Remy's ghost.

Sending a silent warning to Rom, Remy circled the area, tightening the circle every time.

Shit, the guy was closer to Amity than he'd thought.

He knew Rom had already started back, but Remy was faster on four feet. He shot off, no longer caring about making noise.

The men following them knew they were here.

Remy had nearly made it back to Amity when he heard her call out, "Perrin, stay behind me. X, we need to go now."

Remy poured on speed, making sure he sounded like a freight train coming through the woods, heard Rom do the same. Maybe it would give the guy pause.

Remy's heart nearly stopped when he burst into the clearing. A placid pool lay in the center, the outer edge ringed by thirteen centuries-old oak trees.

On the far side of the pond, Amity stood over Cal's crumpled body as Perrin shakily brandished a pair of blades that had to be Cal's. Behind Perrin, X slumped against a large boulder that seemed to have been thrust up out of the earth from below. Remy didn't see any blood on X, but the guy was clearly dazed.

In front of them stood a male who couldn't be more than twenty, his dark hair frat-boy short, his Etruscan features set in stoic lines. He held one hand stretched toward Perrin and Amity as if he were beckoning them to come with him.

Remy didn't stop to think. The man smelled dangerous and stood much too close to Amity and Perrin. He raced toward the man with the intention of taking him down—

And found himself sprawled on the ground when a powerful force shoved at him. It picked him up off his feet and blew him yards away. Luckily he didn't hit any tree trunks on the way or his insides might be spilling out right now.

This *scassacazzo* was strong. And not just physically. He vibrated with power.

"There you are." The guy's tone sounded like they'd just met during a social event. One where they weren't trying to kill each other. "I've been looking forward to meeting you, Remy. And you too, Rom. So glad you could join the party."

"Run," Amity pleaded and it took a few seconds before Remy realized she was talking to him. "Please. He's only here for the two of you. Get out now."

Remy snorted, shaking his head as he tried to clear it. To hell with that plan. There was no way Remy or Rom were leaving her alone so they could run and save themselves.

But the guy was strong. And he had help on the way.

The only choices were to take the guy down… or get Amity and Perrin into the dream plane. The question was, how did they do that when Cal was out cold and X was injured?

Remy made a split-second decision and recalled his pelt. It left him vulnerable for several seconds but the *Mal* merely watched, making no attempt to attack.

"Who are you and what do you want?" Remy began to close the distance between them. The cool air covered his skin in goose bumps but it wouldn't slow him down. In fact, it made him more focused.

The *Mal* shook his head. "You don't need to know who I am. You and your cousin simply need to come with me. If you don't, I'll hurt the women and then you'll come with me. Either way, it works out the same."

Amity drew in a sharp breath. "Remy, don't—"

"I won't hesitate to hurt them," the guy said. "And they'll be bleeding when we leave."

Remy smelled the truth behind his words. He didn't care if he hurt Amity or Perrin. He had one goal and that was to get Remy and Rom.

"First tell me who you are and why you want me."

The guy smiled, something vaguely reptilian about it that made

Remy's skin crawl. "Oh, not just you. Good try, though. No, you and your cousin, who I know is lurking behind me, will come with me. I'm sure you've figured out why already."

Yeah, he knew why the *Mal* wanted them. To make them slaves. *Fuck that.*

But did they have a choice? Right now, the guy seemed to be invincible. Remy had flown through the air like he weighed all of twenty pounds.

They needed X to help Amity and Perrin into the dream plane, then he and Rom would take care of this guy before his backup arrived.

"So you work for the *Mal*. But you're not *Mal*, are you?"

"Again, not something you need to know. You're stalling, waiting for the other men to wake. If you and Rom come with me without a fight, I'll allow the women to live."

Then Remy got an idea. A fucking brilliant idea, if he did think so himself.

He was pretty sure Rom would think it was crazy, but then they didn't have much choice. And not much time to think of anything else. Remy sent the thought to Rom a split second before he lunged for the guy. At the exact moment, Rom called his pelt and shifted into his wolf directly behind the guy.

And just as Remy had hoped, the guy split his focus and his power.

The stream of power he sent at Rom deflected off the controlled magic of his shift but managed to knock him to the side. Remy wasn't as lucky. He caught the blow directly in his chest and staggered back several feet into a tree trunk, where he hit his head. Flashing lights appeared in his eyes but he blinked them away as fast as he could.

Not fast enough. The *Mal*, probably sensing he was most vulnerable, ran at him. The guy's mouth moved, weaving a spell.

Remy knew he didn't want to be on the receiving end of any

spell this guy could come up with. He had a split second to consider strategies before Rom leaped for the guy's throat.

And X and Amity began to finish what they'd started.

Remy slammed into the guy just as Amity began to chant in ancient Etruscan, the alien-sounding language spilling from her lips as easily as English. Remy only understood every couple of words, but he didn't have time to concentrate on that. Rom needed his help.

Remy briefly thought about taking one of the swords Perrin was holding—and found himself holding it a second later.

"Holy shit."

He spared a quick glance at Perrin, who looked as dumbfounded as he felt. Then he forced himself to clear his head and concentrate only on Rom and their ability to protect Amity.

As she continued to chant, Remy lifted the sword and went after the *Mal*.

Rom had his jaws clenched around the guy's arm but was taking an awful lot of abuse from him. The *Mal* looked like he was about to level another spell.

Remy aimed the point of the sword for the guy's throat, figuring that was the most vulnerable spot, and it would cut off his ability to chant. Remy really didn't want to be around when the guy unleashed another spell. And he sure as hell didn't want Amity near here if the *Mal* pulled it off.

A second before he would've skewered the guy, the *Mal* rolled, ripping away from Rom's sharp teeth. Blood splattered and Remy regrouped to take another stab.

Only, the ground rolled beneath him and he pitched to the side just as Rom leaped for the *Mal* again. And missed because the *Mal* stumbled, as well. Rom tackled Remy instead and Remy had to drop the sword to make sure he didn't cut Rom as he caught the brunt of the hundred-pounds-plus wolf.

As they scrambled back to their feet, the *Mal* made a run for

Amity, who had her gaze trained on the pool of water, which didn't seem to be affected at all by the shaking earth. In fact, its surface looked as smooth as glass.

Remy felt a surge of red-hot power blast through his body, a power that wasn't totally his. He sensed a portion of it coming from Rom. And fueling it…

Remy put his hand on Rom's scruff, felt the same power coursing through his cousin.

And, in a flash of insight, knew exactly what they could do with that power.

Amity spoke the last few words of the spell she had wrought with X and watched as the surface of the pool took on the sheen of a mirror.

One great big magic mirror to step through into the dream plane. How was that for straight out of a fairy tale?

Avoiding looking at the fight taking place on the other side of the small pool, she reached behind her.

"Perrin, take my hand and don't let go."

"What's going on?" Perrin asked, but she did as Amity had told her.

The woman sounded frightened but not paralyzed with fear. Good. She'd need that strength in the next few minutes.

"We're going to use the pond as a conduit into the dream plane. Kind of like *Alice Through the Looking Glass.*"

"I stopped believing in fairy tales a long time ago."

"Well, you're about to cross over into Wonderland."

Now Amity dared to look across the pond. And what she saw made her gasp.

Remy had one hand on Rom's scruff. In the other…

Blessed Goddess, in the other he held a glowing red ball of fire.

In the next split second, Remy flung it at the *Mal*.

The fire consumed the younger man and he cried out in pain.

"Amity, go now!" Remy shouted.

"We have to go together. You have to jump."

"I don't know if the fire will contain him while we're gone. Cal isn't—"

"We'll be fine," X said. He'd already gotten to his feet and was hauling a sluggish Cal with a shoulder under his arm. "Go now."

Amity looked at Perrin then again at Remy and Rom. Then she took a deep breath and waded into the water.

Since she'd never done this before, she hadn't been sure what to expect.

She only had time to realize the water was no longer water. And the ground had disappeared below their feet.

———

Rom watched Amity step into the pool—

And disappear as if she was wearing cement shoes.

Blind panic hit him like a bomb blast, and he nearly tripped over his paws and Remy to get into the water.

Disorientation hit him hard, nausea and dizziness combined as he fell.

He sailed through darkness, the light cutting off as if a switch had been thrown. And had just enough time to think *Holy fuck, how the hell far is it to the bottom*, when he hit.

Hard. So hard, he went lights out for several seconds. Which didn't mean a damn thing because, wherever he was, it was completely dark.

Get up.

He had to get up. He had to find Amity. Had to make sure she was okay. Had to trust that when Remy followed, he'd find them, as well.

Pushing himself to his paws, he did a complete body shake, making sure nothing had broken.

A few aches and pains. Maybe a few more pains than aches, but he could stand. And if he could stand, he could walk.

Taking a deep breath, he let his eyes get accustomed to the gloom.

Damn, was it always like this? Had they really made it to the dream plane? Amity would know. He had to find her.

He turned in a slow circle.

For as far as he could see, there was nothing but open space. The ground beneath his feet looked like dirt, but he had the sense that it only looked that way because that's what he expected to see. Which was weird but not as weird as the landscape that started to spring up around him.

Trees, shrubs, brush. A forest, but unlike any he'd ever seen. The trees were misshapen, the trunks bulging in odd places, and the limbs bent in unnatural ways. The bushes were brightly colored and their leaves strangely geometric. And none of them were taller than him.

Very weird.

Don't panic.

Good advice for unintentional interstellar travelers and *lucani* who found themselves in the dream plane. Now if only he had a towel. And Remy complained that he didn't have a sense of humor. Of course, it could be the beginning stages of hysteria.

Where the hell were Amity and Perrin?

A flash of light caught his eye and he spotted what looked like a falling star. Shining bright as it made its way from up there, which was utter darkness, to down here. Which was gloomy.

Then he caught a faint hint of a scent he recognized.

Remy.

He took off as fast as he dared, the tree limbs pointed and sharp—

Shit. Remy would be impaled.

The forest disappeared in the blink of an eye and Remy hit the ground with an oddly muffled thud.

Rom reached his cousin's side in seconds, sticking his muzzle into Remy's cheek. He chuffed with relief when Remy groaned but sat up rubbing his head with one hand and his naked back with the other.

He must have taken the time to put on pants before he'd jumped into the pool. And grab a sword, which lay next to him on the ground.

"Damn. That's really gonna hurt in a little while. Right now, it's slightly less than agonizing. Where's Amity?"

Rom shook his head as Remy stood, one hand reaching up to rub his nape as he looked around then looked back at Rom.

"We need to find her. Can you pick up her scent?"

Good question. Rom closed his eyes, stuck his muzzle in the air and inhaled.

At first, there was nothing. Hell, he barely smelled Remy. It was as if smells didn't exist here.

Panic wanted to build but he forced it down. And concentrated. Damn it, where—*There*. Just the faintest hint but it was her. Then he caught another scent and his heart tripped over itself as he began to run, Remy right on his heels.

Blood.

Chapter 15

THIS WAS HER FAULT. All her fault. Amity never should have agreed to bring Perrin.

When she'd landed, Perrin's head had taken the brunt of the impact against the marble ruins and now her blood stained the cracked stone she'd fall on.

Amity had no idea why the ruins looked so familiar or even why they were here on the dream plane. She only knew Perrin was injured.

"Heal her."

The deep male voice startled her and Amity looked up to find Charun standing over them.

She hadn't seen him in more than a millennium but he hadn't changed. His sharp features and dark, piercing eyes gave him a deadly air that wasn't imagined. The God of the Underworld wasn't known for his mercy.

But the way he was staring at Perrin…

Amity felt something other than simple professional curiosity from him. It rocked her back on her heels for several seconds as she stared up at him. He cared for Perrin, she could sense it.

"Heal her," Charun repeated. "She's going to die. You need to fix her now."

He was absolutely right.

She had to save Perrin, even though her injuries were so severe, Amity might not have any power left for Charun to harvest when she was finished.

She closed her eyes.

"What are you doing?" Charun demanded, his voice a distraction amidst the chaos of her emotions.

"What you told me to do. I'm healing Perrin. Now shut up and let me work. It's difficult to concentrate with all the pain and agony."

"Welcome to my world." Charun's softly muttered words fractured her concentration. This time, she knew she'd heard something in his tone, felt some emotion she wanted to pause and consider.

Yet she knew she couldn't. She needed every ounce of her focus to heal Perrin. Two millennia ago, she would have been able to heal a score of people at the same time. Those days were long gone.

Time to read the writing on the wall.

She'd been avoiding it for so long. These last stolen days with Remy and Rom had been wonderful, but now she knew her time was up. She wouldn't be returning to her men. But neither would she allow Charun to consume her power, what little she had left.

Because truly, she'd only been siphoning it from Remy and Rom. Channeling it from them and using it for her own purposes. Which didn't really make it hers.

Sinking deeper into herself, she split her focus, using her hands to direct the remaining energy in her body into Perrin's.

The head wound had caused bleeding in the brain and there were additional internal injuries. She'd already lost so much blood.

Amity just kept funneling power.

When she was finished… well, maybe Charun would still welcome her into Aitás even though she'd have nothing left for him. Or herself, for that matter.

—⁓—

Remy and Rom ran toward the scent Rom had picked up. Remy prayed they wouldn't be too late.

He barely noticed when the ground suddenly became littered

with ruined marble columns and broken cobblestone roads. He only knew he could sense Amity. She needed them.

It didn't take long to find her. And when they did, neither of them hesitated to rush toward her, even though Charun stood over her.

Rom leaped at Charun, uncaring that the God of the Underworld could crush him with one hand.

"Stay back." Charun flung out his hand, and Rom went flying through the air without being touched and landed with a sickening thud.

With a roar that would have made a demon flinch in fear, Remy ran at Charun. He'd kill the bastard god or he'd die trying.

He got close enough to actually land a punch but Charun grabbed him by the throat and shook him, Remy's feet dangling inches off the ground. "You fool. You're going to kill them both by diverting her attention."

He struggled against Charun's grip, tearing at the strong fingers around his throat. If Charun exerted just a little more pressure, Remy was pretty sure he wouldn't need to breathe because he'd be dead.

He had to try. Had to get to Amity to shore up her strength. He wanted to tell Charun that he needed to go to her, put his hands on her so she could draw power from him.

"I… can help. Let… me… go."

His throat burned with every word as he clawed at Charun's fingers.

When he finally fell to the ground, he knew it was only because the god had allowed him to fall.

"Then do it."

Remy was already scrambling toward Amity. Sitting behind her, he bracketed her between his knees and gently wrapped his arms around her waist. He didn't want to break her intense concentration, but she needed to know he was there. Bending his head, he pressed his lips to her neck and forced his energy into her.

He'd never tried to do this with anyone other than Rom and

only when they were working spells. This was totally different, but it was the only way he could think of to get her to accept his help.

He immediately felt his energy flow out of him and into her. His head began to pound, the throbbing in his temples and between his eyes made him light-headed, and his stomach churned.

The sound of a scuffle caught his attention but he disconnected from everything but Amity. She needed him. And he wouldn't fail her.

—⁂—

Rom knew he had several broken bones, probably a concussion and other internal injuries.

If he shifted, the broken bones would heal themselves, as would most of the internal injuries. If they weren't too severe. If they were… he could do serious damage if he shifted. But he had to risk it.

Someone had followed them through.

He knew Remy was helping Amity, giving her his energy, practically forcing her to take it.

That left him to deal with the *Mal*.

Returning to his skin was always easier than calling his pelt. His body knew its natural state. This time, though, it hurt like hell.

He made no sound as he shifted. Nothing felt out of place, but he looked down at himself just to make sure. Still looked okay.

But now he needed a pair of pants. He'd fight naked but he'd feel a hell of a lot better if he didn't have to. Leather would be—

Leather pants molded to his skin. His favorite pair. He blinked down at them for several seconds then decided he really didn't need to think about it. Not when he had a *Mal* to kill.

He gave Charun a wide berth as he walked over to pick up the sword Remy had dropped. He felt the pull on his strength as Remy supported Amity while Amity healed Perrin.

And hoped his remaining strength would be enough to protect

them. It would have to be. He spared a final glance at Charun, who paid no attention to him. Then he planted himself at Remy's back and prepared to fight. He didn't have to wait long.

The *Mal* stepped out of the gloom, his eyes wide, a crazed look in them.

"You can't escape now, Romulus. There's nowhere for you to go."

"Then I guess I'll just have to kill you. Because we're not going anywhere with you."

"You will. See, Charun made a deal with my boss. He gets Munthukh. We get you and your cousin. When Charun takes the goddess, he'll hand me both of you on a silver platter."

"Not if you're dead."

Rom attacked without warning, hoping to catch the *Mal* off guard as he swung the sword straight at the other man's ribs.

In a flash, the *Mal* held his own sword, deflecting Rom's blow but stumbling back. Rom pressed his advantage, fear for Amity and Remy and furious anger at the entire situation fueled his strength.

But the *Mal* had wiry strength and a fanatic's zeal. He twisted and turned, deflecting every one of Rom's attempts to incapacitate him. Rom tried to draw him away from Amity and the others, tried to trip him up.

But the guy just wouldn't go down. Rom was beginning to feel the strain on his abused body, still not completely healed from the blow he'd taken from Charun.

He took a step back and nearly went down, his ankle twisting painfully.

The *Mal* saw an advantage and took it. He swung the sword at Rom's head, which he blocked, but wasn't fast enough to deflect the next jab. The sword skewered his thigh and he groaned in pain.

And saw his opening a second later as the *Mal* thought he had him beat. As the guy drew back to strike again, Rom surprised him by swinging his sword low. Rom cut him across the left knee, hearing the *thunk* as it hit bone, grinning when the guy dropped his own sword to clutch his leg.

Forcing himself to his feet, Rom pressed the point of the sword against the guy's throat.

"I should kill you now but I want you to deliver a message. Tell your boss he'll never get Remy or me. Tell him if he comes after us again, we won't stop to think about killing. We'll consume him in red flame and leave him to rot for eternity."

"That will never happen. You have no idea who you're dealing with. You don't—"

The words cut off with a gurgle as Charun appeared beside Rom to grab the man's throat. "They don't. But I do. And I'll tell the man myself. Your soul is now mine."

Charun broke the man's neck with one powerful flick of his wrist and dropped him to the ground without a second glance.

"You'd better see to Remy and Amity," Charun said.

Rom turned, his stomach twisting. "*No.*"

Remy and Amity's still bodies sprawled on the ground beside Perrin's.

Rom's heart pounded so hard it hurt, and his stomach threatened to heave its contents.

Not both of them. Blessed Mother Goddess, please. Not both.

He closed the distance between them and dropped to his knees beside them. Charun bent to gather Perrin in his arms then stood, disappearing from Rom's sight.

Remy was closer and Rom reached for him, but he couldn't make his hand close the inches between them. He didn't want to feel Remy's lifeless body.

Amity's hair covered her face. He was afraid to brush it away to see the pallor of her skin.

It wasn't until he felt something drip from his chin that he realized he was crying.

"What the… fuck… Rom."

Rom's gaze snapped back to Remy. His eyes were slits of muddy blue but they were open.

"Remy. *Ceffo*, I thought…" He quickly wiped away the tears before he reached for Remy's shoulders to hold him still. "Don't move."

"What happened? Where's Amity? Perrin?"

"How do you feel?" Rom ignored his cousin's questions, not ready to deal with anything else right now.

"Like I'm in hell."

Rom felt tears well again but ruthlessly forced them back. Time enough for that later.

"No, but close enough. We need to get out. Now."

Rom's gaze narrowed even more. "Not without Amity."

"We won't leave her behind. Do you think you can stand?"

Remy's eyes widened a little more and his lips parted as if he were going to say something.

Then he turned his head. Rom's hands curled into fists but he didn't try to stop him.

With a groan, Remy sat up and reached for her. Unable to stop himself, Rom moved around to her other side and helped Remy lift her.

Her skin was still warm and Rom drew in a sharp breath as he realized she was still breathing.

"We have to get her out of here," Remy said. "We need to get her home."

"Then take her."

Both of them whipped their heads around to Charun, standing behind them with Perrin in his arms. The other woman appeared to be sleeping, but Rom couldn't tell for sure if she was breathing.

"You and Amity may go," Charun continued. "Perrin stays."

Rom knew Amity would fight them tooth and nail not to leave Perrin behind but they didn't have much of a choice. If she was dead, there was nothing they could do to help her. If she wasn't... they'd deal with that situation later.

Rom knew Remy was about to fight with the god but Rom stood, grateful his head played nice and he didn't go lights out again. "We'll go."

"Tell Amity... we'll talk later."

Not if Rom had anything to do about it. But he didn't say that aloud.

"Can you get up?" he asked Remy.

He wanted out of here right away. Then he realized he had no idea how to get out. The intensity of his need to escape escalated until his skin crawled.

Remy got to his feet, looking pretty steady as he cradled Amity in his arms. "So how do we get the hell out of here?"

"The same way you came in."

Charun's voice sounded all around them and suddenly they were drowning.

"I don't know what else to tell you, guys. Let her rest. If she doesn't wake by tomorrow morning..."

Sal shook his head and stepped out of the bedroom, closing the door behind him. He never finished his sentence. He didn't need to.

There was a lot of that going around.

They'd made it out of the dream plane and back to the pond, almost drowning in the process.

Cal and X had been waiting for them, the unconscious bodies of the *Mal*'s guard trussed like pigs on the ground by the side of the pond. When Remy and Rom had surfaced, dragging Amity between them, the brothers had jumped into the pond to drag them out.

They'd had a brief discussion about where to go that consisted of two choices. They chose the safest and headed for the den, where

Cole himself met them at the little house, along with Sal and a *lucani* doctor named Dane Dimitriou. He'd done a complete exam and when he sighed and replaced the stethoscope around his neck, Remy had walked away to look out the window.

He didn't want to hear anyone else tell them they had no idea if she'd ever wake again.

That had been last night.

Ten hours later, Rom looked ready to crack under the strain. That in itself was enough to make Remy want to scream.

His cousin hadn't said more than two words at a time, probably because his jaw was clenched so tight, he could barely speak.

Rom sat beside the bed they'd shared only two nights ago and stared out the window. He only left the room to use the bathroom. The only food he'd eaten had been because Catene had brought it and stood by him to make sure he finished it.

The young woman who'd inherited Lusna's powers as the Goddess of the Moon had attempted to rouse Amity, as had Lusna, Thesan, and Nortia, the Goddess of Fate. None of them had had any luck.

Rom had even refused a direct request from Cole to talk about the two *Malandante* they'd brought back from the dream plane.

Frankly, Remy was glad he'd turned that one down because it probably would've turned into a blood bath. Cole had a couple of guys working on them but so far they'd gotten nothing more than vague threats.

Remy had told Cole that when they needed someone to gnaw on the men to come get him. Cole had promised he'd be the first in line.

Now, the house was so fucking quiet it hurt Remy's head. Which might have more to do with a lack of sleep than anything.

He knew Rom had to be feeling just as bad. Neither of them had slept in more than twenty-four hours.

"You need to lie down."

Rom's voice startled him, he'd become so used to the silence.

His cousin sat on a chair by the side of the bed, one hand wrapped around Amity's resting on top of the quilt. Rom's gaze was glued to their joined hands. Almost as if he didn't want to miss the moment she woke.

Remy had the awful thought that Rom would die in that chair waiting for her to move.

"You haven't slept any more than I have, Rom, what—"

"You need to let her know you're here and you're okay."

Remy frowned, trying to make sense of his cousin's words. Had Rom finally cracked?

"What the hell are you talking about?"

"Can't you sense her? Don't you still feel her? She's here. She just can't find her way back. You need to show her the way."

Remy opened his mouth to tell Rom to snap out of it. That he was freaking him out. But before he did, he closed his mouth and thought about what Rom was saying.

He didn't sound crazy. He sounded as rational as he always did.

And it was rationale that Remy latched onto.

"What do you sense?"

Rom finally lifted his head to look at Remy, and Remy breathed a sigh of relief at the completely sane look in Rom's eyes.

"All the other people, it was too much. I felt her retreating. Maybe now, with just the two of us here…"

Could that really be it? Or was Rom grasping at straws?

Remy slammed his eyes closed and forced out every other distraction but Amity's scent and Rom's presence as they lived inside him.

He latched onto that other sense, the one he knew was Rom's consciousness, and followed it.

"Lie down and *hold* her, Remy. Let her know you're here. I've been trying to reach her for hours but… I don't think she can sense you."

That's why he'd been so silent, so withdrawn.

Uni's ass, Rom had been holding her for hours. Mentally. And Remy hadn't realized. *Fuck.*

Remy knelt on the bed, careful not to jostle her. He forced himself to look, to really look at her. She appeared to be sleeping. Her cheeks still had faint color in them. And not a flush like a fever, but a healthy glow.

Her lungs rose and fell in a slow, steady pace and her expression looked worried. Not blank or slack, but as if she couldn't stop thinking about something and it'd followed her into her dreams.

Hope began to pound like adrenaline through his veins. Toeing off his sneakers, he pulled back the covers and slid onto the bed next to her. Wrapping his arms around her, he turned her onto her side so his chest was plastered against her back.

Tucking her head under his chin, he got her as close as he could, hoping against hope that she felt him. That she sensed he was there.

They'd removed her clothes and slipped her into an oversized T-shirt of Rom's before putting her in bed. Now Remy let his hands rub her bare forearms and thighs, her skin warming beneath his touch.

He held her, losing track of time as he tried to reach her. He didn't realize he was murmuring in her ear until he felt Rom begin to pull away.

"No." He reached for Rom and Amity's joined hands and added his to the mix. "You have to stay too."

After a second, Rom nodded, his jaw loosening just the tiniest bit. And Remy let his hand slide back up Amity's arm.

Lowering his head, he put his lips directly against her ear. "Come back to us, Amity. We're both here. We're not going anywhere. You can't leave us. Not now. We love you."

He felt Rom still even more at that last statement but he didn't move away. And he didn't deny it. Instead, Rom bent over their joined hands and pressed his lips to her fingers.

Remy thought he felt her move, just a slight tremor in the arm holding onto Rom's hand.

And the stillness, that sense of waiting he'd felt from her before was gone. He swore he felt her struggling toward consciousness.

Remy put his mouth close to her ear and dug deep for that well of power he and Remy shared, the power that made them able to defeat a *tukhulkha* demon.

The power they'd always believed was meant for fighting and destruction Remy now channeled to reach Amity.

"Amity," he whispered in her ear. "Wake up now. We need you here with us."

Remy heard her breathing change, a slight hitch that hadn't been there before.

"Open your eyes, Lady." Remy reinforced his words with a blast of power so strong, not even a goddess could ignore it, apparently.

Amity took a deep breath and Remy held his until he heard her take another.

And when she rolled onto her back and opened her eyes, her hazy gaze going first to Rom and finally to him, Remy could breathe again.

"Bossy men." Her voice sounded weak but steady and Remy closed his eyes as his arms tightened around her. "I love you too. Both of you."

Remy couldn't get his vocal cords in gear. Luckily Rom wasn't having as much trouble.

"Good. Because we're not going anywhere and neither are you. We will bind you to us if we have too. We're not losing you again."

Remy lifted up on one elbow so he could see her face. Rom still held her one hand so she threaded her other with Remy's and lifted it to her lips.

Her weak smile made Remy's heart pound. "That's good to hear. How about we start right now?"

The look in her eyes made Remy's blood run hot even as Rom shook his head.

"You need to rest."

She released Rom's hand so she could stroke her fingers across his jaw. "No, what I need is the two of you."

Rom flashed him a look, but Remy figured she was entitled to make that decision.

"I'm not one to say no to my goddess."

Her smile lit him up inside. "Then strip and let me show you how much I love you."

Remy shot off the bed, dropping clothes without saying a word, but Rom only stood by the side of the bed.

"I don't think—"

"Exactly." She grabbed Rom's hand. "Don't think."

Amity rose onto her knees to face Rom, and Remy slipped his hands under the shirt she wore, sliding his hands over the smooth skin of her stomach until he could cup her breasts in his hands.

Leaning back into him, her hands reached behind her to slide into Remy's hair and draw his lips closer to her neck.

He did as she silently asked and put his mouth on the skin just below her ear. She shuddered beneath his hands and her arms reached for Rom, who moved closer so she could hold onto his shoulders.

"I can't stop thinking." Rom's voice had dropped another octave. "About how we almost lost you."

"Then think about how good you'll feel when you're flat on your back and deep inside me."

Aw fuck. Remy's cock throbbed at the promise in her voice. And when she slipped her hand behind her back to stroke him, he groaned.

"And how tight it'll feel with you inside me too."

If Remy had had any hope of holding onto his control, she'd just blown it to smithereens.

Luckily Rom had slightly better control.

"Take her down, Remy. On her side."

And fuck her. Rom didn't have to add that part. He knew Rom wanted to watch first.

And Remy couldn't wait to get inside her. First, he swept the shirt over her head, hearing Rom's indrawn breath as he revealed the beauty of her body.

Then he swept her off her knees and laid her out like Rom had demanded.

He laid down beside her, his cock sliding into the crease of her ass, making her moan as he grabbed her hips and rubbed against her.

"No, watch me, baby," Rom demanded. "Don't close your eyes."

Remy didn't know if she obeyed but she must have because Rom leaned back in the chair and crossed his arms over his chest. His face was set in rigid lines, his eyes laser-sharp as they slid down her body, following Remy's hand as it moved from her hip to between her legs. She moaned as his fingers found her clit and began a slow, sensual assault that had her writhing in his arms.

Her ass rubbed against his cock, inflaming his already fast-burning lust. Damn it, he needed lube. He didn't want to hurt her.

He looked at Rom as he continued to stroke Amity. His cousin was one step ahead of him. He was already bending over and rummaging through the bag at his feet.

Rom tossed the small tube and Remy had to release her to catch it. "Hurry."

That one word, whispered in her voice, nearly had him coming all over her back. As fast as he could, he made his cock slick then slipped his fingers between her cheeks and rubbed the excess against the tiny opening there. When he was sure he wouldn't hurt her, he pressed the head of his cock to the entrance and pushed.

He breached the outer ring and worked himself inside with a slow steady motion. Amity pushed back against him, her hand resting over his as he gripped her hip and sank deep.

When he'd buried himself to the hilt, the tight grip of her ass squeezing him, he knew he couldn't move or he'd go off like a lit firecracker.

But Amity wouldn't stay still. She shifted her hips, making him groan as friction shot quicksilver through his balls and up his spine.

"Rom. Now."

Rom was already pulling his shirt over his head and kicking off his sneakers when Remy gritted out that command.

His jeans and boxers followed just as fast, and he crawled onto the bed, lust making his hands shake.

Spreading his body down the length of hers, he wrapped his hand around her head and brought her forward for his kiss. Their lips met in a hard crush but he couldn't stop to be gentle. And she didn't seem to want gentle.

She ate at his lips, her hands cupping his jaw to hold him to her before running down his chest and straight to his cock. Wrapping her hands around him, she began to stroke him with a strong, impatient rhythm.

If she kept that up—

He reached for her hands, moving one behind her back, where Remy caught it in a gentle grip, and guided the other between his legs. She knew what he wanted and gathered his balls into her palm, testing their weight. His head kicked back as he soaked in the sensation but he couldn't let her continue or he'd come in her hand.

And that was not gonna happen.

Just a few more seconds.

Damn, he loved feeling her hands on his body, especially between his legs.

Maybe...

Remy groaned and he felt Amity's lower body shift, trapping his cock between them.

"Now, Rom. God dammit."

He heard the raw hunger in Remy's voice and knew he couldn't last much longer.

Sifting his fingers through her hair, he tugged her head back until he had a clear shot at the sensitive skin of her neck. He lapped up her taste as he nudged his cock between her thighs.

She was so tight, with Remy already lodged inside her. Each centimeter he invaded was a victory his body craved. Just as he craved the sound of her voice moaning his name, Remy's name, urging them to move, to make her scream. To love her.

"Always," Rom said as he came.

"Love you," Remy groaned.

Amity went limp between them, allowing them to hold her up. "Forever."

Chapter 16

"So we still don't know where they're holding Kari."

Cole shook his head, his mouth set in a hard line.

"No, I'm sorry, Lady Amity. We haven't been able to get them to talk at all. But we won't give up. We'll find her."

Amity had to continue to believe that. If she didn't... well, no sense thinking about that just yet.

Not when the two men she loved so desperately had vowed swift and painful retribution to anyone who so much as mussed Kari's hair.

She still sensed her sister, though the bond they usually shared was muted. Dulled. She had no idea why or even how, but at least she knew Kari still drew breath.

"I'm sure we will." Amity gave Cole a brief smile.

She stood, prompting Cole to stand as well. They'd met in the tiny house in the den that she was beginning to think of as home. Mainly because of the two men who shared it with her.

A smile tugged at her lips as her gaze transferred first to Remy then to Rom, standing on either side of her. They hadn't let her out of their sight all morning, shadowing her every step.

Which, she had to admit, she liked. Being alone for so many centuries would do that to a person.

"Lady," Cole started then paused, as if he knew he shouldn't bring the subject up again but couldn't help himself. "I really wish you would rethink this meeting."

"I appreciate your concern, but I have to go."

Not even Remy and Rom had tried to talk her out of the meeting Charun had asked her to attend. Both of them had gritted their teeth… and started sharpening swords.

She could live with that. She couldn't live with herself if she didn't attempt to bargain for Perrin's release from Aitás.

Hours later, she stood by the gate of Aitás. Only Cal accompanied them, though they were met on the other side by a tall, quiet man whom Cal called Diritas.

Amity didn't even guess until Cal introduced them that the man was his father.

Diritas bowed his head to her, gave Remy and Rom a quick, dismissive glance then took them straight to the gate.

Where Perrin stood between Culsu and Charun. In Aitás.

Amity wanted to reach for Perrin and drag her out, but Perrin's expression stopped her.

"Hello, Amity." Perrin gave her a smile, as if still trying to remember how to do it.

"Perrin, are you okay?"

"Actually, I'm fine."

Amity tried to read any undercurrents the woman might be sending her, tried to read between the lines, but Amity sensed nothing other than calm in Perrin's emotions.

"And… I've decided to stay for a while."

Amity's mouth dropped open as Perrin's meaning sank in. Was the woman under a spell? Had Charun somehow entranced her?

Her startled gaze flashed to Charun, whose hard-edged features held absolutely no emotion. Was this another move in whatever game he was playing?

"Perrin, I don't think you understand what that means. Do you really—"

"I asked her to stay, Munthukh. I am not keeping her here against her will."

Charun's even tone struck no false notes at all. Still, Amity couldn't believe what she was hearing.

"Perrin, why?"

Perrin's lips curved in a slight smile and her gaze flashed at Charun then held. Amity's mouth dropped open for a brief second before she could close it.

"Because I... I find it peaceful here."

"I've given her my word that she can depart at any time," Charun said. "She's not a prisoner here."

Amity turned to Culsu, the Goddess of the Gate, who nodded, pale white hair flowing around her shoulders. "She's staying of her own free will. I've told her the risks she incurs if she stays."

"Amity, I can't thank you enough for all you've done for me but," Perrin paused to flash another look at Charun, "I'm staying. For now."

Amity opened her mouth several times, trying to find the right argument, the right words to get her to leave. But she could come up with nothing.

Instead, she turned to Charun. "Should I continue to be afraid to sleep?"

Did she sense a hint of amusement in him? No, she couldn't quite believe that.

"No. And neither should any of the other goddesses. I've decided to stay where I am for the time being. But the time will come when we'll revisit the situation. I'm not sure how much longer I'll be content to remain here."

And when he finally decided to leave his post, to leave Aitás... nothing would stand in his way. She knew that.

Then Perrin reached through the gate and Amity stepped forward to take her hand, squeezing tight as the other woman nodded. "I'll be fine, Amity. I'll see you soon."

"I'm going to hold you to that. Be safe, Perrin."

—w—

Amity stared at the night sky from her chair on the tiny patio at the back of their house.

In the forest, she knew Remy and Rom were off for a run so she wasn't surprised when a huge gray wolf stepped out of the trees. The girl at his side, however, was a bit of a shock.

"Hello, Lady Amity." Cat stopped several feet away, as if she didn't want to come any closer without leave.

Amity smiled at the girl, even though her chest tightened. So stupid to be jealous of this girl, who was still trying to find her way in a world that had shifted so drastically under her feet.

"Come sit with me, sweetheart. Tell me what's on your mind."

Cat sat next to her, so close Amity could feel the warmth of her body. And sense the soul-deep fear she kept hidden so very well.

Wrapping her arm around the girl's shoulder, Amity pulled her closer as the wolf melted back into the trees.

"I don't want to make them choose between us, Amity. But I sense that I need them."

Ah. Seems they shared this fear. Good thing she'd already made up her mind about a few things. "Then you have nothing to worry about. We're staying. Our people need us, Cat. We won't desert them."

Cat physically softened against her. "Thank you, Lady. I think I'm going to need all the help I can get."

"And you'll have it, dear. I'll see to it."

Remy and Rom walked out of the forest only minutes after the girl left, Tivr glued to her side.

Remy sprawled on the ground at her feet, still wearing his pelt, as Rom shifted before her in a moment of blurred reality. He bent down to kiss her, before lifting her into his arms so he could sit on the chair with her in his lap.

"Did you have a good run?"

"Yeah, until Remy decided he wanted to chase rabbits. Damn things are fast."

A low growl made her laugh as she wrapped one arm around Rom's naked shoulders and let her other fall to the side so she could run her fingers through Remy's pelt.

"You'll need to keep on your toes. I don't want anything to happen to either of you."

Rom kissed her as Remy shifted beneath her fingers until she felt warm, satin flesh. As she kissed Rom, Remy laced his hand with hers and brought it to his lips, pressing a kiss to her palm.

"As long as we've got each other at our backs," Rom said, "we'll be fine."

Amity smiled. They'd be more than fine. "We'll be together. And that's all that matters."

Read on for an excerpt from Book 1 in the
Forgotten Goddesses series by Stephanie Julian

WHAT A GODDESS WANTS

Now available from Sourcebooks Casablanca

DYING WAS SO BENEATH her.

Of course, she hadn't done much living lately, so if he caught her now... Well, that would just suck. Because she'd recently decided it was time to change her ways. Get out more. Live a little. Get laid.

How pitiful was it that she couldn't remember the last time she'd had sex? Or if it had even been any good.

Pretty freaking pitiful.

Thesan, Etruscan Goddess of the Dawn, Lady of the Golden Light, was sick of being a pretty, useless deity. Much less a pretty, useless one usually just called Tessa.

For centuries... millennia... she'd brought light and beauty to the world. She'd guided the sun into the morning sky. She'd seen the rise and fall of empires. Gods had lusted after her. She'd worn out her share of mortal men in her bed.

She'd been worshipped by millions. Okay, maybe millions was stretching it just a bit. Still, she'd had a following, people who'd adored her and who'd worshipped her.

Now she was being chased by a crazed god intent on consuming her powers and leaving what was left of her soul to rot for all eternity in the dreary Etruscan Underworld of Aitás.

That totally sucked.

So did this. Her lungs heaved as she ran through a dark forest, the night sky black. No moon shone above. No stars twinkled. No reflected sunlight gave her even a hint of power.

Her legs shook like wet noodles, threatening to collapse at any moment. The underbrush swiped at her calves, and tree limbs caught at her hair, yanking and pulling.

Peering over her shoulder, she saw a dark shape weaving through the trees behind her. Her heart hurt as it pounded in her chest. Her bare feet bled and ached as she stumbled along.

Oh, she knew she really wasn't running. She was actually asleep in her lonely bed in her home in the quiet hills of eastern Pennsylvania. She knew that because she'd had the same dream for the past three weeks.

Charun, that blackhearted bastard, was taunting her like a high school bully picking on a weaker kid. But Charun's intent wasn't to merely frighten her, though the bastard did get a kick out of it.

No, he was wearing her down, waiting for her to make a mistake so he could pinpoint her location. So far, she'd been able to keep her whereabouts a secret. But when he broke through her defenses, he'd send one of his demons to drag her down to Aitás. To him.

The bastard couldn't come himself. He was tied to Aitás by bindings even he couldn't break. At least, not now.

But if he found her, if he managed to accomplish what she thought he had planned, then soon, maybe, he would be able to break those bonds. And this world would suffer as the demons and the damned escaped with him.

And she'd never get laid again. Damn it, she'd much rather go out with a literal bang than a figurative one.

With a gasp, she broke free of the dream and sat straight up in her bed, blinking at the bright light even though it was… three o'clock in the morning, according to the clock on the bedside table.

She'd left all the lamps blazing in her bedroom. An infomercial blared from the television, and the stereo on the nightstand blasted Puccini. None of it had been able to keep her awake. Probably because she could count on both hands the number of hours she'd slept in the past three weeks.

Damn it, she needed help.

Her nose wrinkled at the thought. She, a goddess, needed help. Wasn't that a real kick in a perfectly fine ass?

"Which won't mean a damn thing if Charun gets hold of it," she muttered to absolutely no one.

Hell, if she survived Charun, she needed to get out of the house so someone could see her fine ass again. Playing the hermit didn't suit her. She'd been one of the original party girls in her day, playing all night before hurrying off to meet the lovely sun each morning.

But now she was a forgotten goddess, her main reason for being usurped by that bitch of a Roman goddess named Aurora—

She took a deep breath. No, she couldn't think about that. Those thoughts led to teeth gnashing and sore jaws.

Still, she'd become a goddess without a true calling. What should she do with her never-ending life?

Oh, she delivered a baby or ten or twenty every year. In addition to being a sun goddess, she also helped bring new life into the world, one of the more pleasurable aspects of her life.

But that left her with a whole hell of a lot of time to fill. A girl could only do so much shopping and have so much sex before it all became so very… mundane.

She wanted to be useful again. She wanted the remaining Etruscans, those who still followed the old ways, to remember that she even existed. And she most certainly did not want to be eaten by Charun.

She needed help. And she knew just the person to help her find it.

"Hang tight… I'm coming. Just give me a minute."

The voice came from the second floor as Tessa stood in the entry hall of the small townhouse in Reading, Pennsylvania.

In front of her, a stairway led along the right side of the house to the upper floors. To the left of the stairway, a hall led straight down the center of the house. To the far left, a doorway led into the front sitting room.

Every inch of the place looked like it belonged to an inner-city *Brady Bunch*, from the '80s-era paisley wallpaper to the colonial blue paint on the trim. Cream carpet covered every inch of the floor, and an umbrella stood next to the small half-round table in the entry.

It all looked so normal, Tessa thought. So middle class.

Until Salvatorus began to stomp down the stairs. Then what would have seemed completely normal to any *eteri*, any nonmagical human, made a complete left turn into mythology land.

At four foot nothing, Sal had the fully developed upper body of a grown man. Wide shoulders, strong arms, nice pecs.

His face was a true marvel of his Etruscan heritage, handsome and strong. And those brown eyes, so dark they looked almost black, held a knowing warmth that always made Tessa smile.

As did the two shiny black horns sprouting from just above his forehead to peek through his glossy, black, curly hair. On any other man, those horns would have been enough to make a grown man choke on his own breath.

On Sal, well, the goat legs stole the show.

Beginning just below his belly button, those legs were covered with hide, a silky chestnut brown fur that was not a pair of pants. No, Sal had the actual legs of a goat.

"Hey, sweetheart," he said as he clomped down the stairs. "Haven't seen you for a while. What's up?"

His deep Noo Yawk accent made her smile grow. But her fear must have shown in her eyes because Salvatorus's gaze narrowed.

"Are you hurt, Tessa?" He descended the rest of the steps on those small hooves so fast she worried for his safety. But he made it safely to the bottom, took her hand, and began to lead her through the house.

"No." *Not yet, anyway.* "I'm fine."

"Well, you let me be the judge of that."

Salvatorus led her to the kitchen at the very back of the house and pointed her toward a seat at the small table there. He didn't speak, not right away, but set about making her hot chocolate, the rich scent of it making her stomach rumble.

Tessa had been here many times before, mainly for parties. She did love a good party, and Salvatorus threw some of the best. But his home also served as a safe house for anyone of Etruscan descent, including those deities who needed his aid.

She'd never sought aid from Salvatorus before. Really, a goddess who needed help? It sounded ridiculous.

And yet, not so much now.

Sliding into a straight-backed wooden chair, she let her gaze wander out the window over the sink and into the courtyard in the back. The August garden burst with color and fragrance that wafted in through the open window, enticing her to draw a deep breath. Roses, herbs, perennials, bushes, and trees bloomed and thrived in Sal's garden, no bigger than twenty feet by twenty feet.

It was beautiful, a testament to the sun's nurturing power and Salvatorus's skill.

Tears bit at the corners of her eyes. She tried to blink them away before they fell, but one escaped and plopped right into the mug of hot chocolate that appeared in front of her.

"All right, babe." Salvatorus slid into the chair opposite her. "Spill. And I don't mean tears."

She lifted her gaze to his. "Did you know Mlukukh has been missing? For more than a month."

If she'd surprised Salvatorus with her statement about another forgotten Etruscan goddess, he showed no sign of it. "No, I hadn't heard. But then Mel has dropped off the face of the earth for years, sometimes decades. She's always returned."

Tessa shook her head. "I don't think she will this time. In fact, I'm pretty sure I know what happened to her."

Salvatorus's eyelids lifted. "And that is…?"

She took a deep breath before leaving it out on a sigh. "I think Charun had her snatched and taken to Aitás where he consumed her powers and left her shell to rot in the underworld."

Now Salvatorus's eyes narrowed. "And you know this how?"

"Because he told me. He told me that's what he's going to do to me as well."

Acknowledgments

To my husband, who never said no when I asked, "Hey, hon, could you come here a sec?"

To my editor Deb, for realizing what was missing.

To Judi, for listening to me think out loud. A lot.

About the Author

Stephanie Julian is the author of *What a Goddess Wants* and *How to Worship a Goddess* as well as The Magical Seduction, Lucani Lovers, Darkly Enchanted, and The Fringe series. She is a member of RWA and Valley Forge Romance Writers and is a freelance feature writer for the *Reading Eagle* newspaper. Stephanie lives in Shillington, Pennsylvania.

Where There's Smoke

by Karen Kelley

The Devil went down to Texas...

Sexy wannabe demon Destiny Carter has pissed off the people downstairs and has been kicked out of Hell. Now she's in Ft. Worth, Texas, with one week to corrupt a soul. Or else.

Lookin' for just One Soul to steal...

When smokin' hot Destiny strolls into The Stompin' Ground bar in a slinky red dress, she has a feeling her assignment might not be so bad. The cowboy at the bar looks pretty darn delicious and oh-so-corruptible.

But Chance Bellew is no ordinary cowboy, and Destiny gets way more than she bargained for when she rubs up against that sexy dark angel perched on a bar stool like sin just waiting to happen...

"Kelley burns up the pages... This book is witty, sexy, and a lot of fun. Readers won't be able to wait to read the next installment!"
—*RT Book Reviews*, 4 stars

"Bestseller Kelley (the Princes of Symtaria series) launches a sultry paranormal series with this smoky, sweet, and surprisingly touching tale."
—*Publishers Weekly*

For more Karen Kelley, visit:

www.sourcebooks.com

Touch If You Dare

by Stephanie Rowe

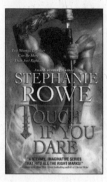

He's just about the hottest warrior she's ever seen...

Reina Fleming really appreciates a man who's on a mission—especially when he's a badass warrior doing his best to impress her. And Jarvis is charmed by the way Reina's magic touch can soothe his dark side.

But when Jarvis's attention puts her job, her home, and her family in danger, Reina has to decide whether love is worth the price...

Enter the nonstop, action-packed world of Stephanie Rowe's love stories—you'll never think of the manly arts in the same way again.

"A steamy, imaginative series that hits all the right marks!"
—Larissa Ione, *New York Times* bestselling author of *Eternal Rider*

"Vivacious characters and witty dialogue... Those who like the works of authors such as J.R. Ward and Laurell K. Hamilton will love Touch If You Dare*"*
—*RT Book Reviews*, 4 stars

For more Stephanie Rowe, visit:

www.sourcebooks.com

Demons Are a Girl's Best Friend

by Linda Wisdom

A bewitching woman on a mission…

Feisty witch Maggie enjoys her work as a paranormal law enforcement officer—that is, until she's assigned to protect a teenager with major attitude and plenty of Mayan enemies. Maggie's never going to survive this assignment without the help of a half-fire demon who makes her smolder…

A hotter-than-sin hero with an agenda…

Declan is proprietor of an underground club and busy demon portal. No way he'll allow his demon race to be blamed for the malicious acts of some crazy evil Mayans. But he's already got his hands full when the sexy witch offers him a challenge he can't refuse…

"Truly a fun, fun story told by a talented author who seamlessly blends paranormal, danger, humor, and love."
—*Night Owl Reviews* Reviewer Top Pick

"Humor, danger, and steamy sex make for an exciting read."
—*RT Book Reviews*, 4 stars

For more Linda Wisdom, visit:

www.sourcebooks.com

Virgin

by Cheryl Brooks

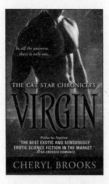

He's never met anyone who made him purr...

Starship pilot Dax never encountered a woman he wanted badly enough. Until he met Ava Karon...

And he'll never give his body without giving his heart...

Dax is happy to take Ava back to her home planet, until he finds out she's returning to an old boyfriend...

As their journey together turns into a quest neither expected, Ava would give herself to Dax in a heartbeat. Except he doesn't know the first thing about seducing a woman...

"An amazing read... hot and explicit."
—*Night Owl Reviews* Reviewer Top Pick

"Virgin is high caliber entertainment from beginning to end—
it hit all my happy buttons and I couldn't put it down."
—*Whipped Cream Erotic Reviews*

For more Cheryl Brooks, visit:

www.sourcebooks.com

Sinners on Tour

Rock Hard

by Olivia Cunning

On stage, on tour, in bed, they'll rock your world...

Trapped together on the Sinners tour bus for the summer, Sed and Jessica will rediscover the millions of steamy reasons they never should have called it quits in the first place...

"A full, well rounded romance... another dazzling story of Sinners, love, sex, and rock and roll!"—Night Owl Reviews Reviewer Top Pick

"Wicked, naughty, arousing, and you'll be craving the next page of this book as if you were living it for yourself!"—Dark Divas Reviews

"Hot men, rocking music, and explosive sex? What could be better?"
—Seriously Reviewed

"An erotic romance that is rockin' with action and a plotline that keeps you on your toes."
—Romance Fiction on Suite101.com